WITHIN THE EMBERS

T.A. REILLY

Editor: Caitlin Lengerich (Instagram: @chronicledbycait)

Proofreader: Chelsey (Instagram: @theimperfectionist)

Cover Designer: Moonpress (Instagram: @moonpressdesign)

H&B's: Amanda Hawkins (Instagram: @eternalgeekery)

Character Eyes Art: Mikki (Instagram: @art.bymikki)

Map Frame: Amanda Hawkins (Instagram: @eternalgeekery)

Couple Art: Belén (Instagram: @belen_digital_art)

❀ Formatted with Vellum

Author's Note

I've always been a reader. I love reading about adventure, romance, and anything fantasy. I love being swept off my feet and dragged into a world of my own imagination. When I wrote *Beneath the Shatter*, I wanted to make it precisely the type of book I would pick up and read. As always, the story begged to be continued. The Vanaiyer Realm had more to share, more to give to its readers. And so, we continue on in the Scattered Destinies Series, as long as you dare to explore . . .

This is a new adult fantasy romance book, and is not recommended for minors. Please consider all content warnings before starting the book.

This book includes content such as: violence, bloodshed, on-page death, profanity, capture, mentions of abuse, instances of physical harm, murder, and explicit scenes (please refer to the Spice Rack for specific chapters).

Reggeon
Sea of Avyz
Estaire
Avyon
Caperdov
Calante
Saltridge Point
Nytestarr
Krymson Forest
Arcelya
Verastarr
Château C

East Engles
Hallyus
VANAIYER
REALM
Dyfinn
Nordak
Kyllios
Vytley Inn

Playlist

◄◄ ► ►►

Way Down We Go - KALEO

Royalty - Egzoc, Maestro Chives & Neoni

Storm - Ruelle

Fangs - Neoni

Dusk Till Dawn (feat. Sia) - ZAYN

Empire Now - Hozier

Who's Afraid of Little Old Me? - Taylor Swift

Elastic Heart - Sia

Up in Flames - Ruelle

Past Lives - BORNS

Vanaiyer Magic Guide

ELEMENTAL MAGIC

Elemental magic is the magic a citizen of
Vanaiyer is born with, gifted from The God.

Shadow Wielder	Fire Wielder
Mist Wielder	Air Wielder
Water Wielder	Land Wielder

POWERS OF THE REALM

Powers only naturally appear in royals. Any
others who possess these abilities have swore
loyalty to the ruler of their land.

Wolvyn Shifters
the power of Verastarr
they have the ability to shift into a larger than life wolf and can
communicate down a bond to other wolvyn

Vamprys
the power of Avyon
they have the ability to move swiftly, their fangs can inject
venom, and their blood heals (though this is not a widely
known fact)

Tidesworn Syrens
the power of the East Engles
they can breathe underwater and feel the call of the sea

Fae
the power of Reggeon
they have the ability to fly and their power allows them to fly
unseen

Gryffins
the power of Nordak
they have the ability to shift into a part lion, part winged
creature

The Lands of Vanaiyer

The Vanaiyer Realm consists of five unique
lands, all connected by the Sea of Ayyz

VERASTARR

Home to the Wolvyn
King: Sébastien Capetian (mated)
(claimed throne by default after the passing
of Adrastan and Kairon de Caude in the
Battle of Nytestarr)

AVYON

Home to the Vamprys
King: Kodrayn Deverell
(claimed throne after his father's
passing by fighting to claim the title)

EAST ENGLES

Home to the Tidesworn Syrens
King: Carawn de Caude
(claimed throne by murdering his brother
and marrying his wife)

REGGEON

Home to the Fae
King: Ryker
(claimed throne when his father relinquished
the title)

NORDAK

Home to the Gryffins
King: Dathrian Demira
(claimed throne by default after his father)

Main Characters of Vanaiyer

The main characters throughout the Scattered Destinies Series . . . thus far.

VERASTARR

Sébastien Capetian
Seh-bast-e-ahn Cap-eh-tea-ahn
King of Verastarr, Commander of Wolvyn Guard, mated to Cass

Cassandra Capetian (formerly Dumont)
Cuh-sahn-drah Cap-eh-tea-ahn
Queen of Verastarr, mated to Sébastien, from the future

Dravyn de Caude
Dray-vin duh Caud-uh
Captain of the Wolvyn Guard, former Prince of the East Engles, mated to Emalyee

Emalyee de Caude
Emma-lee duh Caud-uh
Mated to Dravyn

AVYON

Kodrayn Deverell
Code-drahn Dev-er-el
King & General of Avyon

Kateya Dumont
Cat-e-ah
Cassandra's sister, from the future

REGGEON

Ryker
Rye-ker
King of Reggeon

Other Characters of Vanaiyer

Additional characters who make quick (or lengthy) appearances throughout the series.

VERASTARR

Kairon Capetian
Kai-ron Cap-eh-tea-ahn
Former Heir to Verastarr

Adrastan Capetian
Ah-drast-ahn Cap-eh-tea-ahn
Former King of Verastarr

AVYON

Torryn Ashborne
Tore-in Ash-born
Younger of the two vampry twins

Everett Ashborne
Ever-et Ash-born
Older of the two vampry twins, second to Kodrayn Deverell

EAST ENGLES

Carawn de Caude
Care-ah-wan duh Caud-uh
Current King of the East Engles

NORDAK

Dathrian Demira
Dath-ri-an Day-mir-ah
Current King of Nordak

THE FUTURE

Nik
Kateya's boyfriend

Aerilyn
Air-ill-in
The Dumont sister's best friend

To all the girls with fire in their eyes and a touch of venom on their lips.
And to my sister, the Kateya to my Cassandra . . .

EAST ENGLES

Prologue – One Year Ago

DARKNESS RELEASED me from its clutches as I landed forcefully on my knees. The wooden surface below me groaned from the force as a heartbroken sob fell silently from my lips. Peering up, I found myself alone in a dark space—a space I recognized all too well—which could only mean one thing. Cassandra had succeeded.

I was back in the present. And she . . . she was trapped in the past.

I couldn't believe that it had worked, that the pendant had actually shattered and sent me back to our time—to our home in the East Engles.

The full force of that realization hit me all too soon. *I had made it back. To the present.* My sister however, had not. And I knew that I couldn't live in a realm without her. In a *time* without my sister. I couldn't spend the rest of my days wondering if she was all right, if she'd survived whatever war was brewing in the past, and if she'd ended up with Sébastien. My stomach curled at the thought of never seeing her again, of never laughing with my sister, of never hearing her voice on the phone.

Bile rose in my throat, and I stumbled through the hallway of my dimly lit university apartment as I darted to the bathroom. My fingers clutched the edges of the faded countertop. The pristine porcelain surface of the sink beneath my fingers was stark against my skin, as I hurled the contents of my stomach repeatedly into the sink, wondering what my life had become.

My nerves, scattered.

My heart, broken.

My fate, now uncertain.

Yet, I knew what I needed to do. What I *must* do. I remembered my promise to her. I remembered promising that I would find the next artifact. That I would make it back to her. Whatever Cass had to deal with in the past because of a Void-damned prophecy, I wanted to face side-by-side with her. I didn't want to live in the present when my sister was trapped in the past.

It didn't matter whether I was fated to find the second artifact or not. It didn't matter where on Vanaiyer it was hidden. I *would* find it. And I *would* return for my sister. She might have thought sending me back to our present time was her only option, but I—I refused to accept that. Fuck destiny. I would make my own path . . . prophecy be damned.

Lifting my head up, I stared at the reflection looking back at me, a soft gasp of shock echoed in the bathroom as I took in my appearance. My hair, usually a luscious brownish-blonde color that matched my older sister and mother's, now had shimmering silver-white colored strands framing my face. Tentatively I reached up, touching the locks in wonder; the silver strands coiled around my finger as I grabbed at my hair. *Magic.*

Cassandra had mentioned that the Elder she had visited at the Rise wouldn't stop talking about the importance of a balance in power, a code of harmony, that the magic of our realm lived by. And me, unintentionally tagging along with her to the past, then being sent to the present again while she remained in the past . . . that most definitely would have messed with the balance of power. A balance I most certainly shouldn't be messing with, and yet, here I was.

The rattle of my front door had me freezing, as I heard the

lock click open. No one—and I mean no one—had a key to my apartment other than Cassandra, and seeing as she was trapped back in time, there should be no one entering through that door.

At least . . . I frowned as the door handle began to turn. No one else had been given a key to my apartment before I'd disappeared back in time, which left me to wonder exactly how much time *had* passed since we found ourselves in the past.

Pressing myself to the wall, I slunk through the shadows to the linen closet in the apartment hallway, before slipping inside in an attempt to hide as I slid the double paneled door closed.

Who would be entering my place? And how did they get access?

I peered through the slight crack between the two paneled doors, eyes tracking the outlined shadows as they intruded, entering my apartment with authority and a carelessness I despised. I watched as two men flipped the lights on in my kitchen and began rifling through my belongings. I should interrupt them, stop them from trespassing, yet I forced myself to remain in the shadows, letting the darkness conceal me as I tracked their movements.

"What are we even looking for here anyways?" The man closer to my front door shouted across my apartment.

"Couldn't tell you, the chief just said to search the place for evidence of the use of illegal magic." The other grunted as he began overturning items in my living room, tossing pillows around haphazardly as he rummaged through my belongings. "At least it gets us out of the patrol room."

Emergency patrol officers.

I held my breath as I watched them, praying to The God that they would speak freely so I could gather information about how much time I'd missed.

"With the Nordak Commander breathing down the chiefs back, those girls better pray they're dead," the first man voiced as he dug through my mail, searching for any explanation on why or how we had used magic.

"Dead . . . disappeared . . . vanished," his partner replied with a wry chuckle. "Doesn't really matter what happened to them though. If they so much as show their faces, I could almost guarantee you that they will meet the same demise as their parents—"

My heart froze at the statement. My breath was nonexistent and my body immobile as the words rang on repeat across my mind, a brand over my heart.

Same demise . . . as their parents . . .

What had happened to my parents? How long had we been gone? My parents couldn't possibly be—no. My parents had been fine; I'd seen them the weekend before Cass and I ended up traveling back in time. They weren't—no . . . no, it wasn't possible. They weren't dead. They couldn't be . . .

"Look at this!" A deep baritone drew my attention back to the patrol officers. Pressing my body against the crack of the doors, I strained to catch a glimpse of what they had discovered, and my heart sank. They found my paintings. Those art pieces alone could sentence me to death.

Painting has always been my escape, my happy place. And while painting alone wasn't a crime—not that I thought any form of painting should be—painting scenes of "fairy tales," of a time when magic was used freely before The Fall, certainly *was* a crime. It would be seen as a conspiracy with those who had possessed powers.

I hadn't shown anyone my paintings, not even Cass. I kept them hidden once each one was completed. Those paintings had brought me joy while I dreamed of a time, seven years ago, before The Fall, when magic and power had been free to be used and the Nordak didn't control most of the Vanaiyer realm. A time back in the past when the land flowed with the gifts The God had given us.

"Pack them up. We'll see what the chief has to say about them. At the very least, it proves the girls had an interest in magic."

The patrol officer began collecting *my* paintings. My heart broke as I was forced to watch on from the shadows, unable to stop them unless I wished to reveal my presence.

"How on Vanaiyer did two sisters just vanish into thin air? Not to be seen all month? It just doesn't make sense." The man who discovered my art spoke as he carelessly packed my most prized possessions into large evidence bags.

"Who cares." His partner laughed as they zipped up the bags. "Let's head out, we still have enough time to hit a bar on our way back to the unit."

I pressed back into the shadows as I watched the two patrol officers retreat, the front door slamming behind them as they left. My body trembled as my back leaned against the wall of the linen closet, wooden shelves digging into me as my mind reeled over the information.

Not seen all month.

Interest in magic.

Demise.

If they so much as show their faces.

The words circled on repeat as I failed to calm my breathing, my hands shaking roughly.

Five . . . Four . . . I breathed unsteadily. *Three . . . Two . . . you can do this, Kat. One . . .*

I knew what I needed to do.

Standing on the doorstep, cold pellets of rain seeped through my clothing as I remained frozen in fear, staring at a dark forest green door I had seen nearly everyday of my childhood. The cool chill of the rain was barely discernible through the dread surfacing in my heart. *What would I find behind the door?*

Knowing I couldn't stay here, out in the open, for long, my hand shakily rose in front of me, grasping the metal handle of a front door I had opened countless times before. Only this time . . .

This time it felt different. It felt *wrong*. I didn't want to open the door and face whatever I would find inside, but I did so anyway.

The handle twisted and the door sprung open on its own accord, as I breathed deeply and forced myself through the entrance. Water dripped off my body, soaking the floor as I entered inside my childhood home.

The door shut behind me, causing me to jump as my eyes adjusted to the dimmed lighting peaking through the blinds. With a reminder to myself not to switch the lights on and draw attention to my presence, I walked through the foyer toward our living room. Stepping over scattered shoes, I noted a fallen yellow lamp shattered on the floor, while paintings and family photos hung sideways on our walls.

Dread welled within me as I realized that my childhood home had been destroyed. "Mum?" My whisper echoed through the walls as I crept forward. "Father?" I paused to listen for their voices. "Anyone home?"

Silence.

I turned the corner and my eyes met red. Deep crimson painted the walls, tarnishing the pristine nature of our living room. My eyes tracked over the scene: the blood splattered on our couch, the smeared handprints painting a story across the walls.

I forced myself to breathe. To inhale air. Not to panic. *They could still be okay. They had to be.* I turned, scanning over the remainder of the living room, when a strangled cry fell from my lips.

There, above the mantle, were the bodies of my parents.

Their lifeless forms were now the brutal centerpiece of our family home.

I fell to my knees while the realm as I knew it shattered before my eyes. Tears streamed over my cheeks, and my heart was hollow. A numb feeling overtook me as sobs violently shook through me. My body and my hands trembled from the shock, unable to believe my eyes, *unwilling to believe them.*

Forcing myself to look again, I realized I knew what this was. I knew what their death was, and I knew why they died. We had seen this before, in our own neighborhood.

Shortly after The Fall, a couple four houses down had used their magic. They hadn't had much, just minor, elemental level magic. Parlor tricks compared to the royals and those who swore loyalty to them. We had returned home from school to witness them being dragged out of their front door by a Nordak patrol. As they were shoved onto their knees, they had been sentenced to death in front of the entire neighborhood. A public display; a violent death. Their screams of agony still filled my ears when I thought back on that day. It had been a warning, a threat to the rest of us of what happened when one used magic.

I noted the same black "X" marked on my parents' bodies. It was the Nordak's branding for those who dared use magic without permission. For those sentenced to a public display of death for the use of magic. Which could only mean one thing: our parents had been punished—sentenced to death—all because Cassandra and I had unintentionally used magic, thanks to a Void-damned prophecy.

The jagged slits in their wrists were now dried and caked with their blood, and there was an open gash on my mother's cheek. Tears welled in my eyes before flooding over as my gaze landed on the remnants of bruises and cuts battering my parents' bodies.

I was unable to move. To breathe. To exist in a realm without them in my life.

My body collapsed, sobs shuddering their way through me as I stared at the lifeless forms of my parents. My parents, who had always been there for me. Who made me laugh and taught me how to truly live. Who had been punished—sentenced to death because of me. Because of both of us. Whose bodies now hung on display—

A threat.

A warning to me.

A lesson of what would happen if I dared show my face in the East Engles, or anywhere on Vanaiyer.

EAST ENGLES

Chapter One

SPLATTERED crimson stained my face as my gaze flicked up, praying to The God no one had seen me. That I was alone.

No one thinks to monitor the back alleys of the Capital after dusk. After all, not many people venture outside in the dark anymore, much less alone. The feeling of warm, wet blood slowly dripped down my arm, reminding me of the task at hand. Lifting both hands over my head, I drew them down with force, the dagger within my grasp angled downward as I thrust it into the figure on the pavement before me, hitting bone as I ensured my target was defeated. The beast was dead.

Relaxing, I sank to my knees beside the carcass, breathing a sigh of relief. This was my fifth kill of the month, but the Seefers kept appearing. Their numbers grew week by week with no one seeming to realize. No one but Aerilyn and me.

Today was the anniversary of my family's deaths.

Of my own.

It had been a year since my parents were brutally murdered. Since I had been thrown back into the present day. Since I had lost my sister to the past.

They say that time heals all wounds, but I call bullshit. Time only buries them, it changes you. It takes your soul and twists it until you've become someone you don't recognize . . . someone you no longer know.

My gaze jerked back down toward the Seefer. This one had been young, inexperienced, yet vicious all the same. I abhorred the next part.

The body was still warm, blood seeping from its lifeless form, soaking into its mangled fur. I had to move quickly. If I didn't, the evidence of blood spill would coat the back alley, making it impossible to hide from the Nordak emergency patrols. With a grunt, I grabbed the front paws of the Seefer, matted gray fur itched at my skin beneath my grasp as I hauled its body slowly to the pile of trash bags in the back corner.

I struggled beneath the weight, my muscles protesting as I slowly made my way to the darkened corner of the alley. Dropping the dead weight of the Seefer, I grabbed a full, black trash bag, moving it over the beast, hiding it from plain sight. Exhaustion overcame me as I stepped back, checking my work to ensure that the body wouldn't be visible or draw attention should someone walk by and take a quick glance down the alley.

I paused, satisfied that the Seefer was covered, as I remembered the night that changed my life a year ago . . .

The door had opened hesitantly, Aerilyn's auburn hair peeking through the crack as shock flooded her face when she saw me. The door flung wide open, her hand shooting out and yanking me inside urgently.

"You can't be here, Kat!" she exclaimed as the door shut as quickly as it had opened. "I don't know what the hell happened to you and Cass—and we can talk about that later—but you can't be here. They will find you. They will never stop looking for you until they do."

Aerilyn raced back toward her room, as I froze looking over the apartment she had shared with my sister. Everything had looked the same. As though Cassandra would come back at any minute.

But she wouldn't. I knew that. Aerilyn seemed to know that too.

"Kateya Dumont," Aerilyn snapped from her bedroom as I focused back in on her, walking toward her voice. "Did anyone see you on your way over here? Where did you go before this? Have you tried calling anyone?"

Once she was satisfied with my answers, the real work began . . . and we began to plan my death.

It had been one year since Kateya Dumont's body had been discovered by an emergency patrol. One year since the search for her had ended. One year since I'd become invisible.

Laughter from down the street rang out, and I snapped out of the memory from a year ago, pushing myself back into the corner, praying the shadows hid my body as a rowdy group of boys walked past. I knew I needed to head back soon.

Wiping my blade across my pants, I sheathed my dagger, remaining in the shadows as I headed back home. My phone vibrated as I pulled it from my pocket, the words flashing across the screen.

Aerilyn: 2 down. 3 sightings.

Void-damn. I frowned at her message. The sightings were growing, and when Seefer sightings grew, an attack was inevitable.

Me: I only found 1. We can't hold them off forever.

Aerilyn: I'll get us access. Soon, okay?

I sighed as I continued home. Soon wasn't good enough. We needed access to the Capital Archives *now*. It was our only chance to find buried records of the prophecy. The only chance we had to learn more about the artifacts and the powers they held.

The only problem? The Archives were closed to the public. They had been since The Fall; since the day the Nordak overtook our Capital, Estaire, and began their reign of terror. Which had led us to our current plan; a desperate, risky attempt to get us inside.

Me: Hydrillas at 8?

An incoming call flashed across the screen and Nik's name popped up. I swiped to answer with a sigh, wondering what my boyfriend wanted.

"Hey babe!" A forced chirp fell from my lips. "What's up?"

"Where have you been?" His voice cut over the phone. "I've been trying to reach you for the past hour."

I picked nervously at the dried blood lining my nails, hating his tone. Knowing exactly where I'd been, my response stayed vague. "I'm sorry, time just slipped away from me. I'll be sure to have my phone on me next time, okay?"

"It's irresponsible, Kat, especially with all the attacks. You've seen the latest reports. I don't want it to be your name on tomorrow's list."

A scoff rose within me at his feigned concern, but I buried the noise. "I'm being careful, Nik. You know I am."

"The next gathering has been pushed up to tonight. I'll see you and Aer there, right?"

Shit. "What time?"

"Eight." His voice rang clearly through the phone. "Same spot as two weeks ago, go through the back door, then to the left and down the stairs. It will be the third door."

Well that changes our plans. This *couldn't* be happening at a worse time. "We'll be there." I hung up the phone, not wanting to continue the call any longer.

> Me: Change of plans.

> Me: 8pm tonight . . . the Descendents are meeting again.

> Aerilyn: Void-be-damned.

> Aerilyn: It had to be tonight didn't it? Why wouldn't they sit on their asses and talk it over as the attacks grow?

Aerilyn's anger at the situation matched mine. The Descendents were a group of mortals who bore familial ties to those hunted for or in hiding from the magic that flowed through their veins. They gathered to stay apprised of the advances the Nordak made on our lands; the changes to the darkness flowing through Vanaiyer. Aerilyn and I had joined them not too long after we had faked my death, in hopes that we might be able to uncover more information regarding the ancient prophecy and the potential locations of the remaining artifacts.

Yet, the Descendents seemed content to stay back in the shadows, monitoring but never taking action. Watching without intervening. They read the death tolls each meeting, tallying the number of Seefer attacks and Nordak imprisonments from the comfort of their gathering places.

A gathering tonight was inconvenient to say the least. We needed to get access to the Archives and I wasn't positive I could sit through another meeting discussing the ways in which they wished to help but wouldn't.

Climbing the stairway, the lights flickered, shadows dancing across the walls as I walked up to our third story apartment.

Aerilyn and I moved here shortly after I returned. The rundown complex didn't attract many, and the rarely working appliances were not a selling point. But it kept us off the grid, and out of sight of the Nordak. And that was all we needed.

A home not under the watchful eye of the enemy. A home we could talk freely in.

The key turned in the rusted lock and the door creaked open.

"You're back!" The shout sounded from our bedroom. "Which gives us two full hours to get you ready to go out tonight. And before you say you don't need help getting ready . . . you do."

A laugh fell from my lips as Aerilyn stepped into view. "I need help? Me? Have you looked at yourself?" I stared at my roommate. Her shoulder-length auburn hair braided tightly on each side of her head had abnormal darkened hues coating it. Her face, usually done up with flawless makeup, had dirt smears and matching blood splatters across it. A few cuts and bruises scattered her exposed skin, and her clothes looked as though they would be trashed. Yet even with her current appearance, her purple speckled eyes lit up with anticipation for the evening.

"I look breathtaking and you know it." She laughed as she headed back toward our room.

"Breathtaking may be a stretch. You might have men rushing to see if you need medical help . . . but I doubt they'll be stopping by our apartment anytime soon with us looking like this," I finished as I gestured toward both of our appearances. A buzz distracted me as I glanced down.

Nik: Don't be late.

With a sigh, I tossed my phone on the bed, groaning as it bounced off the mattress and landed on the wooden flooring with an unwanted thud instead.

"What's the boyfriend want?" Aerilyn called out from the other side of the bathroom door.

"Who's to say that was Nik?"

"Come on, Kat," she said with a groan as her head popped into view. "Will you just dump him already?"

"You know it's complicated, Aer," I snapped.

"Look, do whatever you want, Kat. It's your life. Just don't come crying to me when he inevitably fucks up beyond repair, okay? You deserve better than him. You deserve more than the crap he makes you put up with time and time again."

Frustration rose in me as she pushed the subject. An argument that arose often between us and never resolved. It's just, she didn't get it. She couldn't.

My mind drifted back to a place I rarely let it go anymore. To the day I returned from the past. The day my life was altered forever. The day I found my parents' bodies, beaten and bruised.

My hands shook uncontrollably as I rose to my knees, regulating my breathing. Forcing air through my lungs as I forced the tears back, swallowing my emotions. They didn't deserve a death like this. The brutality. The cruelty. Crossing the living room, the carpet squished beneath my feet, yet I refused to look down. Keeping my gaze above the fireplace mantel, I took note of each stroke of brutality painted mercilessly across my parents' bodies. Their blood was etched into the walls, soaking the carpet beneath where they hung.

And I vowed right then to put a stop to this. That I wouldn't stand by helplessly as someone I loved was taken from me due to Nordak forces.

Straining under the weight, I lowered the lifeless forms of my parents to the floor, holding back sobs as I took in the full extent of the torture they endured. Torture . . . they endured because of me. Because of Cass. Because of a prophecy that was etched deeper into our histories than we could have ever known.

They would get a proper burial—a final resting spot—even if their souls had already been claimed by The Void, just as countless had before them and countless more would after them.

They deserved that much at least, I would make sure of it.

I hadn't known what to do or who else to go to, so I stood on the back porch a few houses down, lowering my hand after knocking on the rust colored backdoor. Blonde hair and sharp brown eyes met mine as I stood before my ex, the typical boy next door, covered in my parents blood.

"Hi," I murmured. My voice barely reached him. "I need your help."

No, she wouldn't get it. I knew Aer wouldn't. Even with all that we had been through this past year, I kept that piece of my past buried deep within my heart. A piece I never shared. A secret only Nik had borne witness to.

"Why do you keep pushing the subject? Just drop it, okay? It's not going to happen. He's my boyfriend, Aer. And that's that."

"I'm sorry, Kat. Forget I said anything, okay? It's been a long day . . . the stress of the growing attacks, the last minute meeting; I'm just more on edge than usual."

"We both are," I muttered back. "Let's just get through tonight, okay?"

The chilled air bit at my bare legs as we snuck our way through the back entrance of the bar. Old beer and cheap perfume permeated the air, flooding my nostrils as we pushed our way through the throngs of people toward the designated meeting location. "He said the third door." My voice raised above the low thrums of music toward Aerilyn in front of me as she pushed her way through the crowded hallway, narrowly avoiding a drunken couple as they stumbled through a door in a passionate embrace.

"Are you sure?" she shouted back. "I'm only seeing two doors."

"Yep," I answered. "To the left. Down the stairs. Third door." I repeated what Nik had told me earlier that day.

"Did we go down the right stairwell?"

The buzz in the back pocket of my faded black denim jeans drew my attention.

> Nik: You're late.

> Me: We can't find the door. I thought you said third?

The bubbles appeared on the bottom of my screen typing before they disappeared as I was once again ignored.

"Great," I muttered under my breath. "Fucking fantastic."

"Wait!" Aer stopped abruptly in front of me, spinning on her heel to face the wall. "I think this is it."

"This?" I looked at my best friend as though she lost her mind as I stared at the brick wall in front of me, not seeing a door.

"Yes. This is it." She grinned as she reached her hand out, pushing against a worn, discolored brick on the wall that sprang free under the pressure. And sure enough, the door clicked open and we were ushered into the enclosed space.

Dim orange lights hung from the ceiling, flickering as they lit the area we had entered. The room was already packed with Descendents conversing in concerned tones. Spotting Nik, we pushed our way through the clusters of boisterous members, joining him near the front of the room just as the lights flicked off for a few seconds then back on.

We'd made it in time.

I breathed a sigh of relief as I met the angry, stormy eyes of my boyfriend. The volume in the room dropped as all eyes focused on the front.

"February 15th," the voice called out as he walked into view, his authority taking over the room, just as he did every meeting. His tall frame filled the space, the beige coat he wore a sharp contrast to his peppered hair as he proceeded. "Ashleigh Handrae." His sharp tone carried across the silence. "Michel Vistare. Sarah Coldron. April Coldron. Joshua Dominique. Axender Dravenport. Viktor Haender. Emilee Haender." The man paused for a moment after each name, his hardened eyes meeting those in the room, landing on mine. I stared back, matching his gaze, forcing him to look on as he continued speaking. "Let these names be a reminder. A reminder that the Nordak won't relent until they have full control. That our lives are mere stepping stones to a greater power they seek to access. A reminder of all we have to fight for."

Eight. Eight. Eight.

The number ran across my mind as his voice droned on.

Eight.

As the crowd around me murmured their agreements to his statements . . . *Eight.*

As he continued encouraging the Descendents of power to remain hidden . . . *Eight.*

As they talked about a day when their powers returned . . . *Eight.*

As the night carried on, and they mapped the locations of the attacks . . . *Eight names.*

Eight lives lost to Seefer attacks yesterday alone. And yet, no one did anything. No one stood up for the lives that were lost. No one plotted against the Nordak. No one offered to track down the Seefers. No one looked for a solution.

No one but Aerilyn and me.

I glanced to my side and could see the anger radiating beneath the surface of Aerilyn's face. The clenched fists at her sides, the slight strain of her lips. They did nothing but look out for themselves. For their families. For the power they thought would return to them. But it wouldn't. Not if we kept living like this, refusing to fight against the control of the Nordak.

"Can you believe it?" Nik whispered under his breath from beside me, his knuckles white from how tight he clenched his fists as his breath wrapped around my neck. "They meet. Night after night. They read the death tolls. They know," he growled, lowly. "They know what the Nordak are doing and still, all they worry about is their own power, praying to The God that it returns to them. As if that will help." He sneered. "They're just too weak to admit it. The power isn't coming back; not with the Nordak in control. And The God . . . The God abandoned us the moment he stayed silent as the Nordak overtook Vanaiyer. Their prayers are falling across emptiness. There's no one listening to them."

I remained silent as Nik shook beside me. I agreed with him . . . to an extent.

Did I think The God had abandoned us? No.

Did I hate that the Descendents stood around in the shadows, watching, monitoring, tracking, but never taking action? Yes, I did, with every fiber of my being.

Something would have to change, and soon. Otherwise, there would be nothing left to fight for. *No one* left to fight for.

EAST ENGLES

Chapter Two

THE MUSIC THRUMMED across the space, neon lights flashing to the beat as couples all around me moved their bodies to the music, lost in the sound. Their drunken stupors erased all concerns of the ongoing attacks, of the encroaching danger. Hydrillas was the spot to be on a Thursday night, and my roommate and I knew it. I watched as Aerilyn swayed her way across the room, skillfully eyeing the scene; a predator on the prowl as she searched for our next targets: our way into the Archives.

I had to give it to her, while the method may be unusual, it yielded results with minimal effort. The scrawny Capital workers often came to these clubs after work in search of some overpriced shots of cheap liquor and an easy lay. So it was a near perfect guarantee that we would get access to what we actually wanted: access to the Archives for research—with the added benefit that no one suspected us for entering them.

I crinkled my nose in disgust as Aerilyn sauntered up to two men by the counter, her targets acquired as she dropped her body across the sticky surface, capturing their attention in seconds. With a sigh, I took my cue. Raising my glass to my lips, I threw back the last of my warm, overpriced tequila with a grimace.

Void-damned, that was disgusting.

Reaching her side, I faked a sloppy stumble, slurring my words ever so slightly as I played the game. "There you are, Aer! I thought I lost you, but here you are, talking up the only attractive men in this club." My voice sounded fake, too cheerful, but they drank it up as I took in their appearance. Medium height, medium build. *Average.* All Capital workers looked the same with their short hair, lack of muscle, and obvious Capital involvement. My memory flitted for the briefest second, not to Nik, *my boyfriend,* but to Eryx. My mind still painted the perfect picture of the man who graced my fantasies late in the night. *The first man who ever made me fall in love.* A man shrouded in mystery with a touch of rebellion. Who broke the Palace rules with me, sneaking out in the cover of the darkness as we took on the town, night after night. The man who took my heart by storm with his trimmed chocolate brown hair, green eyes that pierced my soul, and the light splattering of freckles that touched tan skin, fading into the ink that crept up the side of his face. If only he didn't live hundreds of years in the past. My stomach dropped at the memory, one lost in time, along with my sister.

I stifled a groan as I continued. "I need another drink." My voice floated toward Aerilyn as I kept my gaze glued on the man to her right, watching with growing disgust as he hungrily ate me up in my short, black dress, lust blazingly painted across his face. The slight hint of glitter shone across the tight, black material as lights flashed by, highlighting my features perfectly. "You guys up for a round?" I finished sweetly as the song changed.

The man to his side flicked his finger and the bartender lined up four glasses, filling them up with cheap liquor that had me gagging in my mind. My gaze flicked to Aer's as we reached for the glasses with a sly grin. These two would be the easiest yet, and a saving grace that was. The thought of those scrawny fingers coming anywhere near me was revolting.

Two actual shots, and three faked ones later, Derrik and Kiervan staggered as we fought our way toward the exit. Narrowly avoiding the throngs of drunken club goers, I stumbled as someone elbowed me in the back, my body nearly crashing into Derrik's frame.

"*Ohmygosh!*" The slur came from my side as a blonde came into view, manicured pink nails clutching at my arm stopping me. Her shrill voice, heavily painted face, and mini skirt told me all I needed to know about her. "I'm *so* sorry."

"Don't worry about it," I said as I tried to pull out of her claw-like grip.

"Are you sure?" Her voice whined in a sing-songy tune as she rambled, her words swallowed by the beat of the music. "I hope I didn't ruin your dress. It looks *so good!*"

Forcing a fake smile I reserved for pleasantries, I yanked my arm from her manicured grip, turning with force as I dodged a couple entangled in each other and struggled to catch up with Aer, whose bright hair I spotted by the entrance to Hydrillas.

The cool air bit into my scantily exposed skin as I broke free from the chaos of the club, pushing my way into the night.

"What took you so long?" Aer asked as I caught up with the group, Kiervan's arm slung around her as both men eyed me with interest.

"Oh, you know." I shrugged as I stopped walking, forcing my body to curl into the side of Derrick's thin frame, as I feigned adornment. "Klutzy girl, that's all." His hand hungrily snaked around my body, tightening as it touched my midriff and I swallowed back a grimace.

We need to get into the Archives, Kat. Just suck it up, hopefully this is the last time.

Walking alongside the two, I looked around, missing the vibrant colors that once adorned the city. Those colors had faded into history long ago. The stars in the sky no longer twinkled, and the moon's shadow rarely painted the town with its light. Instead, a dull darkness colored the sky in rough strokes, a lingering reminder of the destruction encroaching all around us.

"*So . . . .*" Aerilyn slurred. "What's it like? You know, working in the Capital? I'm sure you get to do just *so* many important tasks there." Her eyes beamed with interest as she stared up at Kiervan.

"I bet you hear all the secrets," I echoed as I pressed more of my weight into Derrik. "Do you get, like, top secret clearance? Access to hidden rooms?" I pushed, praying I correctly judged the level of drunk he had been at Hydrillas. Not too drunk that he couldn't think, but drunk enough that he wouldn't think twice about giving me answers. At least not until the morning, but we'd be long gone by then. A fleeting memory, never meant to last.

His chest puffed with pride as he spoke. "We get access to everything in the Capital *and* the Archives. All the high clearance projects. They trust us with some of the most important parchments."

"Truly?" I wondered aloud with interest, even as I internally rolled my eyes. "You must be quite important to the king if he trusts you with all the high clearance parchments. I've always longed to see the Archives, it must be a sight to behold." I slipped into the conversation casually as I glanced upward, noting the boastful glint in his eye.

Jackpot. I had him right where I wanted him.

"Oh, His Majesty trusts me with a great deal." He breathed into my ear, as we walked along the sidewalk. The breeze wafted by, picking up the alcohol on his breath as his words slurred. "You should see the Archives. When you first enter, the walls snake upward for stories, parchments covering every surface carefully cataloged. Of course, I spend most of my time on the ninth floor in the back. That's where His Majesty keeps the most important records, the histories of our realm, and the details on our political climate."

I nearly shrieked aloud, it couldn't have been that easy, could it? He wouldn't just openly share such confidential information, would he?

But I had what I needed from him, now I just needed Aerilyn to get a key and we would be in. We could research the history of the artifacts, learn how they were scattered through time, and figure out how we could use them to get back to my sister.

A lone shrill called out in the distance, our footsteps quickening their pace against the frost covered cobblestones. My body was shaking with chills as the midnight air bit against me. I was so close to turning around and sprinting home, my bones frozen as we trudged along hurriedly before the two finally turned left, yanking open a door to an extravagant apartment complex.

Warmth flooded my skin as we crossed into the foyer of the complex, my jaw dropping in awe as I took in the chandelier hanging from a freshly painted domed ceiling. The crystal jewels clinked together as the wind circled around them gently.

"Elevator's this way." Derrik's voice cut through my gazing, as I spun, remembering my role, eyes colliding with his.

"Well . . ." I tossed out in response. "What are we waiting for?" The words felt forced—fake—rolling off my tongue, just as they always did as I watched the elevator numbers drop. A stark *ding* reached our ears and the elevator doors swished open for us to enter.

The numbers continued to climb and climb, and just when I thought it would never end, the low hum halted and the doors slid open. Dimmed hall lighting met my eyes as we walked along the carpeted pathway to their apartment and Derrik reached for his keys.

I knew what he expected. I knew what they *both* expected. And yet, we would never let it get that far.

It was the same routine every time. Feign drunk and flirtatious at the club, stumble home in the dark to their place, propose another round of drinks. If Aer had picked right, we would get lucky and they would pass out after another drink, too drunk to remember they had brought dates home. If our timing was off, we would have to resort to other methods. I was not an advocate for our alternate method, but every time, Aerilyn's point held true.

Just make the sleeping potion, Kat, he will be out before you know it.

Her voice would mock as she referred to a potion we had

purchased far from the Capital to easily knock out the men we questioned.

It's either that or let him slip it in you.

Tonight, as they opened the door and led us into their luxurious apartment, we got lucky, watching as they passed out from one drink too many on their couch that would cover a month's rent. Then we snuck away in the early hours of the morning, praying to The God that the key we'd received truly worked.

I woke in the morning to sunlight creeping in through my window, dancing softly over my skin. I loved the first few moments after waking. Moments when the realm was still and calm. Moments before the worries and duties of the day flooded into my mind and forced me to pry myself from the comfort of my bed to be responsible. While I occasionally longed for the days from over a year ago when I could lounge in bed until half past noon, getting up with the sun was now a habit, and I embraced the morning hours, when the realm felt as though all was right.

Pushing out of bed, I began to dress for my daily training session, which would be followed by a visit to the Archives. Pulling my hair back in sections, I began to form two braids down the sides of my head, tugging my brown hair taut in the pleats. Just as I twisted the last hair tie around the remaining hair, my phone vibrated on my worn, wooden nightstand. Nik's name flashed across the screen as I unplugged the device to read his text.

Nik: Morning. I'll be there in 5.

Me: See you then!

Hurriedly tossing on the closest pair of joggers, with a slight grimace as I noticed another frayed edge on them, I grabbed a t-shirt and rushed out of my bedroom hopping into my clothes.

It was rare I overslept, even slightly, but something about the early spring cold front that had hit the past few days had thrown me off. Rushing out the front door of my building, I leaned casually against the gray stone column just in time to spot Nik's matte black sports car turning onto my block.

I sighed a breath of relief as he approached my building, saying thanks to The God that I had made it outside before he had turned the corner. I hopped down the stone stairs and approached his car as it came to a sudden halt. Swinging the passenger door open, I muttered a far too cheery, "Morning," for 5 a.m. as I slid into the leather seat.

Nik's gaze swept over me, causing my heart to flutter as it always did. We had our issues in the past year, and I knew Aer didn't love Nik, but by The God was he gorgeous, with short dirty blonde hair that curled at the tips, piercing brown eyes, and a jawline that could cut stone.

"After last night's report . . ." Nik's serious tone flooded my ears as I prepared myself for another grueling workout. "I thought we should practice sparring. Hand-to-hand combat is still a vital skill to have and something we've pushed off in favor of weaponry lately."

I nodded at his decision. While I would miss the feel of a dagger in each hand, or a notched arrow for target practice, I couldn't deny the truth to Nik's assessment. Hand-to-hand was by far my most lacking form of defense, and while I hoped to never be caught weaponless, one could never train too much. Or at least that's what our twice-a-day training regimen suggested.

"Any particular form of hand-to-hand?" I questioned. "The attacks have continued increasing. The Seefers are growing in population it seems, multiplying in numbers nearly every day." But I didn't add that Aerilyn and I had been tracking the numbers, or that we'd been picking them off one by one. Some things were better left unsaid.

"Kazrah suggested boxing first, ensuring that your stance and form are up to par before moving on to a cycle of complex sparring techniques."

"Okay," I replied with minimal annoyance. "It's not like I haven't done hand-to-hand before, you know."

"Seven months ago, Kat. Seven months is a long time."

"I'm just saying, Nik. I'm not incompetent." I trusted Kazrah, he'd been training us since Aer and I had faked my death and moved across town to our small apartment.

I thought back to the day I'd first met him, fresh rain still coating the ground as I stopped at a newsstand and picked up the local newspaper, scanning it for any mention of our deceit.

The thin pages of the paper shook slightly in my hands as black ink glared back at me.

"ILLEGAL MAGIC WIELDER FOUND DEAD. Kateya Dumont's body was found early this morning outside her family home in Estaire. Let this be a warning to those who seek to embrace the ancient power, death shall be the only release you find."

I held back a scoff as I stared at the words, reading my name over and over again. I was now, legally, dead. Gone. Erased from existence with just a few splatters of ink on some carbon paper. You would think that your death mattered more than that. That it would affect those who knew you more. That it would perhaps even alter the lives of those around you. But somehow, their angry black printed marks just mocked me. My death, though only on paper, was just that: words bound to be forgotten in time.

Happy as I was that our plan had succeeded, that the Nordak scum took the bait we'd laid out, it felt as though I'd lost a part of me. A part of my soul. I crumpled up the parchment, venom bubbling up from deep within me as I threw the paper against the wall.

"Woah." A rough voice came from behind me. "I highly doubt that had the effect you wanted it to. I've got a better solution if you want it."

I took in the man to my side as he leaned against the side of the lamp post. Though I could tell he was older, his sturdy frame and muscles stood out against his peppered hair. He seemed to be about the age my father was. Had been.

"What makes you think I need a better solution?" I questioned, my voice thick with wary intrigue at the strange man's proposition.

"You look as if the realm stole the light out from under you and you have no means to fight back. Yet, from the looks of it, you want to fight back, don't you?"

My eyes widened in shock at his assessment, the accuracy to which he found me, as I watched him with care. Would I regret accepting his offer? Should I accept it so soon after faking my own death?

"You've got two minutes to decide," he stated even as his feet began moving away from me, the distance between us stretching on.

I felt my legs moving to catch up before I could stop them, my voice calling out in a plea, "Wait! Please wait!" I caught up to him at the intersection. "What did you have in mind?"

He simply grinned as he led the way, my steps falling into pace with his.

The car halted with a jerk, the seatbelt clawing at my chest as Nik parked the car, pulling me from my thoughts. I followed Nik, his hand entwined with mine as we entered the tunnels, twisting in a downward spiral before veering to the right, to the same place I had trained nearly every day since meeting Kazrah a year ago.

The training pits were underground, deep enough that the Seefers couldn't scent out the blood, sweat, and tears that covered the dirt flooring. With a sharp push, the door budged, creaking open as grunts filled the air and a musky scent hit my nose.

"Ring three." Kazrah's voice rang out as a greeting. The door closed behind us as I set my mind on the morning's task: clearing the nagging thoughts lingering and focusing on my session. Hopping over the fencing with an ease honed by a year of prac-tice, I took a few deep breaths, running through the stances by memory in my mind, visualizing the outcome of my session. Nik wanted me to train in case I ever needed to defend myself during a surprise attack. But Kazrah, he trained me for the fight that was yet to come. For the kill. And he *never* went easy on me in the ring.

EAST ENGLES

Chapter Three

I'D TOLD Aerilyn everything before we faked my death. I told her about traveling through time with Cass; about the flow of magic in the past; about the prophecy and the pendant; about the Elder and the importance of a balance in magic; and, most importantly, about the two remaining artifacts lost in time.

That had become our mission, our purpose in life for the past year. I needed to find the remaining artifacts, and make it back to my sister before she had to face the prophesied threat of war on her own.

Drenched in sweat, my legs trembled as I stumbled up the last few steps; my body was on the verge of collapsing. Aerilyn had secured the key code for the ninth floor last night and we prepared to enter one of the only remaining areas in the Archives we hadn't searched yet.

We'd been searching for three months so far—four floors underground and eight above. But the ninth . . . the ninth had an extra code to get into the back rooms. Rooms we'd failed to enter for twelve weeks.

Turning the key, I stepped through our apartment door, my body was screaming at me for a break it would not get, as Aerilyn greeted me while she prepared to head out. "Morning! Breakfast is in the fridge. I'm leaving in fifteen. Meet you two blocks south of the west entrance?"

I calculated the distance in my mind. With the route I would be taking to the Archives, that gave me twenty minutes to rinse off and down breakfast before I would need to leave.

"Sounds like a plan," I responded as I tugged open the refrigerator. Chilled air clashed with my clammy, sweat-drenched clothing, causing me to shiver as I reached for the shake. "What flavor is this today?" I threw out over my shoulder to Aerilyn as I took a sip.

"Cinnamon apple and oatmeal, with vanilla protein," she called out from the hall as she gathered her purse. "Oh, and leek."

I spluttered, nearly spewing the contents in my mouth as I forced myself to swallow. "Leek?" I croaked out as I now warily eyed the contents in the glass.

"Yeah, I read something online about the benefits of using leeks against Seefer venom. I'm not sure of its validity yet, but I figured it didn't hurt to have some in our system with the increase in sightings lately."

"Uh-huh . . ." I muttered as I eyed the drink with remorse before continuing to drink it while I walked toward my room. "See you later," I called out to Aerilyn as I chugged down the odd mixture in the glass quickly, shuddering slightly at the thought of the vegetable thrown into an otherwise delicious smoothie.

Twenty minutes arrived all too soon. The cold shower had hurried me along as I dressed in a rush, before dashing out the door. We rarely took the same path to the Archives—preferring for it to look as though we only occasionally met to frequent the library of documents found within its walls.

I took a left out of our building and headed for 5th Street, knowing that the Nordak preferred to patrol the populated streets at night, rather than the mornings; meaning my chances of running into any emergency patrol forces were slim. The morning sun was climbing higher in the sky, glinting softly across arched windows as it rose. Spring mornings like this, with the cool air caressing my skin and the birds playing in the early light, reminded me of the East Engles before The Fall. I loved seeing the reminders in the sky of a time when peace and magic flowed together freely, channeling from each other. It was moments like this that reminded me why I spent every waking moment searching for the missing artifacts. For a way back to my sister, stuck in the past. For a way to end whatever war was most certainly brewing thanks to the artifacts cast across our realm.

The walk to the Archives remained uneventful, with hardly a soul on the streets this early on a Friday morning. With the increase in both Seefer attacks and Nordak patrols, the Descendents had slowly encouraged the citizens to adopt later starts to their mornings. People took to new hours in businesses—opening around noon and shutting down for the day before dusk—allowing folks to return to the safety of their homes before the sun set each day, believing that this kept them safe . . . protected from the grasps of darkness. In reality, it didn't. Since The Fall, people have begun to willingly believe what is presented to them without question. How else would one explain the multitude of historical documents that have simply vanished in the past eight years? Or the lack of questioning that occurred regarding mortal disappearances? Or the extinguishing of those in Vanaiyer who had held elemental magic? Or the death toll that increasingly grew daily, yet was never shared to the public. Rather, it was swept beneath dusty parchments in the Archives.

Knowledge was power, and since The Fall, we'd been stripped of any ties to our past. Most were content to merely exist within the confines of restriction. Yet another reason I knew, without a doubt, that Aerilyn and I wouldn't be able to stop until we found the remaining artifacts. Our only hope being that once we found the artifacts, we would uncover the secrets of our pasts and find a way to put a stop to the terror that reigned in darkness over our lives daily.

I slowed my pace a block over from our meeting spot, checking every few steps to ensure that I hadn't been followed, that no eyes were watching me from the shadows as I met up with Aerilyn.

"Ready?" Her voice chirped as I came into her view.

"Let's pray to The God that this floor has the answers we're looking for. I don't know how much longer we can keep sneaking into the Archives like this before someone catches on."

"There's only two more floors left," she replied. "If it's not there . . ." Her voice faltered at the end, trailing off, but I knew what she was getting at. It was the same thought that ran rampant through my mind in the late hours of the night. If the answers weren't there, we'd be at a dead end; failing at our only goal before we could truly get started.

The Nordak had forcefully stopped all forms of travel within the past year. It would be nearly impossible to gather any other information, to source anything regarding the artifacts. And with the attacks increasing every day, it was unlikely we had much time left to locate the artifacts to begin with.

The doors slid open silently and an older woman briefly glanced up from her desk as we stepped through the entrance, the warm air brushing softly against our skin as we were met with silence. Calmly, we walked in silence to the keypad, typing in the code to the main interior checkpoint—a code we had managed to uncover months ago—and watched the electric silver doors swing to the side after there was a low buzz from the pad.

Entering the inner enclosed atrium of the Archives, I stopped briefly, just as I did every time we visited, in awe of the structure.

The circular structure spiraled toward the sunlight peeking through the glass ceiling. Low lights flickered softly as they floated in the air, a humorless laugh dying on my lips at the thought that the Archives managed to do what thousands of Vanaiyerian citizens hadn't been able to . . . produce magic. As the Nordak had taken our Capital, they had eradicated any use of magic, stripping the city to the bones, yet the Archives still produced magic, though diminished. It was truly a wonder that the ancient structure had been woven so skillfully in its creation that even the darkest forces of our time couldn't strip it of its power.

Glancing at my watch, I began counting down the minutes as we walked our way up the stone steps to the ninth floor. The shelves switched locations, precisely on the dot, once every three hours, hiding themselves in plain sight. And with each magical shift, the impossibility of locating a text grew.

Cool air embraced my skin as we stepped off the winded staircase on the ninth floor, the dusty texts stacked in organized chaos, as though this floor was often left untouched. Weaving our way through the wooden shelves, I stared at the dating system, counting backward in time, yet every time, without fail, the texts halted at the year 500. As if, magically, Vanaiyer had been created in 500 by The God—simply lurching itself into existence. Yet, I knew that the prophecy that kept my sister back in the past had been created at least thirty years before that.

"Two minutes," Aerilyn's voice whispered in the silence as we neared the door she'd been instructed to locate. *Well, not instructed, but informed, nonetheless.*

"Are you sure the key will work?" My voice echoed along the floor and I winced, praying no one had heard.

"Not the slightest clue," she replied with a wry laugh. "But we have no other option, so it's worth a shot."

We came to a stop in front of the door and stared. So simple, just a tinted glass door that blended into the shadows of the dimly lit alcove, and yet, behind this door the answers we'd been searching for could potentially be waiting. I held my breath as Aerilyn stepped forward, pulling a knife from her back pocket as she raised it to her pointer finger, pricking the tip. Blood welled slowly as she closed the knife and lifted her other hand as she stood on her toes, pressing against what appeared to be a chip in the glass. Using her pointer finger, she traced her blood in a familiar triangle symbol while repeating the numbers, "Five, eight, twenty-three, six, nineteen, forty-four, ten."

Neither of us breathed as we waited in bated silence, eyes glued to the door.

Nothing.

Another moment passed, and I could hear the subtle shift of the shelves behind us, as our time began to start anew. Three hours left until the next shift, yet the door didn't budge.

Two hours, fifty-nine minutes.

"Are you sure you did it right?" I whispered, staring at her blood smeared symbol on the door, the crimson color stark against the glass.

"Yes." She hesitated, thinking. "I'm sure. I did everything just as he told me."

Two hours, fifty-eight minutes.

"Well." I sighed. "Maybe he was just too drunk and making it up . . . you know," I muttered, "to get you in bed."

Aer sighed, lowering her palm. "I was just so sure that this would be it."

I stared at the door. We needed this. We needed to get through the door.

So we waited, with bated breath, and yet. The door did not budge.

Aerilyn fidgeted beside me, studying the symbol she had drawn, as she re-muttered the numbers under her breath, checking the order. Looking to the side of the door, I began studying the works, the titles, when a subtle click hit our ears and we froze.

"Did you hear that?" Aerilyn whispered. And I nodded back, watching as the lock slowly spun, as if being unlocked by a magical force, before the door sprang free and we stared inside.

A blue-hued room met our gaze with scrolls of paper littering the space, some sprawled haphazardly across an oak desk in the corner. For a singular moment, we were frozen, in utter shock, at the vast difference this singular room had in comparison to the remainder of the Archives. The chaos that was unbounding beyond the frame.

We sprung to action. Rushing into the room as the countdown continued.

Two hours, fifty-six minutes remaining.

Frigid air met us as the blue hue of the room surrounded our skin, enveloping us while we assessed the room, careful not to let the door click shut behind us.

"I'll take the desk first." Aerilyn's voice softly filled the room.

"Leave everything as we found it," I whispered back, walking to the closest cabinet of scrolls, gingerly opening the amber cabinet doors as the search continued. Shifting through the scrolls, I delicately picked up one, then another, scouring the ancient words for any mention of the artifacts, any mention of the battle that would have been waged all those years ago.

The shelves of scrolls seemed to carry on in an unending fashion, my fingers cramping as I hurriedly shifted through scroll after scroll. My phone vibrated in my back pocket, startling me as I stood to stretch, legs cramping from my crouched position. Nik's name flashed across my screen, reminding me of our plans tonight. Plans Aerilyn had begrudgingly agreed to join in on.

"Nik said he would meet us there at nine." My voice drifted slowly across the room as I continued my search. "Find anything yet?"

"Nothing." Aerilyn's voice hit me with defeat. "But I'm thinking we're getting closer."

"Closer?"

"Yeah," she retorted. "The scrolls here . . . I haven't even come across these in the Archive records and there are a great deal that date back further than any I've seen."

The soft rustle of ancient paper once again filled the room as we resumed our search, my eyes scanning each document that graced my fingers. *Politica. Great War rising. Powers that be.* I skimmed the scroll at hand, searching further down the document—the first I'd seen to mention any form of war rising. And yet, nothing.

A defeated sigh slipped my lips just as Aerilyn half-shouted, "Kat! Here . . . read this one."

Springing stealthily to my feet, I rushed over, excitement and hope welling within me even as I strove to push it down, to remain realistic. I delicately grabbed the scroll from her outstretched hand, my eyes scanning the parchment before they met the first words that stood out, stark against the surrounding ink, *red-hued gemstone*. I took a closer look.

A Great War is drawing near. Death and destruction are on the brink as the Nordak seek the powers of the darkness, striking bargains sealed in blood and lies. A war so devastating our lands won't survive . . . the realm won't remain the same once touched by their cursed power.

"It's a journal entry." I loosed a breath. "One from right before the artifacts were placed into existence it seems." I resumed reading, the soft vibration of my watch indicating that we had twenty minutes remaining.

This power . . . a power unlike any the lands have seen, is capable of calling mauled creatures into existence, of casting darkness across the realm and spreading disease through the soil. We have only one hope. One desperate attempt to spare the lives of our people and to give the future of our realm a fighting chance. A chance of the future.

Three stones: a sacred blue with the water element flowing through, an emerald green that contains life within, and a red-hued gemstone of the lifeblood we preserve and willingly sacrifice. The answer to our prayers, the warrior's power, the final hope, now embedded in the stones of—

The words stopped. I scanned the rest of the document, my heart sinking as I looked at Aerilyn. "The rest must have faded over time."

"That," she muttered, "or whichever king wrote this entry didn't have time to finish writing the contents of the stones before they cast their powers into them, banishing them to the far corners of the realm."

A longer vibration rolled through my skin as I glanced at the countdown on my watch. "We have ten minutes to wipe our tracks." Our actions picked up as we returned the scrolls to the position we found them in, leaving not a trace of our visit in the room.

The cherry-tinted lipstick painted across my lips provided me with a false bravado, a direct contrast to the feeling rising within me as we stood in line at Hydrillas to meet Nik. My fingers grappled with the frayed edges of my leather skirt, the material stuck to my thighs as my mind raced with the knowledge uncovered today.

Three stones, three colors, two remaining chances of returning to Cassandra.

Two chances to try to stop the darkness that shrouded our realm.

I only needed one though. One stone would bring me back to her, the only true family I had left in the realm . . . and not even time could keep us apart now.

"ID?"

I glanced up to the bouncer, flashing my license as a flirtatious smile spread. "Busy night tonight Jace?" I asked the blond bouncer I'd known since my early clubbing days. He was one of the only people in the realm who had recognized me since my return, and as such, had been sworn to secrecy.

"Busier than most, but not as bad as the time Aer packed this place for her twenty-first." His laugh carried over the rhythm of the music.

"That's a night none of us will ever forget, not that she'd let us." My grin grew as I threw a knowing look at Aer, both of us thinking back to fond memories of the raging party she and my sister had thrown years ago. "Nik already inside?"

"He came through around half an hour ago. Probably already has a table for you two."

An annoyed shout came from down the line and Jace lifted the ribbon, allowing us to slip inside the club. The music and flashing lights beaconing us closer to the center of the club.

"Drinks first?" Aer's shout came into my ear over the roar of the music. A nod of my head and we started to the bar, pressing past throngs of clubgoers as we fought our way to the sticky counter. Motioning toward the bartender, we soon found ourselves with two iridescent shots of unknown liquor.

"Bottoms up!" Aerilyn's voice cried as she lifted her shot glass, liquid sloshing on the counter as it collided with mine. The shot hit me like fire and ice, burning my throat before a cool calm settled over my soul. A group of men slid up beside us, Aerilyn's attention drifting as the men focused on her.

"I'm gonna go find Nik." My head angled toward the VIP booths in the back. "Meet me soon?"

Her absent nod told me all I needed to know as I pushed off the counter, making my way across the dance floor in search of my boyfriend. Checking my phone again, a frustrated sigh slipped my lips. No new texts. Nothing from Nik at all since this morning.

Me: Where are you???

Nothing.

Me: I'm at Hydrillas. Jace said he saw you come in.

Me: Heading to VIP.

Nothing.

Sliding my phone back in my pocket, I avoided dancing couples across the floor as I moved closer to the back corner of the bar, skirting the edge of the crowded dance floor. Jace hadn't been lying when he said this place was busier than usual. For a Friday night, I'd never seen it this packed. It was nearly impossible to move across the floor.

A glimpse of buzzed blond hair caught my eye in the shadows and I drew closer, praying to The God that it was Nik. Losing sight of the man, I pushed around a couple, drifting closer to the outskirts of the crowd, eyes pinned to the spot I'd last seen a flash of familiar blond-colored hair. I froze as I spotted Nik. My pulse increased as I watched my boyfriend twist his hands further into raven black hair, tilting the owner's head back for him as he bit her lip, before taking it into his mouth and kissing her. Fury blinded me as I watched in shock as my boyfriend cheated on me. Rage overtook my logical thinking and I stormed over to his shady corner of the club.

"Hello, Nik," I purred, ice dripping from my tone as he whirled around, alarm flashing briefly in his eyes. Turning to the female trapped in his clutches, I extended my hand. "I don't believe we've met." My venomous smile crept across my face. "I'm Kateya. Nik's girlfriend. Well," I said with a sharp glance toward him, "*ex*-girlfriend now; since any man who decides to go out with multiple girls at once isn't really my style. But all the power to you if you can handle being someone's sloppy seconds."

Nik fixed a dark glare at me as I whirled on my heel, his hand snatching out to wrap tightly around my wrist. "What do you think you're doing, Kateya?" He sneered, his grip tightening around me as he tugged me back toward him, his catch of the hour slinking off into the background.

"Breaking up with you," I threw back. "Like I should have done months ago. But thank you, truly, for making this so easy for me."

His scoff crept across my skin with a breeze of unease. "You think you can get rid of me that easily? Huh, Kateya?" His grip tightened as he pulled me even closer to his icy skin. "This is over when I say it is. You don't get to play the pathetic, helpless girl who lost her family and then switch to bitch mode."

"I said . . ." My gaze met his eyes demanding attention, outraged that he dared bring up my family like that. "This." I yank against his hold. "Is." I pulled my arm free from him. "Over." My knee slammed up, colliding with him, straight between the legs. "Forever." His eyes widened in pain as I jerked away from him. I didn't waste another second as I whirled on my heel, forcing my way through the crowd as I broke free—away from him. From my last tie to a past that I would never get back. To a time that would forever be frozen in my mind.

I didn't stop until I locked myself into the far bathroom stall, sinking down to the floor. My hands shook as I stared aimlessly at the etchings scrawled onto the stall door.

Sarai and Ren forever.

F+E=BFF.

The drunken ink scrawling of club goers covered the space, yet I stared at nothing.

We were done. Over. My chest rose and fell, as a stream of hurt tears cascaded down my cheeks. *He'd cheated. I knew things weren't always perfect with Nik, but he . . . he cheated.* A dull pain faded within as I let myself wallow in self pity for the briefest moment, counting down.

Five. *A future with him.*

Four. *The only person other than Aerilyn who remembered my family's existence.*

Three. *The guy who'd been my first boyfriend.*

Tears welled slightly, threatening to fall over again but I held them in.

Two. *The guy who'd help me train to survive a realm of no magic.*

One.

I rose to my feet. I wouldn't lose myself to the darkness; I refused to. So I whispered the same thing I repeated to myself every day for the past year.

I am resilient. I will overcome.

Opening the stall, I stared at my reflection in the dimly lit bathroom mirror, taking in the smudged mascara under my eyes. The girl next to me glanced in my direction. "You okay?" Her brown hair flopped in her high ponytail as she touched up her makeup, pausing for a moment to pass me a paper towel.

"I'm good. Thanks though," I replied, accepting the towel as I began to clean up my ruined makeup. Her eyes glimmered knowingly as her hands went up to her earrings and she began tugging on them, the movement momentarily distracting me from the events that just occurred.

"Let me guess, the ruined makeup involves a guy." She smirked knowingly as she took out her dangle earrings, resting them on the watery counter before fixing the hair around her ear.

"Doesn't all ruined makeup involve one in some way." I forced a smile back toward her, my makeup almost acceptable once again.

"That they do. These things"—she gestured to the dangle earrings now laying on the counter—"can't move without them hooking onto the sides of my head and messing up my hair."

A series of pops echoed through the air, followed by a chorus of alarmed shouts that cascaded into the nightclub. Freezing, we both glanced toward the bathroom entrance, waiting to hear what was happening. That's when I heard it; the growing shrill echoing from inside the club, a shrieking cry that haunted my nightmares. A noise I'd recognize anywhere for the death that followed in its shadows. *Seefers.*

The bathroom door flew off its hinges as a group of half drunken girls shoved their way inside, screaming in terror.

"MOVE!"

"Open the window!"

"No, just take your shoes off! We need to get out!"

"We're fucked. This is where we die!" Their screams ricocheted off the tiled bathroom walls as they scrambled toward the singular window. I cursed my luck. Armed with only a gun and a knife, I didn't stand a chance on my own. The girl I'd been talking to by the sink turned to head into the fray, as I began to move toward the now broken bathroom door. Adrenaline pumped through me as I followed after her. I pushed against the throng of girls fighting for the window, when a glimmer of blue caught my gaze. As if called by the glimpse of color, my eyes collided with the pair of blue earrings forgotten on the counter. With a swipe of my hand, I pocketed the earrings as I charged toward the main section of the club. Toward the screams; toward the beasts.

Blood coated the nightclub floor, the lights had been flipped on as chaos erupted around me. I did a quick scan of my immediate surroundings and noticed Jace with the other bouncers, fending off a Seefer by the south entrance of the club. Another Seefer was mauling someone to my right, their tortured screams flooding the air. Pulling my gun, I thanked The God that the shot was clear, before I aimed toward the mangled gray fur, locking in on my target before pulling the trigger. The shot rang true, hitting the beast between the shoulders. Blood sprayed as the Seefer stumbled, before turning on its heels, locking gazes with me. Its fiery eyes narrowing in on its newest victim. *Me.*

"We need to draw it the fuck out!" Aer's voice shouted out of nowhere next to me. "RUN!" she screamed as we charged toward the east entrance of the club and took off in a full sprint.

The chase was on. I could feel the Seefer gaining on us as the night air hit my skin. I sprinted, cursing my outfit for the millionth time tonight as I veered to the right, skidding to a stop and lining up my shot. Drawing in a breath, I steadied myself and fired again, missing by two inches as the Seefer narrowly leapt from the bullet's path, right into Aerilyn's bullet. Blood sprayed as it went down, enraged snarls on its tongue as we charged the creature, knives drawn. With precise cuts, we ensured the Seefer was dead, before we fled the scene, racing home toward our apartment.

EAST ENGLES

Chapter Four

WE DIDN'T MAKE it out of the comfort of our beds until well past noon. The events of last night, plus our debrief of everything that went down at the club had dragged well into the late hours of the night. Aerilyn had shrieked out of excitement upon discovering that I had indeed dumped Nik for good, which led to a celebratory bottle of champagne being popped, despite it only being early afternoon.

As we proceeded to drink the bottle, we discussed the Seefer attack at Hydrillas late into the night, pondering what led to the attack point being there of all places. While not uncommon, it was far more rare for the Seefers to make it inside buildings when attacking, preferring to stay in the dark alleys and backlit roads.

"Seefers don't plan attacks, Kat," Aerilyn argued. "To plan an attack would mean that the Nordak control the creatures. We haven't found any evidence for that."

"Who's to say they don't, though?" I questioned back. "Seriously, Aer, think about it. It's something we've never looked into. The Descendents haven't even looked into it." I paused to take a breath. "It's always just been assumed that the attacks were random occurrences, but what if we're wrong?"

Aerilyn stared at me, her pale purple eyes tracking mine,

reading the seriousness of my tone. "*If* the Nordak are controlling the Seefers and their attacks, and that's a big *if* . . ." she paused. "Why now? Why Hydrillas? They could have attacked anywhere, at any time."

"I think that's what we need to look into," I said as I walked over to our drafting table we used as a desk, flipping the surface upside down, the map of Estaire coming into view. Studying the pinned flags, the markers of known Seefer attacks, I looked over at my roommate. "Do you see any correlations? Anything that could resemble a connection?"

We studied the map in silence, connecting each of the attack points as I added another red pin for the attack last night.

A gasp fell from her lips as her hand shook. "Kat." Aerilyn paused breathlessly. "Look at this. I don't know how we missed it. It's been right in front of us this whole time."

I studied the map and then glanced toward her as she continued. "Look. *Here.*" She pointed to one marker. *"Here."* She pointed yet again. *"Here."* Her finger shook at each marker. Her hand reached up to the top of the map, flipping the switch on the digital background. *Click, click, click.* She settled on a map overlay, the purple lines illuminating on the desks surface . . . *the ley lines.* I stared in shock as each of the attacks directly hovered over a section of the map where multiple ley lines connected with each other.

"Every attack falls on a ley line," she whispered in horror.

"Almost . . ." My throat felt dry as I continued. "As if the Seefers gain power at those intersections. Or . . . the Nordak can control the Seefers where those lines connect."

"It would make sense." She paused. "Think on the history, the Seefers were creatures born of corrupt magic. They were created by a *Nordak* king hundreds of years ago. The Seefers themselves *are* magic. So why wouldn't the Nordak be able to control the Seefers, since they created them long ago. And, they could be controlling them when they show up at the overlapping sections of our ley lines—where magic would be the strongest."

"And if the Nordak are the only ones who can control magic currently," I muttered in shock. "How would anyone know? No one would notice the spikes of power if they can't even sense it in their own veins. There's absolutely no way for any Vanaiyerians to notice that they are controlling the creatures."

We quickly began marking off the remainder of the intersected ley lines, focusing on the points that would most likely be targeted next. Each marker placed causes our hearts to grow heavy as we realized there could still be another ten attacks that could happen in the Capital.

"But why only at the ley lines?" I questioned. "Why not control the Seefers all the time?"

"Maybe they can't?" Aer's voice responded. "Or maybe we're still missing something, some other piece to the puzzle."

"We need to start monitoring those points." I looked at Aer as I spoke. "Learn the quickest route to each ley line intersection."

"I'll get on that later today," she said, tone heavy with the weight of our discovery.

The fucking ley lines. Why hadn't we thought of that sooner?

Tugging on a creamy colored crop top and black workout leggings, I began pulling my hair back for the gym.

"How long will you be at training today?" My best friend's shout came from down the hall.

"Four hours or so." I frowned as my brownish-blonde hair refused to cooperate with me. "I have patrol for the night shift. Want to give myself enough time to rest afterwards."

"Okay, I've got patrol until 7 p.m., then I'll head straight to the gym."

"Don't let Teaja drive you crazy on patrol today!" I called back to her. "We can catch up in the morning."

"Where'd you get these?" Aer's voice called out as she drew closer to me, before her red hair popped into view, a pair of blue stone earrings in her hand.

"I'd forgotten about those," I replied, my hair finally settling into place. Walking to grab my socks, I continued. "When we were at Hydrillas, there was a girl in the bathroom next to me. She was complaining about them continually getting caught in her hair and took them out. But in all the chaos of the attack, she left them on the counter. Something about them called to me, so I swiped them before I ran out the door to join the fight."

Aer's laughter floated through the room. "You mean to tell me." She paused dramatically. "That in the middle of the *most* chaotic Seefer attack we've had all year . . . you *paused* to grab a pair of cute earrings . . ." she finished, dangling them in front of me.

"What?" I laughed as I swiped them from her outstretched hand. "Can you blame a girl? They're gorgeous!" We stared at the pair of earrings—round, icy blue stones dangled from silver and gold entwined metal. A smaller stone at the top of each earring.

"Whoever she is . . ." Aer started. "I doubt she will miss these if she was taking them off at a nightclub."

"Finders keepers," I whispered as I looped one through my ear, securing the backing and then the other, the air around me settling with a new weight as they hung from my ears, glimmering in the sunlight.

"I've got to run! I'll see you in the morning," she said as she started out the door.

"See you in the morning," I called back out as I stared at the earrings a moment longer, before lacing up my shoes for the gym. They truly were stunning.

Beads of sweat drenched my back as I stepped out of the fighting ring, my limbs shaking and on the verge of collapsing. Even with the long hours spent training, exhaustion grew with every session. I pushed to increase the time spent in the fighting ring; the time learning every throw, each block and maneuver. Every loss I had in the ring was knowledge gained, and every chance to train with weapons meant another life I could protect—could help to save. The scars that speckled my arms and legs told me that I was alive and I was fighting.

A glance at my phone told me Aerilyn would be getting off her patrol shift in two hours. The angry messages from Nik had come in every minute until I'd blocked his number halfway through my workout, relieved at the silence on my smartwatch.

"See you tomorrow, Kazrah." I waved as I pushed open the front door, the evening air cooling my heated skin. Late winter nights had the sun setting far earlier in the evening, casting our land in a blanket of darkness; a darkness that allowed for all manner of creatures to emerge and prowl for longer than desired. Hurrying home, I willed my legs to move faster, stealthier, as I walked through the shadows, avoiding the beams of street lights that would highlight me as willing prey.

Even at this early hour, it was rare to see people on the streets. Most chose to avoid the darkness and the dangers that lurked within its embrace—man and beast alike. They often failed to realize that monsters could be born out of darkness. But more often than not, they are a fabrication of the realm around them. A result of the hardships they've endured. Those same creatures they shy away from at night grace their houses in the daylight.

A car horn sounded in the distance as I rounded the corner to my street, taking each step quietly, but quickly. Fully alert, even as I mentally ran through the list of things I needed to finish before my patrol shift. My thoughts continually drifted back to the piece of parchment we'd discovered yesterday. The prophetic words running rampant in my mind.

A chance of the future. Three stones: a sacred blue with the water element flowing through, an emerald green that contains life within, and a red-hued gemstone of the lifeblood we preserve and willingly sacrifice. The answer to our prayers, the warrior's power, the final hope, now embedded in the stones of—

All that was left was to find the stones. My mind flashed back to my sister; how she said that the necklace just showed up one day. A gift from an elderly woman when we left Verastarr as children. Even with my apartment in sight, I kept thinking back to that—tracing through the facts.

Three artifacts.

Four lands that bound a prophecy.

The East Engles was eliminated because the prophecy had been created on the magic of the land which would mean that its ruler had no need to present an artifact. Cass had found the artifact provided by the king of Verastarr. Which left two remaining artifacts: one blue and one green, from the lands of Avyon and Reggeon.

Cassandra's artifact had appeared to her in the land that it had brought her back through time to. Did that mean that we would have to fly to Avyon or Reggeon to find the remaining two artifacts? Yet even if we did, how would we know that we had truly found the artifacts?

Or, would they simply appear? A random, every day occurrence that one wouldn't think much of, much like the pendant Cass wore around her neck had just been given to her one day. But that left too much to fate, to destiny, and I had no intention of waiting for destiny to intervene.

Opening the front door of my building, I glanced to both sides of the sidewalk, ensuring that no one had followed me home from the training gym. The cool night air playfully nipped at my chilled skin as I stepped through the main doorway and headed for the stairs to my apartment.

My mind briefly flitted to the instance the other night, and the girl that left her earrings on the counter.

If only finding the artifacts was that easy, I thought to myself as I fumbled with the key to my door, my arms shaking from the exertion at the gym. Getting the door open, I dropped the keys onto the counter, before moving to flip the light switch, when a voice cut through the air. "Well, well. Look who finally decided to show up."

My heart froze, my fingers slipping to the dagger around my

thigh as I hit the light switch. Nik's frame came into view as he lounged on my couch, one arm wrapped over the back ledge.

"What the *fuck* do you think you're doing here, Nik?" I seethed as I stared at my ex, sprawled out in a relaxed position in my apartment. "You're not welcome here, and you know it." I took in his little posse of friends. I recognized them, but only barely. There were two on the chairs by the couch, and a third leaning against the hall door frame, a ruthless gleam in his eyes. I was outnumbered and low on strength from training all afternoon.

"I thought I told you yesterday. *I* will decide when this"—he gestured between the two of us as he spoke—"is over. So, *Kateya*." He sneered in my direction, his cold eyes holding me hostage. "Why don't you sit down and let's talk about this like adults."

I scoffed. "Or . . . why don't you get out of my Void-damned apartment. I've got nothing to say to you, Nik. And frankly, Aer was right all along. I should have dumped you long ago."

He moved, quick as lightning, until he towered over me, my back pressed against my kitchen cabinets, cold metal from the handles pressing into my skin. But I held my ground, not ready to use the only weapon I had in hand just yet.

"You listen to me." His dark gaze raked over me, fury in his eyes. "You're fucking everything up. You think we don't know." I froze, my body tense as I wondered what he was referring to. "You think we don't see you and Aerilyn going on patrols; tracking the growing Seefer movement; spending all your spare time in the Archives. We know, Kateya."

I met his eyes, because there was no way he could know everything. There was no way he could know that we were searching for a way to get back to the past, to my sister, that we were searching for the missing artifacts with hopes of helping to stop a long foretold war.

"You know nothing," I spat.

"Really, Kateya. I expected so much better from you. It's honestly somewhat disheartening, come to think of it," he said with a wry chuckle as he nodded his head toward his friend. Walking back to the couch, he continued, "Who do you think got you accepted into the Descendents?" A vicious little smirk told me he had pulled more strings than I'd thought. "But did you ever stop to think why?" he prompted as I tensed, because no, I hadn't. I had assumed that Nik wanted us to help, to fight for the people of East Engles, the people of our realm; just as he wanted to. "Thanks to you two, we now know what the next two artifacts look like."

My gaze flicked to him in horror, before looking over each of the three other men standing in my apartment, the sinister grins on their faces. "What do you want with the artifacts?" My voice tightened, heart thudding heavily as I spoke. My hand moved ever so slowly to my smartwatch, navigating the screen without them noticing. Aerilyn and I had never mentioned the artifacts . . . to anyone. And if Nik knew, that meant there was more lying beneath the surface of the Nordak attacks than we originally believed.

"Well to start, we know that each of those remaining artifacts carry more power than even the Nordak King holds. And, we know that you've been searching for them ever since your sister disappeared with the first one."

A slow, malicious smile spread across his face as he stared at me and my heart skipped a beat in pure terror. I'd never once told him about the artifact, or about the details behind Cassandra and my disappearance a year ago.

My fingers discreetly tapped the face of my watch, once, twice, a rapid double tap, and then I held my finger on it as I prayed to The God that Aerilyn got my message. That she knew our cover had been blown and to not return here.

It had been a backup we'd set in place when we faked my identity, to ensure we could always hideout somewhere if need be. I took three calming breaths, checking each of their positions, sizing up my opponents, not sure if I would make it out of this situation.

One. I walked forward, keeping my eyes on Nik, even as his group shifted from my movement.

Two. My hand slowly grabbed the hilt of my knife.

Three. My other hand slid under the counter, grabbing the gun hidden underneath. I stopped, a slow smile spreading across my face, glimmering silver strands of hair framing my eyes as I pushed the fear into the background of my mind and spoke.

"Whatever you think you're going to accomplish, Nik," I sneered, "you will fail. The artifacts you're looking for . . . you won't find them. They aren't meant for you, or anyone in your little posse. And even if you do get your hands on them, they won't work the way you're hoping they will. I guarantee you that much."

I threw the knife, not even looking as it flew hilt over blade, cutting through the air toward my ex. But I was already moving, flipping the safety off the gun as I fired a shot, the bullet flying toward the male charging for me. I heard Nik's grunt of pain, the knife meeting its target, embedding itself in him. A shout came from my side, and I turned just in time for a fist to collide with my jaw.

Pain erupted across my face as I flew back from the force, colliding with the ground as the gun bounced from my hand, skidding to a stop under a chair. Blinding pain shot across my head as my skull pounded from the impact. I grunted, pushing myself up as Nik rose from the couch, rage ablaze in his eyes as a knife rested in his palm, covered in his blood. "You *bitch,*" he seethed, stalking toward me. "You think you can get away with this? You think you can actually get free of me?"

I scrambled back, closer to the door as I got to my feet, only to be knocked down as his other two friends tackled me, slamming me into the ground with such force that I saw stars.

Nik's face appeared in my vision, towering over me as I struggled against the two males holding me down, thrashing and kicking, but I couldn't break free from their hold. I was pinned down, trapped and cornered. "You will pay for this," Nik bit out as he tossed the knife to the side, the blade clattering against the tile flooring. "We *need* the next two artifacts for our King to rise to his full power. And you . . . I have a feeling you are the very key we need to locate the next artifact. So you won't be going anywhere until you bring us the next two artifacts and tell us where your bitch of a sister is hiding."

Void-damned. My mind blanched at the realization that Nik had changed sides. That he was actually working for the Void-damned King of Nordak. That he was part of the terror that ran rampant in our land.

His gaze turned ruthless, pure obsidian spreading in his eyes as he stepped closer, leaning over me and drew a wicked, curved onyx blade from his side that had me thrashing even more against my captors hold. I thrashed violently from side to side, my limbs protesting the jarring movement as I struggled and failed to break free from the two men pinning me to the floor of my apartment.

I recognized that blade. The curved onyx he wielded was a blade I'd read about in the Archives, a blade talked about in whispered tones when I'd been back in the past in Verastarr.

It was the Blade of Rathmen.

A long forgotten blade that the darkness wielded. A blade the vicious King Vyrnor of Nordak had forged and then wielded as he reigned terror across the realm during the First War. A war of the beginning of times, from the early days of our realm. It was a cursed blade. One that imbued its victims with a form of unknown magic, magic known to make the carrier crazy from its power, once the wielder carved their name into their victim. Magic that made the victim do whatever the blade wielder demanded they do.

I'd seen sketches of it as Aerilyn and I had scoured the Archives for the artifacts.

It was horrifying. The power it held, the lives it could alter; the darkness that flowed through it. The blade had been lost for centuries, allowing me only the briefest moment to wonder how Nik had gotten his hands on the cursed weapon.

The irises of Nik's eyes turned black as he spoke words in an ancient tongue. In a tongue I never knew Nik had even heard of. In the tongue the Nordak had spoken hundreds of years ago. Dark purple tendrils of mist began to radiate from the hilt of the weapon he wielded, coating the blade in a form of dark magic I wished I had never seen. A magic that would only ever be tied to the corrupt; a magic meant to destroy the light.

"Don't do this, Nik," I pleaded as the blade drew closer to my thrashing body, the immovable weight of his friends pinning me to the tile rendering me helpless. I clawed, thrashing and screaming to no avail. But Nik didn't listen to me, was unrecognizable to me as the blade met my thigh, drawing blood.

His mouth didn't stop moving as he continued, repeating words of a long forgotten, ancient curse that mixed with my scream of pain. The air of the apartment dropped in temperature, the purple magic of the long forgotten dark king hummed with hunger in the air. Freezing cold evil met my skin as the blade dug deeper into my leg. Suddenly, Nik began to etch his name across my exposed flesh, a way to indicate who wielded the power of the blade, and who would wield me when the darkness took over. Overwhelmed with agony, my screams reached a new level as the corrupt magic began to sink into my skin. The marks of the Blade of Rathmen singing as he carved the shape of the letter "N" into my flesh.

There was a loud knock on the door, followed by the landlord's angry shout to "Keep the ruckus down" which was the only opening I needed as the men holding me down froze momentarily at the noise. I exploded, adrenaline coursing through me as I twisted to the side with enough force that my joints screamed. I shockingly rose to my feet, only seconds ahead of the four men whose attention was now back on me.

I sprinted, throwing myself toward the back door of our apartment with as much force as I could. I just needed to make it to the back staircase, then down the stairs.

A hand grabbed my wrist, twisting my arm at an unwelcome angle and I stumbled backward, using the motion to ram my elbow into a skull. Pain erupted through my arm once again, but I pushed on as a howl of pain came from the male whose face I just smashed.

My fingers clawed for the door handle. My other arm was barely able to function and I could hardly pry the door open before Nik was there, fury ablaze in his black eyes as his nails dug into my skin, stopping my escape.

I jerked to the side, kicking him with everything I could, even as my leg burned in agony from where my shin hit bone. Turning toward the stairs I began to run when a powerful force rammed into me from behind.

I screamed in horror as I lost my footing, and fell. Air rushed past me as I tumbled down the stairs. The shouts of the men echoed down the staircase as the worn, wooden steps scraped against my skin while I flew down each step with force, unable to stop the momentum.

The rapid rush of footsteps followed me down as I continued my fall, the base of the stairs coming into view faster and faster. But I couldn't break the fall, I couldn't make myself stop the catapult of movement.

My head slammed into the wall at the bottom of the steps, the side of my face ricocheting off the concrete, throwing my head to the other side as I collided to the floor. Dark spots danced in my vision and my head throbbed as a new level of pain erupted from me. I could see small pieces of blue glass shattered by my head as Nik's face began to draw closer into view, a sinister look glinting in his eyes as if he knew he had won.

My head spun rapidly from the collision, and I was unable to speak, to move. A glimmer of bright blue caught the corner of my eye in a shape I recognized in the back of my mind, yet my consciousness was fading quickly. I tried to push myself off the ground, tried to protect myself.

Nik drew closer, the deadly Blade of Rathmen inching toward my skin, humming with a magical hunger to finish what it started.

The ancient words continued rolling off Nik's tongue when an arctic chill swept through the area.

Black mist rolled up from the ground as golden specks began to fly through the air around me, circling my body. A chill that cut to my bones. A chill I'd experienced before.

The mist picked up, swirling swifter as Nik began to reach the bottom steps of the stairs, his towering form lunging for me as the mist encased my body. I let the arctic mist circle me, snaking around my limbs as I welcomed its familiar embrace, it's comforting magic. "Take me back," I whispered to the gold-flecked darkness before I let the pain engulf me, closing my eyes.

AVYON

Chapter Five

I AWOKE with a start to the sounds of blood-curdling screams flooding the air in the distance. Shouts and grunts echoed in reply to the shrill screams. My mind was foggy as I tried, yet failed, to remember what had happened.

Failed to remember where I was.

Another scream cut into the air, my body tensing in response to the unknown danger, my fingers reaching for a dagger that wasn't there, as shivers coursed through me.

Why wasn't the dagger there? Why couldn't I remember anything?

What had happened to me?

A sharp pain radiating from my thigh drew my attention as I shifted my focus to my body for the first time since waking. Blood soaked my leggings, a dark crimson stain stark against the cream colored material. *Was it my blood? Had I been injured?*

I forced the rising panic down as I assessed my situation. Minor cuts appeared on my cropped shirt, a trail of blood dripped down my right forearm. Evidence that I was injured. A dull throb was present on my head, as my fingers collided with an open wound, slowly trickling blood. *Well, that would explain the memory loss.*

Another sharp jolt of pain caused my thigh to spasm as my gaze tore down to my leg once again. Spotting a gash in the material, I grasped the edges of the wet fabric, giving a sharp rip as it gave way and split further. Looking over my leg I couldn't see an open wound. *Someone else's blood perhaps?* The thought crossed my mind as another pinprick of pain pulsed, my hand pushing on my flesh to stop it. Yet my fingers paused. The skin of my inner thigh was raised higher than normal. Something wasn't right . . .

Turning my leg at an angle, I glimpsed the raised flesh, a gasp of shock flooding the air as I stared at my inner thigh, my eyes catching on a perfectly carved letter—the letter N. The silver flesh looked healed. Almost as though it had been there for years, yet the mark had a dark hue in its depth, as though something lurked beneath the surface of my skin.

What the hell was going on?!

My heart rate increased as I frantically searched the remainder of my body, looking for any other cuts, before my skin froze as an arctic chill filled the air. Glancing around at my surroundings, I noticed the sky turning a stormy gray. The clouds rumbled in with lightning speed, darkening the grass I found myself in. There was a forest surrounding me, thick trees bunching together, save for this one circle of grass.

The air dropped what felt like another twenty degrees and I watched as frost appeared on the ground. Not slowly, as it would on a cold winter's morning, but instantaneously . . . as though by magic. The storm began to circle overhead, the wind picking up as icy snow flurries flew down in vicious circles. *What in The God was happening?* The pain in my thigh reappeared, and a chill began to set around me, shivers coursing through my body at the temperature drop.

Another scream pierced the air. That's when I heard it—how I had missed it before, I don't know—the unmistakable sounds of metal clashing and grunts filled the air. *Battle.*

Jumping to my feet, I scanned the ground with increased panic. Where was my dagger? I *never* went anywhere without a weapon. And yet, I couldn't find it. The sounds of battle grew louder from behind me. Or was it to the side of me? *Move, Kateya,* my mind seemed to scream at me. And I did. Picking a direction, I took off in a sprint, pushing my legs to move as fast as they could. Whatever was going on, I didn't want to be found here, that much I knew.

My lungs screamed for air as I continued to push myself, further and further. The wind grew stronger as I ran, thick snow flurries bit against my skin as I pushed on, the frost-covered ground crunching under my feet. I couldn't hear any battle cries over the sound of the howling wind, I just urged my feet forward, knowing I couldn't stop. I'd left a trail behind me, making me easy prey. And with the arctic chill the forest had taken on, I would be dead one way or another if I stopped.

My feet carried me to another clearing, ominous gray storm clouds raging before my eyes as I stumbled to a stop.

No. No. No. No. "Fuck." I scanned my surroundings hopelessly. A damn town. I had run right toward the attack . . . right to the center of the battle. *Why? Why did this happen to me?* Cursing my luck, I turned around, back toward the forest. But not before my gaze caught the eye of a soldier.

I sprinted, feet slapping against the ground as I pushed with everything in me, paving a different path, praying the second set of footsteps confused the soldier who had spotted me—that he wouldn't catch me. That I could hide in time. Crippling pain burst from my inner thigh as a strange heat spread over the scarred portion of my leg. But I didn't have time to think about what caused that scar. Or really, about *who* caused it. Not that I could remember presently. I stumbled, trying to regain my footing as I pushed deeper into the thickets of the now ice-coated forest. *What had happened to me? What was this place?*

I watched in horror as an icy blast of snow flew toward me. *Toward me.* Not down from the sky, but snaking through the forest.

And I froze, just momentarily.

My mind churned as I put the pieces together. My lack of memory. Thick forests of oak and cedar trees. *Flying ice.* And I knew; I just knew. This had happened to me before.

I had traveled back in time . . . I didn't know how. But I had.

All my searching, training, and desperate attempts had paid off. I'd made it back, or at least, I prayed to The God that I had. Which meant I needed to find Cassandra . . . as quickly as possible. If there was one thing I remembered from being in the past, it was that their views on women being alone were vastly different than in the present. The sooner I found my sister, the better it would be for me.

A shout in the distance nabbed my attention and I unfroze, my mind still reeling as I remembered the icy snow blast, now even closer than before. I turned on my heel, desperate to avoid its fury. And I crashed directly into the soldier who had given chase.

My body screamed in protest as I collided into his black armor with enough force to rattle my bones. His hands snaked out around me, a firm grip trapping me in an unmovable hold as I struggled against him. "Let." I jerked to the side. "Me." Another twist in his arms. "Go!" I yelled. When his hold didn't budge, I jerked my head back, staring up to meet his dark eyes. Black lines were painted in stripes across his darker skin, his eyes narrowing in on me with satisfaction.

I stopped moving.

My body grew heavy in his arms as I let myself become deadweight in his hold. His hold on me slipped slightly from my action.

I snapped my head forward, crashing my skull into his. A deep grunt sprang from his lips as his hold loosened just enough for me to fall through. My head throbbed as my feet collided with the frost-covered floor, the wind whipping around us as he clutched his most likely broken nose. I pushed to my feet, wobbling slightly, ensuring my balance was solid before continuing. My legs picked up speed as I sprinted with everything in me away from the soldier.

I knew he would give chase again. I hadn't injured him enough and I cursed my luck once again that I didn't have my dagger on me. Icy snow flurries bit against my skin as I ran, my footsteps through the forest a dead giveaway. I couldn't hide. I couldn't stop. I had no choice but to keep moving. To keep running. To keep pushing. I was the prey . . . and I had no way to defend myself.

"You think you can escape me?" An angry voice roared over the howl of the arctic wind. My heart rate increased, panic and fear setting in. "You're nothing but a Nordak whore." The soldier growled as he closed in on my trail. "I can feel your pulse beating, crying out to me. I wonder how it would taste."

My heart lurched. *Nordak. Hear my pulse. How it would taste.* It hit me so instantaneously I nearly stopped in my tracks. It was only due to my momentum that my legs continued pushing forward at all. Branches slapped at my skin as I realized the gravity of my situation—the death sentence I was racing to escape. The man chasing me—hunting me in the ravaging ice storm—was a vampry. Which meant that I was in Avyon, and he thought I was a Nordak. Most likely believed me to be a spy. And if he found me, he would feed . . . on me. Because this was a battle and no one knew me here.

The sound of a second pair of footsteps reached my ears and a moment later I felt myself flying through the air with the grace of an eagle before I crashed into the forest floor. Cold seeped through my clothing as I felt a weight slam into me, pinning me underneath an imposing form. My body pressed deeper into the ground, my lungs wheezing as I lost the ability to breathe; as I struggled under the rigid form holding me down. A hungry growl sounded from above me. "Well, well . . . what do we have here?" The voice was different, belonging to the owner of the second set of footsteps I'd heard. "Another pathetic Nordak female on the run it would seem." His breath came hot on my neck, my pulse racing as fear flooded my system.

"Get off of me!" I screamed. "I'm not Nordak and I am certainly *not* a Void-damned snack for you to feed on!" I struggled again, trying to move any part of my body. Squirming under his weight as panic welled within me.

"Shut your fucking mouth." I could see his fangs lengthening from the corner of my eye, and I screamed. A rough hand brutally clamped over my lips, cutting off my air flow. And then . . . a memory flitted to the front of my mind. It was hazy and shadowed, but I had the strangest sense of déjà vu. As though I had been held down, in this position, before fighting to get out of someone's hold. Four blurry figures flashed through my mind. I could make out their muffled shouts in my distant memory. I remembered myself being held down as I thrashed and struggled. I remember the feeling of betrayal, of being forced against my will, and of pain. Immense, searing pain that scalded my skin as a dark voice chanted beside me.

What had happened to me? Was that memory the key to me winding up back in time? I knew that memory had to be recent. *But when? Where?*

"Put your fangs away, Baxton." A sneer came from above me and my hazy memory floated away as quickly as it had come. "The prisoners are *not* snacks. At least . . . not yet. Put her with the rest of them." I felt the soldier, Baxton, stiffen at the command, his body rigid as he retracted his fangs and removed his weight from me, careful to ensure I couldn't escape.

"I'm not a Nordak. I don't know why you think I am. But I'm —" I paused, not knowing how to finish that sentence properly, before I settled for the closest truth I could think of. "I'm from Verastarr. I just need to find my sister." My cry fell on empty ears.

With a rough jerk, Baxton hauled me to my feet, laughing at my protests as he tightened his hold on me and harshly tied the rope around my wrists, securing them behind my back so that I couldn't break free. I twisted, struggling against them to no avail, as they merely tightened more with every movement, cutting the circulation until my struggle came to a halt.

Baxton pushed me back toward the direction of the village as I heard the voice of the man who stopped me from becoming a snack, speak again in greeting to someone behind me. It was a deep, rich voice that bit in the chilled air and caused every hair on my body to rise, to listen. "What happened to you, Everett?"

"That fucking bitch broke my nose," the man, Everett, I

presume, replied. "Void-damned Nordak whores. Can't leave them untied for even a moment."

The man who had questioned his compadre laughed. A deep laugh that contradicted the events that had just occurred as he spoke to his friend once again. "Round up the second battalion. Have them head back to camp. There's bound to be more Nordak scum in the surrounding villages."

Everett scoffed. "If I never see another gryffin, it will be too soon."

A hand on my back pushed me forward again as I stumbled over fallen branches in the still ice-covered forest, wondering how I had ended up like this. I had looked for a way back to the past for over a year. A year of researching, of scouring every inch of the Archives for clues on the artifacts. Blood, sweat and tears had gone into searching for a way back. A way to Cass. A way to be with my sister once more. And now, now that I was finally here, I'd been *captured* . . . by Avyon vamprys. By someone who should be an allied with Sébastien.

The cries and pleas grew louder as we approached the outskirts of the village, and I could tell that the ice storm had wreaked havoc on the village's remains. Cottages had been buried in snow or torn to shreds from the wind. Thick icicles had embedded themselves into the ground. But upon closer inspection, they weren't just embedded. The icicles had been used . . . as stakes. A shocked gasp flew from my lips as I stared in horror. The frost-covered ground was coated in red surrounding the icicled stakes.

When I looked closer at the village, I began to take in the unusual aspects of the scene. The snow buried houses deep within, but the ground itself was not covered with snow. In fact, even the ice on the ground was melting away. It appeared that the snow had fallen in large quantities over specific areas of the village. Burying only what it needed to, or what it was instructed to bury. The icicles had only appeared buried deep within bodies, as though someone had the power to harness the ice and use it as a weapon. My mind thought back to when I had been running in the forest. I had seen a gust of angry snow flurries flying with venom in the wind toward me.

And I remembered. They hadn't been falling down from the sky, but rather angrily racing horizontally to the ground. Someone *had* been using magic. Powerful, elemental magic.

Someone who could harness the skies with enough power to bring a raging ice storm down on a village. To bring about destruction and death from something as beautiful as ice and snow. *What sort of vampry had the power to harness the skies? Or was it even a vampry?*

Another sob tore my gaze from my assessment, as I looked in horror to see a line of women all strung together. Their clothes were in shredded pieces, with dirt and blood smeared across their bodies, still visible in the evening light. The sounds that rose from these women shook me to my core as I wondered what *had* happened here. *Why these women had been taken captive? Who the vamprys were searching for?*

A sharp shove hit my back and I found myself in line with the other women. "Wait!" I shrieked in panic as I realized what was happening to me. "What are you doing?! I'm not a Nordak. Please! You don't understand. I live at Ny Palace, with my sister." Alarm continued to rise within me, my eyes widening in fear as the soldier gripped me harder and began to tie my wrists up in line with the others. "No! No!" I screamed, pleading to anyone who would listen. "Don't do this to me." My hands were chained up to the others. Shackles placed on my wrists, the cold metal settling harshly against my skin, stripping me of any remaining freedom. "You're making a mistake!" I pleaded to the soldier as he ensured the shackles were locked securely. "Please! Stop this now!"

A sharp burst of pain radiated from my cheek as the sound of a slap resonated around me. Heat flamed up on my face, the feeling of blood slowly trickling down from my lip stunned me into silence, while I watched crimson fall in slow rivulets onto the ice, staining it.

I don't know how long I stood there, shackled like cattle with the other captured women, staring at the spot where my blood marred the hard ground. The wind howled around us, cutting through my thin layers of clothing—clothing meant for a training pit, not the brutal forces of ice magic. My senses numbed as the chill bit at my exposed skin, my mind going blank as the sky grew darker. The air dropped colder and the shivers began wracking my body. I felt my eyelids grow heavy as I stood there, frozen in place, when all at once, my memories began to unlock. Flashes of my time searching the Archives with Aerilyn, of finding a singular clue regarding the artifacts, of dumping Nik, and of his betrayal . . . it all came back to me in one fell swoop, just as the cold took over.

AVYON

Chapter Six

MY EYES SNAPPED open with urgency. A harsh shout sounded from ahead of me and I instantly remembered my surroundings. Yet, as I looked around again, I noted that the landscape had once again shifted. With the rising sun, I noticed that snow no longer buried the village buildings, the arctic whip of the wind had disappeared, and the air felt warm, as though it was spring—which, maybe it was. *After all, time did pass differently in the past than in the present.* It *had* been winter in the East Engles before I had been transported here; I remembered that now.

Last time I had traveled back in time with Cass, my memories had been intact the entire time. I couldn't figure out what had happened this time to bury my memories in the back of my mind when I had first landed in the past. *Had it been because of what had I endured? From falling down the stairs of my apartment? From the ancient curse Nik had begun to cast over me?* My mind drifted once again to the scar on my inner thigh, the letter N carved in my skin, and a raging wave of anger washed through my body as I thought about what had happened to me.

"Move it," a vampry soldier snapped to the woman in front of me. Her thin dress, shredded to pieces that barely clung to her frame, shifted in the wind as her shaky footsteps hurriedly rushed forward. I watched as her steps faltered, my hands urgently reaching out to help her, to stop her fall. But my own hands came to a jarring halt as rough metal dug into my wrists, the shackles tightened as I tried and failed to break her fall. The soldier to our side let out a mocking laugh as the Nordak woman before me struggled to get back up. My heart felt for her—something that it would have never felt back home in the present with the Nordak forces invading our lands. But I knew that here, in this time, she hadn't been taken captive for her own actions—for something that she had done—but rather, she would suffer for the crimes of the one she loved. Victimized for wrongdoings beyond her control.

I bit my tongue, drawing blood as I remained silent in an attempt to not draw attention to myself. Every fiber of my being screamed to speak up for this woman, to come to her aid, to protect her from the brute in front of us. Yet, I forced myself to remain still; an unbreakable, immovable force. The soldier's eyes flared as they snapped their focus onto me. I sucked in a worried gasp. I could only watch, frozen in horrified terror as his fangs began lengthening, his pale green eyes darkening to a deep emerald as he bared the pointed tips of his incisors in my direction.

His hand whipped out, clasping firmly, unwavering around my forearm. A foreboding chill seeped into my flesh as his hold tightened. His fingers were rough and brutal against my skin. A touch that felt cold, with a hint of unrelenting danger.

Could he feel the beat of my pulse? Was it the scent of my blood that still coated the inside of my mouth that drew his attention to me?

I sucked in a quivering breath as he pulled me toward him while an internal battle raged in my mind, unbeknownst to him. *I couldn't run. Couldn't flee. I could hardly fight in my current circumstance. And I had never felt more powerless, more hopeless than I had in this moment.* With no weapons at my disposal, I had two choices; neither of which would get me far with my hands trapped in heavy bands of metal. I held still, whispering a prayer to The God, as the soldier's calloused grip traced up the curve of my neck, an unwelcome shiver running down my body at his action as I struggled to mask the look of disgust, fear and terror welling beneath my surface.

"Well, well . . ." the deep voice taunted in my ear as cool breath curved around my neck. His fingers splayed at the base of my neck, tracing over the spot I knew he could feel my pulse the strongest. "Not so fearless all chained up now, are you?"

My blood turned cold; my pulse rapidly increasing as his words hit me. *He knew me. He'd been there last night.* Which meant he was one of three vamprys that I'd had the unfortunate pleasure of encountering on my failed attempt of escape. I knew he couldn't have been the first one who'd given chase. And somehow, I didn't believe he was the third vampry, the one who'd shown up and stopped me from becoming a mortal blood bag. Which meant—

"I didn't get to finish what I started last night now . . . did I?" Baxton's sneer came as his tongue touched the column of my neck before trailing down to the base. Panic rose in me, my body tense and rigid at the unwelcome touch. His grip around me tightened, one hand wrapping around my waist as he yanked me closer against his solid frame, pinning me to him as his eyes hungrily devoured me. His free hand trailed over my skin, snaking up my stomach, hitting the underside of my breast as my body revulsed in disgust. *Who did this man think he was?*

He continued to toy with me, his hand roaming over my body while a chilled breath licked at my skin. His fangs were a whisper of a touch against my neck—a reminder of what he had *attempted* to start last night, and I *snapped*.

I would not be a victim, I wouldn't let him hurt me or touch me any longer. I yanked hard against the chains on my wrist, biting back an agonizing cry as searing pain flooded my wrists, while I aimed the movement toward him. My leg kicked up at the same moment, reaching for its target to no avail. I didn't have enough traction, enough room to maneuver. His grip on me was like death, unwilling to release me while I thrashed viciously in his arms.

"Get." *Thrash.* "Your." *Thrash.* "Hands off me!" I screeched as his hold tightened and a dark chuckle surrounded me, filling my ear as he spoke.

"Such spirit . . ." Darkness seeped from his voice as he continued. "What a *pity* you won't be around for me to enjoy it. I like a challenge and *you*. . . you are a fun chase." The glint in his eyes terrified me as I tried to break free from his grasp. I struggled, the chains drawing blood from my wrists as they cut deeper into my skin. Maybe the scent of my mortal blood would bring other vamprys—someone, *anyone*—to stop him from his onslaught.

The women around me did nothing to stop his advances as his hold tightened on me and locked me in place. I drew my leg back, the only part of me he hadn't secured tightly and swung it in an upward motion as forcefully as I could, hitting my target with a deep jolt. A guttural groan filled the morning air, his hands faltering around me as he bent forward, crumpling in a wheeze of pain. But it wasn't enough to allow me to break free. The action merely angered him more.

"You *fucking* bitch." He sneered with fury alive in his eyes as he stood, his fangs rapidly lengthened more, and he pierced them down on my neck with brutal force. Fiery pain seared to life in my body as his teeth tore into the soft flesh at the column of my neck, ripping the pale skin as a strangled cry fell from my lips. I twisted in response, writhing as I tried and failed to break free, but his fangs just clamped down deeper, as he drew long pulls of my blood without permission.

My body felt as though it was on fire, a raging inferno within me, as he continued his assault—a direct contrast to the chilled feel of his roaming hands over my skin, up the curve of my hips, and between my breasts. I felt myself thrashing against him, failing to escape from his grip as he continued to feed from me, his fangs embedded in my flesh.

My head began to feel light, the rapid loss of blood affecting me as he continued to drink at a brutal speed. The smell of iron reached my nose as Baxton withdrew his fangs, his hungry eyes meeting mine as I gasped in horror. Crimson smeared across his mouth, while rivulets of blood dripped from his lengthened fangs. His once pale green eyes seemed near black from his bloodlust induced frenzy. Then, he bit down again. Twin stabs of pain shot across the expanse of my exposed neck. A cry of agony radiated from my lips as I weakened, the fiery feeling alive in my body once more.

I felt as though I was floating, unable to control my limbs. A shout echoed somewhere in the distance, and then someone was there, yanking Baxton off of me with unmatched strength. I felt the rip of my skin as his head was yanked back, fresh blood seeping from the wound. Baxton's snarl filled the air as he was pulled from me, dark scarlet blood dripping from his fangs. *My blood.*

But I was too far gone. My neck seeped blood from the ragged tears he'd left as he'd abused my body in his bloodlust. I felt weak, *empty.*

I was floating, the pain evaporating momentarily, the shouting and anger far in the distance as the realm went black.

When I awoke again, I found myself lying on my back. As my eyes slowly fluttered open, they were met with dusk light peeking in from a beige tent flap that swayed in the wind. I didn't know what had happened after Baxton had forced himself on me, and fed from me. My body shook in disgust from the memory of his clammy hands on my skin, pulling me close, the feel of my blood being sucked from my thin veins leaving blue and purple bruises along the side of my neck.

My wrists were still bound together, my body sore and heated.

"Good. You're awake." A deep tenor met my ears as I shot up, wincing from the lingering pain in my body while my gaze collided with the most stunning amber eyes I'd ever seen. I sucked in a sharp breath of air, mixed signals coursing through me—

intrigue, desire, danger. The need to *run* being the winner. This man, towering over me, dripped of vengeance. Of ruthlessness and power. A dark silver scar ran across the left side of his face. And there were three jagged claw marks that stretched from his hairline to his cheek bones that gave him an air of danger and recklessness, causing me to wonder what had happened to him, while fearing him all the same.

His gaze pierced mine as I studied the male in front of me. I took in the hard set to his mouth; the sharp jawline, covered in a five o'clock shadow, that clenched as his gaze bore into me. His onyx hair was cut short on the sides, and longer on top with a slight curl. My eyes looked him up and down before my gaze collided with his, heat rushing up my cheeks as he still studied me, seeming to wonder how I fit into this picture.

"How is it that you, a Nordak captive, understand me?" His voice questioned in a tone that demanded an answer, yet his face remained an impassive mask giving the appearance that he did not care what my answer would be. "Did you receive an education in exchange for being a Nordak spy?"

I sat up taller, ignoring my body's protest of pain, the side of my neck throbbing as it tore slightly and anger flared in my eyes as I answered. "Well to start," I spat at the man I couldn't seem to take my eyes off of, "I am *not* Nordak. Which would explain my ability to understand you seeing as I speak the same Void-damned language as you. However, I *do* understand the Nordak tongue because one would be a fool to not learn the language of the land that insists on terrorizing Vanaiyer. And." I paused, my throat scratchy as I responded to the dangerously attractive, yet accusatory male in front of me. "I am *not* a spy. I am from Veras-tarr, so I would appreciate it if you didn't treat me like a prisoner of war."

My answer seemed to surprise the man looming over me, the shock discernible from the way those golden amber eyes widened just slightly at my voice.

He laughed; a deep, silky laugh that contrasted the entirety of his demeanor. "You expect me to *believe* that? Truly?" He stalked toward me, kneeling down until he was on my level, a wave of blood orange and cedarwood washed over me as his hardened gaze held mine.

"Do you *truly* think I'm that ignorant? That I would *honestly* believe that you, a female fleeing the Nordak camp we surrounded, mid-attack, are *not* a Nordak spy?" His scoff rubbed me wrong as his eyes dared me to disagree with him, to prove him wrong.

I opened my mouth to speak, but the venom in his glare halted me in my tracks, my mouth sputtering when a fresh wave of pain shot over me, this time stemming from the scar on my inner thigh, and a pained cry spilt from my lips as I crumpled over, grasping at my leg.

His emotionless scoff filled the air as he rose, storming away from me. I swallowed the pain, blinking away the dark spots at the corner of my vision. My gaze unfocused as I tried to pinpoint the location of the retreating man. I said the only thing I could think to say. Something that I prayed still held leverage in this time. "Capetian," I forced out, praying to The God that this would work. The man's footsteps faltered slightly, enough to tell me I had piqued his interest, even as he kept walking toward the tent entrance. "I need to see Sébastien Capetian. He—" I forced the words out as the pain refused to fade, instead growing in strength as stabs of agony shot through me. "He and my sister, Cass. I need to find them. She can tell you I'm not Nordak. She's the reason I'm here . . . I need to get back to her." My voice was fading, my body not yet recovered from Baxton's assault. The burn rose within me, pushing me dangerously close to a breaking point.

The man spun on his heel, his eyes flaring as he assessed me with new interest. "No one calls her *Cass*." He sneered. "She is Cassandra Capetian, *Queen* of Verastarr, to you."

"No," I bit out as spots danced in my vision giving him a funny look as I continued. "She is Cassandra *Dumont*. From the

East Engles. She lived in Estaire with me." His eyes narrowed as he stalked toward me. "And she traveled *back* in time with me, before sending me back to the present . . . without her." He froze, his face unreadable as mine went lax. A wave of darkness washed over me, sweeping me off to a realm where pain ceased to exist, and all I could do was pray to The God he believed me . . .

AVYON

Chapter Seven

I HAD no idea how long I'd been asleep. The concept of passing time was the least of my concerns as I began to fully wake. I laid there, my surroundings a distant blur as I stared at the tent covering, watching as the fabric rippled slightly as the wind blew against it.

The earrings.

I couldn't stop thinking about the simple action that had unknowingly altered my life.

I hadn't even considered the possibility that they were an artifact. But looking back, it made sense. An artifact, appearing before me. The girl from the bathroom, gone as quickly as she'd come. An obvious sign of an Elder tasked with handing off an artifact. I hadn't even given the earrings a second thought, and yet, they'd been tossed onto my path all the same. Destiny, revealing its hand. I'd sought to force destiny to reveal itself to me for the past year, I had never once stopped to consider that the prophecy had chosen me. That my fate had been sealed before I ever knew it.

The tent material rustling slightly overhead was coarse and sturdy, even as the wind whipped against the beige covering. My mind processed the onslaught of memories that seemed to cascade through every time I closed my eyes, and tears trickled from the corners of my eyes at them, mourning the loss of my former life, my old life, my trust. I'd made it back to the past, but not before sacrificing myself to do so.

Nik. The name flashed vehemently across my mind leaving a bitter taste. *He'd tried to ruin me. He'd tried to kill me. He'd tried to use me as a weapon against the very people we'd sought to rescue from the darkness.* He'd failed at the first two, and yet, it was my life that would forever be marked by his actions. *My* leg that he'd carved his initial into. I couldn't help but wonder whether there would be repercussions from his attempt with the Blade of Rathmen . . . He hadn't fully carved his name into me, but would the start—would that first letter—give him power over me even from the future? Could someone else in this time finish what he started? Would it give the darkness power over me?

What would any other man think when he saw the mark?

Even as I thought that, my body tensed, repulsed at the thought of another man's hands on me after the mark he'd left. The memory flashing across my mind like a nightmare. The hands holding me down, forcing the curse on me, stripping me of any freedom as his friends had helped him. The helplessness. My body involuntarily shuddered at the mere thought of a man touching me as Nik had tried to.

Eryx.

The name flashed through my mind and a glimmer of hope peaked into the darkest part of me, and vanished just as quickly.

My mind flitted briefly back to the man who'd captured my attention, *my heart,* the last time I'd traveled back to the past. The man I had confessed to Cass on the last night I'd had with her that I was falling in love with, only time would separate us and I had known that then.

Laughing, Cass teased in response, "So, tell me about the guy. Eryx, right? Is he the one?"

"Maybe." I sighed, as memories of my time with him the past few weeks flooded my hazy thoughts. "Or at least he could have been if we were born in a different time." I let out a strangled laugh as a wave of happiness washed over me at the mere mention of his name. Eryx, the brown-haired soldier in the

Wolvyn Guard. "*He's perfect, Cass. We just, we fit. In a way I haven't with anyone else. It's as though he completes the parts of me——*"

"*The parts of you that aren't whole,*" Cass finished for me. "*Like he embraces the parts of you that you keep buried in a box, hidden from the realm.*"

"*Exactly.*" *I sighed again as I thought about the time I'd spent with the wolvyn soldier who was there the first day we landed back in time.* "*I just wonder what it would have been like . . . if I actually had a chance with him.*"

The memory lingered as I thought of his short brown hair and hauntingly beautiful jade eyes that could melt me with the briefest glance. The curled ink that started across his broad chest and traced up the side of his neck, drifting off by his temple. The way his lips felt against mine as he stole kisses under the dark cover of the Ny Palace, his muscular frame pressed against mine. Claiming *me*. Wanting *me*. Needing *me*.

What would he think of me now? What would he do now that another man had carved himself into my skin wielding dark magic?

Fresh tears soaked my cheeks as sorrow built within me. How had I let this happen? How had I let Nik worm his way into my life like that? And how had I not seen the truth behind who he truly was so long ago?

The tent flapped open and I hastily wiped away the tears that painted my skin, praying that no trace of my sorrow remained while I pulled myself to a seated position as quickly as I could, still being careful since I hadn't yet taken a full inventory of my injuries.

"You're up." A cold voice broke the silence that hung in the tent. Ruthless brown eyes held my gaze as my body involuntarily tensed, sensing danger from a man I recognized from the forest. Everett. The man I'd *headbutted*. A feeling of dread rose up.

His demeanor felt off-putting, as though he wished to be anywhere but here, yet at the same time, his presence filled the space, making it difficult to breathe. I took him in; from the towering warrior's stance, to his muscled arms bulging as one hand rested on the hilt of his dagger, to his thin armor and the faint ebony hue of his skin. His dark brown hair hung in thickly twisted dreads down to the middle of his back, various gold beads and carved bones wrapping tightly into strands.

"I'm sorry." My voice sounded raw—*hollow*—as I spoke. "Should I know you?"

"No." His voice had a cold authority to it as he continued. "Not that it matters, because I know you. Or at least I know who you *claim* to be."

"I—" I began.

"I would advise you to let me speak first." His eyes shot daggers at me as he cut me off. "You claim to know Sébastien and Cassandra. How?"

I stared at him with venom. *Did this brute not believe what I had told the first man? Was it that hard for him to hear what I'd said?*

"Like I told the other brooding vampry before I passed out from blood loss—no thanks to your men," I snapped as I glared at him, not willingly to deal with any more shit from men who thought they could control me. "I am Cassandra's sister . . . Kateya Dumont."

I watched his posture tense, just slightly, his face portraying a hint of surprise that was just as quickly masked with indifference. So quick, one might have imagined they hadn't seen a change in his expression. The slight widening of those dark chocolate eyes and slightest intake of breath. But I had. I caught the split second of recognition in those observant, yet deadly eyes. The moment the man towering before me recognized who I was. And, more importantly, what it meant if I was now back in the past.

"Is that what you wanted?" I snapped. "The answer you were looking for? Does Cass being my sister grant some form of immunity in this hellhole? Or at least the courtesy of not being turned into a blood bag for your foot soldiers?"

I watched as the warrior's nostrils flared, his eyes narrowed at my tone. "I'd be careful what you say to me, *girl*. Who your sister is will not get you special treatment in the middle of war."

"*Girl?* Seriously? Don't insult me like that. And who even are you? Better yet, where are we currently?" My tone raised as I glared at the man before me, my body protesting the exertion of strength.

"You don't ask the questions here." A cold voice cut through the air as the tent flapped open to reveal, arguably, the most hauntingly terrifying, yet attractive male I'd ever laid eyes on. The man from earlier. A man I still didn't know the name of. The ruthless claw marks that scarred his left eye in a jagged formation were a perfect match to his unyielding amber eyes that sent a flicker of fear through me as they cut across my body in assessment. "Nor do you speak to Everett like that."

A scoff slipped my lips before I could hold it in any longer at his tone. "*You* don't fucking tell what to do, vampry filth," I hissed, teeth bared as I struggled to rise, holding myself up so I didn't have to look up at him. Well, look up at him as much, seeing as his muscular form towered over me by nearly a foot.

Those gold flecked eyes captured mine in a chokehold as his lip curled up in a delightfully wicked smile, elongated fangs poking through. "Ah, but you see, Kateya, I hold *all* of the power here. *I* can tell you to *breathe*, and you will. *I* can tell *you* to shut that poisonous little mouth of yours, and you will. And *you*—that's right—*you* will do exactly what I tell you to."

A humorless laugh embraced the air as my words cut through the space between us. "And why's that? Who are you to demand those things of me?"

"I'm the one in charge." His sole answer gripped into me as I watched the towering warrior exit the tent as quickly as he'd entered, the breath I'd been unknowingly holding slowly exhaling with each step he took away from me, from this space. My eyes lifted to the steeled man still remaining before me.

"So, *Everett*," I drawled with a grin, turning my gaze to the man still in the space with me. "How do you fit into the picture?" His mouth fell open, but I continued, ready to dance with fire.

"Wait, wait, wait, let me guess. The errand boy?" I frowned mockingly. "No, no, no. The captive turned lover."

His snarl filled the air, patience wearing thin with my antics. "Ah, that's it. The unfortunate babysitter of General Alphahole's newest captive." I smiled sweetly, the picture of innocence. "But . . . the real question is how you ended up with the unfortunate task of watching me. You must be important enough that you can be trusted, but not important—"

"*Enough,*" Everett's snarl filled the tent as one minute he stood by the center beam, and the next, he towered over me. His hand wrapped around my throat, pressing down just slightly on my already damaged wound, my toes straining to remain on the floor. His fingers tightened while his eyes watched mine like a hawk. "You will listen. And you will listen well," he spat as he threw me down onto the pallet with just enough force.

"Whether your claim holds true or not. This is war. You are not the first 'Kateya' to appear since Cassandra's sister vanished to the present two years ago. Nor will you be the last. And this is—"

Everett continued speaking, his voice sharp as he rambled on, but my mind looped those few words on repeat, over and over again.

Two years ago . . . Two years ago . . . Two years ago.

I sat there numbly. I'd missed out on two years with my sister. Two years I'd certainly never get back. My mind flashed through the harrowing series of events that had occurred in the last year of my life since I last saw my sister. But two years . . . I knew time passed differently in the past and yet, a lot could happen in two years time. And even more could change, not just with Cass, but with the state of the Vanaiyer realm.

I didn't notice when Everett left, nor when a soldier left a tray of stew and bread inside the entrance to the tent. The bite wound on my neck faded to a dull throb as I sat there, all alone, wondering how things had gone so wrong in the past few days of my life.

Wondering how so much had changed.

I awoke the next morning with a start, the side of my throat throbbing as I gingerly lifted my fingers to the damaged skin. They traced over the puncture marks with renewed fury. Rising slowly, I took in my surroundings, noting the emptiness of the tent, the lack of guards inside the space, and a change of clothes folded on the floor of the tent. With the presumption that I was not being held hostage, I carefully changed, taking in the landscape of my body, mentally logging every cut and bruise, its location, and how it would affect my physical abilities. Blessing The God, I was grateful that a majority of the cuts and scratches across my body were surface level and healing shockingly fast for my body. Most were fully healed, only small pink lines in their wake.

Had they given me something to speed the healing process?

My throat took the brunt of the injury, still swollen and most certainly bruised from the vampry's attack. As I pulled on the black leathers laying on the floor, I ran through what I knew.

I made it back to the past thanks to the earrings I'd swiped at Hydrillas. It was likely that I was somewhere in the heart of Avyon—the land of the vamprys—and my sister still lived. Though where she was or how I could get there, I was unsure.

Hair secured in two dutch braids down either side of my head, I squared my shoulders and walked determinedly out the front flap of the tent. Then I froze. An ominous gray sky met my eyes, heavy mist rolling in from the east as I took in the utter destruction of the village the vampry soldiers were camped in. Collapsed gray houses filled my vision; soaked, burnt wood, bending beneath the weight. Tents were perched all along the empty spaces, as soldiers rambled throughout the area. Even the land itself felt as though it had been sucked free of any life; the grass dead and soggy underfoot, trees barren of any leaves. The whole village, stripped of any form of life.

My gaze met with the soldier who stood guard outside the tent I'd just vacated. "W-what happened here?" I questioned in shock. "The land . . . it's as though it's been—"

"Stripped of life," the gruff, elderly voice of the soldier finished for me. I nodded as he continued. "It's all the same. Every village the Nordak inhabit has the same dark feel to it."

"The feel of death?"

"We haven't learned why yet. But each field we wage battle in . . . *dead.* Each village we take back . . . *destroyed.*"

My eyes scanned further, yet the soldiers' words hung in the air ringing true. Each direction, as far as I could see, the land simply ceased to exist. I walked further into the camp, the elder soldier trailing a few feet behind me as I avoided the soldiers rushing around. I began to search for the heart of the camp in hopes of finding the tent of the man in charge. It would have been easier to ask the soldier tailing me, but I knew I wouldn't get an answer. I doubted I was *important* enough to be privileged to barge into the General's war tent.

I felt the eyes of several soldiers tracking my every movement as I wandered deeper into the camp. Their hungry gazes focused on mine, yet for some reason, unbeknownst to me, I trusted the guard tailing me wouldn't allow another attack to happen. The scent of blood filled the air around me, bile rising up within me as I walked by a crimson tent, pained noises falling on my ears. Curiosity piqued my interest and I crept to the side of the tent, peering in through a crack in the coarse material, as my hand flew to my mouth in repulsion. Vamprys, feeding off of others, fangs clamping into mortal flesh, biting down as they *fed.*

Disgust rose within me, yet my gaze watched as a soldier traced his fingers along a woman's exposed throat, circling the crook of her neck, before digging his fangs in. Blood welled, before he lapped at it, the woman's pained noise fading to softer whimpers, her eyes closed as he fed from her. Words escaped me as I watched, disbelief pulsing through me. With no magic left in my time, and hardly any vamprys, I'd never witnessed a feeding before.

"Unless you're looking to offer yourself up, I'd suggest you stay far away from this particular tent in the evenings." A familiar voice sounded from behind me. I whirled around, the elder soldier who'd been trailing me, now stood directly in front of my path. Looking him up and down, I took in the sturdy training leathers he wore, the high ranking emblem over his right shoulder, the weathered skin and wisdom-filled eyes.

"I didn't . . . I've never seen . . . well, I've never seen *that* before." I grimaced at my own words as they struggled to come out. "Is it always like that?"

"Feedings?" His prompt response came. "Yes. You get used to it over time. Can't say I was any more comfortable the first time I saw one of the vamps go to town."

"You're not a vampry?" I breathed with a sigh of relief.

"No, I'm not." Came his chuckled reply. "Been a *mere* mortal my whole life. Didn't ever need no magic to survive the wars we've waged. Just brute strength and a fierce determination to stay 'live."

I smiled softly toward the man, appreciative of the only kind words I'd received since landing here. "I'm Kateya," I offered as I stretched out my hand in greeting, his calloused one closing around mine in a firm grip, as though he didn't know precisely who I was.

"Zaron."

"It's nice to meet you, Zaron." I started as we turned away from the feeding frenzy. "Could you tell me what's happened in the past two years?" The need for knowledge, for traction, rising within me once again. I'd never make it back to Cass on my own if I didn't know what I'd be up against.

"We've been at a state of declared war since Sébastien Capetian was crowned King of Verastarr. We allied with Verastarr and Reggeon after the fatal attack on the Ny Palace that took his father and brother." My heart stopped at the mention. *War. Fatal attack. Took his father.*

"And Cassandra?" I prompted, struggling to push the panic down.

"Ah, the Queen. A fierce one she is, with shadow magic like I've never seen. Enough to rival her mate's control of the mists as they bring protection through the cover of darkness." I released a breath as I stared at Zaron.

My thoughts shifted slightly, giving pause to a word he'd mentioned. *Magic.*

If Cassandra could wield the shadows, that meant that she had . . . she had elemental magic. How had she gotten it? We were mortal, both of us. Had it been because of the artifact she shattered, or because of Sébastien? Could I have magic?

"And the war you speak of?" I questioned, focusing first on the answers I could gather.

"Started right after Sébastien took the throne. We've been battling the Nordak ever since—their hunger for corrupt magic continues to grow. It's likely the East Engles have joined their forces by now."

I smiled gratefully at the information offered, even while I made a mental note that it was off-putting that he would share information if they didn't believe who I was.

"Who's in charge here? A name?" I questioned as we walked through the camp toward the fire at the heart of the encampment. A forming line of soldiers gathered for the evening's meal.

"That"—he sighed as he guided me to step in line for food—"isn't for me to share."

I sighed in frustration as I waited my turn, meticulously taking note of the flow of the camp; the soldiers that rushed back and forth, the captains in a group talking by a smaller fire, and the one other man I knew by name in the camp, Everett, who sat by a man with identical facial features. A brother? Twin? I wasn't sure.

I tracked every movement, the ebb and flow of the vamprys as I waited, plotting my next step: a way to my sister.

AVYON

Chapter Eight

"I DON'T HAVE time to wait until it's safe," I said forcefully, eyes ablaze with an inferno of fury. "Why is that so hard to understand?" I glared at the man before me, matching his stance, as I crossed my arms, standing firm. Just as I had been since I pushed my way into his tent fifteen minutes ago when one of his foot soldiers accidentally gave me the name of the man in charge of the encampment. *Kodrayn Deverell*, a name I recognized from my time spent at Ny Palace. A name rumored to only cause fear on the battlefield. The name of the General of Avyon.

The air in the tent dropped, an icy chill in its place as I continued, anger rising in me. "I'm not here *asking* for your permission." My voice snaked toward him. "I'm *informing* you that I *will* be leaving. I *will* be finding Cassandra. And, most importantly, I will *not* be waiting around here to be a blood bag for the next vampry who gets hungry and can't control their Void-damned bloodlust."

Ice lashed out with precision from the bronzed hands of the man across from me. Sharp blasts of icy flurries that hurled through the air, wrapping themselves around my wrists before I could move. Cold seeped into my exposed flesh as the flurries solidified, forming an intricately-snaked cuff of ice that interlocked in the middle. Glancing down, I yanked on the ice, twisting my arms as I pulled them in opposite directions to no avail.

"Now," the menacing growl came from above me, freezing me in place as I slowly lifted my head, hiding the fear that his voice instilled in me. Angry amber eyes glowered above me. "*Perhaps . . .*" Kodrayn's voice purred around me. "I should introduce myself *properly.*"

I blinked in surprise, shocked that he planned to reveal his identity. "I know who you are."

"Do you?" A slightly devilish grin slid up on the side of his face, a dimple visible as he stared at me as if he knew he'd caught me right in a trap, right where he wanted me. A dimple that at any other time, I would have fallen for. "Go on then, tell me who I am, since you know me so well."

"Kodrayn Deverell," I spat the name from my mouth with a bitter taste. "General of the Avyon Army."

"That I am." His smirk turned dark as he pinned his gaze on me, drawing close enough I could feel the heat of his breath dance across me. Muscles bulged as he crossed his arms again, the movement momentarily distracting me from my purpose here. My body tensed, heat pulsing through me as his eyes held me effortlessly in place while he continued. "And yet, you're still wrong. Kodrayn Deverell, General and *King* of Avyon. And I'd suggest that you show a bit more decorum if you wish to survive your next few days on *my* lands."

Fuck me, I groaned internally at my luck, as I paused, processing the information. I'd heard of the kings of this time. I just hadn't known that the King of Avyon and the feared General were one and the same. More than that though, I remembered something Cassandra and I had been told during our time at Ny Palace. I remembered us talking with Emalyee about the princes, or kings, as some were, and a bond that they had shared since they were young. A pact that I knew she had mentioned Sébastien and his brother had been a part of. That Emalyee's mate, Dravyn had also been a part of, along with two other kings.

The Brotherhood.

Five men, tied together through a blood bond long ago. Five little princes of the lands of Vanaiyer, who'd made a pact when they were young to always be there for each other; to protect each other and always have their backs. A bond of love and sacrifice, that went before their duties to their land. An oath of duty and service to the others, should the need arise.

And I'd be willing to bet that *he* was a part of the Brotherhood. Which meant that I could leverage my relationship with his blood brother's mate.

As a devilish smile of my own crept up, I looked toward the king and the raw power emulating from him; the power that any man with too much magic held and I replied. "Don't threaten me, *Kodrayn*." Fiery heat rose within me as I spoke, venom dancing across my tongue as my words hit their target. "I'm quite certain that if you harmed me at all, you would find a realm of hurt coming toward you. Or does the Brotherhood mean nothing to you?" He stilled, ever so slightly at the mention of the blood bond. "If you hurt your blood brother's mate's sister, do you truly think that would bode well for you?" I matched his stare, fire in my eyes and venom poised on my lips. Unrelenting. Unwillingly to let another male tell me what to do. I felt cool liquid dripping down my wrists as I continued. "Now. I think it would be best if you let me leave." I paused, because I felt . . . I felt *free*. My wrists felt . . . I noticed it at the same time Kodrayn did. The cuffs on my wrists had melted away from the inside out.

His eyes narrowed instantaneously. His face a stoic mask as an arctic wind whipped through the tent, circling me like a predator ready to pounce.

"You will not leave." His voice filled every inch of the space with command as his power surged through the tent causing me to tremble. I could feel it, feel *him*, radiating through the space, an icy presence demanding to be obeyed. "We are returning to Calante. To the Palace. You will be coming with us. There, I will send word to Sébastien."

"I will go *now*," I bit out, not willing to wait any longer to see my sister. I'd missed two years with her already, I couldn't miss any more time.

Cool wind bit at my legs. "No," he commanded, his amber eyes narrowed toward me as he stalked closer, stopping a hair's breadth from my body. I felt the cool touch of calloused fingers across the expanse of my neck and sucked in a shaky breath as he forced my chin up to meet his gaze.

"I will honor the blood bond and ensure harm does not befall you on my lands. But you will not be leaving now. Not until we have confirmed you are who you claim to be."

I scoffed. "You still don't believe I'm Cassandra's sister?" I held his gaze. "What more do I need to do to prove it to you? What do I have to gain from lying?"

I knew the moment I said the last question that I shouldn't have asked it. Darkness crept across his eyes, the gold vanishing as he answered.

"One gains a great deal when they have friends in powerful positions. If you are who you claim to be, the truth will present itself soon enough."

"And if it doesn't?" I questioned, uncertain of what truth he was expecting to be revealed.

"Then we will have a very different discussion. One with a fatal outcome for lying to the King of Avyon."

I stared at him as he spoke, hating that even as the king before me spoke of what would happen to me if I was lying, I couldn't take my eyes off his face. Off the jagged scar that had been carved on his skin, the small flecks of gold floating in his eyes, the dimple indent on the right side of his cheek.

"You won't leave yet." His words drew my attention back in. "Even if I have to keep you locked up every minute, you will travel with the army back to Calante. You will help when needed." He paused briefly. "We are in the middle of war, and whether you wish to leave or not, I will not risk Sébastien's wrath by sending his mate's sister off on her own."

I held my tongue as he spoke. "Tomorrow, we will speak more on how you arrived on my lands, and after that, you will begin training."

I paused, my mind circling over his demands, assessing my options. While I wanted to get to Cass as soon as mortally possible, reality was stacked against me. If there were indeed battles being waged across the lands, my chances of capture were higher than I'd wished. I didn't know how to get in contact with my sister or how to find my way to Verastarr. And at the moment, I had no weapons to protect myself.

"Fine," I resigned. "I will stay and cooperate. I will assist around the campgrounds, and I will even share with you what I know about the artifacts and the Nordak presence that has been growing in the future. In exchange, I'm asking to not be treated as a Void-damned captive or a vampry snack."

"You are currently in no position to be making demands, especially with such a venomous little mouth."

"And yet . . ." I paused dramatically. "Here we are." My emerald gaze held his as Kodrayn regarded me, his eyes searching into the depths of my soul while he considered my requests before a dimpled smirk slowly spread.

"Training starts at sunrise," was all he replied before he signaled and the tent was opened for my departure. A dismissal.

I didn't tell them everything. I don't think I'd ever tell anyone everything. As I sat in the tent, surrounded by men and vampry alike, I knew there was not a chance I'd spill it all. But I told them. I told them of returning home, of finding the strands of my hair a glimmering shimmer of silver from the strain of magic used on my body; of needing to find the remaining artifacts; of the Nordak increase in power; of the Archives and the prophecy pieces we'd put together. I twisted the truth from there. I told them that I slipped and fell. That the earrings I'd worn that day had simply shattered and I'd found myself here, unintentionally.

I looked around the space after I finished my story, at Kodrayn, Everett, Zaron, and the male who looked like Everett. Their faces varied in shades of intrigue and concern. I studied their postures, the hands on the hilts of their swords as they assessed me, watching my every movement to discern if the words I spoke held true.

"Something doesn't add up." The male on the right, the one I'd yet to meet, finally voiced, breaking the silence. He looked at the other three men. "When Sébastien told us about the pendant breaking for his mate, it took precision, timing, intentional force and words for it to shatter. Why would the next artifact shatter so willingly, so easily?" His question echoed the one that had run through my head for the past two nights.

It shouldn't have been so easy. I would know. I'd been there for the first one shattering. Unless we'd had it all wrong. Unless each artifact functioned under a slightly different set of rules. Unless my artifact had been affected by the dark magic from the Blade of Rathmen—a part of the story I kept to myself.

"Do we know which land's artifact it was?" Everett's voice rang out. "Or why it brought her here?"

"Should we search to see if maybe it wasn't fully shattered?" The unknown male questioned.

"What does this mean with the ongoing war?" Zaron's voice cut through the rise of questions.

"You're all asking the wrong questions." Kodrayn's voice rang about above the noise causing his men to fall silent as they regarded their king and General. "The true question is, if she is telling the truth, and the second artifact was not only found, but shattered, why now? Why is this time so vital that the artifact brought her here? What do the Void-damned Elders know that we don't?"

None of his men spoke as we sat around the space, the leather flapping in the wind as the question hung thick in the air around us. A thrum of pain stabbed at my upper thigh, my hand involuntarily grasping at the spot as I grimaced in pain, silently, the concern over the mark on my leg still lingering in the back of my mind.

"We may need to consider Arcelya," Zaron said with a pointed look to his king. "I know it's a dangerous trip and the timing would complicate matters, but perhaps there we could get the answers we need. The pieces of this prophecy are slowly falling into our hands and we aren't prepared for what it may bring once all the pieces have surfaced. We need more answers and only those who walk with fate can give them."

"Arcelya?" Everett questioned. "Have we exhausted all other options?"

The men spoke around me, debating the details of journeying to Arcelya, wherever that may be, as though I was not in the tent with them.

"We'll decide once we return to Calante," Kodrayn's command cut across the tent. "For now, we proceed as planned." With nods of acknowledgement, Kodrayn's closest advisors rose to depart from the tent.

"Come on, Silver. You're with me." Everett's voice sounded as he began to walk out the tent. With the briefest of glances toward Kodrayn, whose gaze was decidedly focused on the maps plastered across the table, I followed Everett out of the tent.

The sun had hardly begun its ascent, and yet sweat beaded along my now clammy skin as I ran. Everett's idea of training seemed to involve a four-mile warm up run before we ran drills. Panting from the early morning heat, I resisted the bile rising within me as the black-tipped tents came into view once again. We didn't stop until we hit the sparring rings mapped out by stones in the dead grass. I collapsed to the ground, my legs shaking and my shirt drenched.

I knew why I was training and how important it was. I knew that since I had been in possession of the artifact, I would now be a target, much like my sister had been when we'd first arrived in the past. It wasn't the first time I'd been thankful for the skills I'd honed in the past year at home, yet I had an uncanny feeling that I was about to get my ass handed to me training with the vamprys—a type of training I'd never encountered before since magic had been stripped from our land back at home.

"Don't tell me you're done already?" A voice sounded from my left as I glanced up, using my arm to block out the sun's rays, enabling me to see who was speaking. "I bet Everett you'd at least make it into the sparring ring."

My limbs protested, wobbling as I stood. "So I have you to thank for the brutal run in the morning sun?" I extended my hand in greeting. "I'm Kateya, by the way. I don't believe we've officially met."

"Torryn." He grasped my hand with a firm hold. "Everett's twin."

"Older or younger?" I replied as I noted the similarities between the two. Dark-hued, bronzed skin that glimmered in the sunlight, long pointed ears, chocolate brown eyes that captured everything, and sharpened canines that protruded with his smile. While Everett's hair was dreaded into thick locks, Torryn kept his hair shorter, opting to cut three lines through the right side of his head.

His deep chuckle filled the air as he replied, "Younger. Not that it should matter. Everyone knows that the younger sibling has more fun."

A true smile graced my lips for the first time since I'd arrived. "Now that . . ." I paused dramatically. "Is the truest statement I've heard. Let's go get you your money." I whirled on my heel, heading to the ring at the challenge.

Grabbing a blade from Everett's outstretched hand beside the sparring ring, I tested its weight in my palm, shifting the blade back and forth as I watched Everett begrudgingly pass a coin over to his twin, effectively losing the bet that I wouldn't even make it into the ring. Entering the ring, I looked back toward the twins expectantly, wondering which of them would be handling this portion of my training, when Zaron stepped into the ring.

"Let's see what type of fight you've got in ya, girl." Zaron squared his shoulders, lifting his blade as he beckoned for me to strike first. Readying my blade, I sized up my opponent, watching his posture, his form; assessing the weight of his weapon.

I struck.

My blade cut through the air, narrowly missing his form as he nimbly dodged my attack, before returning one of his own.

I feigned right, ducking as I spun on my heel, using my short height to my advantage to avoid a blow aimed at my neck. Zaron circled me, tossing his dagger casually before catching it again, his eyes on me the entire time. A grin crept across my lips. Intimidating as he was, I'd trained for this.

He struck, his dagger cutting through the air, flying toward my shoulder as I twisted out of reach, narrowly avoiding the fist that had been aimed at my face. Throwing a jab of my own, my hand collided with Zaron's palm, his fingers wrapping around mine with a yank that sent me rolling onto the ground. My shoulder took the brunt of the collision as I regained control of my hand, recovering just in time to see a dagger launch through the air, causing me to flip to the side.

A move he'd anticipated.

His hand grasped my ankle, hauling me toward him. Throwing my weight, I flipped, twisting his wrist with the motion until I felt him release me. I sprang to my feet, circling him as I calculated my next step. Playing the steps out, I could see the progression, visualize my path, just as I'd been taught. Throw, duck, twist, and kick, before pulling a dagger and fist combination.

But I held back, keeping the full extent of my skills a secret. Instead, I let Zaron move, his fist flying toward my face. With a fast duck, I avoided his strike, leaning to the left as his other fist snaked out, clipping my right, the collision knocking me off balance. I stumbled from the hit, my side alight with pain as I hit the ground, hard.

A grunt fell from my lips as I pushed up onto my elbows, locking eyes with Zaron. "Well played."

"Not too bad, Silver." I looked to where Everett and Torryn stood off to the side, tracking every movement I made.

Nodding, I stood up, taking inventory of the cuts and bruises. Once certain that none of the marks required stitches, I walked over to the twins, watching as Torryn reluctantly gave Everett two silver coins. Another bet.

"What happened there?" Torryn groaned as I approached. "I hadn't been planning to fund Everett's next night in the town just yet."

"How would it look if I took out one of your top soldiers minutes after entering the ring?" I said back. "Do you really want a run for your positions so soon?"

"Now, Silver, that's quite the talk for someone who just lost to another mortal," Everett jibed. "At this rate, you won't be ready to take on a full-powered vampry for quite some time."

"I'll let the General know that she'll be training with the first-year vamprys," Torryn added, a teasing wink aimed toward me.

I fumed, their jokes making my blood boil. My fingers felt as though they were on fire, a prickling sensation that coursed down my arms, before I took a breath, steeling myself.

"Ha. Ha." I stared the twins down. "Are we done now?"

"Done?" Torryn questioned, feigning confusion.

"Oh no," Everett answered, "training has only just begun."

I froze at that. *Just begun* . . .

"But first, Cook's waiting for you at the fires. Said something about needing some help with the morning dishes. But find us when you're done and we will pick up where you left off." Everett turned to the next ring, already assessing the sparring match in progress.

The next day had gone similarly to the first, with the exception that the encampment was now being packed up. I'd been stuck on dish duty following each meal, the constant stream of dishes causing my hands to ache.

While the majority of the men had accepted my presence in the camp, a few still tracked me as though I was their next conquest. Stacking the last of the chipped bowls into the chest, I turned to find myself face to face with a familiar vampry—his fangs enlarging as he blocked my path.

"No protection now, mortal." His growl made me freeze, and I was overwhelmed with a flashback to his fangs on my throat, tearing into my skin. To the black-and-blue bruise that still marred my neck.

My body burned with anger at what he'd done to me, fury coursing through my veins, even as my limbs refused to move. I opened my mouth to tell him off, yet no words fell from my lips.

Weak. Helpless.

The unwanted words slipped into my mind.

"That's what I thought." Baxton's dark chuckle set something ablaze in me. My eyes snapped to him. *I wouldn't be helpless again.* Anger rose in me and with it, a wave of power I hadn't felt before; a calming heat that tingled in my veins, in my very soul.

I glared at the foul vampry before me, my mouth once again opening. This time, the words cut through the air. "How many Void-damned times do I have to tell you to stay away from me?" I growled.

He advanced, his eyes alight with darkness and hunger, but I held my ground, prepared to strike, my hands by my side, ready should I need to fend him off. *He would not touch me again.* Embers sparked through the air hitting his skin, my glance drifted to the fading fire to the side in shock. Hardly a coal was still ablaze.

"Baxton," the voice cut through the air—Cook's voice. "If

you're not looking to help in my kitchen, I'd suggest you take your leave and stop bothering *my* help."

Baxton's sneer sounded as he turned to leave. "You've been marked, *mortal*," he hissed as he left the space. Heat pulsed through my veins at his grating voice, my gaze focused venomously on his back. I heard his yelp of pain before I processed what had happened. A rapidly growing hole spread on the back of his shirt as it . . . *burned*.

His cry of pain drew the attention of a few soldiers nearby. Baxton grasped at the shirt, struggling to remove the material from his body as Cook roughly grabbed my arm. "Let's go. *Now.*"

I spun, gaping at him. "I-I didn't do anything . . ." I trailed off as his grip tightened around my bicep, rapidly rushing me away from the center of the camp. Away from Baxton's cries of pain. "I mean it." I protested against his hold on me.

"Don't say another word." His harsh command came under his breath as we walked toward one corner of the camp. To one of the only remaining tents still standing. *Kodrayn Deverell's tent.*

With a nod to the two guards, Cook walked right into the tent, dragging me along behind him, as Kodrayn looked up. I stumbled to a stop as I took in the four men inside the tent who all happened to be staring at us with various looks of annoyance.

"What is it?" Kodrayn's voice cut through the air.

"It'd be better if we spoke privately, General," Cook replied to Kodrayn, head bobbing in deference. His eyes darted toward the three other men in the room.

I watched the exchange with intrigue, noting how Kodrayn's body, ever so slightly, tensed at the suggestion, the only sign of irritation before a subtle nod of his head had his three closest consultants exiting the tent.

"Care to explain what is so important you require a private audience?" Kodrayn questioned, his face an ever impassive mask as he awaited Cook's answer.

"I told myself yesterday that I was wrong. Seeing things. That it couldn't possibly be." He paused, nervously before resuming.

"We haven't . . . well, Highness, we haven't seen anything like this in our lands for years. Even so, it's still . . ."

"What, Axel?" Kodrayn bit out. "*What* haven't we seen in years?"

"Fire magic." His answer came out in a low breath. "We haven't seen fire magic since, well . . . since your great-grandfather. But she has it," he finished, with a gesture to me.

Kodrayn froze, his gaze switching between the two of us. "What makes you say that?" He directed the question to Cook.

"Last night, the dishes were all dried at a faster rate than usual. They were hot to the touch when I set them up for the night. And the fire raged higher than usual. I assumed I was sleep-deprived. I thought nothing of it until this morning," he continued, "when Baxton . . ." Kodrayn's eyes narrowed slightly at the name. "When he started talking to the girl"—Axel gestured toward me—"I watched as embers appeared out of thin air. Anyone passing by might have just thought they came from the fire."

"But you don't?" His voice cut into Axel's sentence.

"No, Highness. It's not possible. I'd just watered the fire down, there wouldn't have been any embers remaining to spark, and certainly not that close to the girl."

I stood in stunned silence, listening as Axel recounted his version of the story to the king.

"You may leave us." Kodrayn dismissed the cook. "I assume it doesn't need to be said that this doesn't leave this space."

Axel nodded in acknowledgement as he exited the tent. I watched him leave before turning my gaze toward Kodrayn. Opening my mouth to speak, he cut me off with a harsh demand. "Did you know?"

"N-no." I winced at the uncertainty in my voice. "I mean I knew the artifacts held magic; that's how my sister and I were able to travel through time. And that somehow, once they are all together, something will happen. And I knew that since I've been gone, my sister developed an elemental magic. But I wasn't certain whether that came from the artifact or from Sébastien." His eyes watched my every movement, as though he was discerning the truth from the words I spoke. "But no," I finished confidently. "I was unaware that I had received any magic or powers from the artifact. I don't really know what else I can say. I just, I didn't know," I finished lamely.

"I had a feeling some form of magic would arise." I glanced in shock at his words, his amber eyes piercing mine as he continued firmly. "I told you that if you were telling the truth, it would reveal itself."

"Wait, so you figured I would have magic? And you didn't tell me?"

"I had no reason to tell you, not until we saw whether you actually did or not."

"No reason?" I scoffed.

"Correct," Kodrayn replied as he stepped closer to me. "Many have claimed to be Cassandra's sister. But Cassandra's sister would have to possess an artifact to reappear."

"That doesn't explain why I would have magic," I replied.

He sighed before answering. "When your sister shattered the pendant she'd been given, it imbued her with the magic and powers of the rulers who cast the original prophecy. Those who wield an artifact have the power of not just one land, but the powers of the kings who forged the artifact. They have the ability to shift into vamprys, wolvyn, fae, or syrens. They also gain an elemental power."

I simply stared at the man in disbelief. Shocked and unprepared for the truth that he shared. *I had magic?*

"I knew that if you were truly Cassandra's sister, eventually a power or elemental magic would emerge from you. I had not been expecting fire magic though. Perhaps I should have, given that my great-grandfather imbued his magic into the artifact." I gaped. Surprised to realize that he'd recognized the artifact from my description the other day in the tent. And yet, yesterday morning, he'd given no indication that he'd recognized the artifact I spoke of.

"Axel is right, a fire wielder has not graced our lands since my great-grandfather. We will need to test the extent of your magic and powers; begin training you to use them to their fullest extent."

I stared at him, overwhelmed by the information. *Fire magic.* "You can't be serious." I met his gaze. "I don't have magic or powers. I'm a mortal. I always have been."

"You *were* a mortal," Kodrayn corrected, looking at me with a new interest. "What did your sister tell you about the pendant that she shattered?" His question caught me off guard.

"Only that it contained the power to send one of us back to our time." I paused, before I continued on. "I'm not stupid though, I know the artifacts contain magic. That's how we're able to travel through time. That's part of how each artifact finds its owner. And ultimately, that's how we will fulfill the prophecy. Although the prophecy itself . . . that I'm not clear on. I'm still not sure exactly why the prophecy originally came about, or what the Great Four planned to do with it."

His eyes watched mine, the scar across his eye twitching as his jaw clenched. "The artifacts are imbued with magic, yes. The magic within each artifact though, was imbued with power from four of the strongest rulers the Vanaiyer realm has seen."

"Okay . . ." I pushed, wondering what he was hinting at.

"Your sister has already begun to experience the fuller extent of her abilities. And if I'm correct, yours will begin to emerge soon, making you just as much of a threat and target as her." His stern voice informed me.

"*What?*"

"Once the artifact wielder inherits an elemental magic of their own, *and* the powers of each of the rulers of the four lands, you will become one of the most powerful forces our realm has seen."

"You mean . . ." I paused as understanding hit me with force, my body trembling.

"Yes," Kodrayn sighed with slight annoyance, one hand

running through his black tousled hair while he watched me carefully, as though I might vanish into thin air with my new *powers*. "Not only do you evidently have the ability to wield fire, you should also be able to shift forms, whether that be wolvyn, vampry, faerie, or syren. Making you and your sister two of the most powerful shifters in the realm. *And*—"

"The biggest targets," I groaned in understanding.

"Nobody." Kodrayn emphasized. "And I mean *nobody*. Can know about this. Do you understand?" His lip curled into a snarl. "Containing this knowledge for as long as possible means the difference between whether you live or die. Or worse, being taken alive. The fewer people that are aware of our current situation, the better."

I nodded, the gravity of the situation hitting me in full force. My mind flicked to Cass, to Eryx. "What about my sister? Or close *friends*?" I winced at the word, uncertain what to call Eryx after how I'd left two years ago.

"Only those who need to know." His eyes burned into mine, ice lacing his tone as he questioned. "Do you understand?"

I nodded, words failing to reach the air for a moment. "What of the prophecy?"

"What of it?" He returned the question.

"What does it say? Surely the full prophecy has been uncovered by now. I know Cassandra only had the first part of the prophecy. And the Great Four, the four rulers who cast the original prophecy, what was their intent? What do they expect us to be able to do? What was the original war over?" The questions flooded from my lips, unable to stop them once they started.

"The prophecy hasn't been fully pieced together," he answered. "When we return to Calante we will begin searching for the next piece of it. As for what the Great Four hoped to accomplish through the prophecy, I am unsure. That's why we are considering Arecyla."

I had so many other questions. So many things I wanted answered, yet I could tell that Kodrayn lacked many of the answers as well, his brow furrowed as he stared at the maps before him. I stayed silent.

"Tomorrow." Kodrayn shifted, heading toward the tent's entrance, an icy breeze following in his wake. "Tomorrow we begin training your powers in secret."

I hesitated, his form nearly exiting the tent before I spoke up, forcing the words to roll off my tongue. "Baxton," I pushed the name out as the General paused to look back at me. I twisted my hands nervously, my fingers unknowingly brushing against the base of my neck in a motion that had the General narrowing his eyes in anger.

"What about Baxton?"

"I'm sure he's figured it out by now. Shirts don't just magically catch fire." I paused, anxiety rolling off me as I rambled on. "Well I mean, I guess here, they can just *magically* catch fire. But well, they . . . you know. They shouldn't. At the very least, he's no doubt considered the idea that his shirt didn't spark up for no reason."

Kodrayn turned on his heel, not a word uttered in response as he left the tent, leaving me to my own thoughts. To process how drastically my life had once again been altered.

AVYON

Chapter Nine

I GRIMACED, sweat and tears blending together in my eyes as I wiped at my brow before raising my gaze up to the twins—fully humbled from my position in the dirt. We'd been on the road for two days now, traveling to Calante, the Capital of Avyon. Each night, as the camp was made, Everett and Torryn brought me to a secluded location far enough outside of earshot and we trained.

First, we began with a series of drills, standard to those I'd ran through at home with Kazrah. My limbs were screaming in agony by the time we began sparring. The twins introduced a different weapon, and a new type of magic to help me learn to defend myself against every night.

That's how I ended up on the ground each night, panting and begging for relief. I'd learned that while I had been able to rely on my daggers, knives, and a gun back home, there were different weapons in the past. Weapons I'd never trained with before. Using longbows, a mace, and dual-tipped blades were outside of my zone of familiarity and took more time to adjust to than we had.

Not to mention that because magic had long since been stripped from the realm when the Nordak slowly began harvesting the powers, I'd never learned to fight against magic wielders. Magic hadn't been seen in my time since I was a young child.

Kazrah had trained me well. Trained me to be an unrelenting force, unyielding. But we had never trained to combat against the use of magic mid-fight.

It was yet another thing that the Nordak had stripped from us when they harvested the magic and powers from citizens all over Vanaiyer. Not only had they taken our magic from us, but we had no knowledge of how to fight against the use of magic.

But here, now, not only was I expected to anticipate magical strikes mid-fight, but I was expected to return those strikes, *with my own magic.* A magic that I still struggled to wield.

"Again, Silver." Everett's tone broke through my haze of exhaustion as I pushed up from the ground.

"It's a bit easier for you," I bit out, frustration rising within me. "Not everyone can naturally have fangs emerge."

In the two days I'd been practicing, I hadn't been able to draw my powers to the surface and shift to any form. I was beginning to think they just wouldn't reveal themselves at all. Or that maybe Kodrayn was wrong about the artifacts. Maybe it was only Cassandra who would wield the power to shift.

The only time my magic had surfaced since it had been discovered was the first morning after the discovery. I'd exited my tent, preparing to pack for the journey when I found a group of guards in a circle, low murmurs spreading across the camp. I'd approached slowly, cautiously, until I caught sight of what had everyone gathering.

There, in the center of the camp, lay Baxton's body. Fang marks circled his neck, ghastly marks of vengeance that had the guards speaking lowly. But that wasn't the worst of it. Chains circled his wrists and ankles, binding them together. Chains of solid ice. Unmelting ice that held him captive even in death. *The king's magic.*

My magic had soared with relief that I would no longer be a target, fiery heat building in my palms that had formed a ball of fire. I'd turned away as soon it emerged, sneaking away from the throngs of guards to keep the elemental magic hidden.

"Just visualize the fangs emerging and let your body embrace the power." Torryn's voice cut through my thoughts and I snapped my attention back to him with a scoff.

"You know," I retorted. "It's a bit easier if you actually have fangs already. Kind of hard to just envision something out of thin air and make it appear." Frustration rose in me once again as he suggested the same tactic for the third night in a row.

"Let's try something new then." A deep voice cut across the clearing, all eyes shifting to the speaker. *Kodrayn.* A flutter of fear, yet excitement trickled through me at the sound of his voice as he stepped out from the shadows of the trees, black leathers molding to his largely muscled frame perfectly.

"I think we've tried enough for tonight," I snapped, exhaustion and irritation radiating off me, my muscles screaming in protest from the hours we'd already spent training.

"Perhaps," Kodrayn's voice growled in my direction. "You don't understand the severity of the matter. You *will* shift. And you *will* learn to control your powers. Otherwise you will find yourself dead seconds after stepping foot onto the battlefield."

I scowled as I squared my shoulders from inside the ring. Kodrayn stopped right outside the circle of small rocks, marking the training grounds. I watched as he paused, a tattooed arm reaching across his torso as he tugged the shirt over his head.

My eyes tracked the movement, watching the way his chorded muscles rippled as the shirt came off. I noted the expanse of ink across his left side. The tattoo across his pectoral standing out, the five intertwining lines that formed a diamond shape in the center standing out stark, even as they were surrounded by other tattoos. Then I froze, realizing I was checking out the Void-damned General while I should be focused on getting my powers and making it back to Cass. And Eryx, *if he'll still have you*, the thought lingered in my mind.

His muscles tensed as he stepped into the makeshift training ring, and my focus shifted to the task at hand, unsure of what *new thing* he thought to try.

Watching him, I noted the way he moved, the way the moon-light reflected on his cheekbones, the tick of his jaw as his eyes tracked me with predatory intent that sent a shiver of delight to my core.

I was Kateya Dumont and I wouldn't back down from a challenge. Especially when my safety depended on me being able to control the powers I'd supposedly been gifted by the artifact.

"Fine." The word left my mouth before I could stop it as my eyes tracked Kodrayn. "What do you have in mind?"

The question had barely left my lips when he sprung, quick as lighting. I turned to the left, narrowly avoiding his strike, but he was there again, anticipating my reaction and meeting my move faster than I expected. I ducked the next blow aimed toward my throat, yet I hadn't anticipated the blast of his elemental magic, and ice bit into my side. Cold swept over my body as I stumbled back, shock and rage filling my body as I squared up, watching his next step, my body thrumming with the fight.

Kodrayn backed up, slowly circling around me as I tracked his every movement. I watched as his fangs elongated, glimmering points prepared to strike. The wind whipped to my left as a blast of ice flew toward me. Twisting to the side I threw my hands up, trying to shield the wall of ice pelting me, exposing my right side to Kodrayn's advance. I felt the punch to my side before I saw him move. With speed like I'd never seen before, he circled around me, his fangs grazing the side of my neck, drawing a thin line of blood as another wave of ice flew toward me. He didn't stop, as the advances carried on over and over, my body trembling, my level of alertness slipping.

Fury rose in me at his advances. My inability to escape his onslaught angered me. I felt helpless, and I promised myself I would never feel that way again.

My body heated with rage as I barely ducked his next blow, drawing my dagger as I spun toward him. With precise movements, I drew my arm back, before launching the dagger in his direction. Once again, I'd failed to factor in his speed. His movements were graceful as he dodged my strike with ease, clearing the path of my weapon as a blast of ice caught the dagger, twisting it back toward me.

I growled in shock and frustration, the dagger, now surrounded by ice, raced back toward me. I heard Torryn shout something like a warning from a distance. Kodrayn struck a blow to the side of my face that had me screaming in pain as my vision flickered. I stumbled back, trying but failing to pull my remaining dagger from my thigh. The ice began to pelt my skin, pinpricks of blood welling where the ice hit my flesh.

I saw Kodrayn advancing once again, a dangerous glint in his eye as he controlled his magic, and I snapped—my blood boiling as I screamed in frustration. Fire erupted from my palms, a blazing blue flame that hovered in front of me, colliding with the onslaught of ice. They met in the air, an even match as our magics collided, sizzling on impact, but went no further. *Fire and Ice. Equal forces in every way.*

My eyes ablaze, I turned my emerald eyes onto the king's golden ones. "You picked the wrong night for a fight." I sneered in his direction even as I struggled to catch my breath.

"Did I?" His chuckle cut through my core, his chest glistening with a light sheen of sweat as he spoke. "Seems I picked just the right night to watch you come alive. You look so vicious with venom in your eyes."

His own eyes lit in terrifying amusement as I raised my hand, launching the growing ball of blue fire toward him. Ice met my flame, smothering it instantly.

My eyes widened in shock and my determination rose. He charged. Daggers of ice flew toward me as Kodrayn moved in tune with his magic. I threw out my hand, struggling to hold off the ice flying toward me with fire, leaving my other side unguarded once again. There was a burst of pain from my shoulder and I knew his fangs had cut me again. I cried out, twisting, as anger built and I envisioned them.

I pictured the fangs, the pointed ears. I pictured myself a

vampry, as something that could match his speed and power. Something that could terrorize him as he'd been doing to me.

A sharp burst of pain hit me, the insides of my body protesting as power shifted within. I whimpered. An actual Void-damned *whimper* as agony erupted from my mouth. My head spun, my vision twisting black, and then it cleared.

I stared at Kodrayn, a grin growing across his face, the hint of a devilish dimple emerging, and I froze. The sounds of the forest around us became clearer, my ears picking up far off noises I hadn't previously heard. My body felt lighter, more in tune with itself, and my mouth, my gums, held a twinge of discomfort. I raised my fingers to my lips, tracing the outline of my teeth, then winced as I yanked my hand back, staring at the prick of blood welling on my fingertip. I'd cut myself. *No.* My own teeth had cut me.

"*Fuck.*" The noise drew my attention as the twins stared at me. A mixture of shock and awe across their features.

"That's not something you see everyday," Torryn's voice choked out in the silence.

I'd done it. I shifted. I—

I started to panic.

I wasn't a mortal anymore. I was a vampry. I, Kateya Dumont, was a Void-damned—

He struck. Not giving me the time to process the shift—to panic about the change. Instead, drawing me from my shell, forcing me to become who I was meant to be.

I saw him move. Instinctively, I lurched to my right, ducking with a grace I hadn't owned before, avoiding his blow as I twisted my weight. Throwing my leg up, I kicked toward his body. His eyes alight with the fight as he gripped my incoming blow, blocking it with a painful jerk that had me stumbling, my ankle protesting the movement.

I caught myself before I hit the ground. Straightening with feigned confidence, I circled my opponent, watching for any tells as I strived to keep the weight off my left foot. I waited, following his movements for his next strike; for an icy blast of power to emerge.

His eyes held mine, a look of pride and satisfaction I hadn't seen before visible in their glimmering depths, before his gaze shifted over my shoulder to the twins. "She's all yours now."

His gaze turned back to mine. "Seems a little violence is all you needed, *little venom.*" His tone caused my heart to freeze, anger rising at his comment. "Don't shift back until you've learned to master your power more." And with that, he turned on his heel, leaving the clearing as Everett and Torryn approached, ready to focus on the task at hand. Training me . . . but in vampry form.

I stared up at the night sky, shifting my body as I lay on a bedroll —restless and stunned from my evening. *Fangs. I'd had fangs.* My body had been pushed past exhaustion from training tonight, and I knew without a doubt I'd be feeling it all day tomorrow. Even through the exhaustion, I couldn't help but search within me for that little kernel of magic I'd opened today. And I found it deep within me, a little blue ball of power pulsing in my soul.

I smiled, because never again would I be too weak to hold off my attackers. I felt the elemental magic pulsing, its energy radiating through me and thought of how it had felt to shift; to use one of the four powers I'd been gifted by the artifact, the powers from the Great Four. I thought of the heightened senses I'd gain from the shift, the grace and agility. The strength.

A flicker of pain shot through my inner thigh and I *felt* the glow of blue light within me flicker out slightly before growing stronger again. A frown marred my lips as I wondered what that could mean, my thoughts drifting back to the night my life had been altered again. To Nik and his *friends* as they held me down against my will. To Nik, who'd attempted to imbue ancient, dark magic *into* me with the Blade of Rathmen, and I knew. I knew I needed to learn what the mark he'd left meant—what damage it caused. Whether the blade still had the ability to control me if another wielder finished the job . . .

Another bolt of pain came from my thigh as I shifted on the ground, trying to get comfortable.

An owl called out into the night air, the crackle of a fire echoing its call as the stars glimmered in the night sky high above my head. I watched the branches of the oak trees swaying softly in the breeze as they began to lull me to sleep and I dreamt of a familiar tattooed face; of jade-hued eyes and dusty brown hair. Of late nights in a dark corner of the Ny Palace, my body pinned to the wall and Eryx's lips roaming over mine. His tongue ravishing the inside of my mouth, his hands wandering over my body. The scent of lemon and bergamot surrounded me in my mind as I drifted off to sleep, my mind replaying my last night with Eryx on repeat wondering if he'd ever want me again. If we'd be able to pick up where we left off two years ago.

"For the love of The God," I grumbled as the sun blazed down onto me for the fourth day in a row, my skin frying and legs cramping. "Please tell me that we are getting close to Calante."

Torryn's laugh filled the air from the horse beside me. "Not the biggest fan of traveling in the heat?" He teased me.

I shot a look over my shoulder at him. "The heat. The company. This horse." My legs had lost feeling earlier today, the continual journey on horseback had not gotten any easier. I thanked The God that I'd taken up horseback riding in the present, aware of the outdated mode of transportation in the past.

"The company?" He feigned hurt with a glance to the rider in front of me. "Ah, yes." His eyes twinkled as he spoke. "Everett can be a bit much for anyone."

I watched the muscles of Everett's back tense as he retorted. "At least my good looks make up for my lack of company."

"Harsh brother. Just harsh," Torryn jested as I laughed, listening to the twins bicker. A pang of longing ran through me at the thought of my own sister; of the hundreds of conversations we'd had that went similar to their own.

"We'll be at Calante by nightfall." Everett's voice pulled me into the present.

"How long will we remain in Calante before I can see my sister?" I questioned. Praying that the answer was sooner than later.

"Asking questions won't always provide you with the answers you're searching for," Zaron's voice answered, as the twins turned to glance in his direction before pulling ahead.

"Zaron," I replied. A smile spread across my lips at the sight of the man.

"Kateya." He nodded in acknowledgement. "I hope you're faring well."

"Well enough." I glanced in his direction as we continued traveling. "I just hope I can see my sister soon. And Eryx," I whispered the last part of the statement to myself, unwilling to share that piece of me with anyone yet.

"Soon enough," he replied as he regarded me with a watchful, fatherly eye. "Don't rush what takes time. Patience is a virtue. I know you are anxious to be reunited with your sister, but don't underestimate the journey The God has for you."

I smiled softly as we rode on, unwilling to tell him that I was tired of waiting. Tired of *being patient*. I just wanted to see the only remaining family I had as soon as possible.

AVYON

Chapter Ten

AS WE ENTERED the gates of Calante, I couldn't help but stare in awe at the city before me. Calante was located in the middle of Avyon, water surrounding the luscious city on all sides, creating a natural barrier of protection. We rode up cobblestone roads, the streets winding upward on the slightly raised hill the town found itself built on. The slight drizzle of rain only stood to enhance the town's natural beauty, as beads of rain stained the windows and bushes in the city. In the distance, I could see a large gray palace residing at the top of the hill, overlooking the town-homes and shops.

The slow bustle of people reminded me of rainy days back home, as those out and about hurried through the streets. Over-cast skies cloaked the town in the feeling of calmness during a storm, even the air smelled fresh and welcoming.

Stopping at an intersection on the cobblestone road, I watched as Kodrayn and Everett gave commands to the soldiers, a majority of the army turning to head in one direction, while a smaller party including Kodrayn, Zaron, and the twins took a smaller street to the right, away from the center of the town. I watched the soldiers that departed, heading toward the town's center, toward the palace, even as my horse followed the lead of those nearby going the opposite direction.

"Where are we headed?" I questioned as I looked toward the guard to my side, an older man with battle-scarred skin.

"The General's private residence, ma'am," was his curt response.

"Does the king not live in the palace?" I questioned, confusion building as I watched the guard beside me.

"That depends, ma'am. However, it's not my place to divulge the king's dwelling habits." His gaze turned forward, focusing on the road and I understood the guard's dismissal of my questions. I tracked the turns, the incline of the streets, our vicinity to the main gates we'd entered as we continued our climb, away from the center of the town.

The drizzle soon became a downpour, as raindrops began to soak my clothing through, plastering the material against the curves of my body. I shifted in discomfort as the cold seeped into my skin and wished, for the first time since arriving, that I'd mastered this new power I'd developed. That I was able to dry the clothing on my back and stay warm as the rain came down. And yet, a humorless laugh fell from my lips at the slightest kernel of power I was able to bring up when I was not enraged.

The horses ahead began to slow their ascent, and a sigh of relief escaped me as we turned off the path, passing into a small gated courtyard. Water dripped unceremoniously from my clothing, my hair stuck to my face. Glancing around at my surroundings, I noticed the courtyard was surrounded by a few townhouses, all nicely constructed with towering black bricks. The cobblestone courtyard was lined with ivy vines that crawled up the building's walls, decorating the darkness with hues of green and small white flowers that stretched toward the sky. I admired the fountain in the center of the courtyard, a silver stream of water spouting from the mouth of a lion before joining the rain water as it fell down.

A few stablehands rushed out, water instantly soaking them as they grabbed the reins from the group of men who had traveled with us. I swiftly dismounted the horse I'd been riding as we had traveled to Calante and then glanced in the direction of the others, waiting for any indication of who I was to follow.

With a motion of his hand, silver scars standing out stark against bronzed skin even in the rain, Torryn beaconed me toward him. My footsteps hurried, grateful to be heading indoors, escaping the torrential downpour.

I stopped inside, droplets of water sliding down my skin, pooling at the mahogany wood by my feet as I took in my surroundings. The scent of blood orange and cedarwood floated through the hall, surrounding me and making me feel at home. The interior of the townhouse I stood in was decorated with mahogany and black marble. The wood contrasting with the darkened mood. Tall windows with intricately designed metals lined the walls of the foyer as I watched the men head to the left and slowly followed.

Quiet conversations met my ears from three of the four men I trailed after, Torryn falling back to walk beside me.

"Do you all live here?" I questioned as he matched me step for step.

"In one way or another, yes." He paused for a minute before hesitantly continuing. "Kode bought the group of townhomes shortly after he earned the title of King of Avyon. He couldn't stand to live in the same place his family had lived and been murdered in."

My breath caught as I listened to Torryn speak, wondering what had happened to Kodrayn's family, whether he'd had any siblings.

"Everett and I each moved into one of the townhomes next to his once he decided to make this his main residence. Zaron followed suit shortly after."

"Why keep the Palace at all?" I asked as we turned down another corridor. Flickering lights bobbed, floating near the ceiling, held aloft through elemental magic.

"All official business is still conducted there. The majority of our guards, the army, all reside within the Palace grounds. It provides a unified front; shows our enemies that we cannot be phased so easily, despite the brutality of what happened to our royal family. Few outside of Calante are aware of his choice of residence."

"What happened?" I questioned. "To the royal family, I mean."

Torryn looked over at me, his eyes haunted as we entered a sitting room. "That's not my story to tell." The sadness of his voice, the echo of pain, hit me as I stopped inside the door, once again looking around at my surroundings.

A worn green chaise filled one corner of the room, nestled next to a roaring fireplace. The heat radiated across the space and I longed to draw closer to it, let it burn away the chill that had long since buried its way into my skin. A longer couch sat directly across from the fire, with two chairs on the other side of the room.

Heavy curtains lined one of the walls, the now raging thunderstorm battered against the window pane, droplets of water rolling down the glass. Everett and Zaron took seats, despite their less than dry clothing, as I continued to take in the walls and desk, decorated with various trinkets and papers. This place, I realized, had a distinct feeling of being well-lived-in, a feeling of home. Kodrayn settled in, his muscular frame filling the width of the seat, as I watched every ripple of his muscles from underneath the soaked material that clung to his skin. My mind wandered as I envisioned him shirtless; the way his toned skin, honed by years of training, would feel under my touch.

"The missive is on its way." My attention snapped to Everett as I realized I was still awkwardly standing right inside the doorway and slowly inched closer, listening to what the men were saying. "I would suspect we will hear from Sébastien in a few days' time."

"A few days!" My voice squeaked unintentionally in shock, even as I clamped my hand over my mouth. I hadn't intended to speak yet.

Kodrayn's eyes caught on mine as he relaxed in one of the chairs close to the fire and crinkled, almost as if he was amused by my outburst. He continued to hold my gaze, eyes roaming over my face as I rambled.

"I-I'm sorry," I added. "I just. Well . . . I was expecting to hear about my sister's location sooner than that." *Like five days ago,* I thought, cursing the Void-damned past and their lack of technology that would have made finding Cass so much easier. "Isn't there anything we can do to get a response quicker?"

Zaron spoke, addressing me. "Unfortunately, given the times and the continually ongoing battles, there are no other options that still ensure the safety of the message and the men delivering it."

It made sense, I knew it did, but that didn't mean I was any happier at having to wait longer to hear word from my sister—to see her again.

A woman stepped into the room from the other side, Kodrayn's eyes briefly flitting to her as his voice filled the room.

"Always good to see you, Melantha."

"You as well. All in one piece too," she said with a chuckle as she glanced at all four men filling the room, her eyes lingering on Zaron. "All of you. What can I do for you this time?"

I watched the motherly woman, perhaps twenty years older than me, with curiosity in her tone as Kodrayn answered.

"Please show Kateya to the guest room."

With a nod, the woman, Melantha, turned on her heel, a "Come along now," following her as she walked from the room.

"When will I know more about the plans to visit my sister?" I questioned as my feet followed after Melantha.

"Once we have information worth sharing," was Kodrayn's only answer as I walked from the room and down the corridor.

"How long have you known Kodrayn?" I switched tactics, speaking to the woman I'd been instructed to follow.

Melantha paused briefly, allowing me to catch up to her as she spoke. "Oh, I've known all three of them since they were in the nursery. Feisty little boys back then, but a tight-knit trio all the same. Never could separate them," she finished with a laugh.

"That doesn't seem surprising at all," I answered, noting that even now, those three men were constantly together. "And Zaron?" I pushed, remembering the way her eyes had lingered on the older soldier.

Melantha's cheeks heated slightly at my insinuation, even as her voice held steady. "Oh, I'd wager I've known him just as long. Been with the royal family for as long as I can remember."

We climbed a set of polished wooden stairs, winding up to the second story of the townhome. I noticed various pieces of art hanging on the walls, along with the expected variety of weapons used as both decoration and presumably defense. "And you?" Her question drew my attention back to her as we turned into a room on the left. "How long have you known Kodrayn?"

"Oh." I paused, unsure how to answer. "Not long. He's a friend of my sister's—" I stopped, unsure. *Was Sébastien her partner? Mate? Boyfriend? I really didn't know. I had assumed mate earlier, but was that what she considered him?* "Sorry, my sister's mate," I finished.

Melantha looked at me closely, her black hair speckled with early gray as she questioned. "And you, do you have a mate? A bonded in your life?"

My cheeks flushed slightly at her directness. "Um, well." I stumbled over my words, embarrassment radiating from me. "I, well, I had someone. But that's in the past. And now, well, I'm hoping that maybe—" I didn't know how to finish that thought, how to explain that situation.

Yes, I have a man in my life. At least, I hope I do. You see, I met this man a year ago, but actually it was two years in his time. So he could have very well moved on from the crazy future girl who he most likely thought he'd never see again. But since you asked, Melantha, I'm hoping that when I see him again, he will want to pick up where we left off.

By The God, I sounded pathetic, even to myself.

She smiled at my lack of words in understanding. "Vamprys

can be tough men, but there's always some good in them. Just give it time. With the way he looked at you, he will come around."

"Oh, no." I cringed at my forced tone even as heat flooded into me at the thought. "Not a vampry. And *certainly* not any of the men in this house." My mind flitted to the men in the other room, to the fangs and agility, the power that radiated from one of them in particular, but no. "No, someone from the past. We, well, we might have been in love had I been around for longer." My thoughts drifted to Eryx once more—to the first time I'd met him. The day we'd first traveled back in time and he'd captured my gaze, flashing a cocky grin at me as he'd helped me onto his horse.

"Ah," Melantha acknowledged knowingly as she bustled around the room before speaking again. "The bathing room is beyond this door here." She gestured to her right. "You'll find some spare clothes in these two drawers and a few dresses hanging in the closet. I'm afraid they may not be an exact fit, but we'll see what we can do tomorrow. I'll have some food brought up to you once you rinse."

I smiled warmly at the woman. "Thank you," I replied, my thoughts already on a warm bath as I walked toward the door she'd indicated led to the bathroom.

I made my way down the corridor the next morning, searching for the kitchen. The clothes I'd found in the dresser drawers fit well enough. The gray pants flowed loosely against my legs; the slits climbing up my thighs while not revealing too much. The shirt I'd found, however, clung to my form showing every curve whether I wanted it to or not.

Hearing voices, I began to follow the sounds as they grew louder, my stomach growling slightly as the smell of breakfast rose from down the hall.

"We just returned. The men won't be thrilled to head off to

battle so soon after returning to their families." Torryn's voice drifted from where I presumed the kitchen was located and I stopped silently in my tracks, listening in to their conversation.

"I don't see what other course of action we have. Saltridge Pointe is close enough to our border that we risk unwanted attacks on our lands if we don't send aid," Everett returned. An arctic breeze touched my skin as I continued to listen to the conversation.

"We will answer the call." At Kodrayn's command, a ripple of silence filled the kitchen, as I wondered what call they had received. "We will always come to the aid of any of the Brother-hood. Just as they will always come to our aid. Even The Void won't hold against their call."

"They won't receive our missive until today, and even then, the call answers our question," Zaron added. "I will send word for the army to prepare for battle."

Battle? I held my breath, praying they hadn't heard me as I tried to creep closer without being noticed.

"Torryn." Kodrayn's voice sounded through the wall. "Send word back to Sébastien. We can be there in three days." A whis-pered gasp fell from my lips at his words. *Three days. I could see my sister in three days.*

A low growl sounded from the kitchen that sent a jolt of fear down to my core. "Zaron." The frustration rose in his tone. "Deal with her, then meet me in my study."

Shit. How long had he known I was standing here listening. I turned, ever so slowly, attempting to trace my steps back.

Zaron's form filled the hallway forebodingly. "Eavesdropping doesn't look good on you. Especially in a house filled with vamprys." His deep voice echoed off the walls as he stalked toward me, disappointment radiating off him. "Let's go," he said, not even stopping as he passed me.

"Well," I huffed, following after him with quick steps. "How was I to know whether Kodrayn would even share the information with me?"

"Has he given you any indication that he won't share information with you?" His inquisitive tone rang out and I paused, thinking of his question.

"No," I replied, hesitantly. "But that doesn't mean he *will* share it with me. He has no reason to." I thought of Nik, of all the things he'd kept from me without me knowing. The dark magic he'd been harboring the entire time we were together. Right in front of me, and yet I had no idea.

"He has no reason not to," Zaron said. "But Kodrayn is not someone to eavesdrop on. Do you understand?" I stared at the man as he continued. "There's a lot you don't know about him—about this land."

"Like what?" I prompted, curious if he would share with me.

"Do you know how kings are selected in Avyon?" His question shocked me yet intrigued me at the same time.

I paused, trying to see if I could remember anything particular about the selection of the King of Avyon in my own time, but I came up empty. "No," I answered softly.

"In our land, the position of king is earned—won through battle—*not* passed down."

"But his father was king before him?"

"Yes, Kodrayn's father was King of Avyon. And when he died, Kodrayn's royal bloodline merely meant his name was placed in the running to become the future King of Avyon, not that he was handed the throne."

I stared at Zaron in shock. "So he had to fight for the title his father held?"

"Kodrayn fought and defeated every vampry who challenged him for the throne. He won the title through vicious strength, determination, and his magic. There are still those foolish enough to challenge him for his throne to this day. And yet, his ruthless name is wielded as a weapon on the battlefield, his power talked about in tales by the fireside. Kodrayn's reputation precedes the throne. Untouchable, yet uncontested."

"Why tell me this?" I questioned, wondering what his angle was.

"Since you've arrived, you've seen a certain side of our king; a side reserved for his closest friends, for the Brotherhood, and by association, *you*. But the stunt you pulled, eavesdropping on conversations in the hallway, that can't happen again, or you will see a new side to Kodrayn. The side that has enemies praying for death in battle rather than meeting the other edge of his blade. You don't want to be on that side of him."

"I may not wish to be on that side of him, but I will do what it takes to make my way back to my sister. If I have to eavesdrop to get that information then I will. I have spent the past year of my life trying to get back here, to this time, only to wind up in the wrong part of Vanaiyer. Days away from my sister, it would seem. I *will* do whatever it takes to make it back to her," I finished, my gaze clashing with his.

"And he will do what needs to be done to hold true to his blood bond." Zaron's eyes held mine, a hint of a threat lurking behind their depths. "But he is still king, and until you make it to your sister, his word is law. He will share with you what you need to know, but eavesdropping? That is not the path you want to make for yourself, girl. And you'd best keep that in mind, other-wise your stay may feel a great deal less friendly."

I held my tongue, studying the man in front of me, before nodding. "Very well. Point taken." I hesitated for a moment, before questioning. "Is there a library here? I'd like to do some research if that's possible."

"On what topic?" Zaron studied me closely and I swallowed.

Quietly, my voice barely above a whisper, I muttered, "The prophecy that was written years ago. I need to know what it says."

"I will speak with Kodrayn today and see if he has insight on where those particular documents may have been stored."

"Is there any place where I might find more information on the power that was imbued into the artifacts?"

"Not that I'm aware of. There were very few records kept of

the prophecy or the artifacts tied into it. Any documents still in existence have long since been hidden in hopes of staving off the prophecy for as long as possible."

I stopped for a minute as we entered the courtyard. "Wouldn't those documents have been revisited following Cassandra's arrival in the past? After all, she fulfilled the first part of the prophecy, did she not?"

Zaron grimaced as he answered. "That she did. However, there are eyes everywhere. Not everything is worth uncovering until need be."

"Of course," I muttered under my breath. "Please tell Kodrayn. We need to see the second part of the prophecy before we depart from Calante, if it's here. It's vital that we know what could happen next."

"I will give him the information," Zaron answered. "But prepare yourself, for his answer may not be what you wish to hear." I sighed as we walked through a metal doorway, the sounds of grunts and fists on flesh meeting my ears. "Now, I believe it is time for you to focus on hand-to-hand combat in your vampry form."

I froze at his instruction. "You want me to shift and fight, *here?* Where others could see?"

"No one here would dare spread a word regarding what they learn here. And if they do, well, they know their life will be one of pain in the short amount of time they have remaining. Now, shift."

I closed my eyes, blocking out the sounds of sparring around me, drawing on an inner silence as I poked at the kernel of power that glowed deep within my soul. Envisioning elongated fangs, pointed ears, and faster than normal speed and agility, I imagined my shift. Straining, I pulled at the power within me; willing myself to shift into something more. Something stronger than what I already was.

AVYON

Chapter Eleven

MY SKIN still glistened as I exited the training pit from a few hours of exhausting work sparring in my vampry form, only to find the King of Avyon himself waiting for me.

He was leaning against the black brick in the fading light, the green ivy crawling up the wall around him as he stood there with his arms crossed. Amber eyes roamed slowly up and down my body, analyzing every inch and curve of my skin, before they lingered on the pointed tips of my ears, still in vampry form. "Zaron says your skills are beginning to show improvement."

"I should hope so," I murmured as I took in his tousled black locks and the shadows cast over his skin in the evening light. The dark material of his shirt was buttoned, exposing a sliver of tattooed skin across the chords of muscle that lined his chest, causing the slightest flutter in my stomach, and his sleeves were rolled to match the casual style of his shirt, despite the harsh contrast of his face. Drawing my gaze back to his piercing eyes, I swallowed slowly, before continuing. "With the hours of training I've put into the ring this past week, one would hope there would be at least *some* improvements."

"Follow me." His command floated on the evening breeze as he pushed off the wall.

"Just give me a minute to shift," I replied as I closed my eyes, beginning to envision my mortal form, the form I had inhabited my entire life.

"No." The closeness of the command had me opening my eyes as the scent of cedarwood and blood orange flooded my senses, and I found the King of Avyon standing inches from my body. I drew in a sharp intake of breath as I tilted my head back to meet Kodrayn's eyes. "You need to practice holding your shifted forms for longer than just sparring matches."

"You want me to stay in my vampry form?" I questioned, softer than I intended.

"For as long as you can tonight, yes." He began walking, and I willed my already sore legs to follow after him as we crossed the courtyard. "Vamprys have the benefit of heightened hearing, agility, and speed. Learn to rely on these skills. Test the limits of your vampry abilities, the ranges to which you can hear, the softness of your footsteps."

"Where are we going?"

But all I got was silence as I followed him through the dark corridors of the townhome, candle lights bobbing through the air, brightening our path as I strove to rely on the heightened senses I had in this form.

"If you listen closely," Kodrayn continued as we walked through the hallways, taking a turn every so often. "You can still hear the sounds of the training pits, of the men sparring inside the ring. And further than that, you can hear the sound of the water surrounding Calante."

I listened, focusing on the sounds in the distance, and a loud clattering of dishes had me snapping my eyes back at the King as he continued walking ahead of me. I couldn't hear the training pit, or at least, I couldn't focus on that alone yet.

With another turn, we came to a stop in front of a large mahogany door and I watched as he flicked his hand, icy tendrils twisting through the air as they slipped through the lock and the door clicked open. Holding my breath, the door sprung free and we walked into a cool room.

My eyes widened as I took in my surroundings, the series of books and parchments stacked carefully throughout the room from floor to ceiling. "What is this place?" My breath fell in a soft exhale as I admired my surroundings.

"My family's—well, *my*—personal library," Kodrayn replied, and my head twisted to look at him slightly, noting the mistake in his sentence, but holding my tongue.

"How long has it been around?" I questioned as I ran my finger along the spines of the books closest to me, running through each of the titles in my mind.

"A century now." His honest answer surprised me and I looked up at him.

"A century?"

"My great-grandfather started this library before we had any struggles with the Nordak. As the skirmishes began rising, he began to lock down this collection of archives, hiding the knowledge so that we could preserve it. When he passed on, my grandfather, then my father, took over the job of collecting tales of our realm, of our people." I watched him talk as I followed him through the large room, noting the way his muscles tensed as he spoke of his father, the hard set of his jaw.

"When my father was murdered," he continued, the open admission shocked me, "I moved the collection to my residence, to keep the history closer to me."

"It's quite impressive," I admitted. "Any records we have in the Archives in the present have been kept locked up by Nordak forces, the level of difficulty to find anything of value is what keeps our lands from rebelling. The lack of knowledge of what we are missing."

"Knowledge is banned in the future?" The genuine shock in his voice surprised me as I looked over to him.

"Yes," the sigh escaped my lips. "I'm sure Cass has shared some, about The Fall and the Nordak coming into power, harvesting the magic in the lands. But since I returned, it's gotten worse. It's difficult to find records of magic, records of the realm from before the Nordak took over. Information has been censored. Even certain floors of the Archives are restricted. Records don't date back further than the year 500."

Kodrayn's gold eyes followed mine as I continued. "Since magic was banished. No one mentions it, no one wields it. I grew up in a realm where the only people who could wield magic had to be Nordak. And the worst part is that even as things continue to get worse, as people keep dying, everyone seems content to just let it happen."

I stared at Kodrayn, realizing that perhaps I had shared too much, revealed too much about myself. "That's why I need to know what the prophecy says. I need there to be a way to stop the Nordak now, so that we can alter the future of our realm for the better."

Kodrayn was silent for a moment, his face an impassive mask as we continued walking. Whether surprised or shocked by my declaration, I was still unsure.

"This section here." I watched as he gestured toward a section to our right. "This is where we would find any information regarding the prophecy my great-grandfather partook in years ago. Where we will hopefully find the answers you are searching for."

I stared at the section of books and parchments stacked in one corner of the room, hopeful that we would find the next clue of the prophecy. Any indicator of the magic that was cast across our realm long ago, shaping the lives of so many.

Grabbing the first book from the shelf, I coughed as a cloud of dust floated off the shelf. "It wouldn't kill you to open a book more often," I said as I settled into the closest chair, prepared to spend the night searching for the answers I so desperately needed.

"I do often enough," was his only reply as he settled in the seat next to mine, a book in hand.

My eyes hurt, the words on the pages blurring together as we read late into the night. The dim lighting cast flickers on the wall around us, and someone had stopped by to start a fire in the fireplace once the sun had gone down.

Rising from my chair, I walked over to the row of books we'd been scouring, standing on my toes to reach a book just out of reach. I felt a cool wave of air as my shirt rose up, before my fingertips finally collided with the spine of the book I'd been reaching for, only for it to tumble from my grasp once I pulled it from the shelf.

A loud yelp fell from my lips as the book hit my shoulder before falling onto the dark carpet with a thud. Still rubbing my shoulder, I bent down to pick up the tome. As I stood back up, my gaze met Kodrayn's piercing one, already fastened to me. *Great, just great,* I thought to myself as I walked with as much grace as I could muster back to my seat. Because of course he would see *that.*

Settling back into my nook in the seat, I began to flip slowly through the pages, searching for any mentions of the origins of the war, the prophecy.

"How did you get the scar?" Kodrayn's deep voice startled me, drawing me from my research. "The one on your stomach." He directed as I looked at him with confusion.

"Oh." I touched the side of my stomach absent-mindedly as I replied. "That would be from my first kill."

A dark eyebrow arched at my words as he waited patiently for me to continue. "As the Nordak began controlling more of our land, the number of Seefer attacks began to grow. My best friend and I began to track the numbers, noting what days had higher death tolls, how many Seefers had been spotted in the area. We were tired of waiting; tired of seeing the death counts rise every day."

"You started taking them out yourselves," he responded. A

statement, not a question. As if he had already discerned what type of person I was.

"We did." I paused. "I got the scar during my first Seefer patrol. The Void-damned beast got a little too close before I finally killed it off." I laughed now at the memory. "That was the day I learned that blades work best for killing corrupted beasts, not modern weapons. Just wish I'd learned that before the Seefer got a claw on me."

"Not many women would take it upon themselves to patrol for Seefers," he responded with a tone of admiration. His gaze held mine, and I shivered slightly, unprepared for the intensity of it.

"And too many people sit back while those around them die. I refused to be one of them. And so did Aerilyn." I stared back at my book, the words Blade of Rathmen appearing as I focused in on the text, reading on the history of the blade.

"What do you know about the Blade of Rathmen?" I questioned as I looked up from my reading.

"It was forged long ago by the Nordak, intended to be one of the greatest weapons of all time. Said to be able to imbue darkness into its victims, allowing the wielder to control those afflicted by the blade," he answered, a dark tone lying beneath.

"When was it last seen?"

Kodrayn remained silent for a moment before answering. "Not since . . ." He paused as though processing the information with new realization. "Not since the prophecy was put in place."

Void-damned. "It's said to disappear and resurface throughout time." I looked up at him. "If it hasn't surfaced since the Great Four scattered the artifacts throughout time, doesn't that make you want to know why it hasn't been seen?"

"Or how it's managed to stay hidden," he answered me. "And why the Nordak aren't searching for it."

"I keep feeling like we are missing something, something vital to the prophecy. To the war that was once rising with the Nordak. And I can't help but feel we are going to relive what your great-grandfather lived right before they gave up their magic to the artifacts."

We were silent after that, both returning to the texts at hand in hopes of finding the next verse of the prophecy. The next piece to a puzzle laid out before we ever existed. The fire crackled in the distance as my eyes blurred while I scanned line after line, page after page.

I must have drifted off at some point, since the next thing I remembered was moving through a dark corridor, the scent of blood orange and cedarwood drifting over me, as it lulled me to sleep. I heard heavy footsteps and the click of a door opening before we passed through into a warm room.

The soft feel of fabric beneath my skin surrounded me as I was gently set down on a mattress. The moonlight shone through a window, illuminating Kodrayn's face by mine as he began to move back. My hand stretched out before I could stop it, even as sleep tugged at me.

"How did you get this?" I murmured softly in the night air, as my fingers began to trace the edge of the silver clawed scar across his face. Kodrayn tensed beneath my touch, the skin cool beneath the pads of my fingertips as I moved them slowly up each line across his face, feeling every ridge of the mark that lingered, forever etched across him.

He didn't answer, the tick in his jaw noticeable even in the low light of the night. Exhaustion pulled at me, but I refused to give in just yet. "A scar for a scar," I whispered as I pointed toward my stomach. "You owe me."

A hint of a fang peaked through his lips. "I owe you?" he questioned. "A king owes no one anything."

Yet his fingers reached out, calloused fingers tracing the scar across the plane of my stomach. My breath stuttered as his fingertips traced over my stomach, a soft sigh falling from my lips at his touch, at the feel of his fingers dancing across my skin, across one of many scars I'd accumulated over the years. Just when I thought he wouldn't answer, his voice glided over me, his fingers never leaving my skin as he spoke.

"A gryffin attack," he admitted, a hard edge to his voice. "Nearly two years ago, a horde of gryffins were spotted at an outpost. I deployed men to hunt them down. Two escaped and trailed my men back toward Calante. I fought them off, but not without one of the beast's getting a hit in."

"It suits you," I murmured as I drifted away, unable to resist sleep's grasp on me any longer.

AVYON

Chapter Twelve

WE LEFT the very next morning for Saltridge Pointe, the location of Sébastien's call to his Brotherhood for help. I'd awoken the next morning in an unfamiliar room, neither of us having any success in finding any documents mentioning the second part of the prophecy. I guess on the bright side, Kodrayn's great-grandfather, one of the Great Four who got together to create the artifacts years ago, would be pleased to know his part of the prophecy had yet to be uncovered. Not that the knowledge did anything to help us now, when we desperately needed that information.

My thighs ached from the journey and I felt a recurring twinge of pain coming from my inner thigh. I rubbed at the spot, wincing at the spark of agony that rippled from the touch, and I knew I'd need to get the scar looked at soon. Better yet, that I'd need to tell someone soon. A conversation I still needed to figure out how to bring up, and to whom . . . because the thought of telling Kodrayn terrified me to the core. We were just getting on friendly terms, and I'm quite positive that mentioning that I may indeed be harboring corrupt magic from the Blade of Rathmen was not the way to keep a budding friendship, if one would call it that.

Oh hey, Your Majesty. Even though you've so graciously agreed to bring me back to my sister, only because of a blood pact you made as a child, I just wanted you to know, my ex, from the future, cut into my skin with an ancient dagger filled with what is believed to be the darkest of magics our realm has ever seen. But not to worry, if you could just have someone look into it for me, I'm sure it will be fine.

A dry laugh died in my throat at the thought of that particular conversation. So I waited, not quite ready to face that battle just yet, and still hopeful to The God that I would just magically discover the answer on my own.

We had departed from Calante early in the morning, Kodrayn and his men not wanting to delay their arrival to Sébastien's call. The sun was already high overhead as we traveled over hills and valleys. Beads of sweat dripped down from my hairline, my nose overheating slightly from the intensity of the sun while I continually swatted flies away. I'd watched the terrain vary all day. From the lush greenery that surrounded Calante and its surrounding rivers, to the drier hills and valleys we were currently traveling through. The slightest breeze rippled over the blades of dry grass, yet never enough to cool us down as we continued to travel to the east.

I nudged my horse out of line with the bands of men traveling. We were traveling with a far larger number of men than when I had first arrived, and the sheer number of vampry warriors traveling with us set me on edge. I didn't know the details of Sébastien's call for aid, but I knew that an army this large couldn't mean anything good.

Flashes of memories from Nik and Baxton raced on and off through my mind, reminding me to watch my back. I hadn't seen Kodrayn, Everett, or Torryn since we'd left the residence. Thoughts of the prophecy lingered in the back of my mind as I brought my horse to a trot, searching for the trio.

I'd memorized the first part of the prophecy from when I'd first heard it from my sister. Engraved the words that had altered our lives forever into my mind. Always hoping to one day come across the remaining verses of the prophecy.

The power of four melded in three,
Scattered on winds of time,
Forced by darkened powers to hide.

Bonded through secrets and lies,
A shattered acceptance,
Destined to start the beginning of times.

I knew the first two lines. We'd uncovered, during our time in Verastarr, that they pertained to my sister. Which meant that the next two lines of the prophecy, wherever it had been hidden, would pertain to me. The person who'd unleashed the second of the three artifacts. I thought back to the past year in the present, of searching through the Archives with Aerilyn for the prophecy, and I prayed to The God that she was still searching. That she would find a way back to this time with us.

I hated how I left, despite the fact that my winding up back in the past was entirely out of my control and unexpected. I wished I had been given the chance to share what I learned about the earrings with Aerilyn, about Nik, and the dark magic rising among the Descendents. That was truly the only thing I regretted about my arrival back into the past—that I hadn't been able to properly warn Aerilyn; to share with her all I'd discovered on the day we were apart.

The twins popped into view in my peripheral vision, their dark hair in contrasting styles visible as they conversed with Kodrayn.

"There you are, Silver." Torryn's friendly voice rang out as I rode up alongside them and fell into line. I noticed as Everett and Kodrayn fell silent on my approach, both looking more wary of me then I'd seen before. Everett's hand even moved toward the dagger at his waist.

"Sorry to interrupt." I smiled sweetly toward the three, still keeping an eye on Everett's movement, ensuring he didn't brandish his weapon on me. "I was just hoping that you may have found something pertaining to the next part of the prophecy." I directed my statement toward Kodrayn, my emerald eyes holding his amber ones.

The three fell entirely silent, Everett and Torryn casting a subtle, nearly indiscernible glance toward their king before back at me.

"We have." Kodrayn's tone was ice cold as he spoke. Not a hint of the friendly side I'd previously encountered from him last night, causing me to wonder what had occurred from the time I'd drifted to sleep until now.

"And?" I questioned, hope rising that the prophecy may give some indication as to where the last artifact may have been hidden.

"And that is all," Kodrayn snapped, his eyes narrowing in my direction in a look that would have shut me up. But it was a look I was familiar with, one I'd received from Nik time and time again. "We found information."

"Seriously?" I demanded, unwilling to accept his confusing, harsh tone. "That's all you have to say? Was I not the one that stayed up in the library with you late last night searching for the prophecy as well?"

Kodrayn's jaw ticked as his gaze remained on mine. I noticed Everett and Torryn slowly backing off, allowing their horses to drift backward a few paces. Still close enough they could advance to protect their king if needed, but far enough removed from the line of fire. I didn't care. "If I knew what the prophecy was, why would I have needed to search for it? Why would I ask for information on it to begin with? You realize that prophecy has to do with me, do you not?"

Kodrayn's jaw clenched, the scar raked across his now stormy eyes tightening as a blast of cold magic surrounded my skin in warning. I was caught unaware as his power circled me in full strength.

"Precisely." His reply came. "Tell me, *Kateya*. Do you have any indication of what the prophecy means?"

The edge of my name on his lips threw me off guard. He was angered. By what? Me? My presence? My insistence on looking into the prophecy?

"No," my answer felt hollow, concern growing within me. "That's why, you know," I said sarcastically. "I was wanting to know what the next part of the prophecy meant. Kind of hard to know what one's fate is without knowing what the prophecy says."

Kodrayn held his tongue, and I watched as he closed his eyes as though he was steeling himself before speaking to me again.

"My father once hid an important piece of parchment that his father had left for him, and his father before him."

I did the math in my head. Kodrayn's father's father would have been his great-grandfather, one of the Great Four, a creator of the artifact from Avyon.

"I was young at the time, very young, and didn't know what he was hiding. I only knew where he hid it because I followed him as a child one day, sneaking off into the underground tunnels after him, curious to see where he was going. With all our talk of the prophecy in the library yesterday, it got me thinking about the paper my father hid and wondering *what if.*"

I watched him as he continued, his gaze still on the path ahead, constantly scanning off into the distance, searching for any signs of trouble, of disrest.

"So I returned to the tunnels late last night for the first time since I was a boy. Following the untouched paths until I reached the spot where I'd watched my father hide a small piece of parchment, and I was right."

I held my breath, praying to The God that he was going to share the next two lines with me. That he'd actually found the second part of the prophecy.

"Imagine my surprise, when I realized that not only was I right in thinking that he'd chosen to hide the Avyon piece of the prophecy there. But when I read the prophecy, it foretold darkness and danger."

His gaze cut to mine, a predatory glint in his eyes and I looked at him in shock.

"W-what did the prophecy say? What did they foretell would happen?"

Kodrayn hesitated, actually hesitated, before speaking. "The second part of the prophecy spoke of darkness. Of blood and ashes. *Wrath*." He stretched out his hand, passing a worn piece of parchment in my direction.

My fingers reached out over the distance, our fingers grazing as I grasped the piece of paper in his hand. But his palm caught my wrist, holding me tightly in his grasp, as a chill climbed up my forearm, particles of ice touching my skin and then melting as his magic sent a warning over me. Just as quickly, he released my hand and I brought the paper up with a trembling hand to read.

Forged amidst ashes and blood,
A thread of darkness soon to rise,
Bringing with it a bleeding tide.

Elements collide to take on time,
Twisting wings of wrath,
A hand of fury set on a daunting path.

A knot grew inside my chest, making it difficult to breathe as I read, then reread the piece of paper between my fingers. *Ashes and blood. Thread of darkness. Bleeding tide. Wings of wrath.* Each word made my heart beat faster, my fingers clammy, as the same line snagged at me, drawing more concern every time my eyes glanced across the letters.

A thread of darkness soon to rise . . .

I knew the prophecy dealt with me to some extent. My mind leapt to the mark on my leg, the letter etched over my skin, and the sheen of black that tainted the scar. *A thread of darkness.*

Fingers still trembling, I extended my hand, passing the paper back to Kodrayn as I slowly raised my eyes to his.

"Well," I said with a shaky laugh that felt forced, "those weren't the promising words of hope I'd been wishing for."

His eyes narrowed but he said nothing. Minutes stretched by as I fidgeted with the harness of the horse I'd been riding and the silence grew until I couldn't take it.

I broke the eerie silence stretching between us. "You don't— you aren't truly implying that you think I'm the threat, are you?"

"You tell me. You show up here, in my land, two years after your sister arrived, with elemental magic that hasn't been seen in decades. And days after your appearance, I get a missive for help on the battlefront." His pointed look cut into me like a dagger. "What would you think?"

I stared at him, words failing to emerge from my lips as I nervously twisted a strand of silver hair that had fallen loose from my dutch braid. "I . . . well . . ." I paused, truly stopping to think about what I would have thought in his position. "I would think the same." The words came out in a cracked voice, a voice I hated to hear at that moment. One that sounded weak and afraid.

"They aren't the truth, but yes. I would draw the same conclusion that you have," I answered with the truth. It's what I'd been taught to do; read between the lines, seek out the lies that had been spun into our society, find the enemy. "But." I looked at the man riding beside me. "If I had known that, why would I have been searching for the prophecy? And more than that, you know the prophecy was put into place by the Great Four to *help* our realm. Void-damned. Your *great-grandfather* was the one who forged that part of the prophecy, Kode."

"Don't call me that." His snarl sounded from my side. And in that moment, as I looked at the man beside me, I could see his internal struggle. The struggle between believing that I wouldn't cause any harm despite the prophecy and doing what needed to be done to protect his people, his land.

"I came here to find my sister, *Kode*." I smiled, loving the way his eyes flashed as I used that nickname again, and knew I wouldn't get tired of it. "I didn't ask to be a part of this prophecy. I never wanted to be a part of any of this. But now . . . now I am. Just like my sister."

I held his gaze as I spoke. "And you seem to trust Cass. And you trust Sébastien. So why can't you trust that I wouldn't do anything to the detriment of *our* realm?"

He stilled, his entire body going rigid as he looked out into the distance, and I knew that I'd struck a nerve.

His voice was deadly low as he answered. "Did anyone ever tell you how I became king?"

I stayed silent, a soft shake of my head the only answer as he continued.

"Five years ago, I came home from a visit to our furthest outpost, to find the Nordak King had launched a surprise attack on Calante." My eyes widened in shock as he continued. "I came *home* to find my whole family murdered and gryffins swarming the Palace. The few soldiers I had with me, and the Brotherhood, are the only reason we banished them from the city."

"I'm so sorry," I murmured. And truly, I was, because I knew what it felt like to come home to death all too well.

"But," Kodrayn scoffed as we continued riding. "That's not even the best part. The reason the Nordak got through our walls so easily, the reason our Capital was breached, turned out to be my father's mistress, who discovered she could make a few extra coins by sharing the secret entrances to the Palace with a rebel."

The gasp fell from my lips as I stared at Kodrayn. His whole life, his whole family, stripped from him for a few extra coins.

I stayed silent for a few moments, giving him a moment whether he thought he needed it or not. Because that's the thing with pain, it can flare up when you least expect it to, and the lingering effects can last long after.

I decided to forgo empathy, realizing that wasn't what was needed in this situation. "I'm not the enemy here, Kode. I'm not here to bring about the darkness."

"*You* may not be. But something regarding the prophecy and the second artifact, which you shattered, will be tied to the darkness."

"So what?" I scoffed, noticing movement behind me as his second and third came up closer. "Are you just going to keep me as a prisoner? Is that the solution to your problem?" The words dripped out bitterly as I stared at the king before me, because that's what he was in this moment. Gone was the budding friendship from the library. The man who shared his family's past. In its place was the *King* of Avyon.

"No." Kodrayn's voice had my emerald eyes flashing up to meet him. "But you will understand that I have to do this. At least until the matter of this prophecy is resolved once and for all."

Panic flared in me as Kodrayn flicked a hand, his amber eyes darkening as a blast of his elemental magic sprung forth. Tendrils of ice wrapped themselves around my wrists and ankles, forming intricate cuffs as he pulled tight on his magic, the bands holding firm around my skin.

"What the fuck?" I screeched as I looked at him with fury in my eyes.

I twisted against the cuffs, my wrists recoiling against the cold.

Just like that, Kodrayn had done what the last man in my life had done—stripped me of my power. Fury blazed in my eyes, heat welling in me. He thought to restrain me, just because a prophecy threatened his land. I tugged at the kernel of power residing in me, pulling at the tendrils of heat that floated around it as I had begun to learn to do, summing them to the surface.

Blue-orange flame drew to the surface of my palm as I moved to melt the chains of ice he'd wrapped around me.

"I wouldn't do that if I were you." Kodrayn's voice hung in the air, a thick barrier between us. But I ignored his voice, focusing everything in me toward his power restraining mine and let go of the flame, watching as it snaked around the ice securing me. I screamed from the pain that erupted from my wrists, my skin crying out from the reaction.

My voice turned venomous as I looked at the King of Avyon. "What did you do?"

"I warned you." His cold voice lacked compassion as he spoke. "I did what I had to do to protect my people. And until we know whether you are a threat to my land, I will not give you the chance to bring darkness onto my people."

"What did you do?" I bit out again. "Why can't I use my magic?"

"You didn't think I hadn't noticed the first time I used my powers on you." His lip curled up, a near mocking expression on it. "The way your fire collided with my ice, how the chains I fashioned simply vanished, melting from your wrists. So I made a little adjustment, *just in case.*"

"And?"

"Well, it seemed only fitting after our first encounter and that venomous little tongue of yours. I imbued my magic with vampry venom."

My mind reeled. Venom? Vamprys had their own form of venom? "V-venom?" I questioned, confusion high as I tried to understand.

His fangs lowered with a glint as he looked at me and raised his wrist to his lips. With a swift motion, his fangs snatched onto his wrist, tearing the skin enough that blood welled. "See, little venom, there are different types of vampry bites. Ones to feed." He paused as he indicated to the quickly healing marks on his wrist. "Ones to claim"—he motioned with a trace of his finger around the marks—"causing the bite marks not to heal. And ones of defense." I watched as his fangs curved with a wicked gleam, the tips of his fangs turning a golden hue as liquid welled at the tip.

With a motion of his finger, he swiped across the fang, the golden liquid now residing on his finger. "Venom. A form of protection for vamprys, often used as a weapon in war."

I stared in shock. I had no idea there were different bites, much less venom. Thinking back, I tried to recount any mentions of vampry bites in the Archives, mentions of venom. But my mind was blank. We'd hardly discovered anything on vamprys at all. It was as though they had managed to keep the secrets of their fangs hidden in the dark for centuries.

"Why haven't I been taught that yet?" I let the first coherent thought that formulated fall from my lips.

"It's not an ideal form of protection."

"It seems pretty ideal to me," I replied as I stared at the venom on his tanned skin.

"It's not." His reply came. "You have to be close enough to your attacker to sink your fangs into them. And if you're that close—"

"You're most likely already dead," I finished for him, putting the pieces together. "Still." I looked over at him. "It would have been nice to know."

"You aren't a captive." Kodrayn's response shocked me based on his latest action. "But until we know what lies underneath the surface of this prophecy, I won't risk the safety of my men—of my people."

My lips tightened in a line as I stared at him. "If you couldn't access your magic, would you feel like a captive?"

He didn't answer for a moment, and that was all the answer I needed. "Thought so," I finished.

"You're still free to move around, to train. The magic in the cuffs will only flare when you reach for a weapon of any form."

"*Oh*." I replied sarcastically. "How fortunate for me. A girl truly loves to not be able to defend herself as she rides off to what I hear are the early signs of a battle."

Kodrayn spoke again, but this time the statement was not for me. "Let's set up camp for the night."

Everett turned, now passing orders to the towering warriors traveling with us. But I sat there, atop my mount, staring at my wrists in shock.

He used vampry venom to stall what little magic I had managed to begin to master.

AVYON

Chapter Thirteen

THE SECOND DAY of the journey passed the same as the first, with one exception. I now rode with a guard by my side, whether to protect me or keep an eye on me, I was still unsure, but I knew it was Kodrayn's doing. I was surrounded by the banter of vampry camaraderie and jokes, yet few of the warriors dared to speak with me, not after Baxton had been found frozen from the inside out after my arrival to Avyon. But I still had free reign, even if every move I made was under the watchful eye of the king's men.

The rain had begun two hours ago, and what had started as a slow drizzle had now become a torrential downpour. My clothing was soaked through, and shivers slowly made their way across my body as I stared into space, attempting to block out the misery.

I pushed my thoughts toward a warm day, the sun shining on my face, lavender flowers swaying on a rocky coastline. It was a fantasy I sent my mind to on repeat when the darkness began to creep in. I lay on a pebbled beach, my light brown hair swaying in the sea breeze.

"Snuck off again did you?" A deep voice had me pushing up onto my elbows as my head turned and a smile spread across my face.

"I just can't take it, Eryx." A heavy sigh fell from my lips. "I hate it—

139

knowing Cass is out there looking for the pendant; for a way to get us back to our time. And I'm here . . . doing what? Prancing around a Palace? Visiting taverns at night? I could be doing more. I should be doing more."

"And here I thought I was worth staying around the Palace for." His chuckle filled the afternoon air as he bent down, his tattooed arms wrapping around me as he threw me over his shoulder.

"Hey!" I protested as his shoulder jabbed into my ribcage. "Put me down!"

But he didn't. He ran, with me over his shoulder, straight toward the Sea of Avyz. "I mean it, Eryx! Don't you dare!" I screamed as I saw the water draw closer. "You wouldn't!" I half-shouted, half-laughed as water sprayed around his muscular form. My concern for my sister, the pang of uselessness I so often felt, momentarily forgotten.

I found myself submerged in the salty, warm water of the Sea of Avyz. I clawed my way back to the surface, shoving a wave of water toward the only man who managed to cheer me up lately and watched as the salt water slowly rolled down his face. His dark green eyes alight with mischief. The dark tattoos that wound up his face were a stark contrast to the smattering of freckles that coated his nose and cheekbones. My gaze focused in on his lips, the feeling of them every time they brushed against mine, devouring me, consuming—

"We're about to make camp for the night." A low voice cut into my daydream, bringing me back to reality. Back to my drenched hair and sore muscles from two days of traveling. I focused back in, finding that Torryn had ridden up beside me.

"Sorry, what did you say?" I questioned as I turned my attention to him.

"We . . ." Torryn said, dramatically gesturing around him. "Are . . ." The word came out in a long drawl. "About to make camp for the night."

"Ha. Ha." I deadpanned. "So sorry I didn't hear you the first time."

"Honestly, Silver. Not really sure what's more important." His tone was light, even as heat crept into my cheeks, no doubt turning them a shade of unwanted red despite the chill of the ongoing rain.

Torryn's eyes settled on mine with a new intensity. "Or, *who* is more important is perhaps the better question."

I ducked my head, refusing to give Torryn the satisfaction of being right as we pulled up on the campsite. "You never did tell me why the two of you decided on the nickname Silver," I said, switching topics.

Everett reached out from where he'd ridden up on the other side of me. "What else would we call you?" he said while he reached out, fingers tugging against the wet, shimmering strand of hair framing my face.

"How original," I responded lightly while I watched as tents went up quickly around me, warriors scurrying about to secure possessions amidst the ongoing rainstorm. Thunder rattled the ground as a bolt of lighting struck in the distance. The only gratitude I felt toward the storm was the fact I wouldn't have to spar for the night, and could instead collapse on a bedroll and pass out.

I missed my apartment in Estaire. I missed coming home from a long day and lounging on the couch, turning on a chick-flick and just relaxing. Sprawling out on a bedroll that squished from the mud underneath my weight was not my idea of relaxing.

I couldn't sleep. Despite the tent that provided a brief reprieve from the ongoing cascade of rain, my mind was reeling. Mostly at the excitement of seeing my sister tomorrow, I hoped. There had never been any confirmation that Cass was actually at Saltridge Pointe with Sébastien. But if I knew my sister, she'd be right beside her man. I had so much to tell her, and yet, my heart sank at some of the conversations I would inevitably have to share with her. I still hadn't figured out how to tell her about our parents, about what I had faced when I returned to the future.

And I didn't know if I wanted to. My sister had sent me back to the present believing that she was doing what was best for me, her younger sister. But a lot had changed since then.

I had changed since then.

I fidgeted with the cuff of magic Kodrayn had wrapped securely around me. I still couldn't believe he had thought the best course of action was to trap my magic within me, but at the same time, a part of me couldn't blame him for what he chose to do.

He was the king and he had an entire group of people to look after, to protect. In a way, I almost admired that he cared so highly for his people, that he would risk the potential anger of a blood brother's mate when she found out what he did. It was a characteristic that many of the rulers in the present didn't have, but one he clearly held in high regard. In another life, I may have even found Kodrayn attractive had I spotted him at Hydrillas on a Thursday night.

A sharp stab of pain burned on my thigh and I reached out, rubbing at the raised skin on my leg, as a low curse fell from my lips. I hadn't told anyone about my leg yet; about what Nik and his friends had tried to do. But the twinges of pain had been increasing, and I knew I couldn't keep it a secret much longer. I still couldn't believe that Nik had been tied up with the Nordak forces. Or that he truly believed bringing back a dark, corrupt ancient magic would be the answer to getting his elemental magic back.

I laid back down, focusing on my breathing as the pain still rippled down my leg in waves. I tried to close my eyes again, thinking about being reunited with my sister, when another wave of pain, sharper than the prior waves hit me and my eyes flared open.

Only this time, a dark purple mist surrounded me in the tent, an eerie darkness filling my veins as the mist encircled me. I pressed my lips together tightly to keep from alerting the guard outside my tent as my hands reached for the dagger by my side, only to remember I couldn't use a weapon with these blasted cuffs around my limbs. *What in the absolute f—*

I froze as I studied the mist. I'd seen this mist once before. Only once, a little over a year ago. The day that Cass and I had first found ourselves in the past and there was an attack. A group of Nordak rebels had launched a surprise attack with arrows laced with purple mist—*dark magic*. I threw the bedroll off, leaping to my feet as I prepared for the approaching attack. For whoever was preparing to ambush the camp. That's when I saw it, the purple mist. It was . . . *No, that couldn't be right. Could it?* It appeared as if it was coming from me.

I shifted back in the tent, and the mist followed, as though it clung to my being. Moving again, the mist continued to follow, expanding but constantly surrounding my body. Looking down, I found the source, and I watched as little tendrils of mist appeared out of nowhere, surrounding the scar on my thigh.

I steadied my breathing, aware that if I made a noise, I would alert the guards and be in a hell of a lot more trouble. Cautiously, I lifted my hands, the cold feel of ice magic weighing on them as I extended my arms out, reaching for the ominous purple mist swarming my tent.

The second my arm touched the dark amethyst color, it circled my wrists and a sharp flare of pain ignited around the cuff, then the mist vanished instantly. Not a trace remained, as though it had never been there to begin with. I lifted the bedroll, before shifting, searching around the tent.

Was I losing my mind? I hadn't envisioned that, had I?

Grasping the course material of the tent, I slowly pulled back the flap, scanning my surroundings. Nothing.

Slumbering warriors filled the area, low snores resonating in the night air as they mixed with the rain. Not a single warrior on night patrol seemed concerned. I sank back down onto my bedroll, mind racing.

It wasn't a dream. It felt too real. Too vivid. And yet, there was nothing out of place anywhere in my tent. Closing my eyes, I tried to calm my mind, deciding that tomorrow I would try to figure out what was going on with me.

No sooner had I closed my eyes than the tent flap burst open and a raised voice had me springing into an upward position, my hand once more reaching for a weapon I couldn't grab.

"Where is it?" Kodrayn bit out as I stared at him, wide-eyed. His shirtless form was outlined by the hint of moonlight visible in the night sky. His eyes scanned the tent, his muscles tense and weapon poised, ready for attack. "Don't lie to me. I could feel the darkness; the corrupt magic that only the Nordak have dared to use. I felt it in my power when it touched you."

"I—Um . . . I'm sorry. What?" I questioned as my gaze once again caught on the towering man at the entrance of my tent in the middle of the night. My eyes drifted down his still shirtless body, to the hard lines of rippling muscle, his defined obliques, and tattoos that were carved into him. I stared at the intricate detailing of the line work, taking in the strand of black ink that covered the left side of his chest and arm. A rush of heat shot to my core, my body flushing as thoughts of undressing the man before me floated dangerously through my mind.

"Something was here." Kodrayn's voice snapped me out of my reverie. "Some form of ancient magic. It had a wickedness to it that made my magic want to coil up." His erratic eyes roamed every corner of my tent, as if whatever it was would just appear before him so that he could vanquish it from his land.

"I'm sorry, I don't know what to tell you," I lied through my teeth as he studied me in the dark. Because I knew, deep down, that I couldn't tell the man in front of me, at least not yet. I kept my heart rate the same pace, one of the first things I'd learned at the training ring back home, focusing on my breathing so that he couldn't sense the lie radiating off me at that very moment.

Kodrayn stepped closer to me, his cedarwood and orange scent surrounding me as I met his gaze, suddenly all too aware of the shirtless man inches from my body, of the cords of muscle rippling across his broad chest. "Don't lie to me, little venom. I felt the magic hit mine. I felt it touch the cuffs around you, and then, just like that, it was gone."

I took in a breath to calm myself, instantly regretting it as his scent flooded my lungs, washing over me. "I am alone in this tent, *Kode*." I gestured to the small, empty space around us. "You can see for yourself, there is no one else here, except you." I stared at the man while I finished speaking, my mind drifting to thoughts of him, alone in my tent, *alone with me*. And suddenly it became hard to breathe, my pulse began to quicken at the thought of us together in this confined space, at what it might be like to feel his body over—

His eyes narrowed, distrust and unbelief visible, and I snapped back to the moment, instantly focusing on slowly my heartbeat once more.

"If your magic felt something, I'm not sure what it was. But I would venture to say that all the noise you have made since barging into *my tent* in the middle of the night, would have certainly scared it away."

"Something's not right," Kodrayn murmured, although whether the comment was to me or to himself, I was unsure. "Ancient magic needs a wielder, someone controlling it. We're missing something."

"Are you sure it was ancient magic?" I asked the man in front of me, knowing full well that it was. Or, at the very least whatever the mist was, was connected to the ancient form of magic.

"Yes," he replied. "I've only ever felt my magic recoil like that once before, when I got—" He didn't finish the sentence as his jaw tightened. But as I looked at him, I put the pieces together.

"When you got these from the Nordak gryffin." My hand reached out without my permission, tracing the claw mark closest to me across his forehead. It made sense now, why the scar hadn't healed fully. It had come from a gryffin who'd been using some strand of the ancient magic.

His head bobbed as he stepped out of my reach and spoke toward the tent entrance, to someone on the other side. "You're with her tonight. I don't care if you have to sleep in the tent with her. She's not to be alone. Not until we find out what's going on."

My teeth clenched in annoyance as he spoke to a guard outside my tent, but I held my tongue knowing there was no way I could explain the mark on my thigh without seeming even more suspicious now. Everett entered the tent with an apprehensive but apologetic look as he settled himself by the muddy entrance to my tent while Kodrayn left.

"Hope you don't mind company," was all he said before he sat there on guard duty for the night.

AVYON

Chapter Fourteen

MY FINGERS TAPPED in anticipation against my thigh, an unsteady beat, as the rocks of Saltridge Pointe came into view. I steadied my breathing, reminding myself that there was still the possibility that Cassandra was not at the Pointe. But that part of me—the part eternally connected to my sister by blood—knew she was there, and I couldn't contain my excitement much longer. While still uncertain of the battle lurking on the horizon between Sébastien and Kode's men and the Nordak forces, I was ready to make it to our destination.

The warriors surrounding me began to slow their approach as we drew closer to the edge of the cliff. Still hidden under the cover of tall oak trees, the shade of the branches kept us protected as a patrol dismounted and cautiously walked toward the ledge of the cliffside. The rocky terrain cut off at a jagged lip that led to a steep drop on the rocky beach. Large rocks jutted out from the shoreline, mixed with smaller rocks and broken red cedar branches. The overcast weather loomed over the shoreline as fog floated thickly above the sea. The forest, surrounding us on all sides, slowly sloped downward toward Verastarr. In the distance, I could make out crimson red tents. Tents that I knew belonged to the wolvyn. *To Sébastien.*

"Clear." One of the vampry warriors spoke as he returned from the edge.

"We'll set up here." Everett's voice cut over the wind as he looked toward his captains. "Use the trees as cover. We need to remain low to the ground and unseen from aerial views."

"We're stopping here?" I couldn't help the disappointment falling from my words as I looked over my shoulder to where Zaron stood at my left.

"The trees provide the perfect cover from gryffin patrols," his gruff voice answered while he dismounted and began unloading materials.

I followed suit, my movements still feeling weighted seeing as Kodrayn had yet to withdraw his magic. "You expect gryffin patrols here?" I didn't understand why the Nordak would be patrolling these lands, but then again, I didn't understand a great deal regarding the battle we'd been called in to aid. And yet, I had a feeling I would learn more soon enough.

"Yes."

"But why?" I blurted out as I tried thinking of the layout of our realm, of this Pointe specifically, yet nothing of significance stood out. "Of all the places the Nordak could be patrolling, and I could think of quite a few, I don't see the importance of patrolling here."

I studied Zaron as he spoke. "The Barree Rise would be one reason. The ease of access to the northern range path would be a key win in war." He continued unpacking supplies as he spoke to me. "And Arcelya would be the next."

"Arcelya?" The word rolled off my tongue with unfamiliarity. It was a word I'd heard mentioned twice during my arrival, but was never spoken of again.

"A small spot, buried deep in the Krymson Forest that few have discovered."

"Why is it so important? And . . ." I paused as my mind raced with questions. "If so few have discovered its existence, how is it that the Nordak are aware of it?"

Zaron's chuckle reached my ears as he turned to look at me. "Just because few have discovered its location, doesn't diminish its existence. Arcelya is a spot of lore, of fireside stories and whispered tales. Yet, it is real all the same."

"What do they want there?"

Zaron paused, his gaze holding mine as he answered. "What we all want, no? Answers. Answers to the prophecies and fates of old."

"And how exactly," I pushed, gathering any information I could, "does one find those answers?"

I watched the kindness fall from the man's face, a look of pain, *of horror*, replacing the features. "That doesn't matter." His tone cut cold as he resumed his duties around the forming campground. "They won't find what they're looking for."

I made my way through the trees, long blades of grass scratching around my ankles as I searched for Kodrayn or the twins. The vampry scouts had returned a few moments ago and I wanted answers. More than answers, I wanted Kodrayn to be proved wrong. I wanted Cass and Sébastien to hear the next verse of the prophecy and tell the King of Avyon that his suspicions were incorrect. That I was no threat and didn't need to be monitored. Yet, even as I wanted that to happen, a slight inkling nudged against me. *What if he was right? What if I was the thread of darkness that would bring about the bleeding tides?*

"Silver," Torryn's voice called out from my right, "we were just looking for you." I turned, finding the twins strapping on weapons as they stalked toward me, faces drawn tight.

"Is everything okay?" My heart thudded in my chest. *Has something happened? Was my sister not here? Had I come all this way for nothing?*

"We have a meeting with the wolvyn." Everett spoke as I tried to reign in my excitement. "You're to come with us."

"To where?" I struggled to keep my tone level as anticipation built in me.

"Across the border," was Everett's reply as he turned to greet an approaching captain.

I felt the ripple of power shift as we crossed the border, entering into Verastarr. The petrichor scent I'd grown used to that reminded me of the hours after a rainstorm was replaced with an all too familiar scent of lavender and lemon verbena. My heart sang.

Zaron and Everett walked in front of us along with two vampry warriors I didn't know. Torryn stayed to my side, one hand on his sword, as Kodrayn and three other warriors took up the rear.

The camp of wolvyn seemed equal in size to the number of warriors Kodrayn had brought, yet the campsite itself was smaller, many of the warriors opting to exist in wolvyn form, hiding in the shadows of the trees. I could smell the salt in the air, as the waves of the Avyz collided with the rocky shoreline. They were right on the water's edge, a direct target if the gryffin chose to come by sea.

Two large wolvyn approached our group. Their eyes scanned each member of our party with intensity. Their eyes fell to me. I held the gaze of the larger of the wolvyn, watching as his ears perked, and nostrils flared. Recognition.

I knew right away, whichever wolvyn was now leading us toward the center of the campground had recognized me instantly. My fingers pulled at the threads of my leathers, the only visible tell of anxiety radiating from me as we took step after step closer to the war tent.

I scanned the set up, noting how the wolvyn had chosen a location with hollowed trees, perfect for resting while remaining undetected. I noted the shifts between wolvyn and mortal—the small glimpses of elemental magic that flared, and the harrowed look of the soldiers that surrounded us. I'd seen the look before. It was the pained look of men who'd lost too many they called friends amidst an ongoing battle. I kept searching as we walked, trying to get a glimpse of my sister's long, brownish-blonde hair or Eryx's stunning jade-green eyes and tattoos.

I picked up muffled voices coming from inside the dark-red war tent we were approaching. The wolvyn we had followed motioned us to wait as he advanced inside the tent. I stared in awe as he shifted mid-step into the tent. A muscled, tall frame and dusty brown hair replacing fur as he entered.

The low laughs of soldiers sounded to my right and I spotted a group of soldiers playing cards and an exchange of coins around the gathering, presumably for the winner.

Dirty brown-blonde hair caught my eye as I strained to see through the soldiers, and the sight of crystal blue eyes sent me running. My feet took off, flying over the forest ground.

Everett's command telling me to stop sounded far in the distance as I sprinted toward the group of soldiers. A few drew weapons as I darted between them, my mind hardly processing the danger. She was there.

I threw myself against her, my body slamming into my sisters with enough force that we tumbled onto the ground. A loud "oomph" sounded from her as I sobbed. "Cass."

I pulled back slightly, watching as my sister's eyes widened even more, tears forming as she stared back at me; her face a mixture of shock, excitement, love, and pain. "Kat?" she questioned as if she couldn't believe she was truly seeing me . . . that I was truly back in the past.

I stared at her, taking in her familiar features, so similar to mine. The blue eyes with flakes of green. Her hair had grown even longer since we'd been apart. A faint scar across her hairline that hadn't been there before. "I told you I'd make it back," I said through sobs. "I told you," I repeated as my heart felt whole for the first time in over a year. *I told you.*

Her arms wrapped tighter around me, pulling me close, as though she was afraid if she loosened her grip, I would vanish once more. "How did you . . . How are you . . . Why are you here?" Cass stumbled through her questions as she stared at me, tears falling from us both.

"It's a long story, sis."

We laid there, crying on the forest floor in a tight, familiar embrace, surrounded by wolvyn and vampry.

"But you're okay?" she asked as she began to survey me as she picked herself off the ground while I followed suit. "You're not hurt? Injured?" She froze as she noted my wrists and her eyes narrowed as she looked back up to me. "Why"—she paused, her voice colder than before—"are your wrists cuffed?"

"Ahhh . . ." I replied, sarcasm dripping from my tone as I responded. "You can thank the hospitable King of Avyon for that one. He and his buddies freaked out over the second part of the prophecy and decided they didn't trust me not to rain darkness down on the realm."

Cass stared at me, fury and disbelief in her eyes. "But you told him you were my sister?"

"That I did." I smiled sweetly, the type of look I'd given my sister one too many times when I'd been annoyed at her. "Evidently, that wasn't enough."

"We're fixing this now," she demanded. Turning on her heel, she grabbed my arm and yanked me after her. We stomped through the campground back toward the war tent. Wolvyn soldiers darted out of my sister's warpath in fear as she passed. With her free hand, I watched as my sister tore the tent flap open and pushed her way through, me on her heels. Her eyes tracked around the space, the faces of every man turned to her before she landed on Kodrayn.

"Are you out of your Void-damned mind?" she seethed in his direction. Everett and Torryn slowly crept closer to Kodrayn, hands on their weapons even as he flicked his palm, dismissing them. "Who do you think you are, Kodrayn Deverell?" Cass continued her reprimand. "I don't care who you think you are, or whether we are in the middle of a Void-damned war. You do *not* put my sister in cuffs. Take them off of her, *now*." Her tone dropped to one of icy venom as she glared at him.

A flicker of amusement flared in Kodrayn's eyes as he matched her gaze with one of his own. "No." His tone was low and clear.

"No?" My sister scoffed.

"No," Kodrayn repeated, this time with agitation rising in his voice. "As I was telling your *mate*," he continued, his eyes flicking over to Sébastien as he spoke, "the arrival of your sister brings about some new threats with the prophecy. Threats that must be taken seriously." Cass opened her mouth, but he cut her off as he continued. "Whether or not she is your sister, until we get answers, I will not risk the safety of my people."

My gaze flicked from Kodrayn to Cassandra, then to the King of Verastarr. His icy blue eyes already on me as he nodded his head in greeting. I opened my mouth to speak, but Sébastien beat me to it.

"I will not contradict your choice, Kode, out of respect for the Brotherhood and the bond we share because of it." Sébastien spoke as his eyes shifted from his mate to his blood brothers. "But Kateya is also my *mate's* sister." My skin bristled as they stood there, speaking about me as if I couldn't speak up for myself—as if I wasn't right there. "Perhaps, you could alter the restraints, at least while we stand on *my* lands." His voice relayed the message. I might be restrained by one king, but we were now on another king's land. A land Kodrayn had no authority over.

Kodrayn's jaw ticked but he said nothing. Simply nodding his head toward his blood brother as the words of the Brotherhood, the words of the pact they'd made as young princes, "Embers and Ash," fell from his lips.

Sébastien nodded his head in return, finishing the statement in gratitude. "Even The Void won't hold."

I watched as the ice around my ankles shifted, dissolving into thin air, but the cuffs on my wrists remained in place, now altered to reveal two thinly woven designs of icy power, circling around my skin. Testing the limits to see what changed, I reached for the dagger at my side when a sharp twinge of power caused the shackle to tighten, halting my movement.

I glared at Kodrayn, realizing that while he'd removed the ankle cuffs and provided less weight and therefore more movement for my wrists, I was still unable to wield a weapon to protect myself should I need to.

I opened my mouth to say something to him, to contradict his choice of actions, instead I shut my mouth as I caught sight of his amber eyes, still on me, watching me closely as though waiting to see how I reacted.

"Okay, tell me everything," Cass demanded as we sat inside her tent, alone for the first time since I arrived. We'd spent the past two hours listening to battle plans regarding the suspected gryffin attack in the coming days, the number of Nordak warriors Sébastien's scouts anticipated crossing our borders, and potential courses of actions before Cass had dragged me out of the war tent, unable to wait any longer.

"Me first?" I looked at my sister. "What about you? A mate . . . A queen . . . Your powers."

Cass sighed, before answering. "Fine . . . I'll go first. But afterward, I expect every single detail, got it, Kat?"

I nodded as my sister began, sharing everything that had happened from the moment she had shattered the dagger. She told me of the final phase of the bond falling into place, of the bonding ritual that happened. She talked of racing back to Nytestarr and finding the Palace under attack—of losing both Sébastien's father and his brother in less than an hour. She told me how Sébastien had taken his position as King of Verastarr and declared battle on the Nordak. Then she filled me in on the battles, the locations targeted, and the brutality and death that had followed for the past two years since I'd been gone.

"I wish you'd never come back, Kat." Cassandra choked on her words as she spoke. "I mean, don't get me wrong, I'm so happy to see you again and hear your voice. But, Void-be-damned, Kat, I would never wish this life on anyone. The constant days of battle and grief. Of watching those you call friends take their last breath."

"It's not much better in our time, sis." My voice was low as I began to fill her in. My heart broke into pieces as I stared at my older sister. I had already decided, I wouldn't go into detail, but she needed to know. Our parents' deaths deserved to be remembered, even if their two daughters were now hundreds of years in the past. Their deaths deserved to be avenged, and the only way that could be done was by stopping the growing power hunger in the Nordaks.

"Returning to the future. It wasn't what we thought it would be. Time passes differently here than it does at home." Cass watched me closely as I spoke. "While it's been two years for you." I paused. "It's only been a year for me."

"What happened, Kat? What happened when you went back to our time?" Cassandra's brow creased and I knew she knew.

"They knew. I don't know how, but the Nordak knew that we'd used a great deal of magic. And when they couldn't find us, and couldn't punish us for going against the laws of magic . . ." I took in a shaky breath, but I didn't have to say it. One glance at my sister's silver-rimmed eyes and she'd pieced it together.

"They punished Mum and Father, didn't they?" Sorrow filled her voice as she asked.

My head bobbed and a tear rolled down my cheek as I said, "Remember the neighbors down the block? The ones with the faded yellow house and brick driveway a few doors down." Cass's breath caught as she stared at me, her eyes widening. "Remember how the Nordak patrol found them using the slightest bit of elemental magic. They—"

Her hand flew to her mouth, covering the sob that broke through as I reached over and hugged my sister.

"They're gone, aren't they?" Her words came between sobs as we clung to each other, grasping for any remaining threads of our past life, the grief a tangible cloud lying around us.

"Yes," the whimper choked out of my throat. "I didn't even get to tell them we were sorry. I didn't get to explain to them where we had gone; what had happened." Tears fell at a steady pace now as I spoke. "They were just gone. I never even got the chance . . ." I stared at my sister's eyes, tears rolling across her high cheekbones. "I'm sorry, Cass. I'm so sorry. I failed them. I failed you. I just . . . I'm so sorry."

The tent flapped open, black mist filling the opening before Sébastien's head popped into view, his form hovering in the entrance, ice blue eyes landing straight on his mate, on her tear stained face.

"What's wrong?" his low voice questioned, focused solely on her.

My sister smiled softly at her mate, "We'll talk later, Seb. I'll be okay."

He stood in the doorway, gaze lingering on her as though he could physically take away her grief just by staring at her long enough.

"Go, I'll be fine. I have my sister," Cass murmured. After another long moment of silence, Sébastien finally turned around, a tendril of black mist remaining by the entrance of the tent as he left.

"Kateya." My sister's voice sounded strong from beside me as she looked at me, meeting my eyes. "You have nothing to be sorry for. This wasn't your fault. None of it was."

We clung to each other for a while longer, just breathing in the familiar scent of family, of love, of a home away from home. Because that's what she was for me, what she'd always be. Finally, I shared the rest of the story.

I told her of faking my own death and moving in with Aerilyn.

I told her about dating Nik again and joining the Descendents; the Seefer attacks and the patrols we'd started—hunting them off. Of the countless days spent searching the Archives for any leads as to what may have happened with the other artifacts.

"And Cass," I started, "you wouldn't believe what we discovered right before I ended up back in time. The ley lines!" I kept my voice to a whisper.

"What about the ley lines?" Cass watched me, her face a mixture of shock and intrigue.

"That's how they do it. The Seefers, they were always attacking at intersections of ley lines. The Nordak. They were—"

"Drawing more power from the sources of power found in the land," Cass finished in disbelief as she pieced it all together. "I can't believe we never thought of that."

I finished my story late into the afternoon, and Cass and I stared at the stitches holding the tent seams together as we lay side by side on our backs. We'd been silent for the past twenty minutes, quietly pondering everything we had both learned.

"Cass." My voice shook slightly as I took a deep breath.

"Yeah?"

"Have you ever," I started. "Well, has your power . . . Do you have the ability to—" I stopped as my sister shifted on her elbow, facing me on the ground. Rolling to my side, I studied her before trying again. "Remember that day we first arrived in the past? And we were ambushed on our way to the château?" I questioned.

"Yes," Cass answered hesitantly.

"Do any of your powers consist of the purple mist that we saw that day? I know you can control shadows, so I was just wondering."

She was silent for a moment, before she answered. "No. And now that I think about it, I've hardly seen that form of magic be used since that day. Why?"

I told her of the other night as I lay in the tent. Of the purple mist that surrounded me, appearing out of nowhere. I told her about Kodrayn running into my tent shirtless in the middle of the night, saying he'd felt an ancient magic touch his power around me. I don't know why I didn't tell her the full story. Or why I never mentioned I knew where the mist came from. But I told her the parts I could.

"But you didn't tell him about the mist?"

"No." I looked at my sister. "He already thinks I have some thread of darkness in me thanks to the prophecy. I wasn't about to add to that by mentioning an ancient purple mist had floated through my tent."

Cass studied me. "Perhaps the Elder knows more about it."

"Don't tell anyone yet, please?" I asked my sister. "Kodrayn's men are wary of me as is. And I'm sure Sébastien has concerns too." My sister went to protest, but I stopped her. "Mate or not, Cass, my arrival here brings a lot of questions, and he would only be doing his job if he had concerns as well."

She shot me an apologetic look that let me know she was already aware of her mate's concerns.

We sat around a fire eating dinner; Sébastien and Kodrayn talking in low murmurs to the side with Everett, Torryn, and Dravyn close by. Emalyee sat to my right, while Cass was on the other side. The fire crackled softly as the girls chatted, asking me questions about the future, about what I'd learned while I was away. I answered, only partially focused on their questions, as my eyes roamed the camp, coated in dusk.

"Are we distracting you?" Emalyee finally cut in, her eyes assessing me with new interest.

"Sorry," I muttered sheepishly. "What were you saying?"

"The Archives," she resumed. "When you first found the parchment that talked about . . ." But I no longer heard what she was saying.

My gaze had snagged on a pair of jade eyes from across the

clearing. Eyes that I had only dreamed of for the past year. I noticed the look of surprise, of disbelief, before I was greeted by the slow, dimpled grin that spread in invitation. I stood abruptly, my plate falling to the ground as both girls looked at me.

"Oh . . ." I heard my sister's voice from behind me, and felt the eyes of everyone around our fire watching me. But I was only focused on one face as it moved closer to me. And then I was moving, my heart racing as I ran toward the man who had claimed my heart over a year ago.

I didn't stop when I reached him. I threw myself at him, arms wrapping tightly around his neck as my body collided with his and he pulled me tightly against him. The scent of lemon and bergamot enveloped me as I clung to him before pulling my face back to meet his gaze. I took in the tendrils of ink creeping up the side of his neck until they reached his temple; the smattering of freckles that brushed across his tan cheekbones. A new scar cut into his chin, and his dimples grew as his emerald eyes held mine.

"How?" he asked gruffly, his voice thick with emotion.

"Does it matter?" I replied, my eyes tearing slightly as he held me in his arms.

"Yes," he answered in a way I knew meant he knew the cost of me being back here, in this time, with him. "Later. We will talk later." His eyes held mine, before they flicked down to my lips and back up at me. A silent question. I bit my lip shyly, nodding at him. He wasted no time, and needed no further invitation from me.

His lips came down onto mine with a claiming force. He tasted of citrus and salt as he pried my lips apart. Muscled arms wrapped around me, his hands roaming over my back, down to my waist, before circling back up. My hands ran up the expanse of corded muscle across his chest, honed over years of training, as I held him to me, losing myself in him. His tongue forced its way into my mouth, a soft whimper falling from my lips as he explored. I swirled my tongue over his, feeling the warmth of his hard body against mine. His hand tangled itself in my hair at the nape of my neck, the other hand going lower as it slid over my hip.

The sound of a throat clearing loudly to the side had me pulling away slightly, breathless as I turned to meet chocolate brown eyes belonging to Torryn. "Well, Silver, now I know why you've been holding out on us." Torryn's teasing grin was met by a deep growl coming from the man beside me.

"Do you have a thing for watching?" I prompted. "Or was there something you needed to tell me?"

Torryn's breathy laugh filled the otherwise silent space. "Just that you will be needed at the meeting tomorrow morning at dawn."

I nodded briefly before fixing my gaze back on Eryx, my hand slipping into his as I asked, "Someplace else?"

VERASTARR

Chapter Fifteen

A WEIGHT SHIFTED beside me as I stirred and blinked my eyes open to find Eryx watching me sleep. "Morning." I smiled softly as I stared at the man who was making his way back into my life once again.

"Morning. Sleep well?" He breathed against my neck as I woke up.

"With you, always," I murmured, leaning over to kiss the tattooed inkings crawling up the side of his chest. A low rumble came from him as his eyes darkened, heat flaring up between us as I moved my lips higher, leaving a trail of kisses in my wake until I met his lips.

With a growl, he tugged me toward him, a low shriek falling from my lips that he covered with his as I found myself sprawled across his torso, getting caught up in him as his lips roamed over mine, licking and sucking. "Eryx," I sighed against his mouth. "We have to get up."

"We have time," he muttered, his hands tracing circles down my bare back drawing a soft moan from me as I easily gave in. I leaned into him, letting the heat from his body warm me as I lost myself in his lips, in the feel of him. His hands crept lower, fingers tracing tantalizing circles down my stomach, my body now ablaze in anticipation. We'd talked long into the night, falling asleep immediately after, but now . . . Now, I *needed* him. I needed to feel Eryx over every fiber of my being. His hands drifted lower as he nipped at my neck, sending jolts of desire pulsing through me. My hips lifted, back arching in invitation. "Please," I moaned as his hands found my inner thighs, teasing me as they crept closer and closer to where I wanted them to be.

"Good, you're up." Came an unwelcome voice from outside the tent I laid in with Eryx. A disappointed groan fell from my lips at the sound of Everett's voice in the early morning.

"I'm going to kill them. Both of them. Slowly." Eryx snarled as I untangled myself from him and replied to the outlined figure outside of the tent entrance.

"Yes. I'm up, although I have a feeling that you already knew that. Was interrupting necessary?"

"Stop wasting time, Silver." Everett's outline didn't move, so I hurriedly grabbed my clothes and began dressing.

"Silver, really?" Eryx's voice whispered almost angrily at the idea of the nickname as he threw on a shirt, the muscles in his arms bulging against the material constraining them.

"It's no big deal. Let it go, okay, Eryx?" His eyes held mine, annoyance nearly bursting from them.

"For now," he relented. "But after all this . . . when you're mine, no one but me gets a nickname for you."

"Deal," I said with a saucy grin as I opened the tent flap and walked out, running straight into Everett.

"Are you out of your mind?" I looked at him as he led the way to the war tent. "No one needs to stand that close to someone else's tent entrance."

He remained silent, avoiding what I'd come to know as his usual joking banter as we made our way inside to join the others. Taking a seat next to Cassandra, I looked around at who made the cut for this meeting. Kodrayn, Everett, Torryn, and Zaron sat on one side of the makeshift table in the center of the space. On the other sat Sébastien, Dravyn, Emalyee, and my sister and I.

"I think it's time to consider Arceyla," Sébastien started once everyone was gathered. "I know we have been pushing it off for some time, but with all the new information that has come to light, it may be our best option."

"We still have no idea whether the Unseens will even see us, much less be willing to speak to us." Kodrayn's voice rang out.

"The Unseens?" I questioned as I looked between the two kings.

"The Unseens are similar to the Elders," Sébastien answered as he looked toward Kodrayn. "We need answers. And we need them before Nordak makes their next move."

"We have no guarantee the Unseen will give us answers. I'd rather we take our chances at the Barree Rise." Kodrayn's voice rose, a cool arctic breeze causing the tent panels to flap, as he glared at the King of Verastarr.

"Arceyla is closer. If the Unseen don't provide the answers we need, we can move on to the Barree Rise. I don't see what other option we have."

"He's speaking some truth," Everett muttered as he looked toward his General. "We need some answers and we haven't had any success finding them yet."

Kodrayn switched his gaze between Everett and his blood brother. His eyes narrowed in on each of them before he shook his head slightly in reluctant agreement. "We leave tonight then. It's best to travel the Krymson forest under cover of the night sky."

After much deliberation, it was decided as Sébastien spoke the final word. "Dravyn," he said with a look toward his second in command. "You will travel with Kodrayn, Everett, Zaron, and Kateya. It's best that we keep the numbers of the group small. We can't afford to be spotted traveling to Arcyela."

The warriors nodded in agreement as they stood to begin arranging travel plans. I turned toward my sister in shock. "You're not coming with me?" My voice caught as I stared at her. "We only just got back to being in the same place, at the same time."

"I can't, Kat." Cassandra's voice was filled with sorrow. "Someone needs to be here. And, with both of us wielding such unique powers, it's best that we aren't in the same location for too long."

A heavy sigh fell from my lips as I stared at my sister. "And you truly can't convince your *mate* to let Eryx come on the trip? I mean, seriously, sis. What good is having a king as a mate, if he can't even let one man go on a trip with me?" Annoyance flared in my chest once again. I'd spent the better portion of the conversation trying to convince the group to allow Eryx to travel with us, but unfortunately for me, Arceyla was located on the Avyon side on the border, meaning that blood brother bonds and alliances aside, Kodrayn had the final approval on those that traveled with us.

"I'm sorry, sis," she replied, sorrow in her tone. "I know you just got to see him again too. I wish I could do more."

I turned to walk toward the training ring, intent on finding Eryx, as my sister fell into step beside me. "We need to know more," she whispered. Her tone was lower than usual as she continued speaking to me. "You and I. We need to find out more about these powers, the prophecy. What it means for us."

"I know, Cass. Trust me. I've spent the past year of my life researching this prophecy, these artifacts. I'm going to do my best to uncover everything I can about them."

"There's very little information available here. The entire prophecy is shrouded in mystery. If you get the chance to speak with an Unseen privately, you need to learn whatever you can about the prophecy."

"I will do my best," I responded to my sister. "Trust me, Cass. I know we are missing something, some underlying piece to this puzzle of fate."

She stopped, before we entered the makeshift training ring and stretched her arms out, enveloping me in her embrace. "I missed you, Kat. More than you know. I missed you so much. Don't do anything stupid while you're gone."

I laughed as I hugged my sister back. "You too, Cass. You too."

"You're serious?" Eryx nearly shouted as I stood beside him near the training ring. I watched his jaw tick as he stared at me, anger and frustration flashing in his eyes. "Why the *fuck* can't I come with?"

"I'm sorry. I tried." I stared up at him, hating that I was making him mad. "Trust me, Eryx," I said as I reached my hand out toward him, gently resting it on his arm. He shrugged his arm out of my grip, pushing me away as he left the ring.

"Did you try, Kat?" he growled. "Did you do *everything* in your power to persuade them to let me come with you?"

"I wouldn't lie to you." I looked at him, shocked at how he was reacting to the news. "Why wouldn't I do everything I could so you could come with me? Why wouldn't I want you to come with me, so soon after getting you back in my life?"

I watched as he ran a hand through his short hair, a flash of black ink stark on the back of his hand as he sighed, taking in a deep breath.

"Sorry," he responded, frustration still blatant in his features as he apologized. "It's fine. It's just not what I had planned."

"What you had planned?" I stared at Eryx, confusion rising at his words. "You only just found out I was back yesterday."

His fists clenched at his side, then he responded. "Yes, but do you know how long I've dreamed of this? How long I've hoped you would reappear back into my life. And for it to happen just for you to leave so soon . . ."

My heart melted slightly at his words, the fact that he'd been wishing for my return to the past.

"We leave in an hour." Kodrayn's low voice cut into our conversation from behind, as I whirled around to face him. Eryx stiffened at my side, and I could feel the tension between the two men as the King of Avyon stopped in front of us, amber eyes assessing the male beside me.

"She's not going anywhere without me." Eryx's deep growl reverberated from beside me and I groaned internally at the rising argument between the two.

"Is that so?" Kodrayn's voice dripped ice as he stared at Eryx, and I stared in horror as his fangs dropped, a golden-yellow color pooling at the tips.

Eryx didn't answer, he just held his gaze firmly set on the king.

"I'd think better than to order a king, if I were you." His low warning hit my ears as I glanced back and forth between the two men knowing no good could come from this.

"How about we just—" I started, before a growl interrupted me. Although from which male it came from, I was still unsure.

"Where she goes, I go." Eryx's deep voice sounded beside me.

A sinister smirk spread across Kodrayn's lips as he looked between the two of us. "Very well. If that's how you want to play this, fine," he said with a wickedly cruel grin toward me as he spoke to Eryx. "You can accompany Kateya to Arceyla. But if you dare step foot onto *my* lands, I'll let every vampry warrior in the area know you're free game."

Eryx frowned as Kodrayn's words were processed. I knew Arceyla was deep into Avyon territory and from the looks of it, Eryx did too. To accompany me was to sign his life away.

"You're a fucking prick," Eryx snarled as he began to walk away, towing me in hand.

"No. I'm a *fucking* king, and the sooner you accept that, the better," Kodrayn growled back, a blast of icy power unleashing at his command, smacking Eryx in the back as we walked away. I said nothing as I trailed after Eryx, but a glance back told me Kodrayn knew he won, a devilish smirk across his face while he watched me walk away.

Saying goodbye to my sister hadn't been any easier this time around. Still, I thanked The God that this goodbye wasn't forever. It was just for a few days. The five of us had been on our way for two hours now, and were well into Avyon lands once again. The familiar post-thunderstorm smell of the land washed over my skin. Zaron rode at my side with Everett and Kodrayn in front of us. Dravyn had chosen to travel in wolvyn form, scouting further ahead as we journeyed along.

None of the others had muttered a word since we had begun; content, it seemed, to let nature be the only sound accompanying us.

I turned toward Zaron, asking a question that had lingered on my mind since the first night I walked through the vampry camp. A question that plagued me now that I could shift.

"Do all vamprys have to feed?" I forced the question out, shuddering at the thought.

Zaron studied me for a moment, possibly wondering at my interest on the topic, before he replied. "Yes, they do."

"And it has to be . . . well, you know. It has to be blood from a living being?"

Zaron's eyebrow arched at the question, but this time it was Everett who answered.

"What are you hinting at, Silver?"

"I just . . ." I paused realizing that all three men were now focused on me and I wanted to die of embarrassment at the topic. "It's just that, well now that I can shift . . . will I have to as well? Because I can't do that. *I won't.*"

Everett's laugh filled the air as we carried on, while Zaron gave me an answer.

"All vamprys must feed to replenish their strength and agility. They feed from mortals unless they have a bonded mate."

"How come?" I questioned, wondering why mortals would offer their blood to begin with. "Isn't that unfair to mortals?"

"Many mortals choose to offer themselves up."

I stared at the men in shock. "You can't be serious. People volunteer to be fed from, *willing*?"

"It pays well, and many are provided protection as well," Everett answered.

"But why mortals? Why not simply feed from other vamprys?"

Kodrayn's voice filled the air as he spoke. "There are many reasons. The primary reason being that sharing blood between vamprys is regarded as an action reserved to be shared between mates—your bonded."

I remained silent, realizing that made some sense, seeing as among each land, shifters often took on mates, not boyfriends or husbands as mortals did.

"Vampry blood has the ability to heal," he added. "Though we try to keep that ability among our own people, not wishing for our own to be captured and drained for the healing power in our veins."

"What about me?" I asked. "Since I was mortal, but now I'm . . . well, I'm—" *I didn't know what I was considered now.*

"We'll just have to wait and see," Kodrayn replied as he began to refocus his attention to the path ahead. "Only time will tell whether that will be a need you must fulfill."

I crinkled my nose at the thought, promising myself I wouldn't feed, even if the need arose. We rode in silence after that, allowing me time for my thoughts to drift over the series of events that had unfolded in the past week and a half of my life. Allowing myself to process the changes that had occurred.

I still prayed to The God that Aerilyn had received my message before it was too late. That she had made it into hiding and would be able to figure out that I had made it back to the past. I wondered whether my disappearance had caused another flare of magic to appear, if it had alerted the Nordak—the Descendents. But, as my father had always taught us, you can't change a path already paved, you can only build from what's been made.

With a soft sigh, I stretched my legs as far as I could mid-ride, looking around at my surroundings; taking in the rolling hills occasionally visible through empty clearings amid the forest. Tracking our path as we made our way to Arceyla and the Unseens.

AVYON

Chapter Sixteen

I **NOTICED** the moment the terrain began to shift in the early morning light. The trees changed from a dark green hue to blood red. The color of leaves you'd see lining the streets in the fall, yet darker—more ominous. I also noticed the subtle shift in the mens' demeanors, as though a weight had been lifted from them as we walked deeper into the shades of crimson. Leaves dropped occasionally in the wind, floating down and coating the forest ground, creating a sea of red mixed with a low-hanging fog that hovered a few inches off the ground.

"What is this place?" I questioned Zaron as I surveyed our surroundings.

"The Krymson Forest," he answered.

"Looks like we escaped the worst of it," Everett said over his shoulder. "Should be relatively smooth riding from here on out."

"Why do you say that?" I looked toward Everett as I spoke, watching as his destrier slowed to ride beside mine.

"The Krymson Forest is sacred ground. Attacks in these parts of the land are few and far between. The last attack to happen here was thirty years ago."

"Truly?" I questioned. "I thought Arceyla was in the Barree

Rise?" My mind drifted back to the map Cass had showed me the other night and knew I hadn't been wrong in what I had seen. "Wouldn't that open us to attacks from the Whisperers?"

"Ah . . ." Everett began. "It's more complex than that. See the Barree Rise draws a line between Avyon and Verastarr. And through the years, it has become a dwelling place for magical and mythical beings alike. A place of lore and danger. A place where answers are sought."

I nodded while listening intently. So far, what he was sharing lined up closely with what Cass had experienced when I was last here.

"The Barree Whisperers reside closest to the Elder, nestled near the tops of the peaks on the Verastarr side of the mountain range," Kodrayn chimed in from a few paces ahead of us. "Arceyla and the Unseens are located on the Avyon side."

"Why does the Barree Rise contain so many beings with the sole purpose of providing answers for The God? Would that not make them more susceptible to attack?" I questioned.

"Only The God knows why beings of prophetic power are drawn to the Rise. But all magic demands a balance. To reach the Elder, one must survive the Whisperers and make it through the journey without losing their sanity," Kodrayn stated in response.

"And Arceyla?" I prompted.

"Arceyla is a myth in its own right." His tone filled the forest as he continued. "Few have found their way to The Wall. And those that do, must still escape the clutches of the Unseen."

"The Wall?" I started. "Wait. I thought we were going to see the Unseen? Do they not hold the answers?"

"Your lack of Avyon history is truly impressive, Silver," Everett said, a hint of teasing annoyance in his tone.

"Not everyone was brought up in a land of magic and lore as you were."

"The Wall is said to be a shimmering rainbow of falling water from the side of the Barree Rise," Everett supplied. "When touched in the right moonlight, it will reveal scenes on its surface to answer the question one seeks."

"You cannot *seriously* be telling me"—I paused in shock—"that we are going all this way to see a magical waterfall. Not even a person, an Elder . . . *but a waterfall?* How has its location managed to stay a secret for this long?"

Everett's laugh filled the air and a huff sounded from ahead, but it was Kodrayn who answered my question.

"Arceyla is hidden in a valley by the Krymson Forest. The Wall itself, though, doesn't appear to everyone. Some may pass by the valley and never once see The Wall. Others may pass by and see it right away. It chooses those who seek answers from pure hearts and appears to them."

"A magical waterfall with its own defense . . . *brilliant.* And we are just praying to The God that it appears to us?"

"Yes and no," Kodrayn answered, now riding alongside Everett and I while Zaron pulled ahead. "Seeing as like calls to like, it would stand to reason that The Wall may appear to you due to the power you now contain."

I stared at the men in shock as we continued on, realizing that we were truly traveling all this way in hopes that I was some sort of mortal key that would encourage a *magical waterfall* to reveal itself to me. "And the Unseen? What about them?"

"The Unseen . . ." Everett's face grew grim even as he spoke. "They have one foot in The Void as they are part witch and part death itself."

I tensed, whipping my head in the direction of Everett. "Part death? As in like—"

"As in, they have already died. But before they died, they expelled a blast of ancient magic, wielded in a tight web that keeps them tethered to this side of The Void while learning the secrets of those on the other side."

"Void-be-damned . . ." My heart beat faster as I thought about what an encounter with a creature like that would be like. "Why would we possibly wish to meet with an Unseen?"

Everett glanced toward Kodrayn, a deferral to his king to provide an answer.

Amber eyes caught mine, holding them captive as my question was answered. "To learn the secrets of the Great Four." I sucked in a sharp breath. He couldn't possibly be serious.

"You can't possibly think—"

A shrill snarl interrupted me and I froze. My hand darted to the weapon strapped to my side, hovering over the hilt. Dravyn's form came sprinting back toward us, the men around me drawing closer, looking out through the fog, searching for the creatures.

I knew that shrill, piercing noise followed by the low snarls.

My gaze snapped toward Kodrayn's as I dismounted from the horse I'd been riding, a sense of calm flooding through me. "For the love of The God, Kode, remove these Void-damned cuffs. I won't sit around unable to protect myself." I watched his eyes flare at my tone, but felt the tendrils of ice that had encircled my wrists vanish as he called his magic back to him.

Taking up fighting stances, we watched the shadows in the trees, searching for the Seefers I knew were circling. Dravyn's snarl filled the air as the first beast emerged, launching itself toward the wolvyn as he pounced, meeting the creature mid-air. Suddenly, two more sprung from the trees, a third circling behind us. But I didn't give them time before I struck. Twisting my body as I raced toward the closest one, I arched my blade and swung in the beast's direction. A fiery howl whipped through the air as I hit flesh and sliced through the Seefer's shoulder. I whirled as yellowed fangs bared in my direction, the glowing orange eyes watching me.

The sounds of metal and snarls filled the air around me as we took on the Seefers, striking and dodging bared fangs gleaming with venomous poison. My blade arched again as I ducked a blow from the Seefer before me, spinning on my heel. Two more appeared, both cornering me back toward the forest. Reaching toward my thigh, I pulled a throwing knife, twisting it in my free hand as I threw it in the air. I didn't stop to watch if it hit the target. I spun, curving my blade as the other Seefer launched through the air toward me. Dark gray, matted fur flew in my direction as the Seefer drew closer.

Raising my blade, I angled it directly toward its heart, knowing I could escape the onslaught. My blade struck true, digging directly into the beast's heart as he landed atop me, knocking me to the ground with the force of his weight.

I struggled beneath the creature, trapped as black blood leaked from the death blow I'd inflicted. I heard shrill snarls in the distance as they grew closer, but I couldn't break free. My limbs ached as I attempted to push myself free, to shimmy out from under the dead beast.

Then the weight was lifted, and I found myself staring into a blood-speckled face with watchful amber eyes.

"Thanks," I grunted as I accepted his outstretched hand and rose back up. Wiping my blood slicked hands on my leathers, I yanked my blade from the Seefer on the ground just as another Seefer struck. I cursed.

Kodrayn stood to my side, a frigid chill radiating from him as he began circling the Seefer that was advancing, ice magic flowing from him as it raced toward the beast. I stood beside him, weapon drawn. The creature snarled, its shrill sound filling the air as it looked between the two of us. A second beast began to approach, falling in behind the first.

It leapt toward me.

I raised my dagger, the only weapon I had on me, as claws and fangs sped through the air toward me. Pulling my arm back, I threw the blade, praying once again to The God that I hit my mark. The blade struck, missing where I'd aimed by a few inches as the Seefer staggered back momentarily before continuing its approach on foot.

I heard the sounds of fighting to my right, the snarls of the Seefer Kodrayn was fighting off beside me. Then there was a grunted shout from my side, "Catch."

A blade flew into my peripheral and I snatched it from the air, just in time. Ducking, I whirled closer to Kodrayn as the Seefer struck, fangs extended. I twisted to the left, swinging wide as my blade caught the side of the Seefer. *Not enough.* I wasn't fast enough.

I took a deep breath, eyes tracking the beast's movements, my vision catching glimpses of the Seefer attacking Kodrayn to my side, and I envisioned fangs and pointed ears, willing myself to shift.

I felt the flash of pain, the elongation of my canine's and the ease of hearing that came with the shift, and I struck. Moving faster than I thought possible as I targeted the Seefer, blade drawn and fangs bared as I cut its side. Speed and agility overtook me, the ease of movement flooding my limbs as I ducked an outstretched claw and arched my blade, hitting my target as the blade slit the beast's neck.

Black blood sprayed, splattering across my leathers as the creature fell to the forest floor with a thud. I looked up, meeting amber eyes as Kodrayn wiped blood from his brow, dipping his head in acknowledgement. "Glad I didn't have to save your life again."

I smirked at him. "Again? When did you even save my life to begin with?"

His eyes glanced over to a Seefer's lifeless form a few feet from me, the one I'd been trapped under. I opened my mouth to protest that the instance was not necessarily life-saving when Dravyn spoke. "What the *fuck* was that?"

And the moment was over.

The men all turned, heading toward their mounts as we looked at the clutter of mutilated bodies around us.

"That"—Everett paused as he looked toward Dravyn—"was a first."

"We need to keep moving." Kodrayn was already mounting as he continued. "I don't know how they made it this far into the Krymson Forest. But if they made it here and there are more, they already have our scent." His horse took off into a more urgent trot, the looks on the other three men more wary as they followed suit, mounting their own rides.

"I thought we were safer in the Krymson Forest?" I whispered under my breath to Zaron by my side.

"We thought so too," was his only reply as we left the carcasses behind us and pushed toward Arceyla, monitoring closely for any new threats along the way.

We didn't speak for the remainder of the journey.

I sunk deeper under the water, letting the warm silver liquid cover my skin as I scrubbed off the remnants of Seefer blood that still clung to me. We'd made it to Arceyla a little over an hour ago and the men had decided that we would search for The Wall once the sun had gone down. A spring had been spotted not too far from where we set up camp and I had wandered off in hopes of a bath. The group had been cautious following the attack, yet the tension seemed to lessen once we reached the outskirts of Arceyla. The ancient grounds provided a blanket of comfort and security since corrupt magic could not enter the grounds.

The weight of Kodrayn's magic never settled back over me, and I relished the feel of that kernel of blue power swelling within me. Whether the cuffs never returned because he felt safer on ancient grounds, or because in helping defend against the Seefers I proved my loyalties to them, I was unsure.

The warm heat of the water pulled me into its embrace as I settled my body beneath the surface, rinsing every last part of me. Once satisfied that there was no blood marring my skin, I waded out deeper into the spring, letting the dusk light settle over me as I treaded water.

The fading light in the sky glimmered off of the red leaves in the Krymson forest surrounding Arecyla, setting them ablaze. The spring was surrounded by the rocky terrain of the Barree Rise on all sides, creating a secluded nook-like feel as I tilted my head back and stared up into the sky. Clouds drifted by, purplish hues on the edges as night began to slowly overtake the sky.

I don't know how long I stayed there, floating in the silvered water, letting its warmth center me. I knew tonight would likely provide answers. Yet the questions still remained. What if the answers aren't what we hope them to be? Did we truly want to know the answers to the prophecy of old?

My fingers began to prune, signaling to me that it was time to head back to the site we had set up camp for the night. The spring, now illuminated by the moon's light, glimmered as I rose from the water, walking over to my clothing.

The brush to my left rustled as I neared my clothes, causing me to pause, my guard on high alert as I scanned the space surrounding the small spring. A tall, muscled figure with shorter black hair broke through the bushes into the clearing and I shrieked aloud.

"Go away!" I rushed for my shirt, holding it across my body as I stared in horror at Kodrayn's still approaching form. "What the *fuck* are you doing here?" I cried indignantly, my shirt stretching as I tried holding it past my stomach to cover my body.

"Watch your tongue, little venom." His tone cut through me, sending little jolts of excitement to my core as I stared at him, eyes wide.

"You can't be serious right now. My use of cuss words is what you're concerned about? I'm practically naked," I deadpanned, not sure how to put my shirt on without revealing everything to him. "At least turn around so I can put a shirt on."

Kodrayn raised his arms mockingly, but turned slowly as I hastily started to put my shirt on. The Void-damned material clinging to every part of my still-wet body. Thankfully the shirt hung low as he turned back around and started speaking. "You've been gone nearly two hours and the sun has already gone down. We need to start our search for The Wall."

I heated slightly, unaware of just how much time had passed.

As I looked Kodrayn over in the fading light, I could still pick out splatters of blood across his leathers, the speckles that painted his high cheekbones and a hint of remorse flashed through me. I'd taken too long in the spring, and none of the others had been able to bathe, allowing me my privacy instead.

He stood close to me, too close, and I inhaled the scent of him. Cedarwood and blood orange washed over me as I got caught in his gaze.

Amber eyes watched me closely, perceptively, picking up every subtle shift and fidget I made as his eyes darkened. I watched as his fangs elongated, ever so slightly, his tongue darting out to run over the tips. My eyes tracked the movement, getting caught on his lips, wondering what they would feel like over mine.

I sucked in a breath of air, my gaze drawn to his movement as his body moved closer to mine, muscles rippling in restraint. Heat built around us as I clung to his gaze, forgetting where I was, where we were. What we were here to do.

And then he was there, tilting my chin up to him, his lips brushing over mine gently at first, a flicker of a kiss; giving me the chance to pull back, to say no. But I didn't withdraw, I was lost in the smell of him, the feel of his lips pressing against mine, covering mine.

I melted into the taste of him. The feel of his lips over mine, demanding but not controlling. He deepened the kiss, his hand trailing from my chin to the back of my neck, fingers splaying in my hair as his tongue licked over my lips. I felt the slight graze of his fangs and a soft mewl slipped from my throat as he took control. He devoured me, consuming every thought in my mind while he held me against his chest in the cover of night. His tongue swirled inside, tantalizing, teasing in a rhythmic motion, and I forgot who I was as he molded his mouth to mine.

An owl cried in the distance and I remembered myself, a night chill washing over my half-dressed form. I pulled back quickly, his fangs nicking my lip in the process as I stared up at his face. Warm liquid slowly dripped down my cut lip as I stared at Kodrayn, breathing heavily in tandem with him. His eyes dipped to my lip, darkening with an otherworldly look as though he wanted a taste, wanted to consume me, before they flashed back to their gold-flecked amber hue. He took a step back, distancing us.

"Sorry," I hastily broke the silence, taking a step back. "I hadn't realized I'd taken so long to bathe." I moved to bend down to grab my pants and the dagger lying next to them, when I lost my footing. Stumbling precariously, Kodrayn's hand darted out, steadying me as my cheeks heated, this time from embarrassment.

My gaze met his as I whispered a low, "Thank you," mortified that I had tripped over practically nothing. He bent down in front of me, my heart picking up speed as he grabbed my pants and dagger, lifting them to me. I drank in the sight of him, of the vampry king on his knees as his eyes traveled slowly up my legs. Heat prickled at my skin as he continued admiring me, while extending my pants. His hands froze. Head unmoving as he focused in on one spot. I noticed his fists clench around the material of my leathers as his voice sounded, cold and dangerous. *Ruthless*.

"Who. Did that. To you . . ." His tone sent a spike of both desire and fear coursing through me. "Who *made* that scar?" His eyes pierced mine as I snatched my pants away from his hands, backing up. Cold terror plunged through me as I realized that he had spotted the scar Nik had given me.

"It's nothing," I stammered, no longer caring if I flashed him as I struggled to quickly pull my pants up. "Just drop it, okay."

He stood up, towering over me, a predatory gleam in his eyes as he repeated, "Who. Made. That. Scar?"

I gulped as my back hit rock, looking up into eyes that held mine hostage. Waiting for an answer.

"It's nothing, Kode. I injured myself as a child. Seriously, it's nothing."

He laughed, a low humorless laugh that haunted me. "Tell me, little venom, do you truly think I'm that ignorant? Now, who did that?"

I swallowed shakily, trembling under the full scrutiny of the King of Avyon. "My ex, okay?" I stared at him, annoyance blazing inside as I spoke. "He went bat-shit crazy after I dumped him, or so I thought. Turns out he was already an idiot, I just couldn't see it until it was too late and it was my life on the line— until it was his buddies pinning me down on my living room floor. Until it was him, playing around with ancient magic while masquerading as a concerned citizen during the Nordak attacks." The words slipped out, but when I went to retract them, I couldn't. They just lingered in the air between us. A truth I'd never told anyone, not even my sister. But I'd just told him.

"Ancient magic?" His tone went rigid, his eyes narrowing as I realized my mistake. *Fuck Fuck. Fuck.* I couldn't escape this one. "What did you get yourself into?"

Disbelief marred my face briefly as I stared back at him. Did he truly think I had something to do with the ancient magic?

"What did *I* get myself into? Nothing. I dumped him when I found him cheating on me. That's all." I paused, my breath erratic, my heart rate increased as I thought back to a day I kept trying to bury in the depths of my mind. "I didn't know that he and his buddies were messing around with dark magic and allied with the Nordak. I didn't know that they somehow managed to find ancient spells and learned to wield them." I glared at Kodrayn, ranting now as I fully shared what had happened to me. "And I sure as hell didn't know they'd found the Blade of Rathmen." Kodrayn's eyes grew wide with horror as I said the name. "And that they would attempt to use it on me, believing that I already wielded the power of the next artifact." Tears welled in my eyes as I spilled the secret I'd been harboring for the past week and a half to the King of Avyon. "So no, I didn't get myself into anything other than dating the wrong man for the past year. And now . . ." Tears rolled down my cheeks as I carried on. "Now I will forever have this Void-damned scar on my leg, reminding me of a man I used to trust who turned out to be my greatest enemy. A scar that has some sort of ancient magic imbued in it that causes pain to shoot through my leg and a dark purple mist to appear," I finished as I turned to the side, intent to get away from him.

Kodrayn's tanned hand, covered in tattoos, snatched out, grabbed ahold of mine as he pulled me to him. I took in the scent of blood orange and cedarwood hanging around us as he stared at me. "Mist?" His venomous tone cut through me. "When did you find out about the mist?"

I gulped in a breath of air as I squeaked out, "Four nights ago." I watched him do the math in his head, counting back the days, and a low curse fell from his mouth.

"The night at the campsite." He paused, eyes holding mine as anger rippled beneath the surface. "I felt ancient magic that night in your tent."

My voice wobbled as I spoke. "Yes." Swallowing quickly, I said, "I'm sorry, Kode, but you see, I didn't know how to tell you; how to tell anyone really. I haven't even told my sister about the scar, the one person I trust more than anyone in the realm. How was I supposed to tell someone I'd just met that my ex-boyfriend tried to carve an ancient spell into me with the Blade of Rathmen and only failed because I was shoved down the stairs of my apartment while fighting for my life and my earrings shattered. Which by the way, happened to be the next artifact. And now my leg randomly shoots pangs of pain, and a purple mist appeared once, but I don't know why because he never finished the spell," I rushed to add. "You would have thought I was crazy."

"Void-damned, Kateya," was all he said at first as he yanked me by the hand back toward the campsite, my heart sinking with each step we drew closer to the others. "We'll talk about this once we get to The Wall."

I followed him through the forest, red leaves falling in our path as we walked in a deathly silence that stretched too far.

"Did he make the jump with you?" His voice startled me and it took me a minute to realize he was asking if Nik had traveled back through time with me.

"No," I answered. "At least not that I'm aware of. But I'm worried he already did enough damage with the blade before I wound up back in the past," I admitted, shocked at the number of truths I'd openly shared with the man before me.

"His breaths are limited if he did," was all the man beside me replied as we stepped foot into our makeshift campsite.

AVYON

Chapter Seventeen

IT HAD TAKEN us nearly two hours of hiking through the rocky valley, searching various caves and nooks before we'd spotted the iridescent shimmer of water falling. Perched high on a ledge, we began climbing up the rocky surface of the Barree to reach The Wall.

As we drew closer, the surface of the mountainside grew steep—jagged rocks protruding out from the cliffside as a natural barrier to the flowing stream of water. Even in the low light of the moon, the water glistened with the colors of the rainbow, rippling across its surface as it fell gracefully.

My foot slipped as we neared the top, sending a rush of pebbles tumbling down the edge of the winding trail and Everett's hand reached out to steady me. "Easy there, Silver. Would hate for you to die before we even got the answers we're looking for."

"Ha. Ha." I stared at the man before me, thick dreads tied up into a knot atop his head, and his chocolate eyes alight with humor. "I'm not that easy to kill off, trust me." My lips curled into a smirk as we continued our ascent.

"That's because I've saved you twice. Or did you forget that so soon?" Kodrayn's voice teased from up ahead.

"I think perhaps we need to reevaluate your definition of 'saving' at some point in the near future," I joked back while we climbed.

We stopped at the base of The Wall, frozen in place as we stared in awe at the sight before us. A low roar filled the otherwise silent night as the water fell in a graceful curtain, covering the rocky surface beneath as it collided into a pool of sparkling silver-and-purple swirls. The pool itself had a magical pull to it, as though it was a source of power on its own.

"We need to go through the falls." Zaron broke our silence.

"What?" Dravyn turned toward Zaron, questioning the elder man's decision.

"Well, if the tales of this place are true, The Wall only presents answers from the other side of the curtain of water. That way, only those deemed worthy of the sought after answers will be provided with them."

"For a magical *waterfall*," I chimed in, "it sure seems like it thought of everything. Even avoiding unwanted, prying eyes from gleaning answers."

"It was placed here by The God long before our time, so yes, I'd say that it was crafted with every intention in mind," Zaron replied with a huff.

"How do we know when The Wall will provide us with answers?" Dravyn asked.

"*As the crescent moon collides with palms and colored fates, the answers shall relay a tale of foretold time.*" Kodrayn answered as he recited a line. "Our nursemaid used to tell us stories of the ancients each night. This lore in particular was my brother's favorite." His voice held a hint of sorrow as we all turned our gazes back toward the hue of colors falling from the slope.

"Well," Everett said with a shrug, "no use putting off the inevitable." He dove face first into the pool of silvered swirling waters. I found myself holding my breath, praying for the best as the water bubbled, and yet no sign of Everett appeared.

Dravyn edged closer toward the pool, looking for the vampry, and when Everett's head surfaced a few feet off, I began to breathe again. One by one, the rest of the party began to wade into the water. I felt the power within the pool swirling to meet mine as I stepped into its silvery hold. Even the silver strands of hair framing my face seemed to glow and sparkle in reaction to its power as I waded in deeper after the men.

My body thrummed, abuzz with ancient strength and magic that only heightened as I sank under the surface, swimming under the crushing water as it fell. As I broke the surface on the other side, I felt every one of the men watching me with new interest. A silver sheen, glimmering in the moon's light, reflected from my skin.

"Void-be-damned," Dravyn muttered under his breath as he saw me. A low curse echoing from Everett to his left. I began to walk toward the shelf of land, hollowed out behind the curtain of water, where the others were now shaking off silver droplets of water.

"Are we really not going to talk about the Blade of Rathmen?" Dravyn's voice drew everyone's attention and my eyes shifted between him and Kodrayn, then back again. "We have the time."

I sucked in a shaky breath, I hadn't realized Kodrayn shared the information with the others at the encampment, but it made sense with the danger the Blade posed.

"I don't know what else there is to say on the subject, and I don't really wish to relive that night once again." The feel of Nik's friend's hands holding me down on the ground as I struggled against them still made me shudder every time I saw the scar. I felt Kodrayn's eyes on me as I answered, a new look to them I hadn't seen before, a look of concern.

"That blade has been missing for centuries. It was lost during the Great War." Zaron spoke. "No one has seen or held that blade in so long that it's hardly more than a story passed on amongst warriors."

"The blade resurfaces every so often," Kodrayn's voice interrupted, closer to me than expected. "My grandfather used to tell my father stories of it—of its uncanny ability to appear on the brink of chaos and drive the realm into darkness." His eyes held mine as he spoke. "No good ever surfaces when that blade appears."

"It appeared during the Great War?" I questioned, unaware of this piece of information. "That would have been—"

"Right before the prophecy was implemented," Kodrayn finished for me.

"King Vrynor, one of the original kings placed in this realm by The God, created the blade imbued with dark magic after killing five Elders; one on each of our land's sacred grounds. It is rumored that he used their blood to forge the Blade of Rathmen in a furnace of flame from The Void."

"From The Void?" I questioned as confusion swept over me. The Void was where all those whose souls passed on from this life went. It wasn't tied to corrupt magic.

"Yes," Zaron answered. "He snared an Unseen in Arceyla, and forced the walker of both sides to hold open a rift in The Void, so that he could harness the magic in the blood of the Elders."

I stared in horrified shock at the news, at this new piece of information I'd just gained. My mind went back to that night, to the sight of the darkened blade; the wicked gleam that glinted from it as Nik had held it in the air above me, repeating lines of ancient times. Verses that hadn't been repeated since the First War —the war from the original kings of our realm. A war that dated back even further.

I shuddered violently at the thought of him bringing down the blade, at the pained feel of the tip cutting into my flesh, and my thigh throbbed at the memory. I felt a chilled breeze to my side as Kodrayn shifted closer to me, his eyes sweeping over my face, watching me. I forced a small smile toward him, even as my hand subconsciously reached down, holding pressure against the black scar on my inner thigh, the gazes of the other three watching the motion.

"What stopped its use the first time? During the First War.

Something had to have halted its use," I questioned, looking between Kodrayn and Zaron, the two who appeared to know the most on the subject. "Something had to cause it to vanish. To be lost to time once more."

"No one knows," Kodrayn answered in a low voice. "Only that it was by the grace of The God that it vanished when it did, otherwise the tide of the First War would have been drastically altered."

'You mentioned it appeared again during the Great War?" I turned toward Zaron as I questioned.

"Yes," he answered.

"But it wasn't used? It disappeared?"

"Yes. But we don't know whether it disappeared because of The God, as it did the first time, or if it was due to the prophecy," Kodrayn replied. "Regardless, it's a miracle it did, otherwise, a cloud of corrupt darkness and despair would be looming in place of the elemental magic that now flows through our ley lines—"

Ley lines. The thought burst in as I interrupted. "Do you have a map of the ley lines located throughout Avyon?"

"Yes," he answered, an inquisitive look crossing his normally masked face as he assessed me. "Although it has yet to be completed, a few of the lines are hidden to even The Elders."

"Do any lines run through Saltridge Pointe?" *It would make sense for one to run that close to both borders, and not too far from both the Krymson Forest, the Barree Rise, and Arceyla. I don't know why I hadn't considered it before.*

"Yes, a faint one, but a ley all the same," Kodrayn answered as Everett asked, "Why?"

"Back home, we discovered the Nordak targeted attacks around the ley lines of the Capital. Siphoning power from the land to bring strength to the Seefers. It's why so many of the attacks were over before they started. The people of the East Engles hardly had time to defend themselves before being ripped to shreds by the Seefers poisoned fangs." I paused to take a breath before continuing, growing certainty rising within me. "I wouldn't be surprised if the Nordak have been siphoning power from the ley lines like they are doing in my time; harvesting and wielding the power as they need."

"I'll have Sébastien check the locations of past attacks, and cross reference them with known locations of ley lines on our territories," Dravyn responded to me. "He can touch base with Ryker as well. We want to keep the entire Brotherhood informed if that's the truth. If the Nordak are siphoning power directly from the land itself, we need to learn how. To my knowledge, no one has been able to harvest power directly from the land before."

"No one should be able to harvest magic at all," I muttered softly, thinking back to how the Nordak had been harvesting magic from the citizens of Vanaiyer since The Fall. "But they've been doing it for nearly half my life, so it's possible to some extent."

"It's time," Zaron interrupted the conversation as the moon had begun to fall into place. I watched as beams of moonlight broke through cracks in the curtain of water still falling in front of us. The silver liquid turned to a dark purple hue as ripples of color burst across its surface in rhythmic blasts.

But we didn't have time to stare at the change in the water. Bubbles began to rise from the depths of the pool as Kodrayn grabbed my hand, leading me into the water. With the inkling that the power of The Wall would call to the power imbued in me from the artifact, I would be the one to touch the curtain of water.

I felt the cool liquid surround my calves, creeping up to my thighs as I waded in deeper, the King of Avyon by my side. I felt the pull of magic, calling to me; the kernel of power nestled deep within me rising to the surface at its powerful pull.

"Keep your magic down," Kodrayn said from my side as I steadied my breathing, trying to keep the flames swarming within me at bay. "You remember what to do?"

I nodded. It was simple enough, once the moon hit perfectly in the sky, I was to reach my hand directly into the curtain of falling water, focusing my thoughts on the question that we wanted an answer to. I repeated the question over in my mind. *What did the Great Four foresee happening with the artifacts? What did the Great Four foresee happening with the artifacts?*

"Just about one minute," Zaron called from my left, as he appeared to be judging the proximity of the rising moon. I felt the water swirling around us, tugging us this way and that with our proximity to the crashing water. The roar of the fall nearly drowned out his voice as Kodrayn drew his blade. "You ready?" he questioned, his eyes holding mine, peering into my soul.

"Yes," I replied. Holding his gaze, the skin surrounding the clawed scar across his eye tightened as his jaw clenched. I extended my hand, feeling the rough calluses on his own as he held my small hand in his larger one. There was a stark contrast between our skin tones and his tattoos, vibrant even in the moonlight, yet the heat coming from his touch warmed me against the cool temperature of the pool.

He lowered his blade, cutting a thin line on my palm that had me breathing in a sharp gasp of pain as he continued. "Eyes on me, little venom. Focus on your breathing," he said in a voice just for me to hear, capturing my gaze with his, even as he continued the cut. Warm liquid welled in my palm and I cupped my hand, containing the blood as we waited for Zaron's command. I swallowed nervously, praying to The God that we got the answers we needed.

"Now!" Zaron's command cut over the roar of the waterfall and Kodrayn thrust my palm forward as I stumbled slightly from the movement. Opening my fingers, I extended my palm into the flowing wall of dark purple. I felt the power rush over my body as the water pounded against my hand, splashes of water sprinkling onto my face and skin as my palm interrupted the otherwise steady flow of the fall. But, nothing happened.

I don't know what I expected from a magical waterfall to begin with. My realm went black—an eerie silence filling my head as visions of memories began to play rapidly in front of me. *My memories.*

I didn't know if the others could see what I saw as I watched snippets of my childhood flash before my eyes. I saw my family back when we lived in Verastarr. Cassandra and I climbing castle ruins on our last night there. I saw The Fall happen again; Cass going off to university. I saw myself saying goodbye to my sister at the airport; the two of us flashing back through time. I saw us back in the past, saying goodbye forever. Soon after, I relived my parent's death, faking my identity, and searching for the artifacts with Aerilyn. I saw Nik waiting for me in my apartment and me fighting for my life. I saw myself waking up back in the past, only this time in a new land.

And as every one of these memories flashed through my head, I kept asking myself. *What next? What could possibly happen next?*

My head spun as my vision suddenly came to and my palm was pushed away from the curtain of water with a powerful force that sent me flying backward.

Kodrayn shot forward, catching me as I stumbled back. All four men stared at me with various signs of remorse and empathy, and I knew that they too had seen the visions of my memories. They had witnessed snippets of my happiest and most painful moments of life. But no one spoke a word of them as we stared at The Wall, waiting, watching.

"Did you ask?" His voice sounded in my ear, a sharp demand. But it didn't matter, because at that moment, color flashed across the water and we all watched in horror as a battle scene was displayed before us.

Dravyn and Everett cursed loudly in the distance as we could do nothing but watch. Teems of gryffins swooped down in perfect formation across Saltridge Pointe, their wings beating furiously as they shrieked into the air. On the ground, wolvyn and vampry alike fought side by side, battling the hordes of Nordak warriors that stormed the shores. Blood spilled across the pebbled coastline, turning the water a crimson color as the forces collided.

A gasp fell from my lips as I spotted my sister, blood-soaked and clutching her arm, even as she wielded shadows around her, warding off the enemy.

Fuck. Fuck. Fuck. A lone gryffin flew off in the distance, cutting swiftly across the seas. A body, barely visible in its talons as it retreated from the battlefield. The water turned silver once more, a peaceful cascading flow as though it hadn't just shown us a life altering vision of the future that lay before us; whether it be hours or days from now.

"What the hell did you ask?" Kodrayn snarled as he whipped around to face me when the images ended.

"I-I-I'm not sure," I whispered, a noise barely heard over the sound of crashing water as he helped me back to the shelf.

"You're not sure?" His voice reached a new depth as his eyes bore into me. "You had one job. *One.*"

"I'm sorry." I winced apologetically as I looked at the four men in front of me. "It just . . . My memories . . ." I struggled for the words, feeling the anger and fear radiating from all the men. "They just, they began playing in front of me. One by one, so quickly. All the pivotal moments of my life. I don't remember asking anything at all. I just remember thinking *what next* as I stared at the series of memories playing before me. And—"

"And," Kodrayn cut in, answering for me, "The Wall answered that question. It told you what's next."

"I'm sorry." I stared at him. "I don't know what else you want me to say. How was I supposed to know it would read my thoughts? I thought I had to ask a question aloud for it to work."

Kodrayn glared at me, his fangs dropping down as an icy wind picked up around him, swirling angrily around his feet, snow flurries touching the night sky.

Everett stepped between us, palms raised as he looked back and forth. "Enough." His tone cut deep. "We can't change what's been done."

I watched as Everett glared at his king, fangs bared back toward him, the two of them locked in a standoff. And, ever so slightly, the icy winds calmed.

"We need to get back to Saltridge Pointe." Zaron spoke up, his weathered voice full of horror and concern. We had all seen the battle before us. We all knew exactly what we'd be rushing to return to. My heart raced as I realized that none of the others knew. Not my sister, not Sébastien, no one.

Dravyn shifted beside me, the fur of his coat bristling as he remained quiet.

"Why did he shift?" I whispered to Everett, not wanting to set Kodrayn off.

"He's communicating with the others."

I stared at Everett, confusion rising as I shifted my gaze between him and Dravyn. "Communicating?"

"Yes," Everett answered. "The wolvyn have the ability to communicate with each other across vast distances when in their shifted form." A breath of relief flooded my system as I realized at the very least that my sister would be warned about the approaching battle, that she'd have a chance of survival even if we didn't make it back in time.

But the vision still flashed across my mind; the gruesome scene of bodies littering the pebbled beach, blood reaching for the sea as gryffins teemed high above. And as we turned to begin the journey back, I knew it would not end well.

AVYON

Chapter Eighteen

WE HAD TRAVELED without stopping for the past ten hours in absolute silence. Every one of us was tense and alert as we rode through the Krymson Forest at a more cautious pace. My thighs were chafing, despite the riding leathers I wore, from the constant jostle of riding horseback. Sweat dripped slowly down my face, my hair clinging in wet strands to the nape of my neck as we pushed onward. Only when dusk began to fall did they decide that we would stop for the night.

It had been decided early this morning that it didn't matter whether we stayed on the Krymson side of the forest or not. Not after the Seefer attack on our way to Arceyla. A visit with an Unseen would have to wait.

I'd smiled with a breath of relief this morning knowing that despite everything that had occurred in the past two days, Kodrayn had not sent his magic back toward me. Instead, choosing to arm me with an extra weapon as we had saddled up this morning to return to Saltridge Pointe.

"Here's good." Dravyn spoke up, shifting back to mortal form to do so as he indicated to a thickly clustered side of the forest to our right. "The trees here in the forest provide an extra hedge of protection, and they grow sparse for the next half mile or two once we exit Krymson."

At Kodrayn's nod, Everett and Zaron turned off, my mare following suit as we headed into the densely clustered trees. Low hanging limbs scratched against my thighs as I brushed past them, wincing every so often when a particular branch snapped against me from the rider ahead.

"At this pace, we'll make it to Saltridge by sundown tomorrow," Zaron said from behind me, his voice gruff. The tension in my shoulders relieved ever so slightly as I realized that we would return sooner than I had thought, making the long hours of traveling worth it.

Everett and Dravyn stopped ahead of me, dismounting in a small clearing, barely larger than the size of a standard kitchen back home. I twisted my head, looking from side to side before looking back toward Zaron who was now dismounting as well. "Is this truly the best place to stop for the night?"

The older man glanced toward me. "Good as any, I'd wager."

"It's just . . . It seems somewhat small; hard to protect against outside enemies in such tight quarters."

"We'll be fine," Zaron gruffed as he threw a few branches he'd collected in the center of the small clearing, preparing to start a fire.

With a sigh, I followed suit, sliding off my ride as I began to unpack the satchels tied to the saddle.

The fire crackled as we sat nestled around the small flame. While I'd been tempted to unleash that kernel of power deep within me —the inferno that longed to be set free—I held it close, knowing that I should not expose my ability to harness fire in an unprotected forest, not when we still had the advantage of my powers being a secret.

Dravyn and Everett joked across the fire, Kodrayn sitting beside me as Zaron nodded off. "Are you worried?" I started, looking over at Kode's silhouette in the night sky. "About the approaching battle, I mean."

Kodrayn stared at me, eyes softening for a moment at my question before he spoke. "Every battle looks different, and is fought and won in its own unique way. We have no way of knowing the outcome until we have fought our way through it. It doesn't help to let worry and fear seep through the cracks in your armor."

I smiled slightly at his reply. "At home, Aerilyn and I wished every day that a battle would break out. That someone, anyone, would rally the citizens of Estaire and we would fight against the invading Nordak presence in our Capital." I paused, watching the flames lick at the cooled night air. "Now, with the knowledge that a battle is on the horizon, and after seeing what The Wall showed us last night, I wonder if we were crazy to ever pray that a battle would befall our home."

I stared at him, the fire casting shadows on his dark skin. "What sort of people pray to The God for a battle to fall on their land?" my voice broke as I asked the question aloud.

"The kind of people that know that things can only begin to get better once a new light can shine free," he answered. "The kind of person who can envision a better future in the distance."

We sat in silence for a few moments, the reality of what tomorrow and the days after could bring floating on the surface of our thoughts. An owl cried out in the distance as tiny embers took to the night sky, illuminating the branches of the trees towering above us. Pushing off from the ground, I turned toward Kodrayn. "I'm going to, well, you know." I awkwardly gestured away from the clearing, toward the trees and shelter of the bushes behind that as my cheeks heated.

Void-be-damned this was awkward. I cursed my small bladder and the need to relieve myself at the most inopportune times.

He nodded, turning back to focus on his friends while I crept away from them, hand on my dagger as I scanned the trees with awareness.

Branches and brambles scratched at my pants as I walked further away from them, not needing the men and their heightened sense of vampry hearing to entirely hear me relieve myself. Finding a small bush nearby, I awkwardly shimmied out of my pants and squatted down.

Bathrooms. I missed bathrooms—modern day bathrooms. The kind where the toilet flushes and there's a neat roll of toilet paper beside it. The door locks and I didn't have to have a hand on my weapon the whole time. The past may have had the upper hand with its brooding men and thriving magic, but in the present day, they would always have the bathrooms.

Another owl echoed off in the distance and my body tensed as I stayed alert while telling myself to hurry up and make it back toward the camp. I quickly tugged up my pants, wiggling as I pulled the leathers back into place and began to head back in the direction I'd come from.

Bearer of Sapphire Flame, the voice slithered into my head; old and ancient yet young and beautiful at the same time. I froze. Every hair on my neck raised as I reached for the dagger at my side. *You've strayed far from the princes of old, yet still too close. Come, flame bearer. Come.* The voice whispered in the wind yet it was in my head, all around me, surrounding me.

Who are you? I thought back into my mind, careful not to make a sound yet. Not to alert the men of the intruder. *What do you want with me?*

Come. Come and see what those gone and those foretold have shared on winds of old. Come. The voice slithered in my ear as a trail of wind circled by my feet, leaves swirling as they moved to the left, away from camp. I stood, frozen in place; every fiber of my being screaming at me to return to camp, to run and not stop until I was surrounded by the four warriors I'd been traveling with.

Yet, a small part of me told me to follow that voice; to find the answers we'd been seeking. The part of me that remembered Cass telling me that we needed more, we needed to learn more about the prophecy that bound our fate.

Come! The voice was shrill in my mind, and I hesitantly took a step forward, a step away from the camp as I followed the wind's path.

I stopped in front of a burned tree, the charred remains protruding from its trunk. The wind had stopped, and in its place, *nothing.*

Are you out of your Void-damned mind, Kateya? I berated myself as I tread deeper into the unknown forest, with only a dagger in hand. *What the absolute fuck were you thinking?*

"Welcome," a voice slithered aloud across my neck from behind me, "Bearer of Sapphire Flame, chosen of destined times, bringer of the darkened tides."

I froze, slowly turning around as I held my blade in front of me, pulling with any power I had at the kernel of flame within my soul, prepared to fight. And my soul truly fled my body. Before me, stood a cloaked figure, uncannily resembling a woman, but not. Her face was devoid of shape, of bone structure, and a grayish-green tint covered what would have been her skin. Browned, decaying teeth jutted from a few spaces in her mouth, black taloned claws protruded from where her fingernails should have been as she hunched over.

The next instant, the face of a beautiful woman with shiny black hair hanging in thick curls and luscious red lips replaced her features. Slim hands and trimmed nails in place of taloned claws.

I gasped. "W-What are you?" My hand trembled slightly at the unknown creature. The knowledge that I should cry for help once again raced through my mind, but I pushed it down.

"Smart girl," she crooned. "Wise not to call for help when you are called on by a walker of both sides."

Freezing, my eyes narrowed in on her as I stared. "You're an Unseen," I said in a whispered breath as I beheld the wickedly cruel smile that appeared on her lips.

"Deyanira," she replied proudly. "And you will heed the

message the fates of old have for you; the words that fall from the lips of those pleading mercilessly on death's doorstep. Heed and prepare, for fate has a way to ensnare."

I watched in horror as her eyes rolled back in her head and a vision began playing in mine. A vision of the king's of old, the Great Four gathered together in secret. I watched as they began chanting, a prophecy of fate being woven into their words as the artifacts lifted higher and higher in the air. I recognized the words, the beginning lines of the prophecy that had started to unravel with my sister.

The image changed, and a hulking man dressed in all black, with tattoos across his face and arms screamed at a withered form chained to the floor. *A magic assessor.* I realized as the vision continued to unfold. The assessor, bound in chains, was pleading, promising anything in exchange for his life. It shifted once again, and I found myself in a dark forest, but when I looked up, it was not the sky that hovered above the trees, but stalactites. I was in a cave and a voice began rising around me. I turned to see a glimmer of amethyst purple on tattooed arms, arms I'd seen a minute ago with the magic assessor. A gathering of men surrounded him as an amethyst artifact, a bracelet cuff, began to rise high in the air, much like the artifacts the Great Four had. He spoke, his voice loud as he repeated the words three times over, dark purple mists swirling around him as he said:

> When three of time meet one forsaken,
> Storms ablaze shall rage,
> Painting the skies with crimson stains.
>
> Unleashing The Void of fates,
> Three to four, and four to five,
> Until only strength remains.

The forest returned to view, Deyanira with it, as she stared at me. "Heed the words of times forgotten, prepare for darkness coming." And then she was gone, sucked back into the land, into The Void itself, as quickly as she'd come. I took off sprinting.

My feet moved as fast as I could force them to as I dashed through the forest, finding my way back to the camp. My lungs burned, but I pushed myself, panic spreading through my body at what I'd just seen; at what I witnessed from the past.

I burst into the camp, wide-eyed, and stared at the four men before me, gasping for breath as every last one of them leapt to their feet, weapons drawn as they scanned past me for the unseen threat.

"What happened?" Kodrayn's deep growl hit me first, his concern washing over me, and icy gusts of wind circling over my body protectively. His demand was closely followed by Everett and Dravyn's questions on where the threat was.

"I saw—" I gasped a mouthful of air. "I met—" Another gasp for air. I motioned with my finger, signaling that I needed a moment while I proceeded to unceremoniously bend forward, hands over my knees as I dry-heaved onto the ground. Everett jumped back, and I shakily stood back up, wiping my mouth on the outer edge of my shirtsleeve.

"From the beginning," Kodrayn guided as I met his piercing amber eyes and he motioned for me to sit down, sensing the threat was no longer with us.

"I heard a voice, calling in my head," I began as I recounted what had happened in the last few minutes. I told them of Deyanira and the visions she shared with me, of the tattooed man who had imbued ancient, dark magic into a cuff. Of the cave with the forests, deep under our lands. I was not interrupted once in my story as Kodrayn muttered the name of a former King of Nordak, a king alive during the Great War.

And as I finished the story and looked around the fire, I was met with four sets of troubled eyes as they stared at me in utter shock. "I think," I said, looking at each of them, before holding Kodrayn's gaze, "I think that there's a fourth artifact. Only this one, isn't prophesied to bring salvation to Vanaiyer. I think it's cursed to bring on the downfall of those tied to the artifacts prophecy, until only one person remains."

"It lines up." I could barely hear Zaron's voice over the sound of the fire. "My father told me tales of the destruction that followed the Great Four's deaths. The King of Nordak went on a rampage that was only stopped once he was believed to have sacrificed a great deal."

"If what this Unseen showed you is true," Kodrayn said, eyes hardening as he met the other warriors' gazes. "This upcoming battle is only the beginning of our problems. And until we find both of the remaining artifacts, this war will never cease."

I swallowed, my breath caught in my chest as I looked around at the grave, somber faces of the men before me. Of men hardening themselves for a warpath that could only bring destruction and death. And I knew that tomorrow couldn't come soon enough. None of us would be getting any sleep.

VERASTARR

Chapter Nineteen

IT WAS early evening when we arrived back in Verastarr. The campgrounds bustled with warriors preparing for a greater battle than first expected. We rushed straight to the war tent when we arrived, those who had stayed behind joining us to hear of all we had discovered on our journey to Arceyla, and to plan our next steps in a greater war foretold long before any of us had been born.

"I'll go," Emalyee interrupted into the night air as we sat around the mapped-filled table in Sébastien's war tent. We had been trapped inside for the past four hours since our arrival back to the camp on the Verastarr side of Saltridge Pointe, discussing the possibilities that arose from a curse being placed over the ancient prophecy. The ultimate decision was that we needed someone to go searching for the fourth artifact. While we were uncertain what time it would appear in, it would stand to reason that no matter what time it should appear, it existed nonetheless.

"No." Dravyn's voice was cold as he stared at Emalyee from across the space.

"Why not, Dravyn?" she answered sweetly—almost too sweetly. "I'm the best option we have and you know it." She glanced around the space before meeting his eyes as she continued. "None of you can go; you'd be too recognizable no matter what land you traveled through. They certainly can't go"—she gestured to me and Cass—"and I have just enough power to be able to shift and remain undetected, but not enough power that those who cross my path will be suspicious of me."

"I won't allow it," Dravyn argued as his king cut in.

"She's right." Sébastien held Dravyn's eye as he spoke. "Her wolvyn abilities allow her to check in with us throughout her travels, but they aren't detected as easily. And she is the only one of us that can go with minimal risk."

"What about Everett or Torryn? One of Ryker's men?" He gestured to three men I'd yet to meet in the back corner of the tent. Ryker it seemed had also received a missive of aid from Sébastien and had arrived two days prior to our arrival back at the Pointe.

I looked around, doing the math once more before opening my mouth. "What if," I started, then froze as twelve sets of eyes swiveled on me. I swallowed thickly, calming my breath before continuing. "What if Emalyee goes." I looked toward her, gratitude swimming in her eyes at my suggestion. "But one of the twins and one of Ryker's men accompany her. That way—"

Dravyn interrupted with a protest, but this time Kodrayn spoke up, a chilled breeze sweeping through the tent. "Let her finish."

I flashed a brief smile of thanks at his gesture as I carried on, looking at Sébastien. "When Cass and I first arrived in the past, you told us that it was an unsafe time for anyone, especially as a woman. That stands to reason, that times are even more unstable now, and Emalyee traveling on her own may raise suspicions on its own." I knew I was right as I noted a few men nod briefly.

"Emalyee has the ability to shift. With the resources we currently have, it makes sense to bring one of the twins. They won't be as recognizable as you four"—I pointed to the Brotherhood—"but they are strong warriors and are vamprys. One of you three"—I spun toward Rykers men beside him—"assuming you are all fae, would provide additional abilities for the journey, while still allowing them to travel mostly undetected."

Every man in the tent stared at me with an assessing gaze, and as my eyes flickered over to my sister I noted the hint of pride welling in them.

"It's settled then." Kodrayn's eyes flicked between his blood brothers before glancing at Emalyee. "You'll leave tomorrow."

I lay curled up in Cassandra's tent, having promptly kicked the King of Verastarr out after telling him mate or no mate, I needed time with my sister. I couldn't quite tell if he'd adjusted to having his mate's younger sister around yet, but the crinkle of amusement around his eyes told me he was warming up to the idea.

"I missed this." I sighed as I moved, snuggling into my blanket more.

"You missed *this*? Truly?" She gestured to our surroundings with a laugh.

"Obviously, I did not mean I missed sleeping on the floor with a battle coming our way." I groaned as I stared at Cass. "I missed *us* though. Remember when we were younger? How every night we would sneak off into each other's rooms when Mum and Father had gone to bed."

Cass laughed from beside me. "And we would pretend we didn't know how we ended up there the next morning." She shifted on her side pinning me with one of her patented older sister looks, "So, you and Eryx, huh?"

"We'll see." I looked at my sister. "What if we can't pick up where we left off? A lot has changed, you know. *I've* changed." My mind flashed briefly back to the night at Arceyla, to Kodrayn's lips on mine. Something we had yet to talk about since.

"Well, there's plenty of other brooding men surrounding you lately." Her eyebrows wriggled as she looked at me. "Kode,

Everett, Torryn, Ryker . . . just saying, you've got your choice of men."

I scoffed. "I think I've had enough alpha males to last me a lifetime." I forced humor into the statement, but my mind snapped back to Nik during the last few months of our relationship.

"You never did tell me," Cass said softly from beside me. "What happened with Nik, I mean."

I thought about my confession to Kode, the only person in the realm who knew what truly happened to me with Nik, and as much as I loved my sister, I wasn't ready to share that part of me with her yet.

"Maybe another day?" I stared at my sister as sleep began to lull me in.

"Whenever you're ready, sis."

I wiped my brow with the side of my shirt, arms on fire as I nimbly dodged yet another strike from Kodrayn, only to find Everett swooping in from the other direction. His blade halted a few inches from my chest as I sucked in a breath.

"Come on, Silver. You've got to do better than that."

"Again," was all I muttered as I raised my sword, staring at Kode's eyes. My arms shook as I tracked his movements to my left even as Everett pounced from the other side of me. I ducked, dodged, and struck as I circled the ring with the two. I felt Kodrayn shift to my right, whirling on my heel as he used his unnatural vampry speed to block my strike and instantly combat it with a counterstrike.

I whirled on my heel, arching my blade as I parried, our swords clashing between us, our faces inches from each other's, separated only by our blades. I strained against his force, holding my weapon firm, our eyes locked on each other. His gaze flickered briefly down to my lips, and his eyes darkened, fangs elongating as they focused on me and my stomach fluttered.

"You plan to keep staring at my lips? Or should we resume training?" I teased, my lip curling up.

"I don't plan to keep staring, little venom . . . I plan to ravish them again, and soon." Kodrayn's low reply washed over me and my breath caught in my throat as I stared at the vampry before me.

A blur of motion caught my peripheral vision and I pulled back, Everett's dagger flew past me and I turned to my other opponent. The moment gone as quickly as it had come. After an offensive strike to Everett's side, I whirled on my heel to face Kodrayn again and my eyes caught on Eryx across the training rings. Jade green orbs held mine as they took me out of the ring, and I lost myself in him. I felt a blade touching my throat and those jade orbs turned a stormy, dark green.

"I'd suggest you keep your eyes on the enemies in a fight, little venom." Kodrayn's low voice growled into my ear as he pressed the blade tighter into my neck, a warning before he relented, allowing me to breathe.

We hadn't practiced shifting since we'd first arrived at Saltridge Pointe, with too many eyes around the sparring rings that may catch drift of my powers. But my limbs still ached as I walked out of the ring, sweat dripping down my flushed skin as I found Eryx waiting for me outside of the makeshift ring we'd been sparring in.

Reaching up on my toes, I leaned in, brushing my lips gently against his, feeling the scent of lemon and bergamot enveloping me. "Want to go?" Eryx questioned, eyes roaming over me as I pulled back.

"Go where?" I questioned, staring up at the man in front of me rather than the two behind my back.

"Someplace alone." His eyes lit up suggestively and my face burned at his tone, heat rising in my core at the thought, but a frown appeared on my lips as I looked at him apologetically.

"I can't right now. I'm sorry."

"Why?" Eryx's tone shifted just slightly, a hint of annoyance rising.

"I have . . ." My gaze drifted over his shoulder to where Kodrayn and Everett waited in the distance. I couldn't explain it to him; that even though I couldn't practice in the ring with my powers or magic, we'd still been practicing my shift in Kodrayn's quarters, mastering the speed at which I shifted between forms.

Given that I had the unique ability to shift between multiple powers, it was taking more time to master each one. It also meant that I had to learn how to call on all the vampry features when I wanted to switch, rather than just elongating my fangs as most were able to do. Not to mention, attempting to somewhat master my elemental magic was trying in and of itself.

"You're joking, right? What reason could you possibly have to spend more time with *them* now that you're in Verastarr?"

"It's complicated." I sighed in frustration, wishing I could just tell him everything. But I couldn't yet, not until this new threat with the artifact was figured out. I couldn't, *right?*

"What aren't you telling me?" Eryx's voice dropped low and cold as he held my gaze.

"Just drop it, please," I whispered softly as I turned to walk away. His arm snapped forward, his fingers tightening around my wrist as he yanked me back toward him.

"Drop it? You go off for a few days with those guys. You constantly train exclusively with them. You're always sneaking off into their tents. And you want me to just *drop it?*"

"Yes, Eryx. That's precisely what I want you to do."

His hold tightened as I struggled against his grasp.

"Let her go." An icy voice sounded from behind me.

"Now," a second one echoed, and I knew that Kodrayn and Everett had heard every word of our conversation with their vampry hearing.

"And look who shows up," Eryx mocked as he looked between

the two men and me. "She's mine. So back *the fuck* off." He snarled as he stared them down.

I felt Kodrayn's power before he unleashed it, but I moved faster. With a sharp twist of my wrist that sent a twinge of pain up my arm, I spun, aiming a kick toward Eryx to let go of me without injuring him crucially and turned away from all three of the men. "I can handle myself, thank you very much," I said to no one and all of them as I walked away, still feeling the impression of Eryx's hand on my wrist, long after it was gone.

VERASTARR

Chapter Twenty

I ROLLED TO MY SIDE, staring at my sister across the space from me as the evening light began to creep in. "It just wasn't . . ." I paused, struggling to find the words to describe what weighed on me. "It wasn't right, I guess. You know those nights, when you know you're making a mistake. But you stick with the decision anyway, even though the outcome isn't going to be what you want." I stared over at Cass.

"Yeah. That's usually when it's best to just walk the other way."

"That's what it was like with Nik. But he was . . ." I struggled, tears welling up as I thought back to when I first got back together with him.

"He was the only piece you still had from your life before we traveled through time."

I nodded as I whispered, "What if it's like that with every other guy?"

"Kat," my sister breathed, and as much as I loved my sister, I regretted bringing the topic up at that moment. I hadn't meant to in the first place, but somehow she always drew these things out of me.

"Never mind. Forget it, okay?"

"Okay, okay . . ." Cass drawled as she lounged on the floor of her and Sébastien's tent. "Remember that trip we took four years ago in the spring?"

"The one to the Innerlands?" I questioned, propping up on my elbow as I rolled to look at my sister.

"Yes! That one. And how you were *so* scared to tell Mum that you left your entire suitcase back at home."

"Oh gosh," I groaned. "Maybe it's best we just leave some things in the future," I protested as she continued.

"No, but seriously. Remember how you were so worried about telling Mum? You went two whole days wearing the *same* shirt and thought she wouldn't notice."

"And?" I stared at my sister, wondering where she was going with this story.

"*And* the whole time, I told you that you just needed to actually talk to Mum, and that if you did, things would be okay and she would get you new clothes for the trip."

Mhmmm. I mumbled as she continued, "Well . . . have you ever considered that maybe that's what you need to do with Eryx?"

I glared at my sister, eyes narrowing at her insinuation. "Eryx doesn't need to know everything."

"Would it hurt if you just told him some things? Think about it, Kat, you were gone for one year, but for us it was two. Two long years. He deserves some bits of your past if you want a future with him."

"Well he's certainly not going to get any bits if he keeps getting all defensive just because I'm training with Kodrayn and Everett."

"*But,*" my sister sing-songed as she held my inferno of a gaze, "it would save us all the Void-damned trouble of having to tiptoe around the two of you quarreling if you just opened up to him about what happened in your past."

"We're not *quarreling,*" I quipped.

"Really?" she responded, her eyes crinkling in amusement.

"Then I guess you didn't just storm off the training ring after practice."

"I didn't storm off," I muttered. "I angrily left two bickering boys to hang out with my lovely sister." I smiled sweetly in her direction.

"Speaking of bickering boys," Cass continued. "What about Kode?"

"What about him?"

"Well . . ." she paused, hesitating.

"Just say whatever it is, Cass." I nudged my sister with my toe. "You know you will anyway."

"It's just, you two have been spending a lot of time together. Are you sure there's not something going on there?"

"You know why we've been spending time together, Cass," I answered quickly, my cheeks heating at her insinuation.

"Yes, yes. You've been *training.*" She mocked indignantly. "I'm just saying Kat. There are plenty of other warriors who could train you with your powers. Just seems like there could be something more."

I ducked my head at her comment because Void-damned, she was right to an extent. I thought back to when he kissed me, the feel of his lips on mine, claiming me. To the way it felt when we sparred, and how he brought out the best in me in the training pit. To the fact that he was the only one I'd shared the whole truth with since arriving back in the past.

"There's more," Cass half-shouted, "isn't there?"

"There is *not* more," I answered quickly, before muttering the next part half under my breath, hoping she didn't hear. "We kissed, but it was just that. A kiss."

"*And?*" Cass nearly shrieked, her shadow magic flaring slightly as we were engulfed in darkness for a split second. "How was it?"

"Calm down. You'll put the whole camp on alert." I laughed as I stared at my sister.

"Well," she prompted.

"It was . . ." I paused because Void-damned, it had been good.

The feel of his lips brushing against mine, consuming every dark part of me.

"That good, huh?" Cass finished for me after my prolonged silence.

"It doesn't matter," I answered. "I'm with Eryx."

"Are you?" she questioned. "Is it official?"

I stared at my sister, hating my decision to come here after training for the second time today. "No, okay. It's not official. But we're meant to be together."

"Two years ago, yes," she replied softly. "But what about now? Is he what's best for you?"

I opened my mouth, but Cass held up her hand, stopping me. "I don't have anything against him, Kat. And if he's who you choose, I will support you in that decision. All I'm saying is, consider all your options. You're a different person now than you were two years ago. That's all, sis."

"Okay," I replied as I started to stand. "I'll think about it, Cass."

I walked slowly through the camp, sidestepping every so often to avoid stepping on wolvyn tails as I made my way to the center. The sun had faded, a soft blue now painting the sky as a cool salty breeze coated my skin. I hated that Cass was right. I needed to talk to Eryx, to tell him about everything I had gone through since I'd been sent back to the present. What the past year of my life had been like and all I'd endured to make it back to this time, this place, with him and Cass.

Yet, that small part of me, buried deep down in my soul, where I didn't like to look too long, told me not to. Begged me not to bare my soul to yet another person, so soon after the last time. I took a deep, shaky breath and pushed onwards until the scent of lemon and bergamot enveloped me and I was standing close to Eryx's towering frame.

"Hey," my voice nearly squeaked from nerves and I instantly clamped a hand over my lips, embarrassment rolling off me in waves. *For fucks sake, Kat. Get it together. He's just a guy.* "Can we talk?"

Eryx eyed me warily, most likely concerned where I was going with this.

Who says "Can we talk?" Come on Kat. You're not trying to end it with him . . .

"Don't worry," the words rushed from my mouth. "It's not bad. I just, well, can we just, well . . ."

"Talk?" he finished for me, dimples appearing as his grin widened. "Let's go," he said, grabbing my hand to lead me away from the fire, toward his tent.

I didn't speak until we'd entered his tent, my fingers fidgeting as I anxiously stared at the man in front of me. *By The God, he was gorgeous.* I looked into his dark green eyes for a little while longer, losing myself as I let thoughts run rampant in the back of my mind, dreaming of his lips on mine, the scorching heat that rose every time we collided.

"Well," he looked at me with a new sense of seriousness, "you wanted to talk?"

"Right," I began, "I thought, well. I figured I owed you an explanation. For the past year, or two years technically for you, but the past year for me . . ." I continued on, recounting what had occurred back home in the East Engles. I told him about the Seefer attacks and the Archives. About Nik and the dark magic. But I didn't tell him about the earrings fully shattering; about the powers I'd gained. Not yet. I'd wait for that one, at least for a little bit longer. Kodrayn's comment about not sharing about my powers unless absolutely necessary nagged at me making me second guess whether I should share with him or not.

But what harm would sharing with him do?

Maybe in the morning, I reasoned, *once he's processed this first.*

"So." I looked at Eryx as I finished my story. "I owe Kodrayn and Everett for taking me in. For bringing me back to my sister safely."

Deep green eyes held mine as I finished speaking, "I don't have to like it." He spoke for the first time since I'd started my story. "And I don't appreciate how protective they are of you. You'd think you were bloodsucking vampry filth as well with how much they hover."

"Eryx," I protested.

"The ancient magic, it's truly inside you?" He switched gears as his face grew blank, unreadable.

"Yes, at least I think so."

"And you're positive it's dark magic?"

"I mean," I hesitated briefly, "as positive as I can be. The words Nik chanted were ones I've never heard before, but they seem familiar to an ancient text I once read." I struggled, grasping at the empty space in my head as I tried to remember where I'd read them but couldn't. "And the purple mists, I've only ever seen those around the Nordak and their darker magic."

"What did he say as he used the Blade of Rathmen?"

"I-I don't know. I can only remember a few words. *Dagthan cer visan. Fayra ite vitos.*"

I watched Eryx as I said them, noting the hardly discernible flicker that raced across his eyes, almost as though he recognized the words I had said. "Do you know what they mean?" I asked.

"No, and it's probably best we don't," Eryx bit into the night air. "What symbol did he carve?"

"Symbol?" I questioned, knowing full well I hadn't mentioned a symbol.

"Yes." His tone grew a bit stronger as he spoke. "Most dark magics utilize symbols or shapes to begin the process of wielding the power. What was he carving to imbue his power?"

"I . . ." I paused, because I actually didn't know. "I just assumed he was writing his name. I read somewhere in the

Archives that magic wielders could control those who they engraved their name on with the blade."

Eryx went silent, his eyes cautiously studying me, with a slight flickered gaze toward my inner thigh, then back to meet me. His lips tightened, the dimples usually visible disappearing as his face grew taunt. "I'm sorry, I wish I knew more."

A smile slowly grew across his lips, "Don't worry about it, Kat. Our knowledge of the ancient magics used in the First War is minimal at best, and most of it was lost to time. How could you know more? How could any of us know more?"

"I just wish I did," I confessed. "I wish I at least knew what Nik was trying to do; what he thought he'd accomplish through using the ancient magics."

Eryx's hand slid up my thigh slowly. "Whatever he was doing, he failed and in doing so, sent you here, to the past. To me." His grin appeared nearly wicked with delight as his other hand cupped my neck, angling it back. Next thing I knew, his lips captured mine in a claiming kiss. I inhaled his scent of lemon and bergamot, my fingers tracing up his back as he pulled me closer to him. I leaned into him more fully, getting lost in his kiss, in the repetitive swirl of his tongue over mine, the sharp pangs as he nibbled on my lower lip, playing with it between his teeth.

His hand twisted its way through my silver brown hair, and with a yank, he pulled my head back. A low moan broke free of my lips as he trailed kisses lower down my neck, heat rising from my core as his hand held my head firm.

I whimpered as his tongue licked along my collarbone, his other hand sliding up my outer thigh, tracing slow circles as it moved higher. I pushed myself closer still, feeling every muscled line of his firm body as he pressed harder against me, consuming me. My mind emptied of thoughts, my body ablaze as every thought, every need was focused on him. *Eryx.* The man I'd dreamt of in flickers of time over the past year.

And he was here, his fingers now drifting up my torso, meeting the curves of my breast and another low moan fell from my lips, his name with it as I soaked in his touches, his kisses, every mark he left across my skin. Because I'd made it back to him, and this . . . this was real.

VERASTARR

Chapter Twenty-One

"MORNING." I smiled as I rolled over, staring up at Eryx's broad shoulders, admiring the inkings across his skin. He was already up and dressing for the day while I snuggled myself deeper into the blanket for just a moment longer, soaking in the morning air.

"Morning," his reply came as jade-hued eyes held mine from across the tent.

"You sleep okay?"

"Same as every night," was his short reply, his eyes watching mine closely, and I knew his thoughts were already churning, any hope of a slow morning gone.

With a sigh, I opened my mouth again. "You want to talk again, don't you?"

"It just doesn't make sense, Kat." Narrowed green orbs held mine as he continued, "If those earrings were truly the second artifact. Why aren't you out searching for them? Why hasn't Kodrayn or Sébastien sent out a patrol of men to scour the lands for where it landed? Unless . . ." His voice dropped off and he looked at me in a different light.

I held my breath, praying to The God that he both did and didn't guess the truth. If he guessed it, I technically wouldn't have told anyone, which meant that I listened to Kode's advice, but would still be able to talk to Eryx about it.

"You already have it, don't you?" His accusation hit me, my heart hurting at his tone, even as a bit of joy grew from his smile.

With a slow nod, I responded. "I do, I'm sorry Eryx. I was told not to tell anyone else, even you, and I wanted to tell you, I really did. But it's all just so new, and I figured there was no harm in waiting. You understand, don't you?

"Well, I know now," he said, the sharp tone still lingering on the morning air. "So maybe you could share the rest now? You realize this changes everything. What powers and elemental magic did you receive? Are they the same as your sister's?"

"We haven't uncovered the full extent of my powers." I matched his gaze, keeping my tone calm. "That's why I've been training with Kodrayn and Everett. They've been helping me shift, although I'm still not too good at it." A small chuckle fell from my lips.

"You shift into a wolvyn like Cass?"

"No . . . Well, I mean, I think I should be able to. But I arrived in Avyon, so the first shift I've learned to do is to shift to a vampry."

His head nodded, almost calculatingly, as he processed the information I was sharing. "And elemental magic?"

I lifted my hand slightly toward him, a small flicker of sapphire flame sprouting as it hovered above my palm, dancing in the air. "Fire."

"Fire hasn't been seen in decades." His eyes widened at the realization. "And who all knows this?"

"Cass, Sébastien, Kodrayn and a few of their closest men," I responded. "The more people that know—"

"The more danger you're in," Eryx finished for me, his face an unreadable mask as he regarded me with a new level of intrigue. "Why don't they have more men protecting you?"

"I can fight, you know." I shot him a pointed look. "Plus, too many men in the middle of a war camp brings extra attention—

unwanted attention. It's best for me to slip by undetected, for now. There are too many spies in the vicinity."

"That," Eryx said, "there most certainly are."

A horn sounded low but clear, three times, and shouts arose from the camp. My head swiveled in the direction as I asked, "What does that mean?"

"That," Eryx responded as he stood and began moving, "means the enemy is approaching. We will go to battle soon. *Very soon.*"

I scrambled to my feet, my heart pounding. *War.* We were going to *war.* "I need to find Cassandra." I hurriedly dressed, as I began to walk toward the entrance to his tent.

"Kat," Eryx's voice stopped me mid-step as I turned back to look at him. "I want you by my side today. I can't afford to have something happen to you."

I smiled as I walked out the door to find my sister.

My nerves were calm as I walked out of the war tent packed with men from all three lands, following my sister and her mate, shadows and mist already circling their feet. I ran through my weapons subconsciously, touching each one strapped to me as I had every night back home before hunting Seefers. A shout from ahead made me lose count, and I began to mentally check the list again, my fingers once again tapping each blade attached to my body.

"I don't think they're going anywhere just yet, Silver." Everett's voice sounded to my left just as I touched the last blade, confident I was as prepared as I could be.

"Ha. Ha."

I turned to stare at him, noticing the gathering formations of soldiers behind him as he asked, "You ready?"

"Ready as I'll ever be I guess. Not going to say that this is what

I had in mind while I searched for the artifact to bring me back to this time."

His gaze flicked over to my sister and her mate, shadows and mist circling the ground below them. "It's all she's known since you left. All we've all known in our lands for the past two years. She's handled it like a Void-damned goddess."

"I'd expect nothing less from my older sister." I smiled at her as she ran through her weapon check the same way I did—the way our father had taught us to. A pang of remorse shot through me at the thought of him; at what fate had dealt to my parents. This prophecy, the larger war that was brewing, needed to end.

My name was called, and I turned toward Cassandra. "See you on the other side," was all I said before I walked over toward where my sister stood with Sébastien, Dravyn, Kodrayn, and Eryx.

"Kateya." Sébastien's voice interrupted the group and I turned to meet his icy blue gaze as the King of Verastarr spoke to me. "I want you with Dravyn. Don't leave his side today, understand?"

My eyes flicked over to Kodrayn, iced flurries swirled across his skin as he nodded in approval of the statement.

"Okay." I nodded and smiled at Dravyn.

Eryx's voice cut through as he looked between Dravyn, Sébastien, and Kodrayn. "I'd like to remain with Kateya as well."

I caught Dravyn's apologetic look before Sébastien even spoke up. "You know your place, Eryx. The third battalion wing has been doing well under your control. Kateya will remain with Dravyn."

"My forces will come in from the west," Kodrayn said as he looked between his blood brothers. "Ryker, you bring yours in from the north. As they arrive we'll funnel them into the beaches here." Nods went around as they began clapping each other on the backs, saying their goodbyes.

I turned to my sister. "I know. I know we can't fight in the same area on the field." We'd spent too long discussing it this morning—the benefits—but more importantly the risks of keeping the two of us together. With the amount of power we had combined, we'd be a near unstoppable force, but also the sole target. "But I wish we could, sis."

"Me too, Kat. Me too." Cassandra wrapped her arms around me in a hug. "Don't you dare do anything stupid, I only just got you back."

"Me?" I laughed as I looked at my sister, silver rimming her eyes.

"I'm serious, Kat. I need you. Be safe out there and trust no one."

"I will, sis. Don't worry about me. I'll see you on the other side of this. We'll both be all right." I forced a smile as we prepared to brave battle.

The first of the drums began beating, a steady, daunting sound as they slowly grew closer and the ships broke the fog, coming into view. I fought the urge to turn right back around and run for my life. I couldn't count the number of ships with the fog lurking in the distance. Dark purple bannered flags flew in the wind, drawing my gaze up, up, up. That's when I spotted them. Hordes of gryffins flew in tight ranks above the ships, their golden wings beating against the wind as they approached.

Shouts and commands sounded from around me. I felt Dravyn tugging at my armor and focused in on him.

"You ready, Kat?" His voice sounded far off, but I nodded anyway as I followed him into formation, preparing for the first of the Nordak to break ground.

Kodrayn walked up to my other side, his familiar scent washing over me as he pulled me near him. "Whatever happens." The seriousness of his tone shook me. "Don't find yourself alone. If you lose sight of Dravyn in the chaos of the battle . . ." Kodrayn's voice was commanding and I tuned in like a soldier, listening to every word as if it would be the difference between life and death—and at this moment, it could very well be. "Find me. No one else, you understand? You find *me*."

I nodded as a shout rose from the front lines. Kodrayn clasped Dravyn on the back, the words "Embers and Ash," falling from his lips followed by Dravyn's reply, "Even The Void won't hold," rang in my ears as Kodrayn walked away to join his formation, and I knew. The fight had begun.

My limbs had grown heavy. Blood soaked the ground everywhere I turned; my own armor splattered in remains of gore and guts as I turned toward the next enemy, raising my long sword. I could feel my arms wobble slightly, yet I steeled them to the oncoming blow, blocking the strike before whirling on the attacker and striking back. Duck, parry, block, strike. The circle went round, each strike draining me of my remaining strength. I felt his blade nick an exposed piece of my flesh where my armor came together and cried out in pain, even as I pushed through.

Spinning on the Nordak man in front of me, I bared my teeth, careful not to let my fangs poke through, as I was not ready for a shifter fight. I twisted my blade, arching high before undercutting at the last second. I felt the blade collide with flesh and bone, as well as the slight resistance I hit before my blade cut clean through and I turned, looking away from the life I'd just taken.

I sucked in a gasp of breath, my limbs screaming in agony and realized, I couldn't see Dravyn. I couldn't see any of the Brotherhood, actually. I whirled, looking in vain for any glimpse of red or black flags, or emblems. *Where were they? Where were they?*

A guttural shout sounded from behind me, and I twisted to see Kodrayn in the distance. Crimson blood soaked his dark blade, his eyes flickered up as they met mine from across the clearing, and I sucked in a breath. And then he was shouting, and I turned just in time to narrowly avoid being shredded into pieces. I raised my sword to fight as the Nordak before me shifted, golden feathers and fur appearing before me as he pushed off from the ground, darting toward me.

I drew a dagger from my side, pulling my arm back to launch the blade toward the beast when it fell from the sky, a black tipped feather with ice magic surrounding it protruding from its neck. *And that made three times he'd saved me.* I pushed forward, not giving it time to fight before I slit the beast's neck, blood pooling as it died before me.

My gaze cut up as I assessed my situation. I saw shadows and mist circling on the rocky shoreline of the beach and knew my sister must be up closer to the frontlines of the beach. A shriek from above had my gaze turning upward as I watched in horror as a fae warrior battled mid-air against a gryffin. My heart stopped; black taloned claws raked down the fae warriors chest, a guttural scream falling from his lips as he plummeted toward an untimely death. His body landed in a heap on a rock, and I knew he hadn't survived the fall.

Kodrayn was closest to me, and per his orders, I knew I needed to remain close to him. I couldn't be alone on the battlefield.

I began weaving my way through the fighting, my arms growing heavier with each blow as I struggled to make my way toward where I'd last seen the Vampry King fighting alongside his men.

Arching my blade in front of me, I swung a final blow, the side of my blade slicing skin and pushed on, but I couldn't spot Kodrayn anymore. I spun in a circle, nearly positive I'd made it to the location I'd last seen him in. But nothing.

I kept my blade drawn, as I paused momentarily for a breath of air when a hand grabbed me from behind. Twisting, I raised my blade higher, preparing to strike when a voice called, "Kat!"

My hand faltered as I faced my enemy, only to realize that I'd stumbled upon Eryx.

"Where's Dravyn?" His voice cut over the cries and clashing

of iron surrounding us. "How'd you end up this far south on the field?"

"I don't know. I lost Dravyn some time ago. I was trying to find Kodrayn but I can't seem to see him anymore." I looked around, realizing now with more clarity that he was right. I'd made it further toward the south end of the battleground. My sister, who had felt closer to me earlier, was now a black cloud in the far distance.

"Where are all your men?" I questioned as I glanced around our immediate vicinity, noticing that there was an increasing number of gryffins approaching and we were most certainly outnumbered. "We need to do something!" The urgency rose in my voice.

"The fighting was too thick, over half my battalion was taken out by a horde of gryffin flying overhead!" Eryx shouted. The few men he had remaining were mid-fight against Nordak foot soldiers.

"Kind of like that one?" My voice faltered, my hand shaking as I pointed to the horde of gryffin flying closer toward us; dark golden wings beating in the air, a noise I knew I'd never forget, grew closer and closer.

I turned toward Eryx, genuine fear rising in me, replacing the battle calm I'd held on to throughout the day. "What do we do?"

"We're too far out of reach from the others. We're going to have to take them on our own."

How did I lose Dravyn? How the hell had I ended up here? In this situation? I took a steady breath, knowing that panicking would not save my life.

"Keep your back against mine, that way we are always guarded from one side." I turned from Eryx, feeling him press his back closer toward mine. I raised my blade above my head, holding my arms steady as I prepared for the diving squad of gryffins.

My lips mumbled a prayer to The God as I wondered, for the first time since seeing Eryx again, why I couldn't have fallen for a man with powers or elemental magic. Something that could help us, since my magic was not strong enough to wield as a weapon and would only give me away.

The gryffins grew closer, fanning out on their descent. My eyes tracked every movement, watching and waiting to see where to strike first. Confusion spread as I watched some of the gryffins land further away from us, forming a circle around us.

"What the fuck?" I shouted over the noise of the ongoing battle surrounding us. "What are they doing?" Eryx didn't answer as a gryffin swooped lower, flying over us, but not attacking. They were toying with us. Taunting us. Waiting to strike.

My arms shook, the weapon in my hands growing heavy as I began to grow antsy. Something wasn't right. Something was off.

"Brace yourself," Eryx said from behind me as a gryffin swooped in once again, this time getting so close that I could feel the air from the wing beat hit my face. And yet, it flew upward again, not striking.

"Something's wrong," I muttered toward Eryx who still stood by my back. "We need to get out of here. Something feels off."

"Everything's going exactly as planned," Eryx sneered in a cold tone I'd never heard before that had my heart stopping in my chest. Then a flash of pain rammed into the back of my skull, and my vision went black.

NORDAK

Chapter Twenty-Two

EVERYTHING HURT. That was the first thought that entered my mind as my eyes fluttered, followed closely by the realization that I couldn't move. And with that, my eyes snapped open and sunlight blinded me. I tried to look around, only to realize that I was thousands of feet above the ground.

A scream ripped from my throat—or, it tried to—only my mouth was gagged, leaving the muffled cry for help with nowhere to go. I struggled to break free, twisting and thrashing my body around, when a loud cry from overhead froze me in place, causing me to notice the black talons that wrapped around my body.

Panic clouded my pain-addled brain as I realized I was in the *talons* of a gryffin and began to thrash even more, needing to break free. The vise-like grip tightened, my lungs screeching for air as I realized that even *if* I broke free, the only freedom I would find would be whatever came after death. The ground rapidly moving thousands of feet below me confirmed my realization.

I stared at the realm as it passed by, helpless and trapped as my captor flew through the clouds. The continued pressure of the talons digging into my injuries from the battle, mixed with the throbbing wound on the back of my head, built until the pain reached a breaking point, and I welcomed the black tunnel that overtook my vision.

When I next came to, I didn't know precisely *where* I'd been taken. But I knew *where* I was: a dungeon. Metal bars surrounded me on three sides, the only wall of stone being the outer wall of the cell. As my eyes struggled to open, they began to adjust to the dimly lit space that reeked of death and decay. I struggled to move, the sound of chains following my movements as I attempted to push myself up into a seated position. I tried to recall how I'd ended up here. What exact events had resulted in this outcome. However, every time I thought back to the battle, it's like that last little bit of information was just out of reach. As though I should know what happened, and yet, I didn't.

Pressing my back against the brick wall, I used the chilled stone to push my way upright, wincing at the loud metal scraping against the floor as I did so. A dampness began to soak my clothing as I settled into a seated position, my head throbbing as I leaned it against the stone and looked around fully.

The space was hardly lit. My eyes, now fully adjusted to the lighting, allowed me to see the row of metal caged cells across the hallway from me. I noticed limp frames in various positions, chained in similar manners to me. Looking to my left, I found the cell occupied, a figure with long hair covering her face, curled in the corner.

"Hello," I whispered, my voice hoarse as I tried to be quiet, but the figure didn't stir. "Hello?" My voice sounded a bit louder. Still nothing.

I moved slightly, the chains shifting, and that's when I noticed it. There was a low thrum coming from the chains around me, the slightest vibration that caused me to pull my wrists up closer to my face, studying the material wrapped around my arms. The iron chains seemed to have an intricate amethyst marking surrounding them, the thrum radiating from them. "What in the . . . ?" I muttered as I stared at them closer.

"They're spelled." A hoarse feminine voice sounded from the cell beside me. I turned, startled that the voice spoke up, and noticed the female next to me had lifted her head to regard me. "They prevent us from using any elemental magic or shifting powers we may have. To keep us weak. Helpless." There was an emptiness to her voice.

I felt inside me, pulling for that small nugget of power that had started to grow within me since I'd arrived in the past, yet it faded in the background, dull and unreachable. "How?"

"No one knows. But if you try to use your magic while chained, the iron sears into your skin." She lifted her arms, angry red welts appearing around the shackles and I grimaced at the pain she must have endured.

"I'm Kateya," I whispered.

"I know who you are," she answered as I startled in shock. "I heard the guards bragging as they dragged you in. 'Bagged the flame bringer . . . don't know how he found the sister with the second artifact.'" She looked me over. "So you're her?"

"Unfortunately," I muttered. "And you are?"

"Soraya," she replied tiredly.

"Soraya," I echoed the name. "Where are you from?"

"I was from Verastarr before they captured me and left me in this dump."

"Where in Verastarr?" I questioned. But she didn't answer as we both heard a key rattle in the distance. I noticed how Soraya curled up, making herself small and unnoticeable as heavy footsteps thudded closer and closer to us. Suddenly, they stopped in front of my cell. I shifted my gaze, looking up at the two guards who stopped in front of the door.

"Well, well." The taller of the two men sneered. "Look who's finally up." The other man fiddled with the key in his hand, before turning the lock in the keyhole. I watched, helplessly, as the door sprung free and he walked through the cell, stopping directly in front of me.

He bent beside me, the reek of fish flooding my nostrils while his key unlocked the walled side of the shackles. I didn't fight him, I didn't question where he was taking me. I bided my time; watching, waiting for the perfect moment to strike, while knowing I wouldn't be able to escape just yet.

"So silent." His jaunting tone hit my ears, yet I kept my lips shut as we walked down the hallway, holding my head high as I took note of my surroundings; memorizing every step, every corner we turned until we left the dungeons behind.

I don't know how long I waited, standing in front of a black metal door surrounded by four guards, before the door finally opened. I was pushed through the door frame, stumbling slightly as I moved further into the space and recognized it for what it was meant to be. *A throne room.*

The whispers started from the multitude of occupants in the room as I was led forward. I noticed the richly-dressed men standing in the room, weapons hanging on all of their belts, and the females dripping off their arms. Finally, I spotted him—the king.

I knew who he was before he even introduced himself to me; his reputation preceded him, not only in this time, but in the future as well. I'd stumbled across his name too many times to count while Aerilyn and I had scoured the Archives throughout the past year.

King Dathrian of Nordak.

We stopped a few feet from the dais, soldiers lining each step up to his throne as I studied the King of Nordak. Oiled black hair fell in tightly coiled curls from his head, a matching onyx crown with sharp points rested atop his head. He sat, clothed in light-weight armor over gray leathers as his hawk-like eyes watched every move I made.

"Kateya Dumont." My name rolled off his tongue, and I cringed at how it sounded coming from his lips. "What a pleasant surprise it is to have you here, *in my court*."

Pleasant, I scoffed internally. *Yes, pleasant is exactly the word I would use to describe waking up in Nordak.*

But I remained silent.

"I'm sure you have lots of questions." His face curved into a wicked smile as dark eyes met mine. "Allow me to provide you with some answers," he finished as he beckoned with his hand and footsteps sounded from my side.

My head swiveled and I froze, heart sinking as I was met with familiar jade green eyes and words instantly flashed free in my mind. "Everything's going exactly as planned." That's what he'd said to me on the battlefield. *"Everything's going exactly as planned."*

"Kateya," Eryx's cold voice purred toward me. A tone I'd never heard him use toward me before as he stopped by Dathrian. I simply stared, and my heart shattered into pieces while I struggled to maintain composure. My mind continually raced as Eryx looked me up and down. "It was fun while it lasted, was it not?" He chuckled, a dark chuckle that filled me with dread. "But now . . . now I have far better things in store for you."

"Why?" I heard the crack in my voice, the only indicator of my heart breaking as I stared at the stranger before me.

"Why?" He scoffed. "Because I could. Because *we* could." He gestured to his king.

"Tell her the story," King Dathrian cut in as he urged Eryx on. My gaze switched between the two men and I forced myself to breathe. *In. Out. In. Out.* The panic rising in my stomach had me wanting to vomit, and my fingers shook at my sides as I struggled to keep my fists clenched together.

Eryx's dimples grew as a sinister smirk spread across his lips.

"It was shockingly easy." He stared at me, watching my body for any signs, any tells of pain. "I was just a young soldier, new to the king's army when I accepted the task. And when we attacked Verastarr, I found Sébastien and pretended that I was a poor villager boy who'd lost his parents and home in the recent attack. I was taken in at Château Comptal, none the wiser. After all," he drawled, "who wouldn't believe the *poor, orphaned* village boy. I trained with the soldiers, rising in rank; waiting, watching, informing, until the moment came."

He walked closer to me, and I nearly stopped breathing when he stopped in front of me, lemon and bergamot rolling over me in disgust. "That's when you and your sister came along. And it was the perfect opportunity." Eryx bent down, his breath fanning over my neck. An action that once made me swoon, was now repulsing as I glared at the man before me. "All I had to do was send the message and the attack was planned. You remember, don't you? What was that little piece of information you shared with me?" His smile grew malicious, and my heart plummeted as I recalled what he was talking about.

It had been the night before Nightloc and I'd been talking to him in the grass courtyard. I'd had a glass too much and had shared that we were from the future. That a magic pendant had brought us back in time, and now my sister and I were trying to locate it to go back to our own time. *I'd been so stupid. I hadn't thought anything of it at the time, naively trusting everyone at the Palace.*

"It was the perfect setup, and when they found the pendant just before your sister, it made her capture all the sweeter." My blood boiled, power raging in me as I realized what he was implying. That *he* had provided the intel needed for my sister's capture. And worse yet, that *I* had been the one to give the information away.

I snapped, fire rising within me as I tried to unleash it on him. Yet the second I attempted to unleash my power, iron seared my skin, a guttural cry falling from my lips. I called my power back, staring in horror at the forming red marks as Eryx cruelly laughed, carrying on with his tale.

"However, Capetian and his brothers had to fuck up the plan when they ambushed our camp, stealing your sister and the pendant back. So I waited, and watched, and kept waiting, keeping my hand hidden until the next moment struck." He looked at me, his jade eyes glinting as he continued. "And wouldn't you know . . . guess who showed up at our campsite unexpectedly." My heart sank as I realized. He was talking about me. *I* was his stroke of luck. And I . . . I had given him every piece of information he'd needed to set me up.

My chest felt hollow as I stared in horrified silence at the only man I'd ever truly loved, who'd just destroyed every last piece of my heart with one story.

"What do you want with me?" I looked over Eryx's shoulder as I addressed his king.

"Everything," he said coldly, "until there's nothing left of you but raw power for me to harvest." My blood chilled as I stared at the man before me. Every fiber in my being screamed at me to run, to get out, to escape this nightmare. But I couldn't. I was trapped in a cage of their confines, and I knew there'd be no escaping any time soon.

Eryx looked at me, delight swarming in his eyes while he spoke. "We want to uncover the full extent of your powers, exactly how much magic your soul holds, how much magic the Great Four put into each of the artifacts; to see what the breaking point is, and once you reach that point . . . only then will we break you, until you are nothing but a vessel of power for us to wield."

"Again!" the voice shouted across from me in the ring as I was forced to draw on my fire power over and over. I'd been brought into the training ring early this morning, instructed to bring my magic to the surface each time the command was given, while also holding on to my vampry form.

When they first made me shift, I could only hold the form for a few seconds, the searing pain of the iron cuffs brandishing my wrists as I utilized my power. I buried the pain in the depths of my mind, knowing that as bad as it was, it was nothing compared to the pain of losing my parents when I'd first returned home, nothing compared to the pain of what Nik had done with the Blade of Rathmen. And, certainly, nothing compared to the pain of Eryx's betrayal. I became numb, a hollow shell, focused only on following the continued order to wield my flame.

Magic assessors in the darkened corner of the training pit watched on as I was pushed to my limits, forced to draw on my power over and over again so they could determine the strength and might of the power imbued into the artifact I'd shattered and taken possession of.

"I. Said. Again!" the voice shouted once more when he didn't see flames appearing in my palms instantaneously. But my will was fading, and it was all I could do to mutter over and over to myself, *I am resilient. I will overcome this.*

My arms shook as tears streamed down my face and I lifted my raw wrists. Of course, they'd left the shackled cuffs on, testing the limits of their spelled cuffs against the power imbued in me from the artifact.

I drew in a shaky breath, as I searched deep within me for that diminished ball of power, begging it to come forth and let its flames flicker to life in my hand. I didn't know what they hoped to gain from this test; from me repeatedly calling my elemental magic to the surface, but I planned to find out.

I stared at Eryx, at the man who broke my heart, my hands wobbling as I called forth my flames. My wrists burned in protest as the iron cuffs sunk deeper into my skin while I launched my fire toward the target hovering in the air twenty feet from me. It was a test to assess the extent of my abilities, something I had hardly begun to practice with Kodrayn and Everett before the battle took place. I watched as the sapphire blue fiery ball hit its target before I let the pain take over my body, washing over me with its nonexistent feeling of numbness, and I became a shell of myself. I let the pain engulf me as I threw fire, time after time until I lost count and my magic shriveled up inside, causing me to collapse on the ground from burnout.

NORDAK

Chapter Twenty-Three

"STAY STILL," Soraya's voice pleaded from the dimness above me.

"I'm trying." I gritted my teeth through the unbearable pain. My arm was bloodied and cut from today's *training session*. And I found myself with my back pressed against the rusting metal bars of my cell so that Soraya could help clean my wounds. I'd learned a great deal since I'd been unwillingly brought to what I discovered to be the fortress at Kyllios—one of the main headquarters for the Nordak.

"Keep it down," a voice whispered from the darkness across from us, "we can't afford them discovering."

"We know," I muttered back through clenched teeth. "*I know,*" I whispered even softer, the words reaching no one. If any of the guards in the dungeon discovered that we had a few healing aids hidden amongst the cells they held us hostage in, we would all be punished. The healers only mended us to the extent that Eryx and the other commanders instructed, which as it turned out, was never fully.

"What did they do to you up there?" Soraya's whisper came from behind me, and I hissed when she applied a salve on my torn arm.

"It's not *what* they did," I whispered back. "It's what they hope to find when they break me."

Her scoff filled the silence. "Then you can't break."

"I know," I resolved. "Pain is just pain. I won't give them part of the key to destroying our realm." Because that's what I would be doing if I broke. If I broke while they tested the extent of my powers, I gave them the opportunity to harvest my power easily, and I still needed to discover how they harvested the powers. We needed to know how in order to fight against it.

"Your arm needs to rest. Try not to put strain on it the next time they drag you to the pit. Use your other arm if you can."

"Thank you, Soraya." I held the girl's gaze before she bobbed her head and began to hide the meager supplies we had managed to sneak into these cells.

It had been five days since I'd discovered that there were others in this dungeon. Others like me, just not as powerful as me. The Nordak soldiers had picked off wolvyn, vamprys, and fae alike over the past two years. What must have seemed like random occurrences of missing men to the other lands, had been the beginnings of a captured army being starved and tested in these cells.

Powerful shifters, captains, guards, and now, me—one of the greatest weapons of all. No one had been able to figure out what they were collecting soldiers for, or what they were testing the extent of our powers for each and every day. But I'd had a feeling we would discover the answer sooner than we were prepared for.

"We need more supplies, we're running low already," Soraya murmured to the earlier voice which belonged to a fae captain named Cainu.

I jerked my head to the side, making out her outlined figure in the darkness. "We're running low, *already*?" The words dropped from my mouth.

"Yes," she murmured in resignation.

"We can't afford to attempt to get more supplies at this time." Cainu's voice sounded loud enough that we could hear him. "If another fae is injured this fortnight, it will look suspicious." I'd learned that when it could be afforded, a fae warrior during training, would feign injuries brutal enough that they were sent to the healers. When their luck aligned, the healers would leave the room for a few seconds, which allowed them to smuggle a few healing ointments and hide them utilizing fae magic until they were returned to their cell. It couldn't be done too often, which led to supplies running low quicker than we could afford.

Three days ago, I'd been sent to the healers chamber after a particularly brutal magic wielding session which had left me drained of all strength and energy. I'd arrived at the healers in a state of unconsciousness and in a stroke of luck, had been assigned to the healing apprentice who had forgotten to secure my iron shackles to the table since I'd been out when I arrived.

It had been that day, as I lay on a cot in the dark, that I decided I was no longer staying, I refused to be a pawn in a battle already written among the stars. So I waited. Once the healers apprentice had been called away for an emergency, I counted the minutes before forcing my weakened body to rise.

Rummaging through the chamber, I'd swiped just a few healing ointments and bandages—all materials I may need on my escape from Kyllios and once I'd secured all the items in my clothing. I began my escape, thanking The God that all the healers were focused on the Nordak warrior who had been brought in from a patrol gravely wounded.

I knew the number of steps it took to make it from the prison cells to the training pit, and the steps from the pit to the healing chambers. I knew precisely how many floors above ground I was, and that a jump from the fifth floor wasn't survivable, but the third floor, if I landed properly, would only sprain my ankle. The second floor was my best option, but I wagered that I would be discovered missing before I had the chance to make it to the second floor, meaning I'd need to jump, land properly, and hurriedly find a hiding spot before they noticed I was gone.

I'd made it down one floor before being spotted. Two before I was captured again and my brief hope of freedom was destroyed. The only saving grace was that they'd brought me right back to my cell, without searching me. So we'd distributed the healing supplies I'd managed to swipe and ensured we kept the materials well-hidden unless they were absolutely needed.

I had been called to the training pit that night and I knew, the moment I'd stepped into the ring, that Eryx had heard about my attempted escape, and he was not thrilled.

I'd been forced to enter this deadly pit every day since Eryx had captured me, but today . . . today felt different. The guards escorting me to the training pit whispered in low tones, as I struggled to catch drift of their conversation. The phrase Moyros Festival continued to be mentioned, and I made a mental note to bring it up to the other prisoners when I could, fearing the worst of the impending event.

The pit had a new energy to it, as though it was thrumming, coming to life with a darkness I hadn't experienced before. My palms shook, the ball of power deep within me—that I'd come to recognize and know so closely in the past week—felt as though it was shrinking in fear.

Eyes of jade that haunted me in my sleep cut in front of my line of vision, and I set my face as I tilted my chin and met Eryx's gaze. The familiar tattooed ink across his face caused me to now recoil in disgust.

"Today." His smile was different. There was an eagerness radiating from it, and his fingers twitched in *excitement?* No. Anticipation. My stomach dropped. "I've been waiting for this day."

Eryx circled me while he spoke, his voice taunting as he walked behind my back, and my muscles tensed, waiting for the strike. "Ever since I first laid eyes on your sister's powers." He stopped in front of me again. "I always envisioned the two of us controlling the realm in terror together, through your sister's power. But who would have thought that it would be you, here, in place of your sister." I clenched my teeth in anger as his voice drove on. "This works too, does it not, *Kateya*? Why rule together, when I can just control you?"

"*You*," I sneered, unable to control myself, "will *never* control me."

His fist collided with my cheek, the blow nearly knocking me back, but I'd been ready for it. I knew it was coming. And I let the pain fuel me, channeling it into resolution not to break.

"We'll see about that, *darling*." His gaze shifted upward briefly into the darkness of the pit, then back to me. "I'd like to introduce you to your newest *friend*. I suspect that controlling you will be far easier after your encounter." A piercing shrill cackled from high above me. My gaze flickered upward in uncertainty, but I saw nothing, save the darkness hovering as it always had.

When I looked back to where he'd been standing, Eryx was gone, leaving me alone in the training pit. "Coward," I snarled as my insides butterflied. The darkness that had so often framed the ceiling of the pit was now descending and pure dread began to rise within me. My upper thigh had a familiar pinch of pain that had me grimacing as I slowly watched the approaching darkness.

I had no weapons, save my elemental magic and my power to shift. And so, I called on it, this time however, I willed myself to be fae. To be swift and powerful, but more importantly, to be able to fly. I imagined large wings expanding over the muscles of my back. It was a shift I'd made on my third day here after seven hours in this ring. I'd spent my nights in my cell talking with the fae soldiers, asking about how they shifted and controlled their wings. I learned the best way to fly, how to control your powers while in fae form, and how to use the wind to my advantage.

The ripple of power coursed over my body, my back stretching as shiny silver wings sprouted from my back and I unsteadily began to push off the ground. The wings beat furiously behind me, lacking the grace I'd seen in fae in the past as I stumbled into flight, but I held my own as my wings lifted me higher off the ground. I could feel the twinges in my back muscles as the wings expanded with each beat and I grew steadier.

My heart froze as I stared toward the darkness hovering in the sky near me and watched in horror as a figure began to take form in the cloud. A tall woman emerged from the dark, with long legs and lithe arms, flowing hair, and a form that felt oddly familiar to me. Almost as though the creature was calling to me.

The creature began to move closer to me as I drew on the power within me, calling on the sapphire flames that danced beneath my surface, tuning out the continual scorch of pain from the iron shackles.

"Such power," a voice danced in the air, and I stared in shock as the voice surrounded me; the creature never closing the distance. "What a pity that you haven't used it how it was meant to be used. I can use it . . . I can use you. Your power is not so different from mine, *Bearer of Sapphire Flame*." The voice taunted me and my wings stopped beating.

I fell momentarily, wings flailing at its words, before the drop in my stomach as I lurched downward caused me to snap out of the delusion I'd felt. Because there was no way it was possible. And yet, the voice that crept toward me sounded exactly like my mother's voice had.

It was noticeable. The reason why the figure seemed so familiar. It *was* my mother, but at the same time, it was *nothing* at all like my mother. Gone was the love that radiated from her tone, the warmth that so often cascaded from her—the happiness and joy.

This darkness, this creature, whatever it was, had taken on my mother's persona. Perhaps to bond with me, to throw me off center. Abruptly, it struck. Purple tendrils spewed from its gaping mouth and charged toward me. Streams of amethyst spiraled rapidly toward me, snaking from the sky. I pushed harder with my wings, urging them to propel me upward to the ceiling as I tugged at the tendrils of flame licking at my palms. Bracing myself for the pain—the scalding sear of iron on my wrists, which came from calling on even more of my power—I threw my hand in the direction of the amethyst tendrils, urging my sapphire flames to split their way toward their target.

I watched in horror as the dark purple tendrils simply ate my flames, the fire fizzling away to nothing upon contact with the ancient magic found within the creature battling me. A dark laugh sounded from below, and I could only assume Eryx was watching the fight. I gathered my strength, twisting as I cut through the air, intent on avoiding the tendrils of darkness that shot toward me.

The figure that had once resembled my mother now had the appearance of a beast with tentacles like an octopus shooting from its mouth. I'd never seen a creature like this, had no knowledge of its powers or abilities; no way of knowing how to best fight it. A creature that could shift forms as I did, but to unimaginable beings of dreams and nightmares who fought with corrupt magic.

I flew to the side of the pit, willing my fire to rise again, as I imagined a rope of fire shooting toward the creature and circling its tendrils to halt the advance. Flames leapt from my skin, a scream of agony erupting from my lips as I expelled the power and watched it dart forward to follow my command. I stared, praying to The God for a miracle as they began to circle three tendrils; the flames still ablaze as the rope wrapped around them. A smile began to creep up my face as I hovered in the air. My power fizzled around the beast before flickering out entirely, and the smile fell from my face just as two tendrils of darkness hit me from the other side in full force.

My back arched, my body too stunned from the collision, and from the darkness now circling my tanned skin to do anything. My wings stopped beating as though they couldn't do anything against the creature surrounding me, and I fell, plummeting to the ground, unable to break my fall as I collided with the floor. My vision flickered out, a cool feeling falling over my skin and the sense of control fleeing my body was all I could feel. A figure began to outline itself in the distance, floating to me. Only, it was me; a darker version of myself with sharp, jagged teeth protruding from its mouth as it began to speak, its shrill voice calling to me, "I'm done playing games, Bearer of Sapphire Flame. You have what I've long sought. And now, now I shall take what should be mine."

I lay there, motionless on the ground as memories slowly played in my mind. Memories filled with happiness and joy—ones I thought of so often with a smile on my face—began to alter. A memory drifted by, one of Cassandra and I climbing castle ruins long ago in Verastarr before we moved; of us laughing while we raced to the top, grappling our way over the stones. I frowned when the castle was set on fire, flames dancing down toward us as we raced to the top. Darkness descended on the ruins as the fire began snaking toward us. My sister screamed and began to fall. A hoarse shout echoed from my voice as I tried to reach my hand out to her, only for her to slip through my grasp and fall into the darkness.

Instantly, a new memory flickered by. I fought against the creature's tendrils as I tried to retain my memories; as I tried to remember the happiness, the moments in life that had brought me infinite joy and held on to them so they couldn't be snatched away. All of a sudden, a wave of pain radiated from my inner thigh, fiery pain that collided with the cold mist surrounding me, and my memories went dark.

NORDAK

Chapter Twenty-Four

MY SOUL TEETERED on the brink of life, closer to The Void than ever before as Eryx paced in front of me. It was all I had in me to hold my head up and meet his gaze while he spoke.

"Your power is as good as ours now. The God will be pleased with the power you present at the Moyros Festival." His grin widened, the tattoo on his face appearing starker, darker as he glared at me in victory. "Just remember that tonight."

"Tonight?" I questioned, my head spinning after being forced to demonstrate the extent of my powers over and over again this morning. But I didn't get an answer. In fact, he didn't say anything at all. I watched as Eryx walked away from me, shoulders held high, as pain coursed through my body, my limbs heavy and numb before I was led back to my cell.

"What's the Moyros Festival?"

My head swam as another burst of agony emerged from the wound on my back that Soraya was tending to.

"Moyros?" a voice echoed from two cells over, concern laced in the deep tone.

"Yes," I muttered. "I heard two of the guards mention the name the other day, and Eryx told me earlier today that I was to be the center attraction for the festival tonight."

"*Void-be-damned.*" The low curse came from across the hallway. "I thought they outlawed that festival decades ago." Cainu, the fae captain emphasized.

"Not here. The bloody bastard of a king continues to let that tradition live," the prisoner down from us, Mathas, muttered.

"What's so bad about it?" Fear slowly rose within me at their tones.

"Long ago," the captain began, "the Moyros Festival, was a festival the lands held honoring their dead. It was typically held after great battles and wars. The people of the land came together to remember those who had gone off to join The God in The Void."

"The bodies of the dead were collected after the wars and typically burned while those who remained on this side of The Void danced and sang in remembrance of those who had given their lives," the deeper voice added.

"That doesn't sound concerning," I admitted, a wince falling from my mouth at Soraya's ministrations.

"Sorry," she whispered, her voice just above a whisper.

"It wasn't at first," Cainu replied as he continued his story. "When the Nordak King began playing with ancient magic before the Great War, however, they altered the course of the festival. They still *honored* those that had died in battle, but they did so through a recreation of the deaths."

"They often selected an enemy prisoner to fight and reenact the battle to the death," another voice chimed in.

"They *what?*" My heart thudded in terror as the men around me spoke.

"The *festival* became a death sentence to the prisoner selected. A way to *honor* their dead through the death of the enemy."

"You . . ." I swallowed thickly as I stared into the dim light. "You can't be serious."

Silence met me for a moment before the fae captain spoke up. "That's why the festival was outlawed. Laws were put in place to ensure that no lands in the Vanaiyer realm partook in the Moyros Festival ever again."

"With all the battles and skirmishes occurring," Soraya spoke up from beside me, her voice soft. "It's not surprising that the Nordak decided to reinstate the *festival*." She sneered.

"If I'm the center attraction . . ." I swallowed, my voice quivering as my mind processed everything I'd heard today. "Then I suppose that means—" I couldn't finish the sentence, and the silence that filled the cells around me echoed the quiet thoughts running rampant in my mind. *Eryx planned to have me fight to the death.*

"Here," Soraya whispered from beside me as something sharp struck my palm. "Take this and hide it well."

I looked down at the object to notice the pale bone carved to a point and froze. "I won't be able to get close enough to kill whatever I'm faced up against, not with these chains." I raised my arms in a near defeated sigh toward her.

"No," she replied, her tone stronger but sorrowful. "You won't be able to kill *it*. You're the only one who's even survived against the beast. But that"—she wrapped my hand around the bone as she spoke—"that is for you. You'll be too weak to fend the beast off for long. They've starved and trained you to the point of breaking. Take matters into your own hands."

I froze, recognizing what she was saying. "I'm not going to *kill myself*. I promised my sister I would be alright. That I'd see her again after the battle," I whispered harshly, in shock at the girl beside me.

"If you get the chance to before *it* kills you. Take it." Cainu's weathered voice echoed across from me. "It's the only way."

"The only way for what?"

"For them not to be able to harvest your magic," he finished.

Harvest my magic?

"What do you mean?" I questioned, confusion laced in my tone. "There's no way the Moyros Festival is how the Nordak King has been harvesting magic."

"No, Dathrian doesn't harvest magic through the festival. If he had been doing it through the festival, it would be too noticeable. He does it through his beasts," the captain replied. "If his creatures of darkness kill you, it gives him a window of time to harvest your magic. That's how he's been growing more powerful. He's stealing the magic of those he captures. But you . . ." The captain fell silent. The only sound in the dungeon was the scurry of rats across the cobblestones. "If you die, he has the opportunity to gain so much power. But *only* if you die by one of his beasts on a quarter moon."

"*If* that's true," I replied, "why is this the first I'm hearing of this?"

"We thought you knew." Soraya's voice said quietly from beside me. "We all know."

"How does everyone know this?" I questioned, alarm growing. "How is it that Sébastien, Kodrayn, and Ryker don't know about this?"

"They couldn't know," Mathas responded. "No one knew until we were captured and began putting it together."

"How long? How long has he been doing this? How long have you been here to witness it?"

"Too long," Mathas responded. "But when I was captured, I heard of his plans from prisoners long before me and began to put the pieces together. Dathrian is strategic about it. He captures people from outposts, from village ransacks. Never enough for the royals to take note that their people are being swiped out from under them."

"Void-be-damned," Cainu cursed from across the way.

"A-And he's just able to siphon magic right from us?" I questioned Mathas, gathering that he knew the most on the topic.

"He must have his beasts do it. No one knows what they are,

but from what we gather, when they draw your memories from you, the ones of joy and replace them with nightmares, it makes it easier to harvest the magic. We still don't know how he does it though—how he manages to harvest it for himself."

I wondered whether he had the Blade of Rathmen, whether that was aiding him in harvesting magic from the people of Vanaiyer. Or if there was some other weapon, forgotten in lore, that aided his wickedness.

"We've lost ten men to the beasts during the quarter moons since I've been here," Soraya murmured from beside me.

My head jerked between the two of them, then toward the others closest to me as I realized. They'd accepted death. They knew what would happen to them here, that they were destined to die during the Moyros Festivals. The only question was which one.

"I–I had no clue," the words came out in a hollow whisper.

Her cool hand tightened around my palm, the carved bone pressing firm against my skin. "If you can end it before they do, the king can't harvest your magic. You can't let him harvest your powers, Kateya. It will doom us all."

I leaned my head against the damp stones, the chill seeping into my hollow chest as I realized that tonight, I would be fighting for my life, quite literally. I tried to draw on happy memories, distracting my mind until the guards came to collect me, yet most of the memories I tried to recall sent me spiraling down. I didn't know what to do. *Could I fight off the beast? And even if I won, was it truly winning, or just prolonging my life for a few more days until Dathrian tried again? Was it better to end it now or risk dooming the realm if my magic was harvested?*

A silver tear fell down my cheek, then another as I buried my face in my palms. The metal chains clanked as I curled in on myself, wishing for my sister, for my parents, for Kodrayn to show up and make a joke of saving my life once again, despite the fact I wasn't the in-need-of-rescuing type. *Hell,* even the twins would be a welcome sight.

"If you do anything stupid tonight," Eryx sneered from my side. "I will personally gut you myself. Do you understand?" he snarled as I looked at him.

"Do you truly think threatening me with death as I prepare to face death tonight is going to scare me?" I replied, my emerald green eyes meeting his from behind his mask.

I'd been dressed in all black, with flowing pants that had slits up the side. A criss-crossed pattern held the slits closed along my upper thighs. A matching black shirt clung to my curves, the material silky and soft, offering me no protection whatsoever.

My hair had been braided tightly into two plaits down my head. The silver pieces framing my face braided into their own two mini strands decorated with silver beads. My face had been painted with intricate black marks around the lace mask that covered my face from my nose to forehead. And from the glimpses I'd caught in the window, the marks closely resembled the tattoos I had so often traced along Eryx's face. An outfit designed to match his, as though I was his, and not a captured prisoner walking toward death.

Had I not been captured and still in metal shackles that excruciatingly slowed my ability to use my magic, I may have found the outfit to be one that I'd select for a night out. Yet the weight on my wrists, the raw, red skin surrounding the cuffs, were a constant reminder of the times I'd been forced to use what powers I could even muster with my magic being restrained.

Eryx's grip tightened on my upper arm as he tugged me forward into the open air of the courtyard, the dusk air of Kyllios hitting me for the first time since I'd been brought here. A cool breeze whipped across my exposed skin, as a shiver crawled over me in the night air.

I carefully took in the crowds of people, the dancing and

laughter that surrounded the otherwise barren courtyard. No flowers lined the edges of the buildings, no signs of light, or life. A cold exterior to match that of their ruler. And suddenly he was there, walking toward me, and the crowd stopped.

The laughter and music died instantaneously as Dathrian, King of Nordak, stopped in front of me, his gaze cold and calculating. "Our guest of honor has arrived," his voice rang out across the courtyard, and a chorus of cheers rose to greet him. The music began again.

"Do not disappoint me," Dathrain sneered, not toward me, but toward the man at my side, Eryx.

"I believe you shall be quite enthralled tonight, My King," Eryx said, in a tone I'd never heard him use as he took my hand and led me along with him.

My body internally protested as Eryx led me around the courtyard. My breath was shaky, my hands fidgeting with the criss-cross design on my pant legs as Eryx took his seat and I stood to the side of him. I felt the weight of the bone on my chest—the only place I'd been able to hide it with easy access so it wouldn't be seen. The weight of a decision I'd soon be forced to make.

I watched the dances, the soldiers moving along the outer edges of the courtyard and realized that the palace was impenetrable. There were guards stationed at every entrance. Even if I managed to escape the beast, there was no way I'd be able to escape the gates.

I felt Eryx's hand on my skin, and flinched as he pulled me toward him, leading me toward the line of masked dancers. My heart rate increased, as I knew what came next.

"Enjoy your last dance." Eryx's cold sneer fell into me as he tugged me toward him and we joined the throng of dancers.

"*Enjoy your last dance,*" I mimicked as I was passed on from him to the next dancer—a Nordak soldier. I let the rhythm of the music calm my soul while I prepared for what was next. My body swayed to the beat as I was passed from dancer to dancer, the distance between Eryx and I furthering as we moved as a group to the rhythm of the night; my mind finding inner peace, just as it always did before a fight.

A cool breeze floated by, casting chills down my skin as a taste of cedarwood and blood orange passed by me. I looked around slowly as I danced with my current partner, but noticed nothing unordinary. I spun to the music, my body swaying to the beat even as my soul felt hollow.

The music shifted its pace, the rapid tempo increasing as I was passed into my next partner's cool hands. I felt it before I even glanced up, an ember of magic flickered to light deep within me, the heat drawing closer to the surface with a new determination. I didn't focus on the cool hands of my dance partner, but on growing the ember burning within. That is, until the words, "Four times is a bit much for someone who doesn't think she needs to be rescued, isn't it, little venom," whispered into my ears. "Be ready." Before I could look up, before I could see if the amber-eyed gaze of the vampry king was watching me, the next dancer was there, taking his place.

As the music crawled to a stop, the song ending, the dancer to my left pointed me in the direction of Eryx.

I contemplated running, right then and there, but when I took a step toward my jailor, the muscled form of the man I'd been dancing with bumped into me, jostling me as I walked through the crowd of dancers.

I felt the missing weight between my chest just as Eryx approached me, and my nostrils flared as I spun my head, looking for the thief. Someone had been watching me. Someone, had known what I had been instructed to do tonight. That I'd been given the weapon as a means to end the harvesting before it began. *He'd been watching me.* And he'd stopped my only chance. My heart rate increased, and I thanked The God that gryffins couldn't detect the shift in my pulse like the vamprys could as I was led toward the training pit by Eryx.

I was defenseless, weaponless, as I was shoved into the training pit. A hush fell over the crowd. My eyes shifted, searching the crowd as I looked for anyone that would help me. But there was no compassion, no empathy, just soldiers hardened for battle. That's when the darkness emerged.

I stared at the darkness before me, a force that caused fear to rise in so many, but had become a known factor in my life. I didn't waste time, because I had none. But I thanked The God that I had fought the beast before, not to the fullest extent that I could, but I'd learned enough through the pain these past weeks. And I knew how to strike.

My elemental powers were close to useless against such a creature, the flames only ever causing a momentary distraction before being swallowed in the dark depths of the creature I fought. So I chose flight, having learned that flight and speed were my strongest allies against the beast.

Wings sprouted from my back in a now familiar ripple of muscle and pain as I envisioned a fae form and pushed off from the ground. I blocked out the jarring screams and insults being hurled from the crowd as I faced my opponent and froze mid-flight.

The darkness stood before me, towering above me in the form of a vampry. "Bearer of Sapphire Flame, it is time that I wield you; time for your power to be mine and you to cease." Its voice flowed from the shadows, a low voice that sounded too much like one I'd thought I heard not minutes before . . . the voice of the Vampry King.

Had I imagined his voice before? Had I actually smelled Kode's calming scent while I danced? Or had it all been an illusion? Had my battle with the darkness started long before I entered the pit? Had it been priming me for this fight with the sole purpose of stripping me of any hope of freedom?

I didn't know, but I didn't have a chance to think any further on the topic because, at that moment, purple mist spewed from its mouth, tendrils of barbed magic snaking their way toward me and I was put on defense.

It was the only method of survival I had. In all my sessions against Dathrian's beast, I'd never found a way to fight back against the creature . . . only defend. And so, defend myself I would, until my last breath.

I flew high, twisting in the sky as I dodged the barbed tendrils aimed for my heart, soaring out of their reach as I flew straight toward the wall of the pit before dropping mid-flight, watching the tendrils above me crash into the wall.

I heard the crowd roar in protest as my wings caught flight once again, and I pushed into the air, catching the breeze as I dove under the beast's vampry form, raising a ball of fire I knew would only distract it momentarily. I threw the roped blue flames toward the creature anyway, its enraged cackle behind me. I approached the wall, protecting my back, waiting for its next strike.

The tendrils of its next attack lashed out faster than I'd anticipated, my wings launching me upward before I torpedoed into a dive, avoiding the amethyst magic on my tail, but I'd failed to catch sight of the next round fired on me. A strike of mist hit my left wing as I dodged the impact from my right, sending me spiraling down to the ground, landing in a thud on the ground.

Pain erupted from my wing, the left one bent at a precarious angle, crimson liquid pooling on the ground as blood spewed from the angle of the wing and I knew it couldn't be good. I could hear the mists circling down, focusing on my fallen form, the crowd cheering at my fall, but I pushed to my feet even as the beast's shroud of darkness grew closer. I envisioned my vampry form, the elongated ears and fangs, the speed that came with and made the shift. I screamed as I shifted, whether from the angle of my wing or the iron sears on my wrists from my use of magic, I didn't know.

I knew I couldn't hold out much longer. My limbs felt like noodles and my inability to utilize my power to the fullest extent meant every shift, every glimmer of flames, ignited a burst of burning pain around the shackles entrapping my power. The tendrils of darkened purple shot through the air once again from the beast's mouth as the ones from above drew closer to me, and this time I couldn't move fast enough. I felt the icy grip of ancient magic wrap itself around me, colliding with me in such force that I crashed to the ground. I braced myself mentally, even as I struggled against the darkness, twisting and turning as I tried to free myself.

I felt the darkness towering over me as I stared at the form of the beast, watching it shift from its vampry form to that of a gryffin—a powerful gryffin that towered above my fallen form, and the cold began to seep in. I tried to raise my arm, to protect myself; to cast out any magic I could for protection, only my limbs couldn't move. I couldn't fight, I wouldn't have even been able to end my own life if I'd still had the sliver of bone on me.

My vision began to grow dark as the beast hovered over my body, my memories pushing to the front of my mind as a mental battle began. I forced myself to switch each memory, replacing the memories that began to spring up in my mind with my nightmares; with memories of Nik, of the Seefer attacks from back home, the memory of my parents' deaths. It could take my nightmares and make them worse, I didn't care. But it would *never* take my joy again.

A ripple of pain coursed through my body, a familiar pain that had me clenching my teeth as purple mist began rising from my body—from my inner thigh—from the mark Nik had forever left on me. It was the same mist that had appeared weeks ago in my tent.

I watched, helplessly, as the amethyst mist rose from my body. Amethyst mist that was nearly identical in color to the tendrils of mist the beast unleashed. I watched as they collided with the tendrils of purple tethered to the creature. It was the *same* ancient magic. The thought crossed my mind as the two mists tangled and twisted, mist on tendrils of darkness, before they began merging into one. They rose up higher and higher into the training pit, racing toward the ceiling. The entire crowd watched, voices screaming in anger at my unfair move, while the ancient magic sparked and danced across the dark ceiling. Just before the magic collided in full force with the top of my imprisonment, the mist disappeared. Vanishing into the air as though it had never been there, Dathrian's beast along with it.

The crowd fell silent, their eyes darting between my battered form in the pit and King Dathrian on his throne before the training pit. I shakily rose to my feet, my legs swaying, blood dripping from various parts of my body as I attempted to steady myself—to stand firmly on my feet before the king.

I was alive. Alive. I had survived.

My gaze met the kings. With anger and defiance in my eyes, I stared at him, and watched as a dangerous smile slowly formed on his lips, curving up wickedly. We locked eyes, my gaze holding to his cold, hard one. I had survived, but I couldn't tell whether I'd outsmarted his system or walked right into his plan. Right into an awaiting trap.

With a flick of his hand, two soldiers surrounded me in the pit, the crowd cheering at my captivity.

I tried to fight their grip. Tried to break free and run away, but I couldn't. I couldn't do anything as the beating my body had taken began to take a toll on me. My left arm writhed in pain, my body weak from blood loss. I couldn't escape now. I wouldn't make it more than a foot in front of me.

"Take her back to her cell," the king commanded as I was dragged toward the door to the side of the training pit. I scanned the crowd, nearly begging for someone, anyone, to help me; to stand up for me. I had fought the kings beast, and I had won, but that meant nothing to these people. It didn't matter if I had died tonight or not, because one way or another, my life was controlled by the King of the Nordak.

I tried struggling, raising my feet to kick the guards away, but my body refused to listen, refused to do anything I wanted it to. I searched through the crowd as we approached the doors, praying to see a glimmer of amber-speckled eyes in the distance, only to be pushed through the fortress doors.

NORDAK

Chapter Twenty-Five

IT WASN'T the subtle tunes of music from the festival that woke me, nor the damp chill seeping into my blood-stained shirt, but rather the sound of Soraya crying in the cell next to me that first caused me to stir.

"Soraya?" I whispered in a cracked voice, my head foggy and unfocused. The sniffled cries continued, and I pushed my voice over the noise. "Soraya . . . what's wrong?"

Her form shifted as haunted eyes met mine in the dark. "Y–you're still here. You shouldn't be here. You can't be here . . . you can't."

"Apologies," I murmured through the fog of pain, "for living." My head throbbed and I noticed that my leg was in more pain than I'd ever felt before. The injuries sustained from being thrown from the sky, the most likely culprit.

"I–it's just . . ." She paused, hesitantly. "If you're still alive. They'll come back for one of us. I–I'm not ready to die." Her sniffles continued as I stared at her, trying to find a glimmer of compassion buried somewhere deep within me.

"I don't think you'll have to worry about that," I forced out and met her gaze. "I think my *demonstration* was enough of a show to keep the king occupied for a few days." I lifted a hand to my pounding head, only to immediately wince, dropping my hand as I glanced at the shackles.

Blistered, red skin stared back at me, and I knew the injuries would never heal properly. My wrists would be forever scarred from being forced to wield my magic in cursed iron.

"What did you do?" she whispered, but I fell silent at the question. *What did I do?* I didn't even know how to answer that question. How to explain the purple mist emerging from me during the festival, which I would guess was all the answer the King of Nordak needed to know. I truly had no idea what would come next.

"I—honestly . . ." I paused, looking at her. "I'm not entirely sure, but whatever happened, it changed everything."

"What do you—" Soraya stopped. We both stopped, pressing ourselves further into the darkness as we heard the ever-so-subtle note of boots on stone. I held my breath, not allowing myself to move even an inch as I listened to the steps growing closer, closer, then stop. My heart thudded heavily in my chest, my pulse racing as I braced myself in anticipation for what came next, refusing to look up at the guards stopped in front of my cell. Not wanting to give them a reason to injure me further than what I'd already sustained.

Keys jangled, before grating against metal, the sound stark against the silence of the dungeon. They clattered some more, the scraping drawing the attention of others, when a deep voice spoke. "Void-be-damned. Give me the keys. How hard is it to open a lock?"

"Just give me a minute, I've almost got it," a second voice answered.

I sucked in a breath, and knew I had to be dreaming, because those voices were too familiar and they certainly didn't belong here, in the dungeons of Kyllios. The lock sprang free and the door was pushed open silently. The scent of cedarwood and blood orange washed over me for the second time tonight, and I relaxed, my body sagging against the damp wall in relief.

"Kateya," a low voice murmured as I looked up and found amber eyes peering into mine, assessing every inch of my face before holding my gaze. "How badly are you injured? I know the fall must have left you with a broken bone from your splintered wing. Can you move?" His eyes narrowed in on a few cuts I knew were across my arms, and one still bleeding on my cheek. The anger brewing in his golden eyes caught me off guard.

I stared at Kodrayn, my mind refusing to work. I had to be dreaming, right? There was no way that he was truly here, in front of me.

"Silver," a voice sounded from my other side and I slowly moved my head, pain lancing through my body at the motion and saw Everett standing before me. "We only have ten minutes. Can you move?"

"I—" I started, before realizing I didn't exactly know if I could move or not. "I'm not sure." My voice sounded hollow and far off, empty as I answered their question.

Drawing on my strength, I willed myself to stand. Pushing off the ground, I slowly began to rise when an agonizing jolt shot through my body and it took everything in me not to cry out as I nearly collapsed back onto the ground. Strong, muscled arms caught my fall.

"Shit," Everett's voice sounded in the distance as my mind grew fuzzy, the pain still coursing through my body while Kodrayn supported my weight. An argument sounded in the distance and I struggled to keep up with the banter through the pain. I caught fragments of the conversation as I struggled to stay conscious.

"I have to, it's the only way." Kodrayn's voice cut through my pain-addled brain.

"Fine, but she's going to resent us for it," Everett bit out.

"I'll take her resentment any day if it means we get her out of here alive." Kodrayn's voice sounded distant as I tried to focus on his words.

"I'll start working on the shackles. We need to be quick."

"I'm sorry," Kodrayn said as he moved into my line of vision, "but it's the only way to heal you quickly." I stared at him blankly, confused at his words. I watched as he brought his forearm up to his mouth, and a silent cry fell from my body as he bit firmly into his arm. Crimson welled on his tattooed skin, but he was already moving his arm toward me.

My mind began to process what he was doing, and I tried to shake my head, protesting his actions, but I was too late, or too tired. Suddenly, he was pressing his arm against my lips, forcing his blood into my mouth. The scent of iron mixed with the metallic taste of him washed over the inside of my mouth, but I refused to swallow it. I *refused* to drink vampry blood. There weren't many lines I drew, but *this*, this was one.

"Swallow, little venom." His words fell over me in an almost soothing tone and my gaze cut to his, even as he held his wrist firmly against my lips. "Vampry blood is the only way for you to heal enough for us to get you out of here."

Everett still worked on the cuffs around my wrists, as I struggled feebly against Kodrayn's arm to no avail.

"Please." The word fell from Kodrayn's lips as his other hand rose up, slowly, tenderly stroking soft circles on my neck. I nearly froze from his tone alone, my eyes pausing a fraction of an inch, at the look on his face. I saw the traces of panic and concern laced across his face with every second I refused to listen to him. And so I did.

I felt it trickle down my throat, the warm trail it made into me. And as I obeyed his command, I felt it. I felt the healing that began to course through my body, the wounds that slowly began to knit themselves back together; the haze of pain that began floating away from my body, the rush of energy and revitalized strength that flowed into me. *His strength.*

"Got them." Everett's voice sounded clearer, and Kode finally removed his forearm from my mouth.

"Do you trust me, little venom?" the King of Avyon asked as he extended his tattooed arm toward me. Tentatively, I reached out my own hand, grasping his extended hand and allowed him to assist me up.

"Five minutes," Everett murmured as I stood with Kodrayn's help.

Looping an arm around my waist for stability, the three of us began exiting the cell when I stopped, turning to face Kodrayn.

"We," I whispered with force, "can't just leave them here. They're your people, and Sébastien's, and Rykers. They need to be freed too." Both Everett and Kodrayn looked at me, before glancing around at the figures outlined in the cell's surrounding us. "I won't leave them," I protested, weakly trying to halt my body from moving.

My body shook, still not fully healed, but I tried to hold my ground. I looked from Soraya to the fae captain I'd become acquainted with, and could see their silver-rimmed eyes, as though they knew they wouldn't be leaving with us.

Kodrayn's jaw clenched, the scar across his eye twitching slightly as he looked over the people locked up, before his gaze settled on the fae captain's and a flicker of recognition swept over his face. "I'll do what I can," he said only to the captain. "Ryker doesn't have enough men to fly everyone to safety. We barely had enough to spare for this mission." The fae nodded as though he understood whatever message Kodrayn was relaying to him, but I didn't.

"You have to free them," I pleaded with Kodrayn, but the look I got when his amber eyes met mine, ablaze with pain and fury, silenced me.

He turned back to Cainu. "We'll do what we can. I promise you that."

I looked between Kodrayn and the captain, then I turned to Everett. "Give me the keys."

His gaze turned apologetic as he looked over my head toward his king. I lurched forward, hands outstretched as I tried to swipe the keys from his side.

"We have to go, *now*," Kodrayn commanded from behind me and I spun toward him.

"If we can't free them all, I won't be leaving without her." I pointed toward Soraya, crouched in the corner of her cell, watching with sadness in her eyes. "And before you say no," I snarled in a whisper toward Kodrayn, "without her, I wouldn't be alive. There wouldn't have been a *me* to rescue if it weren't for her. I *owe* her for my life . . . *you* owe her for my life. If she doesn't come, neither do I."

I held my ground, my emerald eyes sending daggers toward the man in front of me until a heavy sigh fell from his lips and he nodded toward Everett.

"Make it quick, we need to keep moving."

Relief flooded my system as Everett hurriedly freed Soraya. I watched as Kodrayn passed the keys into the fae captain's cell, exchanging a few brief words with him, and then we were moving; the two vamprys ushering us through the hallway as quietly and swiftly as they could.

Our movements passed in a blur of motion, my mind still sleep deprived and exhausted from what I'd endured. I barely noticed the change in scenery as we exited the fortress, and found ourselves in the fresh air, late at night. The music from the festival was dying down, the streets less crowded. Even the guards stationed on duty were less observant, the beer and whiskey they'd spent the evening drinking, taking a toll on their systems.

We walked through the streets undetected, even as we approached the gates of Kyllios. I held my breath as we walked through the gates, both men looping their arms around Soraya and I, causing our gait to change. To those on watch, we looked like two couples, stumbling home drunk after the festival.

And as we walked toward the forest, my mind raced. It couldn't have been that easy, that simple, this whole time. There had to be a catch, something. Something was off. This was a dream . . . it had to be. We approached two horses, tied to a tree in a strange forest where the trees had no leaves despite the season.

"K–Kode," I whispered the name as we began mounting the horses. "Something's wrong," I forced out.

"We're fine, little venom, trust me."

"It shouldn't be this easy." I tried to turn in the saddle to look at him, but the angle mixed with my exhaustion made it impossible. "Something's wrong," I tried again, but they kept moving, quickly mounting the horses behind Soraya and I, and then we were off, moving swiftly through the trees, the only thing to light our path being the quarter moon hanging high overhead in the night sky.

The steady rhythm of the horse began to fall in sync with my exhaustion, and sleep tugged at my body. As the night breeze swept over me, mixed with the scent of cedarwood and blood orange, I realized what was wrong; why this felt too easy. It was a dream, it had to be. Because in no realm would it have been that easy to sneak two prisoners out of a dungeon cell in Kyllios.

As sleep called out to me, I embraced the dream, drinking in the momentary peace it provided me, the happiness and hope. "Thank you," I murmured to the night air as sleep took me under.

NORDAK

Chapter Twenty-Six

I AWOKE to sunlight hitting my eyes and a firm arm wrapped protectively around my torso, holding me securely in place. Soraya's voice rambled on in front of me, and I caught little snippets of her story as she told Kodrayn and Everett about her time in captivity. Turning my head slightly, I took in the cloudy, overcast day casting shadows across the forlorn forest we were riding through. *It wasn't a dream. He was here.*

"Welcome back to the land of the living." Kodrayn's voice rumbled behind me, and my heart warmed at the sound of his voice.

"How did you—when did you—why—" I stopped, my cheeks flaming at the lack of a complete sentence.

"Want to try that again, little venom?" he purred from behind me and I angled my right elbow back slightly, jabbing him in the ribs.

"Ha. Ha," I deadpanned before my tone turned serious as a rush of questions filtered through my mind. "When was it first noticed that I was missing?" I questioned as I pushed my memories back to that first day on the battlefield when I was captured by the man I thought I loved.

"Dravyn first made a comment to me once we crossed paths

on the field, about a half hour after you got separated. From there, we split up, trying to locate you as quickly as we could." He paused, his breath touching my neck before he continued. "Ryker spotted you first, but even then, we couldn't be positive about what happened, or where you had been taken."

"Eryx," the name dropped from my tongue in an arctic breeze.

"What about him?" Kodrayn's sharp tone cut into me from behind, his voice rumbling as my back pressed against him. *So they didn't know.* My heart sank at the thought of having to explain that unfortunate mistake to him.

"Later," I forced out, tears welling in my eyes at the thought of sharing what I'd endured; at everything I had been put through since the day of the battle. I felt Kodrayn's hand tighten on the reins around me, I could see the veins in his forearms pulsing, but to his credit, he didn't push the topic further.

"We sent out scouts that day, and by the time we got word, you'd already been brought to Kyllios."

I stayed silent, listening to his side of the story as he explained how they'd managed to locate me.

"We thought we'd be able to break you out in a day's time, but we couldn't keep up with the number of times they had you brought to that *training pit.*" My body tensed at his words, every fiber of my being recoiling at the thought of that arena where I'd been forced to encounter the unknown beast. "When we heard about the Moyros Festival, we knew that would be our best shot at freeing you, so we waited and prayed to The God that you made it to the festival."

I remained silent, staring at the gray tree limbs as we rode past, feeling as dead on the inside as the trees passing by looked. Everett and Soraya had fallen silent in front of us, yet I paid them no heed as I slowly opened my lips and shakily began. "On the battlefield . . ." I paused, my hands shaking in my lap, but it was hard to control them as the memory of that day reentered my mind; as the thought of Eryx betraying my trust sprang back up.

A cool hand traced a circle down my wrist, before he wrapped his hand over mine, squeezing slightly, staying in place firmly around mine. I breathed in Kode's calming scent of blood orange and cedar.

"Take it slow," his voice rumbled behind me. "I'm here. I'm listening. Tell me everything."

I steadied my breath, relaxing as his thumb rubbed circles over my skin, before I began again. "Once I lost Dravyn, Eryx found me. We were surrounded by a group of gryffins, with no way of escaping. I was certain that's how I was going to die, when I was struck in the back of the head." I stopped, not wanting to say the next part, but forcing myself to anyway. They needed to know. They needed to know everything. "By Eryx," I murmured the name so quietly they may not have heard had they not had vampry hearing.

A sharp icy breeze whipped by as Kodrayn struggled to contain his anger at my words. Small icicles speared the trees around us. A sarcastic, hollow laugh fell from my lips. "Turns out, Eryx has been conspiring with the Nordak King since he was first enlisted into their army. He was placed as a spy at the château in Verastarr and slowly gained Sébastien's trust."

I continued my story as we rode. Pausing when I needed a moment's reprieve from the horrors of what I'd endured. Kodrayn's body behind mine offered the only reminder that I had indeed been rescued from that prison cell. "The creature," I continued. "I don't know what it is, but Dathrian created the beast through ancient magic. And once it's done attacking you physically . . . once it strikes and gets you into a vulnerable position, it takes your memories, but just those with happiness in them. Then it alters them to only feel hopeless, devoid of any joy. It all becomes a nightmare." The hollowness of my voice rang out as I finished sharing about the trials of battling the unknown creature, forcing myself not to think of the memories I'd lost, of the memories forever altered.

We fell into a silent rhythm and continued our trek through

the forest, everyone on alert, knowing that our absence would certainly be noticed by now. Soldiers would be on patrol for us— or more particularly, for me. *The Bearer of Sapphire Flame.*

"Why are we stopping?" I questioned as we slowed down near an inn on the outskirts of the forest we'd been traveling through. I took in the wooden structure, shaped almost like a glorified tree-house, with branches extending off the sides of the building and small wooden window sills hovering off the sides. It fit in with the forest, yet felt almost out of place at the same time.

"We'll be safe here for the night." Kodrayn's voice rumbled behind me from where I was nestled into his larger form.

"Here?" I questioned, looking at the inn in the middle of nowhere. "Truly?"

"Yes," he answered, dismounting and then assisting me down. A middle-aged woman bustled out of the inn, quickly beckoning us over.

"Come, come. No time to linger. We must be quick about it." She ushered us inside, the horses being taken from us as we entered the inn. I had no time to even take a look around before she was pushing us through the kitchen and a dusty pantry until she lifted a floor board and beckoned us to go through.

I hesitated briefly, as she spoke urgently, "On with it girl, we haven't got all day."

I stepped down into the darkness. Feeling along the wooden railing, I guided myself deeper down in the space, praying to The God above that this wasn't how I met my end.

A flame flickered in the distance and then came ablaze. It took all of my control not to shriek as I came face to face with another soldier. I drew my fist, prepared to defend myself when Kodrayn's voice rang out quietly, "Jace, my man, good to see you! Any news from Ryker yet?"

I studied the man more closely, his blond hair was cut short and he wore leathers with Kodrayn's emblem across them. I breathed a sigh of relief. The soldiers down here were Kodrayn's men. He hadn't come alone, he'd brought back up.

"Nothing new, Your Majesty." He nodded his head toward his king. "Had you been a day or two later, that may have been a different story. The men are getting a bit stir crazy." I looked past his shoulder, noting the six other men in this cramped underground space with him.

I turned toward Kodrayn. "Where are we? Why were we just rushed into an underground cellar?" My hands picked at the material on my leg, stress slowly rising in me at the trapped feeling I once again felt here. *I'd just escaped one prison cell, I was not about to be trapped in another.*

He must have felt the panic rising in me as he replied calmly, "We're fine, this is a safe house."

"A safe house?" I was shocked.

"Yes, the top portion of this inn is for Nordak soldiers and townspeople. But deep underground, we've had this safe house in effect for the past decade for any missions revolving around Kyllios." I was too stunned to speak. "We've had men stationed here while Everett and I entered the fortress to rescue you."

"Why?" I choked out.

"Ryker and the other fae could only fly so many of us to Kyllios without being detected. He's been waiting at the coast, a two-day ride from here. I placed men here at the safe house to make the journey to keep them updated."

I stared at the vampry, shocked by the amount of detail that was needed to go into freeing me—saving *me*.

"Go and rest with Soraya. We will be leaving shortly to head to the coast."

I nodded at his words as I walked over toward the only other female in the room and laid down on a worn mattress beside her. Exhaustion clung to my body as we laid next to each other, the sounds of each other's breathing lulling us to sleep while I prayed to The God that the nightmares from my time in Kyllios didn't come back to haunt me.

The sounds of hushed conversation drew me from my sleep, but I kept my eyes closed as I listened to the voices speaking.

"If what the innkeeper says is true . . ." Everett's voice stood out in the conversation. "We need to at least go and check it out."

"It could be a trap," another voice, Jace possibly, emphasized. "If the narelle flower is actually real, why would the Nordak King not already be in possession of it, or have killed off its existence?"

"Still, if it has the ability to ward against the Fantom, we are going to need all the help we can get," Everett said. *Fantom? Was that what the unknown beast was called? Had they learned more about it?* I wondered as I feigned sleep, letting out a deep sigh.

"It's a day's trek inland, and with all the patrols out searching for the girls, it's a high-risk journey if we go," Kodrayn voiced to the men with him. "But if what Sylvia says is true, and this narelle flower helps to prevent the effect of the Fantom for long enough to kill the beast before you succumb to its powers, it may very well be what we need to help win this war."

"And if it's all a lie to get us caught?" Jace interrupted.

"Then we have to be ready," Kodrayn demanded.

"Jace and I will go with you to the field." Everett spoke in commander mode. "The others can take Kateya and Soraya back to Ryker and we can meet them there in five days' time. That way they will know when to expect us."

The room went silent for a minute, presumably as the soldiers waited for final orders from their king.

"Anything you want to add, little venom? Or are you merely content to eavesdrop on yet another conversation of mine?" Kodrayn's voice rang out a bit louder than before and I froze at his words, my eyes snapping open in alarm as I met his amber ones.

"I . . . well, I . . ." I stuttered in response.

"You didn't mean to eavesdrop?" Kodrayn's gaze held mine, a flicker of amusement coursing through them at my slightly panicked state.

I took a deep breath and looked at him. "If you're going to go off in search of a mysterious flower that will potentially prevent the effects of *that creature*," I spat the word even as my voice trembled slightly, "then I'm coming with you."

His eyes widened, whether from shock or amusement, I wasn't sure.

"I'm coming with you, Kode. And you can't stop me." I paused, matching his gaze, glare for glare. "I was the one who had to endure weeks of torturous fights against the creature. I was trapped in a cell, at the mercy of Dathrian, *of Eryx*." My voice shook then, liquid welling in the corners of my eyes as I looked down to the ground, reminding myself I wasn't there anymore. "If there's any way to help prevent others from facing that same fate, from having to endure the fights during the festival, I want in. I can't—I won't let anyone else suffer like I had to; like everyone in those cells has been forced to. I need to *help*."

"No." His word cut in quickly, too quickly. As though he already knew what I would want to do and had decided I couldn't come. "I won't risk it, not with all of Nordak on the lookout for a vicious woman with silver streaked hair. Not after all you've endured; after everything they forced you to do." I caught the flicker of anger mixed with concern wash over his face as those amber orbs stared at me.

"It wasn't an option." I glared at Kodrayn, even as tears I could no longer hold in trailed down my face. "*I'm coming with you.*" I held his gaze, narrowing my eyes and his gold-flecked ones peered back at me, a hint of pride flickering through them.

I watched the vampry approach me, long legs carrying him over in a few steps as I stood up to meet him, determination set across my features, hands resting against my hips. I noticed his men in the background turning away, giving us privacy while we spoke, their distant chatter filling the air of the small room.

His eyes narrowed in on me one last time, assessing me, before he spoke. "Very well, you can come with." His lip curved in a smile that told me I wasn't going to like what he had to say next, so I didn't let him say it. I beat him at his own game . . . or at least, I tried to.

"It wasn't up to you to decide, *Kode*, but thank you all the same." I smiled sweetly at him.

"Ah . . . I wasn't finished, *little venom*." He smiled back at me and took another step closer. His hand drifted up, touching my forehead as he brushed a stray strand of hair out of my face, wrapping it carefully behind my ear.

I heard my own intake of breath at his action, the flutter of butterflies that dropped to my core. His fingers continued, trailing along my neck until they reached the tip of my chin, tilting it up to meet his gaze.

"You can come with me, but only if you allow me to heal you fully first. I'm not bringing you with us when you have injuries that could bring you further harm." His gaze trailed down to my wrists, where the still noticeable injuries and scars from the shackles remained.

I watched his other hand touch my wrist, and my body flinched, my reaction causing his eyes to turn molten, anger blazing across his features. But he kept his hand there, on my damaged wrist, calloused fingers slowly tracing circles across the raised flesh of my arm, as his eyes captured mine.

All at once he was leaning in, his gaze lowering to my lips, just briefly, and I found myself holding my breath, praying to The God that he would kiss me again. Wishing to feel his lips pressing over mine. Wondering what his fingers would feel like tracing circles over other parts of me.

Instead, I was met with his breath on my neck, causing me to shiver as it fanned over my skin. "I mean it, little venom. You're not going anywhere until you feed . . . *from me.*"

I held his gaze, staring him down, just to realize that he wasn't budging on this. "Fine," the word fell from my mouth in frustration and desire. I knew he was right. I knew anyone in their right mind wouldn't *willingly* journey further into enemy territory while still injured, but that didn't mean I had to *love* his vampry solution to my injuries. A solution which involved me *feeding* from him.

NORDAK

Chapter Twenty-Seven

WE ONLY STARTED SLOWING DOWN ONCE
Kodrayn was convinced that we were approaching the location
the innkeeper had provided. After traveling on foot since last
night, having left the horses hidden in a bouldered formation of
rocks to ensure we avoided unnecessary detection, my feet were
killing me, and I found myself wishing I hadn't agreed to go on
this journey with them. I knew I needed to do this for those after
me who would have to face the Fantom—as well as for me and all
I'd endured—but Void-damned my feet hurt.

Jace, who I'd learned was Everett's second-in-command, went
ahead of us, scouting the area in search of a field that would only
be visible at night's peak, until we finally stumbled across a small
clearing surrounded by trees. I wondered, as I stared at the clearing, how these flowers had begun to grow here, in this secluded
location, hidden from bypassing travelers. And still, I couldn't
shake the feeling that something didn't add up about these flowers,
nor the feeling that we were missing something very important in
the middle of this.

I stared in awe at the field as it took my breath away. How, in
the middle of this decaying land that would forever haunt my

nightmares, the most beautiful sight I'd ever seen managed to grow, I would never know.

I watched as the night breeze danced through the narelle flowers, their light purple blossoms dancing in the moonlight. Each flower bud had a soft glow around its petals, illuminating it as it radiated light in the darkness. They grew in little clusters scattered in the clearing of the trees.

A truly perfect location, hidden from the main paths, surrounded by tightly clustered trees, with only a small clearing to grow in, and only blooming at night.

"Wow," I murmured as we all came to a stop in front of the field, careful not to disturb the flowers. "They are . . . breathtaking." I couldn't help but stare at them in wonder.

"As are you, little venom." Kodrayn's voice was little more than a whisper from the left of me and heat bolted through me at the words. I ducked my head, dipping my eyes as heat fanned across my face from his comment, because there was no way he meant that. Not with how I looked after these past few weeks . . . not with all the scars that covered my skin; the lack of food and bathing I'd had.

I felt the heat of his body draw near, the scent of cedar before me, but didn't meet his eyes until his hand reached up, his thumb tilting my chin to meet his eyes. "I mean it, Kateya." His gaze pierced mine and I wished in that moment that we were alone, just the two of us, in this magical field. I wondered what the vampry king was capable of; if his hands, if other *parts* of him were just as skilled as his lips had been. My heart rate spiked and I noticed the moment his vampry senses detected the shift in my heartbeat, his eyes darkening as his fangs elongated ever so slightly.

But we weren't alone, and we had a task to accomplish before any Nordak got the chance to locate me.

I looked past the towering man in front of me, pushing down my desire and brought my focus back toward the field again. "So how are we to gather them?" I stepped back from Kodrayn as I finished my sentence, waiting for instructions.

"Sylvia said to harvest just the blossoms, leaving the flower stalks free to sprout new buds. Then to store them in these." Kodrayn lifted up his hand and revealed dark cloth bags. "Once harvested, she said they can't be exposed to sunlight, so we must keep them in the dark until we can prepare them for use."

"Is it that easy?" I questioned, sure there'd be a catch; something to trip us up. "Just harvest the flowers and store them in blackout bags?"

"So she claims," Kode answered. "We can each take a corner of the field. Fill your bag with as much as you can." He handed each of us a dark bag to collect the narelle buds.

Jace stepped forward, a motion of his hand for us to wait as he scanned the field. "I'll go first." He cautiously took one step forward, and another deeper into the clusters of flowers.

We waited, watching with bated breath to see if this was a trap, if Nordak forces would swarm forward as he walked through the clearing. He bent down, his hand reaching out as he grabbed one flower bud, his fingers closing around the node where the stem and bud met, and he pinched, the flower springing free. We watched as the flower fluttered up from his grasp, floating in the air as it spun in a circle, glimmering dust fluttering down to the ground around Jace as we all stared at the flower.

When the narelle appeared to still, hovering in the air above its stem, Jace tentatively reached out, plucking the silk flower out of the air and stashing it into the bag, securing it.

"All clear," his reply floated on the wind over to us.

"It seems too easy . . . too simple, does it not?" I whispered from the edge of the clearing.

"It does," Kode's reply came from beside me. "Let's be quick about it. We have no idea what will come from this."

So I moved, following Everett into the field, and carefully picked blossom after blossom, gently packing them into the bag on my side, praying to The God that this flower provided a solution

—some form of defense against the Fantom beast Dathrian had created out of ancient magic.

After collecting as many narelle flowers as the bags would hold, we returned to the boulder of rocks where we had hidden our horses in the early hours of the morning. With the knowledge that Nordak forces were sure to be searching the forests in hordes, we hurriedly packed up the campsite, carefully ensuring every bag of petals was tightly secured from the sun's touch.

"What did you do?" Kodrayn's voice cut in, distracting me as I secured the bag of flowers to the horse's satchel.

"What do you mean?" I looked up toward Kode as I finished tightening the straps and smiled at the look of concern across his features, wincing as a cut on my lower lip reopened and the taste of iron slowly seeped into my mouth as it bled.

"To your lip." He walked closer, his gaze narrowing in as he studied my lip, his eyes darkening as the scent of my blood lingered in the air between us.

"Oh," my cheeks flushed as I remembered the embarrassing incident I'd had early that morning. "I . . . um, well . . . forgot I had fangs." I laughed sheepishly. Being in vampry form constantly was normal enough until I did an everyday action like brush my hair behind my ears and my hand hit a pointed tip, or, in the case of today, bit too hard on a piece of bread and bit into my lip, effectively splitting it.

His hand reached out, cedarwood and blood orange wrapping over me in a cool chill while his thumb brushed against my tender lower lip, which was fully split. My breath stilled as he gently traced across my lip, my heartbeat pulsing at his touch. My body didn't move as he slowly wiped away the bleeding droplets of fresh blood that stained my lips. I flushed at the action, at the feel of the pad of his finger on my lip, at his finger now coated in a layer of my blood. Entranced, I helplessly watched as he raised his thumb to his lips, slowly putting his finger into his mouth, sucking it as he cleaned away my blood from his skin. *I couldn't breathe.*

Amber eyes captured mine as he withdrew his thumb, his fangs elongated from the taste of my blood on his lips. My breath hitched as he stared at me, his expression unreadable. And in that moment, I wanted nothing more than to feel his lips on mine, the weight of his body over me. I wanted *him.*

"You need to feed," Kodrayn murmured softly, breaking my trance as the thought of feeding sent a chilling spike of fear through me. I'd only fed twice before, and both times had been out of necessity due to my injuries. I'd fed just enough to heal my body but not a drop more.

"I'm not a full vampry you know," I quickly replied, my desire fully diminished at the thought. "I think I'll be fine." I'd been traveling in my vampry form since we'd arrived at the inn, in hopes that my scent would be masked by the presence of the other vamprys I was traveling with, and thus holding the Nordak at bay for as long as we possibly could.

"Using that much power every day is draining you," he answered in a nonnegotiable tone. "You haven't trained nearly long enough to hold a shifted form constantly without expelling a great deal of power and diminishing your supply. You will burn out if you don't replace the energy exerted, as any vampry would," he finished as he held out his forearm. I stared at the arm outstretched in front of me, admiring the swirled ink that crept up the side of his body, and the veins that snaked under his skin, pulsing as though they called to me.

"Fine," I sighed, knowing he was right. My strength had been fading quickly, and I struggled to remain in my vampry form everyday to help avoid detection. I could feel the well of power within me growing smaller each day we traveled, the blue fire still there, just fading, distant.

I stepped closer, inhaling the scent of cedarwood and blood orange, the scent of *him,* and letting it calm me as I closed my eyes, praying to The God that this time would be easier. I still struggled with the concept of biting into someone with my fangs to draw blood.

Kodrayn pulled me into his arms, holding me securely against his chest as he stretched one arm out again. Taking a deep breath, I tightened my grip on his arm, lowering my head until my fangs hovered just over his inked skin. I froze in place, relaxing slightly in his hold, in the support his body provided me, and stared at his veins pulsing.

"Any day, little venom," Kodrayn's voice purred from some-where above me, and I bit down, sinking my fangs into his fore-arm. The scent of his blood flooded my nostrils as I tentatively drew from him, warm liquid coating my mouth. I sputtered, once, twice, causing small droplets of blood, *his blood*, to fall onto his arm.

"That's it, little venom. Just like that." His voice rumbled over me as his blood hit my system, his energy and power washing over me.

I was lost. Lost in the feel of him, in the *taste* of him. It was like I was drowning and floating at the same time, my mind solely focused on him; on the way his blood, his power felt in me. My thoughts shifted to what he may feel like inside me in other ways. On what it would feel like to have him *in* me, moving in me, just as his blood was now.

I imagined him on top of me, his bare chest honed with chords of muscles pinning me down. His hands in my hair, on my arms, his body over me as he moved within me. Taking me. Claiming me. Making me his.

I felt hungrier, desire building in me as I drew from him. I moaned against his arm as I continued to feed from him. My body drew closer to him, grinding up against him as the feel of his blood strengthened me, driving me higher. I could feel every sensation, every movement of his hands over my back as I fed from him. My body tightened with raw need as I felt him harden against my back, his thick length present as my skin tingled with the overflowing desire coursing through me, for him. I couldn't get enough. I couldn't get—

I felt my head be pulled back by a firm hold.

"That's enough," the soft growl sounded distantly from above me.

"No," I sputtered as my fangs dislodged and I raised my head in confusion, in protest. Warm liquid dripped from my fangs as my brain began to clear and the feeling of pulsing need ebbed.

I stared at the man in front of me, at the restraint evident across his face as need, embarrassment, and pleasure washed over me in waves.

"What the *fuck* was that?" I asked when I could finally articulate a sentence.

"That was the feeling of bloodlust," Kode answered as his arm began to heal over, the fang marks fading before my eyes.

"That didn't feel like bloodlust, that felt like—" I trailed off, unwilling to voice the intensity of the feelings that had been coursing through me.

"Like you couldn't get enough?" He questioned, his voice darkening. "Like you wanted nothing more than to give in to your impulses—to be consumed, controlled, and devoured the way you deserve to be."

Heat flooded my cheeks as my breath caught in my lungs and I stared weakly at the man before me, the man voicing every urge I had felt just moments before.

"Well?" he questioned.

I swallowed, my face burning as I nodded in response. "Yes, it felt just like that."

"It's quite normal among vamprys, especially those not as experienced in feeding, and those feeding from other vamprys."

"How come you didn't—how come we didn't—" I stumbled over my words as I stared at the vampry before me.

"Because, *Kateya*," his voice wrapped around me, his eyes darkened, and his fangs lengthened slightly. "When I act on those *urges*, it won't be because of a bloodlust induced desire. It will be because you want me to consume every part of you until you can think of nothing but your need for me."

I froze, speechless as he smirked at me while I processed his words.

After time seemed to stretch on for eternity, words finally flowed through my lips. "That's never happened to me before," I replied, my body still high on him.

"The only other times you've fed, you were gravely injured. Your healing instincts took over, ensuring the energy gained went straight to repair your body, your injuries." Amber orbs held me as I processed.

"And this time?"

"This time you were replacing energy spent. Your body didn't need to heal any major injuries," he finished as he began to finish preparing the horses, leaving me to come down from my feeding frenzy.

NORDAK

Chapter Twenty-Eight

I NEARLY CRIED at the sight of the inn when it finally popped into view. I'd spent all day pressed up against Kodrayn as we rode back to the inn, dying of embarrassment. My mind kept replaying this morning, the feel of his blood coursing through me, the thoughts of his body on mine, *in mine*. My body grinding up against him as I was overcome by bloodlust. My heart rate spiked every time the thoughts reentered my mind, causing Kodrayn to tense behind me, noting the shift in my pulse each time my mind strayed to thoughts of him.

Thankfully we'd made it back, dismounting before we walked through the gate. Or at least, we'd made it back to somewhere I could safely rest for the night. As we walked undetected through the gate leading to the main entrance, my eyes caught Kodrayn's before trailing down to his lush lips, and for a brief moment my thoughts flickered back to this morning; to the feel of his fingers across my lip and I nearly moaned aloud.

He approached me, stopping just inches from my body. A cool breeze floated across my skin as he reached up and pulled the hood of my cloak further down my face, ensuring my hair and features were covered before we entered the inn.

"I see your journey went smoothly." Sylvia greeted us as we walked through the door to her inn.

"Indeed." Kodrayn's answer was short and to the point, not wanting to risk any ears listening in. "We'll take two rooms and a hot meal."

I watched as both Everett and Jace monitored the few guests at the inn, most already halfway to a drunken stupor judging by the time of night.

"I'm afraid I only have one room and a cot available at the moment," she answered, an underlying tone of warning in her voice.

What about the underground cellar? I wanted to ask, but kept my mouth shut as Kodrayn looked between the two other men and answered.

"Very well, Jace here will take the open cot," was his only reply as he waited for Sylvia to lead the way. I followed, squished between Everett and Kodrayn as we made our way through the space.

This was the first time I'd seen the inside of the inn, and I took in the half-crowded bar tables, as well as the smell of warm bread and stale beer wafting through the space. The dusty wood planks underneath our feet creaked as we walked by, yet hardly drew a glance.

We followed Sylvia up a short set of steps, on to the second level of the inn, then down a long winding hallway. At the end of the long hall, we came to a stop by the last door. I watched carefully, shoulders still tense, braced for a fight as the middle-aged woman opened the door to a cramped room with a singular cot and small wash basin in it and gestured for us all to go in.

Wait, what? I felt as though I was certainly missing something as Kodrayn, then Jace stepped into the room. Everett nudged me from behind, and, with a confused look, I stepped through the doorway, half-expecting magic to take over and miraculously enlarge the room we found ourselves in.

The wooden door screeched and I heard the lock click shut.

Kodrayn and Everett moved once Jace ensured the door was secure.

"What—" I started but I felt Jace's hand wrap around my mouth, effectively shutting me up. My eyes bulged as I looked between the three men, wondering what the *hell* was happening.

I watched as Everett walked around the outskirts of the room, hands moving subtly at his side. That's when I noticed a layer of air lining the room, trapping us within it. When Jace finally removed his hand from my mouth, I inhaled deeply before glaring at each of the men. "What in the Void-damned hell is going on?"

"Watch that pretty little tongue of yours, little venom." Kode drawled as he leaned against a wooden wall. "All secure?" he questioned with a swivel of his head to his second-in-command.

"We're good, for now," Everett answered.

"For the love of—" Kodrayn glared at me briefly as I spoke. "What is going on?"

"If you had a bit more patience, Kateya," he purred my name as he spoke, "I would have explained. Inn accommodations vary depending on the time of day one arrives. If there are no people currently in the inn, you will be ushered to the safe house underground. However, if there *are* other guests residing in the inn. This last room here has been secured as an additional safe house room," he informed me.

"And we are *all* sleeping in this small space?" I questioned, gesturing to the room that was barely the size of a bathroom back home.

Everett moved to the far side of the small room, before he pressed a small notch on the wood paneling and a soft spring moved. I stared in shock as a door pulled open, leading to a small set of steps. With a grand gesture of his hands, Everett indicated teasingly, "After you, *milady*."

Hesitantly, I walked toward the door, following the short series of steps upward into a larger room with two beds in it. Because why wouldn't there be a secret room in the inn in the middle of Nordak territory. A dry laugh nearly fell from my lips at the thought. I spun on my heel, looking at the two men who'd followed me up the steps to the room.

"And where will you both be sleeping?" I smiled ever so sweetly toward the men as I plopped myself unceremoniously onto the larger of the beds.

"Don't think too highly of yourself there, Silver." Everett laughed as he turned to head back down to the smaller of the rooms.

I took in the small wash basin in the corner, the two beds with faded quilted mattresses atop them, and the wooden windowsill close to the larger bed.

Turning to Kodrayn I questioned, "Do you mind if I have a few minutes to wash up?"

"Just don't take as long as you did in Arceyla." His low voice wrapped across the room as he turned to head down the stairs.

Turning on the faucet, I let cool water stream onto my hands, taking in a deep breath for the first time in weeks.

I laughed softly at the table, surrounded by Kodrayn, Everett, and Jace as we enjoyed a round of drinks. While all three men were still alert, it felt nice—normal—to do something as simple as have a beer with them. And I couldn't help myself from wondering what it would be like, if we weren't in the middle of ongoing wars and this was just an everyday occurrence, what it might feel like to just be normal for once . . .

The warm liquid ran down my throat with a slight burn, the drink far stronger than any I'd had back home at the clubs with Aerilyn. Everett laughed beside me as the three men chatted.

"Another round?" Jace questioned as he stood to head to the counter by the kitchen bar. Everett nodded from beside me in agreement.

"I think I will head up." I smiled apologetically toward the men as I stood, saying goodnight, my head already slightly abuzz from the beer I'd had. Weaving my way through the crowd, I made it to the stairs when I noticed his presence behind me.

"I think I can make it to the room on my own, Kode. You don't need to follow me," I murmured to the towering figure behind me.

"Last time I let you out of my sight . . ." He didn't finish the statement as he followed me up the stairs.

"You know," I drawled, as I turned the handle to the first room. "Following me up here might give people the wrong idea." My cheeks heated slightly, knowing I was playing with fire as I walked through the door.

Kodrayn surveyed the room, before securing the door behind us. "And who's to say I want to give people the right idea, little venom?"

I froze, heart pounding in my chest and turned to stare at the man in front of me. I watched as Kodrayn's form moved closer, and my heart skipped a beat as I took in the towering man before me. I admired the muscles that rippled beneath his fitted shirt, and the way his eyes darkened as they skimmed over every curve of my body; the cedarwood and blood orange scent that enveloped me every time he drew near.

He was suddenly in my space, his breath hot around my neck as he nudged me forward, through the small door that led toward the upper bedroom. My body came alive under the touch of his fingers, splayed across my skin as we made our way up the stairs. We barely made it up all the steps before he turned me, pressing my back against the wall and his hands started roaming over my skin.

My pulse quickened, desire pooling as he touched my hips, his grip firm, controlling. Then he trailed his hands up my sides, taking in every inch of me. Without warning his lips were on mine, capturing them, commanding my attention as he pried them apart. I kissed him back with equal passion, my tongue prodding against his lips, demanding entrance, which he gladly provided, letting me explore the insides of his mouth as his hands explored every curve of my body.

I moaned into his mouth as his hand traced under my breast, firmly squeezing as he took control of the kiss, probing my lips to open further for him, to let him in fully. Heat built in my core as we moved closer toward the bed, bumping into a table, then hitting the windowsill. His hands wrapped firmly around my hips, lifting me up as I propped myself against the edge of the windowsill—cool night air hitting my back as his hand shifted.

Kodrayn paused briefly, lifting the hem of his shirt with his arm to remove it in one motion. My heart froze as I stared at the masterpiece that was Kodrayn. Rigid muscles honed by years of training lined his chest, mixed with the swirled ink of his tattoo across his left pec, drifting down his arm.

He closed the space between us once more, his left hand tangling in my hair as he tilted my lips up to collide with his. My legs wrapped around his torso involuntarily, as I held myself closer to him. I *needed* to feel him, the cool touch of his skin mixing with the fiery touch of mine. Another jolt of need coursed through my body, and I kissed him recklessly, without a care in the realm as I got lost in the feel of his hands across my skin.

His lips trailed down my cheek, pressing fevered kisses down the line of my jaw, drifting slowly toward the column of my neck. Each kiss caused my body to shudder beneath his touch, coming alive for him. He paused, licking a slow trail with his tongue back up my neck, my body shuddering under his touch before dark gold hungry eyes met mine. "Do you trust me, little venom?" His voice, low and husky wrapped around me. He'd asked me this once before, and I hadn't answered him, but this time, I did.

"Yes," the word fell from my lips breathlessly as I held his gaze, fully trusting, *falling* for the man before me. "With everything in me."

My body tensed slightly as I caught sight not just of his grin, which was slow and seductive, but of his fangs. They had grown longer as he ran his tongue across them, an action I noticed he did for me to show me he meant no harm.

"Kode," his name fell from my lips, a plea, a need, as I stared at him, at his fangs, my heart beating for him.

His hand tilted my neck back slowly as he placed one, two, three kisses before he sucked the skin of my neck, drawing a low moan from me.

"So fucking sweet, little venom," he murmured against my neck as I moved my hips, struggling to get closer to him, to feel his hands roam over every inch of my body. "Breathe for me," the words were hardly out of his mouth before he struck.

I felt his fangs pierce the side of my neck, sinking into my flesh as I cried out. Arctic ice collided with fiery flames as he sucked, drawing from me. He may have been ice, but I was fire. And together—*together*—the inferno of flames racing within me combusted. My body writhed under his attention as his hand traced circles around my hip and pleasure flowed through my body. I moaned, squirming against his skin as he continued to draw from me.

"More," I whimpered against him, the collision of fire and ice building as he left his mark on me, his fangs still deep in me.

I felt the material of my pants give as they sprung free, night air brushing across my heated skin as a lust-induced haze built around me. Kodrayn lifted his gaze, feral eyes meeting mine as blood dripped from his fangs. *Blood. My blood.*

His eyes held mine as he asked a silent question, his finger tracing circles across my inner thigh as he did so. With a nod of my head, his fingers swept across my center, a jolt of icy electricity coursing over me and low moans from both of us filled the air.

His fingers traced over me, building the intensity as our tongues collided once more in a dance of power and need. I drank him in, getting lost in the cedar and orange scent that clung around us. His fingers circled my center building me higher and higher, the pressure building until I couldn't take it anymore.

"Kode," I breathed his name once more, a cry, a demand, and

he met it. His eyes were dark and hungry as he held my gaze. He struck once more, thrusting his fingers in at the same time his fangs struck that sweet spot on my neck. I screamed my release, losing myself to him as the realm shattered around me. Tiny embers danced in the air around us as I lost control of my magic, my senses, myself.

I barely recognized he was moving, carrying me carefully to the bed. My mind buzzed in a satisfied state.

The door creaked open a few moments later and a voice carried over the room. "Void-be-damned," was all the voice murmured at first. "At least tell me the two of you are dressed if I have to share a room with you." Everett's pleading tone sounded as he entered the room.

My head shot up and embarrassment radiated from me as I glanced between him and Kodrayn. "We didn't, well . . ." I stuttered looking between Everett and Kodrayn, both of whom had amused looks on their faces as I floundered with my words trying to make my point.

"You didn't *what*?" Everett answered as I looked to Kodrayn for help.

"Yes, little venom." Kode laughed at my embarrassment. "What *didn't* we do?"

"Oh fuck off," I groaned as they laughed at my expense. "I'm keeping the bigger bed." I smiled, satisfied with myself as I sprawled out on the bed closest to the window. "You two will have to share." I rolled to my side, shutting my eyes as I tried to block out the two men only feet from me.

"We'll see about that," was Kodrayn's only reply as the mattress dipped beside me.

"There is no 'we'll see about that,'" I muttered from my side. The light flickered from the table and then switched off, leaving me in the dark with the two vamprys.

I stared at the ceiling for a long moment, trying to fall asleep, the knowledge that they were both in the same room as me, and Kode in the same *bed* as me, was new. I laid beside Kode, my heart rate beating quicker as we lay next to each other, doing our best not to touch, especially with Everett in the next bed.

We'd slept near each other in campsites many times, but never in the same room, much less the same bed. Right after . . . after we . . . after he ruined me for any other man with how good it felt when he touched me; when his fingers traced across my skin; when his fingers thrust into me. My pulse rose as my fingers drifted up to my neck, still tender from the mark left just moments earlier, and reveled in the feel of pure bliss it had created.

My thoughts drifted as I envisioned what would have happened if Everett hadn't returned to the room. I pictured him throwing me onto the bed, caging me underneath him as he trailed kisses down my writhing body, fangs nibbling across exposed flesh. His fingers kneading the soft skin of my breasts before tracing lower. A breathy moan nearly escaped my lips when I envisioned him slipping his fingers through my waistband, fingers grazing—

"Void-damned, little venom . . ." Kode cursed from beside me. "Whatever you're thinking about, *just stop*." His growl came as his arm wrapped firmly around me, tugging me against his bare chest, surrounding me with his warmth as I drifted to sleep.

NORDAK

Chapter Twenty-Nine

THE POUNDING INCREASED in my dream, over and over until I awoke with a start, realizing that the sound was actually coming from downstairs. Bolting upright, I looked around only to notice that Kodrayn was already moving down the stairs and Everett was quick on his heels.

"What's going——" I stopped at the silencing look Everett gave me as he headed down the stairs. Grabbing my weapon, I quietly followed after the men, stopping on the bottom step as I listened to the hushed whispers coming from Jace at the door.

"Leave . . . now . . . Nordak guards . . . ten minutes . . ."

I caught snippets of the conversation and quickly rushed back upstairs to pack up the meager belongings we had with us.

Someone had spotted us and knew our location.

I grabbed the few spare outfits we had, shoving them into cloth bags and safely secured the dark bags filled with narelle flowers, ensuring they were hidden from view. As I rushed about the room, collecting our weapons, I caught a glimpse of myself in the mirror and froze.

My brownish-blonde hair, framed with silver, vibrantly glowed in the candle light. But what caught my attention was the mark across my neck. A dark red bite mark with two prominent fang markings at the top marred my lower neck. I raised my finger, running my hand over the injury Kode had inflicted in our moment of passion when I stopped, drawing closer to the mirror.

I'd expected my skin to feel raw and irritated around the mark, yet my neck was smooth, as though there was no injury at all. When I looked into the mirror, *it was there*. I could see it clear as day: a bite mark.

"Silver, we need to go." Everett's voice sounded from the stairs and I turned from the mirror. I'd worry about the mark later. For now, I grabbed our belongings and darted down the stairs after the men.

"Where are we going?" I looked toward Kodrayn, his eyes widening in primal satisfaction as he skimmed over my neck before he answered.

"We've been located. We'll get an early start on our travel plans, but will have to go a different route back to where Ryker is meeting us."

I nodded as we began to sneak out of the room, down the back doorway of the inn. Carefully heading down the steps, we ensured that our footsteps were near silent until the cool night air touched our skin as we exited the inn. Moonlight glowed across the forest as we swiftly began moving through the trees. I drew on my vampry speed to match the pace and sprinted through the forest in silent steps.

I watched as the outlines of trees blurred by while we ran. I'd rarely run utilizing my vampry abilities, yet every time I did, I was in awe at the agility and speed that came from the shift. My legs hardly burned as I pushed them to lengthen my strides, easily doubling my normal stride as we moved through the forest. With fae-like hearing, vamprys had the ability to hear far more than the average mortal, picking up noises far in the distance. It still surprised me, each time I shifted, the differences in senses and how much more heightened they were.

We pushed on through the forest, narrowly avoiding fallen limbs and rocky clusters, until even in vampry form, my legs were protesting each movement and my lungs were screaming for air. Pausing for a brief break, I leaned against a withered tree, head between my knees as I held in the vomit threatening to spew forward, knowing that even my vomit would be a trail for the Nordak hunting us to follow.

"How . . ." I gasped for breath. "Much . . . further?" The words fell from my mouth in a pant.

"A few more miles and we should be able to rest for awhile," Everett panted beside me.

"The majority of the search parties will be out in the daylight since Kateya's been spotted. We'll need to keep low and travel at night," Kodrayn added, his breath barely strained as he spoke.

"How are you not . . ." I panted looking at Kodrayn. "Out of breath," I finished, still wheezing.

He shot a devilish smirk my way as he responded, his tone teasing, "You'll find my stamina is quite impressive."

"Too bad I haven't had the chance to experience it yet," I quipped back. "Not sure if I actually believe you."

He was there in an instant, his towering form encroaching on my space as his voice dropped low. "Soon, little venom. And once you do, I guarantee you won't be making jokes anymore."

I didn't answer, couldn't answer, as we began moving again, racing through the forest at a speed I'd never dreamed I'd be able to match.

I collapsed into the cave unceremoniously, my legs quite literally giving out as I lay down on the ground, immobile.

"I don't think we train her hard enough," Everett said with a low laugh to Kodrayn while I gasped on the ground like a fish out of water.

"I—I train—" I couldn't even finish the sentence as I lay on the cool rocky surface, letting the stone lower my body's temperature. I didn't move until the men had set up camp for the day, and we could watch the early dawn light peek through the cracks of the small cave.

The space was cramped, with hardly enough leg room for the four of us inside, and not quite high enough for Kodrayn to stand at full height. The cave sheltered us well from the outside realm though, blocking out the sounds of any creatures in the distance and keeping our whispers trapped within.

"We'll pack up at dusk and head east once the sun's down," Kodrayn informed our small group. "With any luck, they'll have less patrols out in the dark so we should be able to move with less cover."

"Wouldn't the gryffins be able to spot us from the sky?" I questioned, feeling like this was an obvious concern we should be factoring.

"No," Everett replied with a slight laugh.

"Gryffins are known to have poor night vision, meaning the majority of their night patrols are in mortal form on foot, which is in our favor," Kodrayn added.

"That's quite fortunate for us." I grinned.

"Every power has a weakness," Kodrayn responded. "All magic needs to maintain a balance."

"Right," I murmured. "Cass always talked about how she was told all magic demanded balance." I paused for a moment, thinking about it before asking, "What's a vampry's weakness? I mean . . . you can run faster, see clearer; your hearing is far better, you have fangs, and can heal others with your blood. I don't see a weakness there?"

Amber eyes watched mine for a second, before he answered. "Our weakness is also our strength . . . *blood*."

"Blood?" I questioned, unsure how that was a weakness.

"Where other powers are weakened and restored merely through sleep, we need to feed in addition to resting. When in battle, or on journeys, we must ensure that we have viable options for feeding. Some lands, such as Nordak, even go so far as to poison the blood of their people to prevent the vamprys from feeding."

I fell silent, contemplating his answer for a while. "What about me?"

"What about you?"

"Well." I hesitated briefly, collecting my thoughts before I decided to continue. "If I can shift into a vampry, wolvyn, syren, and fae, and I have elemental magic as well, what's my weakness? Or do I have multiple weaknesses? I'm not a full-fledged vampry, so I don't have to feed."

Kodrayn and Everett both remained silent, looking at each other, and back at me.

"You know, don't you?" I replied.

"We've been attempting to discover the same thing with your sister. We knew there had to be a weakness, but we weren't sure what it was. That is, until you ran into the Unseen."

My mind drifted back to that night in the Krymson Forest and my conversation with the Unseen. "You think that the additional artifact she mentioned ties into our weakness," I realized as I stared at them.

"Yes," Kodrayn replied, "we do. Whatever Emalyee discovers, we think it has the ability to destroy you and your sister."

I fell silent, listening to the light breeze cut through the cracks in the rock while I processed their words. After a few minutes of silence, I spoke again and began to stand. "I need to go . . . um, you know." I gestured awkwardly toward the forest.

Jace stood across from me. "I'll go with."

"I don't need someone to accompany me, you know." I looked between him and Kode.

"He'll go with," Kodrayn growled toward me. My mouth drew into a tight line, but I didn't argue. Turning toward the entrance, I carefully walked outside, Jace right behind me as we trekked through the forest.

I stepped carefully over fallen limbs and brushes, avoiding the thorn-filled patches of ground as I moved further from the cave, toward a well-hidden area of privacy.

"Just, um . . ." I looked behind me, at Jace. "Wait over there, I guess. I'd like a bit of privacy. Maybe try to not . . . well . . . to listen. I don't know what it's like with vampry hearing and—"

"I get it," Jace cut in, saving me from my rambling. "I'll be over here. Close enough, but far enough for some privacy."

"Thanks," I replied through a tight smile.

I walked away from him, ensuring I had enough privacy. Once I was done, I walked a few steps further, dipping my hands into the creek that I'd located and washing some water over my face and hands. The cool water felt fresh and cleansing on my hands and face as I cleaned the grime from traveling through the forest.

I was nearly done when a familiar voice halted me in my tracks, and terror coursed through me. "That bitch will get what she deserves once I get my hands on her again," the voice growled in my ear. I whipped around, hand on my dagger as I looked for the man that haunted my nightmares. And yet, I saw nothing out of the ordinary. Absolutely nothing.

Jace stood a good distance away, with his back turned, but body rigid as though on guard. I began to relax, hurriedly finishing drying my face as I stood and blended in with the forest around me, when I heard it again. "The things we have planned . . . we will be unstoppable." My heart stopped, and I knew I wasn't imagining things, somewhere, somehow, Eryx was here.

Fear and dread coursed through my body as I stealthily began moving back toward Jace, careful not to make a noise. *Eryx is here. Eryx. Is. Here.* The words ran over and over in my mind as fear took hold of my body.

I felt a cool, icy tug in my soul and all of the sudden, another voice cut through my mind, growling in response to my thoughts. *What do you mean, Eryx is here?*

I nearly shrieked aloud at the low question coming from my mind from yet another voice I recognized.

What in the Void-damned . . . how the hell am I hearing your voice right now? I responded in my mind.

The question, little venom, his voice demanded of me. *What. Do. You. Mean. Eryx is here?*

Is this some vampry trick? Some power you have? I was confused about how I could hear him in my mind.

Kateya, Kodrayn's voice growled into my mind, sending shivers across my body. *What do you mean?*

I heard the voice again, closer to the wind and started moving closer to Jace. *He's here. I can hear him. I don't know where, but somehow he's here.*

"Jace," I whispered as quietly as I could. I watched the vampry turn toward me at my whisper, and I watched as his eyes widened in pure terror as his hand flew toward his blade. I watched as he gripped the weapon, screaming at me to run.

Out of nowhere, my realm fell dark as purple mist surrounded me. And this time, a new memory sprung up; a memory of me at a tavern table with Kodrayn, Everett, and Jace. A memory of us laughing and joking as we shared beers and swapped stories. All of a sudden, the memory altered, purple mist weaved itself through the memory, ripping the happiness to shreds as joy and laughter was replaced with horrified terror. As Seefers barged into the inn and began wreaking havoc on the guests. A scream ripped through me as I tried and failed to hold on to the happiness of the memory, to keep the joy alive as the Fantom pried it from my grasp. I heard a panicked growl in my mind. The sound of my name being roared by Kodrayn. Except all I knew was hurt.

NORDAK

Chapter Thirty

THE WIND WHIPPED through my hair at a terrifying speed as I came to, panic rising in me as I struggled to move and realized that I was once again in chains. Twisting my hands and legs, I realized I couldn't move any part of my body more than an inch in any direction. I couldn't be captured again. I couldn't endure one more day in Kyllios. This *couldn't* be happening to me.

I thrashed, screaming and yelling as I struggled to break free, but the caw of the gyrffin holding me only seemed like a laugh as it took me with it, higher in the sky. Further away from land. *From Kode.*

I fought harder, yanking at the metal grating against my flesh as I struggled to free myself. Left, right, left, right. I shifted back and forth, attempting to break free. My screams refused to relent as I jerked myself around, ignoring the wind biting against my skin as we cut through the clouds.

After a series of sharp twists, an angered caw sounded from above me and I felt the talons holding me firmly in place release their grip. Suddenly, I was plummeting through the air, falling swiftly toward the rocky terrain below me. Wind whistled by me as I fell, fast and deadly. My scream reached a new level of terror as I realized I was plummeting toward my immediate death.

I passed gray clouds as I hurtled through the air, unable to shift with the amount of chains surrounding my body. I was unable to break my fall, unable to save myself. Panic rose to a new level, my hoarse screams falling empty of the wind as I dropped.

Kateya, the voice cut through my mind like an arctic breeze just as sharp talons wrapped sharply around me, digging into my skin as my plummet to death ended abruptly. My body jerked to a painful halt and I found myself, once again, in my captor's grasp.

Kateya, the voice in my head growled again, edged with panic, and my heart calmed a beat. Just one, but enough for me to focus on the cool thread of ice within me, wrapped around the flaming ember in my soul.

Kode? I questioned back in my mind, testing to see if I could truly hear him. Talk to him.

Did that Nordak piece of—

I didn't let him finish.

I'm not injured, at least I don't think I am. I felt a rush of winter air wrap around me internally at my words.

Do you know where you are?

I looked around, taking in the rocky, gray terrain filled with a mix of leafless trees. I could scc the lifeless coast of the Sea of Avyz to my left.

Not yet, I responded. *I'll keep watching until I can give you a reference.* I swallowed as the wind continued beating against my face, the chill from the altitude causing me to shiver continually. *Until I find a reference point, you owe me an explanation. How can I hear you in my mind? Can all vamprys do this?* I asked the questions, needing something to take my mind off the fact I'd been recaptured, at least until I could figure out how to free myself once again.

Kodrayn was silent and worry rose within me.

Kode? I tried again.

Remember how you said you trusted me? he asked and wariness rose within me.

Yeah? I questioned back, not sure I was going to like the answer he gave me.

Not all vamprys can speak through their minds, only bonded vamprys have the ability to speak to each other.

Bonded? I nearly screeched back. *We aren't bonded. I've literally only known you for like . . .* I paused to do the math, unsure exactly how much time had passed. *Not even two months?* I thought back on his words from a moment ago. *Wait. Did I miss something? What does this have to do with trust?*

Kodrayn remained silent for a minute, and I felt the anxiety rising in me as I waited for his reply. Finally, he spoke. *Every land has mates. However, each land mates in a different way. In some lands, bonded mates are a stroke of destiny, a path offered. For your sister, wolvyn mate through three phases that ultimately results in them forming a mated bond. In other lands, such as Avyon, bonds are formed. They are a choice, a decision two vamprys make to become bonded to each other. But once the choice is cemented, it's irreversible.*

How? I asked through the bond.

The reason vamprys rarely, if ever, choose to feed from other vamprys is because the beginnings of a bond can be formed once they've both exchanged blood with each other from a feeding.

But we've never—

I stopped, not finishing the sentence as my mind processed back to the other day. I'd fed from Kodrayn the other morning before we made it back to the inn, and that same morning, my lip had been cut. He'd wiped the blood from my lip, and brought his finger to his mouth, cleaning it in front of me. My mind shifted to later that day, to when he'd fully fed from me in the bedroom at the inn that night. *Okay, so we've exchanged blood,* I finished.

A bond can be formed within a twenty-four-hour window of the blood being in both vamprys' systems. Once it's in your system, all it takes is for a vampry male to initiate a claiming mark on the female. Before I could speak, an image flashed across my mind, but from Kodrayn's perspective. I watched as he asked, "Do you trust me?" and I saw myself nodding that I did, telling him I did with everything in me. I watched my body press against his as he licked up my neck, I saw his fangs elongate fully, biting down into my neck. Warm heat rushed through my body, my core tightening at the memory as I watched the scene replay in my mind until it ended.

You mean that you biting me initiated a bond between us? I questioned.

Me biting you the second time as you came apart on me initiated the bond, yes, the heated growl came from my mind, as though he too was affected by the scene that had played out in front of us. *If you noticed, the marking on your neck is fully healed, layers under your skin.*

I paused thinking back to when we'd urgently been packing our belongings at the inn, remembering how I'd stopped in the mirror, staring at the marking but when I touched it, my skin had been smooth.

The wind chilled briefly, and the gryffin holding me darted downward at a swift angle as it flew past the cold pocket of air, my stomach lurching before its wings evened out.

What the absolute fuck were you thinking? I snarled down the bond toward Kode. *You seriously thought unknowingly bonding with me was an okay idea to run with? I know you're a king and all, but seriously, Kode? Why did you bond with me?*

I was thinking, he snarled back, *that we were in the middle of enemy territory and should anything go wrong, we'd have a way to communicate with each other—a way for me to protect you. Don't worry.* He paused. *The bond hasn't been fully formed yet. You can break it once we're back in Avyon if that's what you wish.*

What do you mean it hasn't been fully formed? Confusion laced my thoughts as I asked the question.

Our bond is there, present and intact, but it's not at its full strength, he shared. *And it never will be unless I claim you in every way. Making you mine fully. Claiming your body and soul, just as you would claim mine.*

My body heated at the thought, at what it would be like for him to claim me, even as a pang of remorse flooded through me as I thought about his words. He'd bonded with me, for my protection. To give me a way to communicate with an ally in a war.

Now, the growl reverberated in my mind, *you need to do everything*

in your power to ensure that Eryx and Dathrian remain unaware that you are
bonded. If they find out, they will try to dampen the bond at your expense.

Eryx brought me right back to Kyllios, the ominous gray walls as threatening as ever, and dragged me before Dathrian once again. Only this time, the look of wicked fury on the Nordak king's face was enough to terrify me more than ever before. Enough to make me wish that I had indeed plummeted to my death on the flight back to Kyllios.

"Thought you could get away, did you?" Dathrian sneered as he towered over me, his presence alone darkening the throne room. I didn't speak. I refused to answer him, to give away my dignity by responding to him.

"Answer me!" he roared as his fist struck my cheek, his ring colliding with bone and my head snapped to the side as pain lanced across my face. I smelled the copper scent of my own blood before I felt the cut that appeared across my face.

When I refused to answer, Dathrian stepped closer, his form towering over me as he peered down at me, a black taloned hand tilting my neck up, forcing me to meet his gaze. I watched his eyes narrow in, focusing on my neck, and I froze.

Kode. The panic laced through my tone as I sent his name down the bond. *He's spotted the mark.*

Who's he? Kodrayn's voice flowed across my mind with a commanding reassurance only he could muster. Only I couldn't answer, not yet.

"Well, well." Dathrian snarled as his finger traced over the mark on my neck, taloned nails digging deep into it. "Looks like someone had a little bit of fun on her adventure outside the gates, didn't you?"

Fury blazed in my eyes as I met his gaze. "So what if I did?" I sneered back. Dathrian turned his head toward a guard and I took the moment to mutter, *Dathrian.*

Void-be-damned. Whatever you do, he can't know that you're bonded to me. We'll force him to think that it's someone else.

"Bring in Caaz," the king's command echoed across the walls as a soldier marched off to obey the orders.

A towering figure entered the room minutes later, as the guard behind me shoved me to my knees. Blonde hair was braided down the center of an otherwise shaved skull. Black inkings decorated the sides of his scalp, creeping onto his face in a similar style to Eryx's own tattoos. Hawk-like eyes surveilled me while he approached, stopping before me and his king.

"Your Highness," the man, Caaz, inclined his head in deference to the Nordak king.

"Let me introduce you to Kateya Dumont, sister to Cassandra Capetian and wielder of the second artifact's powers." Dathrian said.

Dark eyes whipped to mine and I realized that this man had a vendetta against me or Cass.

"Find out who she's bonded to." Dathrian looked me over before continuing. "By any means necessary."

The grin on Caaz's face grew as he studied me from head to toe. "I believe, your sister had the pleasure of acquainting herself with my brother, Luk Eldritch, before her *mate* ended his life."

Oh shit. Oh shit. Oh shit, I murmured to myself, internally panicking. *This is not good.*

What is it? Kodrayn growled into my mind and I realized I had no idea how to shut off this bond. How to shut him out of everything I thought or felt.

Caaz Eldritch. He knows Cass, or at least—

His brother did, Kodrayn finished. *Luk was the one who captured and tortured your sister when you were first here. He's going to try to pry into your mind and see. We need to paint him a picture of what we want him to see. Do you trust me?*

Yes, I replied, knowing that I did fully trust him, even though he formed the bond without my knowledge. I trusted Kode with every fiber of my being. I felt a chilled breeze whip across my mind just as Caaz turned his full attention on me and struck hard. An invisible blast struck my skull, a scream slipping from my lips as a fiery jolt of pain ripped into me. I struggled to breathe as I felt the clack of claws against my skull, searching, prying, hoping for an entrance into my thoughts, my memories.

The claws raked across my mind, the agony causing me to cry out once more, tears streaming down my face as Caaz searched and pried for any crack. I felt the chilled breeze of Kodrayn's powers barricading my thoughts and protecting my memories.

Hang on just a bit longer, his command coursed through me. *I'm going to open a crack for him to see what we want him to see.*

The claws tightened their grip on my mind, squeezing with such force the pressure had my head feeling like it would explode. I couldn't contain my screams. The claws paused, scrambling for a hold in a small crack of my mind. Caaz pressed in, sifting through the information, cataloging what he needed to know, what he was searching for.

After a few more long moments, the pressure relented. My mind relaxed as the claws retreated from my body. Caaz turned his wicked smile toward the king and barked a laugh.

"The Avyon whore bonded a soldier in his army." He laughed. "Not even a captain, just a foot soldier that traveled with them to break her out of here."

The king's laugh joined his and I sighed with relief as their attention momentarily drifted.

They bought it.

"Now I know why you wanted to hide that piece of information so badly," Dathrian mocked. "Your esteemed sister, mated to the King of Verastarr. And *you* bonded to a peasant soldier in Kodrayn Deverell's army."

I pressed my lips into a tight line, pretending to be embarrassed by my choice of bonded vampry.

"Take her back to the dungeon," Dathrian commanded the

soldier behind me. "Have her cell double secured and tighten security around the dungeon."

The soldier nodded, saying, "Yes, sir," before hauling me up to my feet and yanking me toward the door. I stumbled against the strength of his grip as he led me toward the black metal door at the end of the throne room.

"Wait," Eryx's voice commanded, and my blood froze as the guard halted mid-step. Cold calculating footsteps approached us, the click of his heeled boots grating on my nerves with every step he took. He stopped before us, and his vicious smile appeared in my peripheral vision as he lifted his hand holding a small vial up for me to see.

"Can't have you communicating with your *beloved vampry* now can we?" He pried my mouth open and crammed the contents down my throat despite my struggles. Holding my jaw together, he waited until he was sure I'd swallowed before turning on his heel. "Take her away, now."

I was being dragged away, back to the darkness of a cell I'd only just recently been freed from.

NORDAK

Chapter Thirty-One

SILENCE MET my ears as I stirred slightly and my memories came rushing back to me. The bond. The Eldritch. The vial.

Kode? I whispered into the bond. I could still feel the icy chill of his presence intertwined with my fiery one deep within me. Silence.

Kode? I tried again, praying to The God that he could hear me; that the vial Eryx had forced me to take didn't actually work. That we still had a way to communicate.

The silence down the bond wasn't promising as I strained against the hazy effects of the contents still in my system.

For the love of The God . . . answer me you fangy idiot. This was your Void-damned idea after all.

I see being captured hasn't made your tongue any less venomous, hmmm? Kodrayn's voice quipped through my mind and I nearly cried with relief that I could still hear him.

Making jokes about me getting captured from right under you now, are we?

I think I'd remember if I had you right underneath me, bonded, Kodrayn answered, his voice deep as he spoke. *And if I had you there, not even The Void would be able to steal you away from me.*

Kode. I replied, unable to say anything else in that moment as my thoughts momentarily pictured the scene he painted in my mind.

He laughed. *Anything to keep you hopeful, little venom,* Kodrayn's reply instantly sobered me a bit.

How are we able to still communicate if they forced me to drink a vial to block the bond?

I'm King of Avyon. Kodrayn's prideful snarl filled my mind and I nearly chuckled at his response. *The concoction their healers have created may be strong enough to block common vampry bonds, but not the bond of a king. I felt the poison as soon as it entered your system, but was able to draw it out.*

Draw it out? I questioned. *How?*

Vampry blood heals, little venom.

Not trying to state the obvious here, Kode. But you're not actually here. It's quite literally impossible for your blood to be in my system when we are in two separate places.

Rare, Kodrayn responded, *but not impossible through the bond.*

So you're telling me that you're able to heal me through our bond?

Yet another reason I initiated the bond in the first place, Kodrayn answered, and I fell silent at his reply. *A way to ensure I could always keep you safe, protect you . . . save you.*

Why?

The silence that stretched after my question lingered long enough I'd nearly assumed I'd lost him, when a slow response answered.

Many reasons. Our realm's battle against the Nordak has gone on since long before Sébastien declared war officially. He paused and I began to wonder why he was pausing. *When I lost my family to the Nordak attack five years ago. I knew. I knew even before I saw their bodies that they must have endured hell. My siblings, my mother, all tortured by Nordak soldiers. And for what? They didn't steal our throne, they didn't overtake our land.* The venom laced in his voice hit me as he spoke. *They were murdered in cold blood. So when you were captured, I understood the terror, the pain that you must have endured, the same torment and anguish that my mother and sister felt before they died.*

I was silent as he spoke. Shocked and angered at what had happened to him, what he'd had to endure.

I couldn't let that happen to you again. I refused to let another person I held close be put in that position, alone. I heard the whimpers and cries in your sleep while I held you in my arms when we traveled to search for the narelle flowers. I could see the fear that flickered through your eyes that you try so hard to keep hidden, buried deep inside. So once I knew that you no longer carried an attachment to that idiot, I did the only thing I could think to help you, in case this circumstance ever occurred. I stayed silent at his words, at the amount of attention he paid to details I thought no one noticed. *Now rest, little venom.*

Tears slowly rolled down my cheeks at his words, at the thought and care he'd put into his actions, to help me, to save me.

"How'd they catch you this time?" A gruff voice sounded from across from me, and I looked up to meet the familiar eyes of Cainu.

"We were spotted on our way back to an inn." I began to share the story of how I'd been recaptured by Eryx. "Made it a day's run from there before another patrol caught wind of us."

"Soraya made it?" the fae captain asked.

"Yes," I whispered, relieved that at least she wasn't back in this hellhole with me. "We split up on the first part of the journey, she should be safely across the Avyz by now," I said with a smile that didn't quite reach my lips.

"Who's the new guy? They brought him in yesterday with you." He gestured to the cell beside me and my head whipped to the side, following his indication.

"Jace," I cried softly. His short blond hair was matted in crimson, and several large gashes covered his battered form. He'd been beaten, tortured, no doubt. I tried shuffling my body toward his limp form, only to be halted in my tracks, barely able to move.

"I reckon they shortened the links in your cell after last time."
Cainu spoke again. "You know him?"

"Yes." Tears fell slowly as I stared at Jace. "He was one of
Kodrayn's men, he helped to rescue me. He didn't deserve this."

"None of us do."

I fell silent, momentarily stunned at the truth of his words.
None of us do.

"I thought Kode gave you the keys to the cells when we left?" I
prompted, bringing my attention back to the man in front of me.
Now curious as to why they were all still here.

"He did," he answered quietly. "We've been biding our time.
We had planned for a departure two nights ago, until we caught
talk of being transported across the Avyz."

"Where to?" Curiosity laced my tone as I waited with bated
breath for his answer.

"An outer point in the East Engles. Sounds like Dathrian has a
meeting set up with the king of the East Engles."

"And you're waiting for what? To be shipped off to more
enemy territory?" I questioned.

"We're waiting for a better opportunity. An easier escape," he
answered confidently.

"And you're so sure this is the best opportunity?"

"It's the best we've been given. I've been here for awhile now,"
the captain answered. "This is as good an escape route as we'll get
here. I'd rather face the beasts in the depths of the Avyz than
dodge gryffins on their own land."

"Then that's the plan we'll have to go with," I answered, resignation in my tone.

"What do you mean?" he asked, staring closely at me. "Don't
go off doing anything stupid from now until we leave, girl."

I smiled sweetly. "I won't do anything stupid, trust me." A key
rattled in a lock further down the hall, and I shimmied back into
the corner of my cell, but not before I lifted my wrists enough to
point to the marking on my neck, the claiming Kodrayn had left,
his imprint, branded across my skin, ensuring the fae captain

understood my message. Ensuring he knew we had a way to communicate to the outside realm.

I couldn't breathe. My lungs screamed in agonizing protest as Eryx's hand tightened around my throat. I'd been dragged to the all too familiar *training pit* before dawn this morning and thrown in front of Eryx.

He stood in front of me, leering as his form towered above me while rage and vengeance took over his features.

"You think you're clever, do you?" He sneered toward me, his grip on my throat unrelenting as tears welled in my eyes. "Bonding a vampry. We both know you only did it as a last ditch effort to save yourself in the future."

I said nothing, my eyes glaring back at the man I'd formerly been in love with.

"It would have been so easy for you." His voice was harsh but had an underlying tone; one I was familiar with. "All you had to do was love me . . . we could have ruled the realm with the power inside you."

His grip loosened and I spoke. "Correct me if I'm wrong, Eryx, but you're *not* king. I wouldn't have ruled by your side, whether I bonded with a vampry or not," I snarked, bracing myself for the blow that didn't come.

"You think you know everything, don't you." His eyes glinted as he spoke. "Your friends, your sister. They have no idea what's coming for them . . . no idea what lengths we have gone to so that we can control the realm."

"You'll never control the entire realm, Eryx." I sneered. "Just like I'll never give up my powers." I bared my fangs, ignoring the blisters forming on my wrists from the iron shackles. "Darkness never wins. You just chose the wrong side of the war, and when it ends . . . it will be your body broken on the battlefield, not mine."

His fist collided with my face, blood spraying from my nose as pain lanced its way through my body and I cried out, staggering back.

"What the fuck just happened?" I heard Kode's growl, a terrifying mix of concern and vengeance in the back of my mind, but I couldn't speak. I focused on my breathing, lifting my eyes to meet Eryx's as I bit back pain.

"Hurt me all you want, Eryx," I spat, blood dripping from my nose as I straightened to meet him. "You won't get what you want, not from me." His fist flew toward me again, colliding with my side as I tried, yet failed, to duck the blow. I felt the crack on my ribs, wincing as they broke. My brain clouded over, agony pulsing throughout my body, but I didn't have time to struggle before his fist hit me again, the ring on his knuckle causing a cut to form on my jawline.

My vision teetered, stars forming in my eyes as I fought to keep consciousness, as I fought to stay awake. *I can't black out, I can't.* "I mean it, Eryx." Sapphire flames rose to the surface ready to strike as I stared at the man before me. "I'd rather die than let my powers be harvested by Nordak filth."

What. Happened. Kode's demand filled my mind with more insistence. An icy sensation seeped through my body, radiating from deep within my soul. Then, I felt the blood stop flowing from my nose, the pain across my face withdrawing, and a slight smile graced my lips. *The bond.* Kodrayn was healing me through the bond, even though I hadn't replied to him yet.

"You may get the chance to choose." Eryx's smile turned feral. "But let's see what you have to say shortly. Perhaps after today, you will be willing to perform the power harvest on the quarter moon."

My stomach dropped as I looked over to the pit doors being opened and Jace's beaten form was dragged through them. "Jace." The word fell from my lips as I gave away the value of the man before me, and Eryx's eyes lit with victory as he walked away.

Answer me, little venom.

But darkness swarmed the ceiling of the training pit, and I watched in horror as not one, but two figures began to emerge, creatures of corrupt magic springing forth from above the shadows.

I'm sorry, Kode, was all I murmured down the bond as I struggled to build a wall in my mind, blocking him out. I wouldn't let him feel the pain, I wouldn't let him know what happened in this *training pit.* I refused to be the one to make him feel that. To make him bare witness to my torture.

I could still hear his roar of protest as I put the last blocks up in my mind. It was a weak wall, but a wall nonetheless. I willed my body to shift, my fae form taking flight as I raced toward Jace, praying I made it to his side before the Fantoms did.

"Get behind me!" Jace shouted as I approached. I could hear the pain laced in his tone. His fangs were bared as his eyes tracked over me, to the Fantoms closing in on us.

I dropped beside him, refusing to shelter behind him as we prepared for a fight, the first tendrils of corrupt magic already snaking through the air toward us.

"We don't have any of the flowers, do we?" I asked, hardly above a whisper as I stared at the tendrils racing toward us.

"No," he replied.

"*Fuck,*" I cursed, knowing my flames alone couldn't fight off the creatures. "Elemental magic doesn't work very well against them," I finished, as Jace lifted his arms beside me.

"If I push the tendrils off enough, can you distract the Fantoms themselves?" His voice cut through as wind whipped around us. I nodded as his magic shot forward, knocking the tendrils back on their descent toward us.

I pushed off, launching myself skyward as Jace's magic fought against the ancient power racing toward us. Calling on my own magic, I willed my flames to life, directing them toward the Fantoms as I rose to meet the creatures.

I cut through the air, twisting side to side as I flew, dodging the new tendrils of power that they cast toward me, toward us. The

Fantom's split, their forms separating as they divided to strike. I lurched in the air, narrowly avoiding a plummet to the ground as a strand of power whipped from my open side.

I heard Jace's shout in the distance, but kept focusing on my target, on the beast before me. An agonized scream sounded from below, bile rising in my throat as I turned briefly, glancing down to see purple tendrils surrounding and trapping his body as he fought against them; the Fantom gaining on his struggling form rapidly.

"Look ou—" The words died on my lips as something struck me from the left and then I was falling.

I screamed, wind howling in my ear as I fell toward the ground. I spread my fae wings as far as I could, praying they slowed my fall as purple mist circled me, a cloud of dark magic on its heel.

I hit the ground, bones cracking as I landed with such force. My head smacked against the side of the ground causing my skull to ring as my barriers slipped.

You thought you could block me out, little venom? Kodrayn's furious snarl whipped through my mind, clashing with the ongoing ringing. *No one shuts me out, especially not my mate. And definitely not when you need me most.*

I couldn't speak, I couldn't move as the Fantom descended on me and I could feel it latching on to my power, searching for that ember of blue sapphire buried deep within my soul. The ember entwined with my mates ice. *Fantom,* was all I managed to whisper down the bond before the Fantom was there. I heard Kode's voice in the distance, but the darkness was already closing in on my mind, memories springing to the surface.

Darkness flooded over me and I was back at the inn, pressed against the windowsill with Kodrayn before me. I knew this memory, I loved this memory. I wanted to keep this memory.

Kode's fingers were tracing over me, building with intensity as our tongues collided once more in a dance of power and need. I wanted more of him, needed less space between us.

I drank him in, getting lost in the cedar and orange scent that clung around us. My back arched as his fingers skillfully circled my center, building me higher and higher, the pressure building until I couldn't take it anymore.

"Kode," I breathed his name once more, a cry, a demand, and he met it. His eyes were dark and hungry as he held my gaze. He struck once more, thrusting his fingers in at the same time his fangs struck that sweet spot on my neck. I screamed my release, losing myself to him as the realm shattered around me. Tiny embers danced in the air around us as I lost control of my magic, my senses, myself.

The door burst open, gray shadows creeping into the room. That's when I heard it, the shrill screech off a Seefer. Alarm flared in my eyes, as two Seefers appeared in the stairwell as though by magic, fangs bared as they snarled at us.

"Focus on me, little venom. On me," Kodrayn spoke and I froze, staring at him. Because this . . . this hadn't happened. Somehow, the memory had been altered, changed.

Kodrayn's eyes were dark and hungry as he held my gaze, a devilish grin as he eyed me, caging me between firm, muscled thighs. His fingers were back on my skin, teasing me, distracting me. My core tightened as his hand began to touch me, and my nipples pebbled as an icy breeze swept across my skin teasing every sensitive, aching spot. I screamed in pleasure, as he thrust his fingers back inside of me, edging me on as his fangs danced across my exposed flesh and I lost myself to him—my bonded. The Seefers began to vanish, retreating from the doorway, and we were moving toward the bed.

"How are you doing that?" I questioned, stunned with what was happening. I panicked slightly, my heart rate racing as I began to remember this was all in my mind, that I was actually lying, surrounded by corrupt magic in the training pit. That Jace was somewhere there too, losing his memories as we fought against the Fantoms.

The walls of the inn caught fire, flames engulfing the wood as the Seefers reappeared in the doorway, only this time there were more, creeping through the doorway as they began to lunge for Kodrayn.

"Focus on me, little venom." His words hit me as he tossed me on the bed

without a care in the realm for anything but me; unconcerned for the Seefers aiming for him. "It's all in your mind, so take control of the narrative of this memory, don't let the Fantom control you. You control it."

I stared at him in confusion. "Is that even possible?"

"Let's find out." He threw a cocky grin my way, his breath fanning across my neck as he spoke. "Unless you have a better idea?" But he didn't give me time to answer before he flipped me over on the bed, heat coursing through me at the action.

I felt his fangs tracing along the column of my neck, licking over the tender spot where he'd claimed me. I shifted on my knees, my body pressing up against his as his weight covered my back. I squirmed, need building within me as I felt the hard length of him pressing against me, pulsing for me. I moaned when his fangs sank in just below the claiming mark he'd imprinted on my neck, my body writhing against his. I felt each ripple of his firm muscles against my back, every feathered kiss on my skin, and the feel of his fangs tracing over exposed flesh while his arm wrapped around my body, circling my center, teasing me, distracting me.

Pleasure built within me, desire pulsing through me as his finger teased my entrance before pushing in, and a mewl of pleasure rippled through me. I moaned louder, moving my hips to match his strokes as his finger moved in and out slowly. He began to pick up the pace, and my heart rate increased as desire built within me. I wanted more. I needed more. I needed my mate—my bonded.

"Kode," I pleaded his name, a command and a question at once as his body shifted behind me, lining himself up. "I need . . . I need you."

"I've needed you since the moment you stepped foot on my land. I've waited to make you mine since the moment you opened that venomous little mouth of yours. And I'd wait the rest of my life if it meant I could make you mine."

Desire coursed through me at his words, at the feel of him so close to where I wanted him to be. I felt his breath across my neck, tingling over his mark. "Now," he growled lowly as he shifted us slightly. "Grab the headboard, little venom," his voice snaked through my hair, my body ablaze as I obeyed his command. He didn't waste any time before he thrust forward, filling me as I screamed his name in pleasure. I revel in the feel of him, stretching me, filling me as he claimed me in yet another way, consuming every thought, every need, as he thrust deeply into me.

I awoke in my cell to darkness, the memory of the inn running through my mind, a memory I wished so desperately to recreate, in person, with the man I'd bonded to. Assessing my situation, I found my body battered and bruised yet significantly less injured than expected. He'd healed me. *And, I was alive.* With a quick glance to the cell next to me, I could tell Jace was too. We'd survived, at least for now.

NORDAK

Chapter Thirty-Two

TAKING A DEEP BREATH, I built a sturdy barricade in my mind, funneling all my thoughts behind the barbed wire fencing and cement just like Jace had been teaching me to do in the past two days. The first day back, fighting the Fantom in the pit, Kode had been furious and concerned when he felt the pain radiating down the bond as I attempted to keep my mental walls up.

So, I had taken matters into my own hands and began to learn how to effectively block out the bond, not needing him to know the gruesome details of what was happening inside the gates of Kyllios. Angered ice had stormed down our bond when he discovered I was working on building up walls in my mind. However, even the Vampry King hadn't been able to refute my need to barricade my mind from enemies—to protect myself mentally.

Today's task was different from the others. I stood in the training pit, just as I had every other day. Only this time, this time I had been given a weapon. I didn't understand why until the barricaded door opened and a wolvyn entered the pit.

My blood turned cold. I *knew* this wolvyn. I *knew* this man. *Dovan.* He'd been captured six months ago and was held three cells down from mine. I couldn't fight him. I *wouldn't* fight him.

I began to back away. My footsteps moved in a backward

motion as I inched further from the wolvyn and closer to the door I'd been led in through. That is, until a sharp metal rod prodded me in the back, halting my progress. Glancing behind me, I noticed two Nordak soldiers standing guard, preventing me from exiting the ring.

The wolvyn growled, lowering on its haunches as he crept closer toward me, stalking me. Analyzing me, as if I was prey about to be eaten. But I refused to be the prey. *Not this time.*

I took my stance, assessing my opponent, blocking out the fact that I knew Dovan. I'd heard stories of his children back in Verastarr, of his little boy, Theo, and his mate. His teeth bared as his snarled growl filled the training pit and I raised my dagger, prepared to strike.

He launched, flying through the air, and I shifted, meeting him mid-strike as claws collided with fur. My forelegs burned, metal searing into my fur as I attacked the wolvyn in the same form, baring my own fangs toward him. Claws raked down my back and I whimpered as I turned, striking his exposed underbelly as he leapt toward me.

Shifting once more, I strained against my wings, willing myself to push higher into the air, separating myself from the wolvyn to catch my breath. Warm blood trickled down my back from the mark the wolvyn had left and my muscles protested the movement. My wrists once again burned in agony as the metal cuffs vibrated against my use of power, but I kept my mental shields up, careful not to let the pain overload my barriers.

I froze in horror as the wolvyn pushed off from the ground, purple mist surrounding his form as he lifted into the air. "What in the Void-damned—" I didn't have time to finish the sentence before the wolvyn struck again, colliding with me in mid-air as I raised my dagger to defend myself. Arching the blade, I swiped toward his neck, missing by an inch as his claws raked down my arm.

I needed speed, agility. And I wouldn't get enough in my fae form. Diving toward the ground, I willed my wings to push faster.

I skidded into the ground, graveled rocks grating against my skin as I shifted once again, staggering slightly. I raised my hand, willing my flames to the surface, my wrists screaming in pain as I hurled my fire in the direction of the wolvyn.

But just like the Fantom, the second the flames hit the target, they vanished, disappearing into thin air. I couldn't use my magic in this fight. Darting to the side, I waited, watching as the wolvyn hit the ground, stalking toward me as we circled each other, waiting for one another to pounce.

I feigned left, watching as the wolvyn pounced, while I darted to the right, spinning on my heel as I whirled around then brought my dagger down. My blade hit bone as I pressed deep, a high-pitched whine filling the air. The wolvyn finally collapsed, the purple mist vanishing from its body.

I collapsed to the ground, my body in agonizing pain, my fingers numb as I held the wolvyn's head in my hands. "No, no, no." Tears streamed down my face as I petted his matted fur, willing him to wake up, to take a breath. But I knew my aim hit true. "Please, please come back. You have to come back. You have to make it home."

A dark laugh echoed from the other side of the pit. I spun, seeing Eryx walk onto the gravel. I raised my dagger, smashing the hilt against the side of my skull, effectively knocking myself out before he could make me fight someone else. I embraced the darkness and the dreams that followed.

The stairs of my apartment complex towered over me. "Whatever you think you're going to accomplish, Nik," I sneered, "you will fail. I guarantee you that much." I threw the knife, watching as it flew hilt over the blade, cutting through the air. But I was already moving, flipping the safety off the gun as I fired a shot, the bullet flying toward the male charging for me. I heard Nik's grunt of pain, the knife meeting its target, embedding itself in him. A shout

came from my side, and I turned just in time for a fist to collide with my jaw. Pain erupted across my face as I flew back from the force, colliding with the ground as the gun bounced from my hand, skidding to a stop under a chair. I grunted, pushing myself up as Nik rose from the couch, rage in his eyes as a knife rested in his palm, covered in his blood. "You bitch." He seethed, stalking toward me, I scrambled back, closer to the door as I got to my feet, only to be knocked down as his other two friends tackled me, slamming me into the ground with such force that I saw stars.

Nik's face appeared in my vision, towering over me as I struggled against the two males holding me down, thrashing and kicking, but I couldn't break free from their hold. "You will pay for this," Nik bit as he tossed the knife to the side, the blade clattering against the tile flooring. His gaze turned ruthless, darkness spreading in his eyes as he drew a wicked, curved onyx blade from his side that had me thrashing even more against my captors hold.

I recognized that blade. It was the Blade of Rathmen. A long forgotten blade that the darkness wielded. A cursed blade that imbued its victims with a form of unknown magic. Magic known to make the carrier crazy from its power. I'd seen sketches of it as Aerilyn and I had scoured the Archives for the artifacts.

Nik's pupils turned black as he spoke words in an ancient tongue—in the tongue the Nordak had spoken hundreds of years ago—and dark purple magic radiated from the hilt of the weapon he wielded.

"Don't do this Nik," I pleaded as the blade drew closer to my thrashing body, the immovable weight of his friends pinning me to the tile. But Nik didn't listen to me; was unrecognizable to me as the blade met my thigh, drawing blood.

The dream shifted, and I recognized the tacky yellow paint job coating the walls before I heard the voice speaking to me. "You'll make it through this." Aer's voice flowed over me. "Just like everything else. Just trust me, Kat, it's all gonna work out."

I laughed in response to my roommate's statement as I lounged on the sofa in our living room sipping one of her disgusting smoothies. "It's all gonna work out? Really, Aer? Do you not see me?" I gestured down at myself. I was in lounge shorts and a cropped t-shirt that said "Innerlands - where the sun *never sets and the parties never stop." A shirt we'd purchased with my sister on our girls getaway weekend, three years ago.*

"Yeah, girl, and you look hot." She smiled, her auburn red hair bouncing in the sunlight as she plopped down on the couch beside me. "It always works out. You know it will. It may not feel like it right now, but I know you'll make it through this. We'll make it through this together. It's you and me until magic is restored to the realm." My roommate smiled at me from across the couch and I laughed, tossing the pillow in her direction.

"You and me, huh?" I laughed as she flipped through the channels, talking about our plans for the evening.

I shivered in my cell. My hair, bloodied and matted to my skull as I pressed myself against the brick wall. The sound of rats scurrying across the floor, and the slow drip of damp liquid, were the only sounds I could make out, other than the rasps of our pained breathing. I knew my internal injuries were healed by Kode based on my ability to sit up easily. Which also meant he was fully aware of how badly I'd been hurt. My stomach spasmed, hunger gnawing at my insides. I couldn't remember the last time I'd eaten a full meal—*a warm meal.*

I know what Dathrian's next move is, I sent down the bond after waking up an hour ago and overhearing the guards speaking amongst each other while they changed shifts.

You truly think that's what I want to talk about right now? Kodrayn's enraged snarl came down the bond.

Well I, for one, thought it to be a pressing matter. What could you possibly prefer to talk about while I'm being held captive?

You shutting me out when they took you to the training pit. Or, more importantly. He paused, then spoke again. *Nik.* His singular reply came down the bond, sending ice down my veins as I heard the name on his tongue.

Nik? I questioned. *What do you know about Nik?* I knew I had shared a little with him when we were in Arceyla, but had I ever given him a name? I couldn't remember.

Is he dead?

I wouldn't know, Kodrayn, I answered frustratedly, not entirely wishing to be talking about Nik. *He's in the present. How on Vanaiyer do you propose I find out if he's still living or not?*

I paused for a moment, thinking his question over again before asking. *How do you know about Nik?*

You dreamt about him. He was towering over you on a stairwell, with the Blade of Rathmen in his hand.

You saw my dreams? I nearly screeched down the bond. *Don't you think that's a little bit of a privacy invasion there?*

You blocked me out of your thoughts, he growled angrily back at me, protectively. *And judging by the numerous wounds I spent healing over* your *body, sharing dreams should be the least of your concern.*

I blocked you out so you wouldn't worry, I quipped.

You were half dead when I finally gained access to the bond through your dreams, little venom. I don't like finding what's mine half dead and bleeding out in a prison cell.

I paused at his wording for a moment, flashbacks of the most recent *training* session I'd endured running through my mind. I wondered what Dathrian was testing my powers for. What piece of information he was hoping to gain from me.

I know where they are moving to next.

You must not be hearing me right if you think we are done with this conversation, Kateya. I will hunt down every last man who has caused you pain. I will kill them all. I will kill him for putting his hands on you. Him and all his little friends, starting with that gryffin scum Eryx.

I could feel his fury radiating down the bond.

Kode, I pleaded down the bond, *I need you to listen to me. As flattered as I am that you wish to kill every man who has caused me harm—a list which is growing by the day—I don't have much time to tell you. Dathrian will be moving me, along with most of the other captives, north.*

I felt the icy chill of his magic come to life deep within me before his words reached down the bond. *Where is he taking you?*

Dyfinn.

That far north? Kodrayn's voice hesitated as he spoke. *Do you know what he plans to do? Anything you've been able to figure out would help us gauge where to attack.*

Turns out, I replied, *the guards speak pretty freely around here when they think that the Avyon whore can't get in touch with her bonded. Dathrian seems convinced that the artifact mentioned by the Unseen is located in the East Engles. I'm not sure what is leading him to believe it's located there, but he is set on searching the East Engles until the artifact is in his possession.*

Void-be-damned. The curse rang down the bond and I sensed his frustration. The frustration we'd all feel if Dathrian found the artifact before us.

I thought Emalyee was searching for it? Or at least seeking out clues toward its location.

I felt the hesitation, even as his answer slowly trickled down. *She was. We haven't heard from her in a few days. We have no idea if she's managed to locate the artifact's position.*

I knew what he left unsaid. We didn't have the time to wait for her to locate it. Hell, I hadn't had the time when I'd spent the past year of my life searching for the artifact that brought me back here.

If Dathrian finds that artifact before us . . . I couldn't finish the sentence.

He won't, little venom, he won't.

You don't understand, Kode. I emphasized to him. *Dathrian . . . he's invented something new. Something that will alter the course of this war. He . . .* I swallowed, unsure how I would be able to voice this next part. *He can take a power and manipulate it with ancient magic. He can control it.*

What do you mean? Kodrayn demanded.

In the training pit, he forced me to fight against a wolvyn. Someone I knew, someone I didn't want to harm. When I shifted to my fae form and took flight, the wolvyn flew, surrounded by ancient magic, and attacked me in the air. I couldn't control it. There was no humanity left in the wolvyn, he was himself, but yet not, I finished lamely, unable to describe exactly how altered the wolvyn's personality had been when fighting against me in the pit.

I had no choice, I choked out in a whisper down the bond, tears welling in my eyes, then falling over in large rivulets as I told him. *When I close my eyes, I can still feel the blade sliding through his fur. I knew him, Kode. I spoke to him a few cells over from me almost every day I was here. I met his mate, his son, back in Verastarr. How do I—What do I—I . . .* couldn't finish the sentence. I couldn't find the words as shame and sorrow overcame me.

It's better that way, for him, Kodrayn said, his voice soothing, understanding, as he carried on. *He won't have to remember fighting his own, he won't be tortured anymore. Trust me. You ended his suffering.*

It doesn't feel that way, I replied, bitterness rising in me as I spoke. Resentment of myself for the action I'd been forced to take. *It feels like I stripped him of his life. Like I took him away from people who loved him.*

His life would never be the same even if we managed to get him free of the ancient magic Dathrian wielded onto him. Trust me, little venom, you did the only thing you could do for him.

I lay there, immobile as I let Kodrayn's words wrap over me, praying to The God that he was right. That I had done the right thing for the wolvyn, and that his soul wound up in The Void safely.

Cainu's voice drew my attention as he spoke barely above a whisper. "Have you relayed the information?"

"Yes," I whispered back, aware that Jace was paying attention as well. "We need to bide our time, at least until we get more concrete information."

"We don't have much more time," Jace growled from my side. "We'll be dead soon if we don't escape this hellhole."

"Our best bet is to escape by the Avyz," I replied, inclining my head toward the captain who'd been here longest, formulating our escape.

"We have the keys," Cainu reminded us quietly. "Now we just

need to wait until we are close to the East Engles but far enough they won't search for us."

"They're going to search for us the moment we vanish," Jace's voice bit out in frustration. "They're going to search for *her*."

"Then I will stay behind," I muttered. "I won't let everyone else lose their chance at escape because of my powers."

"Like hell you'll stay behind," Cainu whispered from across the hall. "It's all of us or none . . . we leave no one behind."

A few voices echoed their agreements from the cells down.

"Then what do we do?" I murmured, unsure how we would all manage to break free.

"For now, we wait. We see what we learn in Dyffin," the captain replied. "And when the time is right, we will go together."

EAST ENGLES

Chapter Thirty-Three

DYFINN, to no surprise, looked the exact same as Kyllios had. Drab gray walls stripped of color, a chilled interior, and the same lifeless feel to the gated city. It didn't surprise me though, not in the least. Every part of Nordak seemed to give off a forlorn, forgotten feel that had you wishing you would never return to its soil.

The air was chillier here, and the thin clothing I had on was not doing much to spare me from the temperature of the place as I huddled next to Jace in a large cell. That, perhaps, was the biggest difference between Dyfinn and Kyllios. They only had one prison chamber here, and we were all kept together, huddled side by side for warmth in the Northern Territory of Nordak.

When the guards left us, I would expel increments of my magic, letting the fiery flames trapped within me burn to life, warming the otherwise frigid room they kept us in.

The power blazed to life within me, humming and thriving as it was expelled from my palms, blue flames flickering in the dark- nesses. The shackles on my wrists were so frozen from the temper- ature that even their power to curb my magic was faltering, enabling me to use my powers for longer periods of time without the excruciating pain that so often accompanied the use of my power.

"They'll take us to Estaire next," the fae captain gruffed from my other side. "We can escape there."

"No," I whispered, ensuring my voice was kept low. "Not Estaire." I knew the landmarks of my homeland all too well and knew that Estaire was an unlikely location for us to travel. "It's too far of a journey. They'll meet somewhere else, somewhere closer to the Northern Territory of Nordak."

The captain turned his head, studying me as though he didn't believe me. But I'd run the math over and over in my head. They wouldn't risk meeting in the Capital, even if they were meeting with the King of the East Engles. "There are too many risks," I insisted quickly, careful my voice didn't carry. "Too much potential for spies to catch word of the meeting, of their search for the third and fourth artifacts."

"Then where?" Jace asked from my left, but I didn't know. My flame died out. The flickering embers of light fading and trapping us in the darkness again, the howling wind whipping against the outer walls.

What's the closest point to Dyfinn? I shot down the bond, praying to The God that Kodrayn had a map accessible.

Hello to you too, little venom, his voice purred down the bond.

Kode, I responded, *I'm serious. What's the closest city, landmark, anything to the Northern Territory?*

Give us a minute.

Us? I asked down our bond.

Us, he replied. *The Brotherhood, and your sister.*

My sister . . . I hadn't seen her in so long. Hadn't allowed myself to think of her much these past few weeks, focusing instead on simply staying alive, and making it to the next sunrise. I leaned my head against the brick wall while I waited, instantly regretting the decision as cold seeped into my skull causing a fresh round of shivers to course through my body. I inched closer to Jace, pressing my side against his in an attempt to keep warm.

Hallyus, his low voice whispered down the bond.

That's where he's taking us, I replied confidently to Kode.

How can you be sure?

It's his only option, I shared. *Think about it. Dathrian needs to stop in the East Engles, at the very least to deploy men to search for the fourth artifact. With the number of gryffins he's traveling with, they need to rest, and they don't want to be spotted. The King of the East Engles, if allied with Dathrian as you believe him to be, will not want any spies to be alerted of their meeting—*

They're going to meet in the ancient city, Kodrayn interrupted.

Ancient city? I questioned, having never heard of an ancient city in the East Engles, despite having lived there for most of my life.

Yes. Outside of Hallyus, there's a city of ancient ruins. If lore is true, the ancient practitioners of magic met there to conjure spells and test the balance of magic. It's not quite sacred ground, but it's ground that most would choose not to venture to, he replied.

Giving them the privacy they need. I added, realizing that if he was right, we'd just narrowed down the location of their meeting. *We leave tomorrow morning. Is that enough time for your men to get there?*

We'll work on our plans now. Kateya . . . The hesitancy in his voice gave me pause as I listened, noting the concern that laced his usual tone. *Once we settle on our plans, I won't share them with you. We've already seen Dathrian's love of using Caaz Eldritch against you. Knowing the plans puts you at more of a risk, you'll just have to trust us. Trust me. I will stop at nothing to get you back. Nothing.* His voice was firm. *I'll never stop saving you, little venom. Even when I know you're fully capable of saving yourself.*

Just promise you'll tell me the moment you need me, need us, to do something, I responded.

Only if necessary. I'll see you soon, Kat. I nearly took an audible breath at the use of the nickname. *But after this, let's try to take a break from me saving your life, hmmm?*

Saving my life? I teased. *I'm quite positive I'm still very much alive, no thanks to you.*

His laugh sounded down the bond, but my heart stuttered,

knowing that joking aside, I was still very much at risk. And I stood to lose so much more if this went poorly.

"I know where they are taking us," I whispered to those closest to me, knowing the word would be passed around. "We need to be prepared, at any given moment, once we arrive."

I fell asleep to the sound of an icy breeze cutting harshly across the outer wall, the sound lulling me to sleep as my mind wandered.

Warm lips clashed passionately with mine, heat rising within me as the scent of cedarwood and blood orange wrapped around my body.

"Mine."

Kodrayn's voice echoed in my mind as his lips claimed mine once more, trapping my tongue between his teeth before sucking on it. I melted into the feel of him, my hands drifting up his muscled chest, tracing the tattoos inked across his shoulder as he deepened the kiss. I moaned into him, running my hand back down his chest, feeling each rigid line of the flat plane of his body.

His hand wrapped through my hair, tilting my head back, giving him more access to me—to my neck. I felt his lips feather kisses down the column of my neck, each one sending a jolt of fiery heat pulsing through my body. I pressed myself into him more, feeling his length hard against my stomach. I moaned again at the heat of it. He paused, lips hovering over the mark he'd left on me the last time we were together, a hungry look in his eyes as he licked around the claiming mark, dark eyes flicking up to meet mine once more. "You're mine, little venom, don't ever forget that."

I cried out as his fangs bit down on me once more. My nails dug further into his back as he drove me to a new level of need . . . of desire. A lust-induced haze washed over my body, the sensation of his fangs on me, on the mark he'd left—

A hand shook against me, causing me to stir in frustration. "What?" I nearly growled toward my left, my fangs springing forward in an involuntary shift to my vampry form.

"Whatever you're dreaming about," Jace muttered in annoyance from my side, "stop. You're setting off inconsistent sparks of fire embers and your pulse is running rampant, driving every vampry in this cell close to a bloodlust frenzy."

Embarrassment lit across my skin as I ducked my head. "Sorry," I whispered toward him, shutting out my surroundings. Leaning my head against the wall of the cell, I let the chilled temperature help reduce the simmering heat ablaze within my core, calming the embers raging within me.

Why'd you stop, little venom? Kode's voice echoed down the bond, and I froze. Shit. I'd forgotten that he could see into my dreams, that he could be *part* of my dreams. *I'm quite a fan of what came next, the little sounds that poisonous mouth of yours makes under my touch . . .*

I groaned at his invitation to return to the depths of my dreams. *I nearly lit the cell on fire with thoughts of you,* I murmured to him instead.

I see nothing wrong with that. He answered down our bond. *For all I care, you could light the Void-damned realm on fire, just as long as you never stop having dreams of me like that.*

My cheeks burned as I focused on lowering the raging fire within me, trying my best to shut down my thoughts of him.

My skin was numb from flying as we touched down right outside Hallyus, the familiar view of sandy shores somewhat at odds with how I felt after having spent the past few weeks in a land of ice and death. The beat of wings began to fade as, line by line, gryffins landed in formation across the coastline of the East Engles, remaining in their gryffin form.

"Void-be-damned," the fae captain's words fell next to me. "You were right."

"I know," I whispered hoarsely, almost wishing I hadn't been as I stared at the ancient city for the first time. Towering ruins of yellow stones covered the expanse of the inlet city. Fallen stones and bare palm trees lined the streets from a distance. I looked closer, noting the remnants of bones littering the pathways of the city, and the Avyz, usually sparkling and clear as it lapped against the shore of the East Engles, didn't even move. The water simply rested eerily against the shoreline, there but at the same time, not there.

"This place feels haunted," Jace whispered from my side, and I could only nod my head in agreement as I continued scanning the location we were meeting at. There were no birds in the air, no sea creatures near the coastline; not even a breeze flowed through the palm fronds as we stared at the ancient city.

Then I spotted movement in the distance, my body going rigid while I watched, unable to draw a weapon as three figures formed, moving closer toward our position. Dathrian stepped forward, head held high, and waited for the approaching men to come into view.

The center figure towered high over the other two, and as he came into view, I recognized the dusty brown hair and similar facial features. But the sharp, perceptive gray eyes stood out the most. Eyes I'd seen many times during my time here in the past. *Dravyn's eyes.*

"Carawn De Cauda," Jace whispered by my side. "King of the East Engles."

"How did he become king?" I softly murmured, careful not to let my voice be heard.

"He murdered his brother, then forced his brother's wife to marry him and took control of the throne." *Dravyn's uncle*, I realized as I stared at the man beside Dathrian in shock.

I watched as emotionless eyes scanned the Nordak army and finally settled on mine, peering into my soul with wicked intention before he motioned toward me with a flick of his hand. I felt the gryffin behind me shift, pushing me forward toward the King of the East Engles.

Holding my head high, I stopped in front of Carawn, my face void of emotion, my mind barricaded as I studied the man before me.

"Well, well," the cold voice drawled. "If this isn't a delightful little surprise." His eyes narrowed on the silvered mark on my neck, annoyance flickering across his features. Cold, dark hands tilted my chin up as he traced his finger across the mark deep beneath my skin. "Pity you couldn't be more useful and bond with the Vampry King. All the same, you'll be excellent bait once we reach the shores of Verastarr." He sneered before pushing me back toward the guard behind me.

"Keep the vampry whore locked up until we leave tomorrow."

Tomorrow? I schooled my features, careful not to give my thoughts away. If we left tomorrow, that didn't provide much time for Kodrayn and Sébastien to arrive. It would mean that the people of Verastarr would be unsuspecting—open to attack.

"Now, Dathrian, let's talk about the missing artifact you seek." Carawn's voice held a malicious glint as the two walked off, further into the ancient city.

EAST ENGLES

Chapter Thirty-Four

I WOKE to the low pound of drums clashing with alarmed shouts and the beat of wings. I'd been kept separate from the other captives, residing alone in the center of the ancient city ruins. The drums sounded again, and I recognized them. Hope welled inside of me at the steady beat I'd only heard once before in my life, but would recognize in an instant from the way it scarred my memory. The sound of war.

I reached down the bond toward Kodrayn, praying to The God that I would feel his icy touch down it. And yet, just as the night before, I felt nothing but darkness—an empty void that I'd come to hate. I twisted in the chains holding me secure against the post, but just as every other time, there was no give.

I was trapped, unable to defend myself in the middle of a war, stuck until someone freed me. I screamed, my throat hoarse as I attempted to make my voice carry over the beat of the war drums to no avail.

As time dragged on, I could hear the clashing of metal on metal, as well as the screeches and cries as the battle grew closer, surrounding me. I began to recognize the sounds of gryffins striking fae warriors mid-air; the clash of the wolvyn colliding with Seefers. I could hear the lifeless, hollow screams of agony of warriors captured by the Fantom beasts we'd traveled with, and I prayed to The God that Kodrayn had found a way to utilize the narelle flowers we'd collected.

My wrists bruised around the cuffs while I still struggled to break free, when suddenly the door burst off the hinges. I watched helplessly as a Fantom attacked a fae soldier, striking and blocking until the fae anticipated an advance wrong, and the Fantom lurched forward, its mist-like tentacles wrapping itself around the fae, nearly swallowing it in mist. I cried, tears streaming down my cheeks as the fae before me screamed through the mist.

I was unable to help him, unable to use my magic to protect the soldier. I collapsed against the post holding me hostage, remorse and anger coursing through me as the Fantom fled from the room, already in search of its next victim.

Pushing myself up, I tried scooting closer to the fallen soldier, attempting to grab any weapon from him I could find. I strained hard against the metal holding me when I suddenly got a new idea. Calling on the fire raging within me, I let it burn in my palm, ignoring the pain I'd come to expect when using my power. Carefully shaping the fire, I snaked it over to the fae warrior, wrapping the flickers of flame around the handle of his long sword and dagger as I slowly brought them to my side.

Triumphantly, I picked up the handle of the sword, placing my chain flat against the ground and lifted the blade high above my head before bringing it down, with as much force as I could muster, directly on the metal chain. I stared at the tiniest scratch the blade made in the chain link and groaned with frustration. This wouldn't work, I wasn't strong enough. *Not like this.*

Sucking in a deep breath, I shifted into my vampry form, garnering the extra strength from the shift as I raised the blade above my head and struck, again. And again. And again. The crack in the metal slowly began to grow with each strike as I worked to free myself, and then the link gave away. "Yes!" I shouted in relief, my arms shaky as I stared in victory at the broken link, freeing my left arm.

"Well this is interesting," Eryx snarled as he stepped into view, Dathrian and Carawn stepping out from behind him. I raised the blade in my hand, prepared to defend myself, only to watch as Eryx looked at me, his eyes daring me to attack him.

"You truly think you can defend yourself against *me?*" he mocked as he lifted his hand, swiping it through the air. A gust of wind barreled into me, knocking the blade from my hand. I sagged against the ground, struggling to catch my breath as I tilted my head up to stare at the three men before me.

Do you know where they are holding you? the voice called down the bond and I nearly cried in relief. Kodrayn, he was here. He would find me.

I'm in the center of the city, trapped in a building. But be careful. Eryx, Dathrian, and Carawn are here with me.

Kode didn't need to respond. I could feel the anger pulsing down the bond in furious waves as I focused back in on the men in front of me. Taking a calming breath, I began to pull on the flames within me when a voice cut across the room.

"Oh, I wouldn't do that," Carawn snarled as he stalked closer to me. "Not yet anyway." I went to pull on the magic within me anyways, refusing to sit there helplessly.

Liquid tendrils of water shot from the ground, controlled by Carawn as they snaked toward me. I struggled as the ropes of water began to wrap themselves around my wrists and legs, pinning me to the ground. Water surrounded my palm, making it impossible for me to move, to call on my magic. Fire and water canceled each other, rendering me useless. I felt water trickling across my cheeks, until it stopped over my mouth; any scream, any noise I made, swallowed.

His footsteps approached, closer and closer until he stopped right beside me, bending down so his eyes met mine. "Now, that's more like it." His voice filled me with dread as I glared at the man before me, unable to do anything to stop him. "I think it's time to play, Flame Bearer, and once we're done, we'll let you bring your fire out."

My eyes widened in horror as he pulled a curved blade from a sheath at his side, a blade similar to the Blade of Rathmen, but not the actual blade Nik had used. He flicked the blade in my direction, effectively slicing a line through the side of my pants. I stared, shocked as his grin grew, before he turned to look over his shoulder.

"You were right." Carawn's tone shifted, wicked excitement radiating from him. "Whoever did this was certainly in possession of the blade. They opened a portal of magic inside her, ready to be used."

I struggled, trying to move, trying to break free. Nothing gave.

"I think it's time we test the extent of the Rathmen's magic in you." Carawn grinned as he raised the blade above his head.

KODRAYN! I screamed down the bond, just as the blade collided with the scar on my thigh and purple mist floated in the air. My body grew numb as the mist surrounded my body, engulfing me in its darkness. I could see Carawn in the distance saying something, but couldn't make out the words. My mind dulled as the mist surrounded me, then Carawn's voice grew louder, infringing on me, embedding itself in my mind. My bond retreated to the darkness, the ember of fire within me flickering out before lighting anew. And then, everything was altered.

I stood, my body alight with power, with strength. The mist vanished back within me. I was ready.

I turned my head toward the man in front of me, the blade in his hand still angled toward my body, as I dipped my head and spoke, "What next, master?"

Amethyst engulfed me as I took on the battlefield, free of shackles. The weapons at my side were wielded with careful precision as I took on my enemy. I struck, ducking and dodging before landing fatal blows to my opponents, efficiently rendering them useless.

The realm stilled, and I felt a command coursing through my body. *Burn.* And so I did.

I raised my arms, drawing on the sapphire flames alight within me, angling my wrists toward the targets, and struck. Fire flew from me as though a part of me, of my being. The heat coursing through my body merged with the darkness, sending strike after strike to any who dared approach me. I shifted faster than before, switching forms as I took on my opponents.

Dodging a wolvyn launching through the air toward me, I spun, arching my blade as it caught its underbelly, the whimper brushing past me as I sent a blast of fire over toward the wolvyn. Orange-blue flames engulfed the flying creature, and it fell back to the ground.

Two Seefers fought beside me, their shrill snarls bringing pleasure to my ears as we continued paving a path through the battlefield, the single command still in the forefront of my mind: *burn.*

I raised my palms, wielding blue orbs of flame as I launched the fire toward any who dared step in my path. I could feel the heat sizzle off my skin, the strength that vibrated freely from my power now that the iron cuffs had been removed. I had been freed to use my magic, free to light the realm on fire.

"Well this is an interesting turn of events, *little venom.*"

That voice. I recognized it through the haze of the command I'd been given. Spinning on my heel, I studied the target. Piercing amber eyes held mine hostage as I surveyed my enemy.

I raised my hand, waiting for the next command, when Eryx stepped up to my side. *Wait.*

My hand dropped, as I faced the man beside me; a soldier, a warrior—ready for their orders.

"Kodrayn Deverell." Eryx sneered as he eyed the Avyon King. "I'd say I was surprised. But you've been a pain since this bitch arrived."

I waited, uncaring about the words exchanged. My mind focused on the command I'd been given. *Wait. Wait. Wait.*

I don't know who struck first; one minute my mind was

focused on the command, the next, I processed the fight before my eyes. I watched through a purple-hued haze as a flash of fangs where bared and swords met, crashing into each other. Duck, strike, block, parry. The two circled each other viciously. Eryx went for a strike to Kodrayn's left, which was blocked swiftly as the vampry moved with speed the gryffin couldn't match. Long swords clashed with brutal force as they continued their advances. Duck, strike, block, parry. Muscles bulged and sweat coated both the men, yet no warriors came to their aid. A chilled wind whipped through the air, ice flying toward Eryx. An advance that was dodged as his own elemental magic came to play, the winds he controlled slamming the ice away from him.

I stood, frozen in my command, unable to move as the man I couldn't place, and the one who commanded my actions collided in a show of power, strength, and vengeance on the field. Their elemental magics collided in vicious strikes against the other. I watched as Eryx controlled his magic, the wind circling Kodrayn's neck, cutting his air supply. The Vampry King staggered for one brief moment, before his magic was flowing over the gryffin, pellets of ice shattering through his windy barricade, shredding into his skin. Kodrayn didn't stop there, his dagger raised and ready to throw—

Attack. Eryx's command rattled through my body and my arms moved toward the target.

I heard Eryx's laugh as I launched the first dagger toward the amber eyed man, but I didn't wait to see if it struck its target, I was already moving, spinning the sword in my palm before I struck. My arms reverberated against the clash of metal on metal as he blocked my blow. Eryx's laugh sounded from the distance again, but I struck, then ducked. Stepping to the right, I matched the man, the King of Avyon, step for step, block for block. As though he knew my every move a second before I made it. Twisting to my right, I spun, arcing the blade when a flat blow to the back of my legs caused me to stumble.

I spun and fell to the ground, rolling with the deftness of years of training; I flipped back up, pulling my last dagger from its sheath and rolled into a standing position right in front of my target. I watched as those gold eyes narrowed, focusing in on me, on the purple hue around me, and then they narrowed in on my neck.

Distracted, my target was distracted.

I struck. Arching my fist to the right, I feigned an attack before thrusting my blade into his left side. I felt the weight of his body tense as the blade drove in, his head falling toward me as his body grew closer. When suddenly, fangs pierced the right side of my neck, and I screamed in pain, as they dug deeper, into a spot so familiar.

My life flashed into perspective. The mark on my neck, the fangs digging in, *Kodrayn*. The word fell into my mind with clarity as my eyes began to clear.

Stay with me, little venom.

I collapsed to the ground as he pulled away from me. I watched, unable to speak as the man in front of me, *my bonded*, ripped the dagger out of his side, the wound already healing from his blood while he drew his second sword and turned on Eryx.

I stared in silence, my mind racing in overdrive at what I'd done, what I'd been *commanded* to do; at the deaths caused by my hands, my blades, *my power.* Kodrayn circled Eryx, a predatory glint in his eyes. I watched as he flicked his hand, a casual motion that had ice shooting up from the ground creating a frozen wall surrounding us, barricading the three of us in a pit much like the ones Eryx had forced me to enter—separating us from the rest of the war raging on around us. That's when he struck, leaving no time for the gryffin to shift as he arched his blades through the air with years of honed strength and sliced them in a crossed motion.

I watched as pure rage filled the face of the man I'd bonded as he attacked, strike after strike. He put Eryx on defense, his vampry agility and speed giving him the ability to strike, time and time again, without allowing Eryx a moment of reprieve. The air around me chilled to an arctic temperature, icy gusts of wind swirled down on Eryx as Kodrayn raised his blade against the man who'd lied to me, captured me, and tortured me.

Eryx's own blade met Kode's, the two weapons clashing with strength and power as they continued to parry, paying no heed to the battle in full force around them. Two more powerful strikes and I watched as Eryx stumbled back, falling against the side of the iced wall that entrapped us.

A longsword of frozen ice appeared within Kodrayn's hand, the arctic weapon solid, shimmering with a faint hue of magic as the King of Avyon raised the blade. Eryx's eyes widened and he struggled to rise, the ice of the wall surrounding his skin, rendering him immobile.

Kodrayn stepped closer to the man, his ice sword already moving in an arcing motion. I watched as the sword speared Eryx's abdomen, his guttural groan filling the air as the iced sword remained lodged in him. Kodrayn hadn't killed him, not yet.

Eryx's eyes filled with pain, blood seeping from his stomach as he stared past Kodrayn to look at me. "*Him?*" The accusation flooded over me. "You chose *him?*"

Kodrayn paused as though he had all the time in the realm as he looked over at me and I struggled to my feet. "What difference does it make who I chose? It would have never been you after everything you did to me," I spat.

"He can't protect you." His eyes flicked between the two of us as he spoke again. "Nothing will save you from what they have planned once they harvest your magic. Nothing." His wheezed breath filled the air as he spoke.

I heard the sound of metal being drawn and looked toward my bonded, the man who had saved me more times than I'd wished. The man who'd freed me from the control of Carawn's corrupted magic. I saw the fear in Eryx's eyes as Kodrayn raised the sword above his heart, ready to plunge the blade through him.

But he didn't. Instead he spoke, venom laced in his tone, and addressed the man bleeding out before him.

"You don't get to take what's mine, touch what's mine, harm

what's *mine*, and live to breathe another day." His snarl filled the air as his sword was plunged into Eryx's chest, ending the life of the man who'd captured me in one fatal blow.

All I could do was stare as Kodrayn turned toward me, blood splattered across his armor. The wall around him dropped—the rest of the battle coming into view—but I had no words. My mind was barely able to comprehend what had occurred as he lifted me into his arms, holding me to his body, and walked across the battlefield toward their camp.

"You're the only thing in the entire realm that matters to me, Kateya," Kodrayn's voice rumbled. "I would do anything for you. I will never stop saving you, even when I know you can do it yourself. You're it for me, Kateya. It's only ever been you."

My body was unresponsive, functioning on autopilot as he set me down in front of Everett and then turned to head back out onto the battlefield; back toward the war still raging.

"About time, Silver." Everett wrapped his arms around me, and I followed him numbly. Unable to process that I was free, truly free. "If you were gone any longer, I might have thought you actually didn't like us."

I let him lead me through the camp, my body shaking, my mind running circles while the haze cleared from me.

"H–He's really gone?" The tears fell down my face in a continual stream as I stared at him.

Everett stopped walking, his hands turning me into him as he held me before speaking. "He's gone Silver. He's gone."

EAST ENGLES

Chapter Thirty-Five

I CLUNG TO MY SISTER, holding on to her as if I would never see her again. "I'm sorry Cass, I'm so sorry."

My sister pulled back from me slightly, her face dirty and hair streaked with blood from the battleground. "What on Vanaiyer are you sorry for, Kat?" Confusion alight in her eyes as tears welled in them. "None of this was your fault, absolutely none of it."

I took a deep breath, emotions running rampant through me as I stared at my sister. "It's just, Eryx . . . Nik . . . The Fantoms . . . Us being here. None of it should have happened—"

"Stop." Cassandra interrupted me. "Just stop, sis. You're not at fault here. You don't get to blame yourself for something bigger than we could have ever thought."

"I just . . . I'm so happy to see you again, Cass. I don't know what I'd do without you."

Cassandra's smile lit up, and she pulled me back into her arms. I leaned my head on her shoulder, both of us sobbing as we clung to each other, not willing to be separated even an inch.

"I didn't think you would make it in time," I confessed to my sister in the darkness of the night. She released me and we both stared into the distance, spotting the rows of fires on both sides of the city. Armies, ready to wage war once again when the sunlight touched the sky.

"It was close," she admitted. "And to make it here as quickly as possible, we had to sacrifice the number of battalions we could transport."

I turned to look around at our numbers, comparing the number of fires on our side to those in the distance, and saw what she meant. We hardly had half the number of fires. Half the number of people.

"How will we . . ." I started, not wanting to voice the rest of my sentence.

"I don't know. Sébastien and the others are discussing that right now," Cass answered me and I could sense the worry in her voice, the strength and determination, yet the fear of a leader.

"Shouldn't we be there then?" I questioned, knowing that we should. That we should be helping to plan the next steps of this fight. That they needed us to play our part.

"No." My sister looked over toward me, authority in her tone. "You need to rest, Kat. What you've gone through, what you went through today . . . Rest. Take the night. This fight, this war, it will be here tomorrow, and for many days after."

"But—" I started, only for my sister to cut me off.

"I'm serious, little sis. I've got this one. Take the night to relax, okay? You just made it back to me, to us. I can't lose you again."

I nodded reluctantly.

"Plus." She half grinned in my direction. "If you still feel the need to be a badass warrior, the battle will go on."

I smiled slightly as I started to walk toward the tents on the far side of camp. "Fair enough." My mind felt hazy as I walked away, and with each step, I prayed that I'd be able to mentally recover. That I'd be able to pick up all the little pieces of myself I'd lost over the past few weeks, the past year, and mold them back together again.

I tried to tune out the groans and cries of the injured, the screams of pain as healers tried their best to stitch together wounds and mend injuries inflicted by ancient magic. It was nearly too much to handle though, and the cries of pain tore through me in agony.

I passed by the center of the camp, walking by the soldiers in line for rations of bread and stew. I noted their looks of anguish and exhaustion in the firelight as I passed. A look I'm positive was mirrored on my own face. But I couldn't stomach the scent of the stew, nor the taste of food after the day we'd endured.

A faint trail of blood orange swept by me, and I turned to find Kodrayn heading inside a tent that I recognized to be a vampry feeding tent. A wave of jealousy washed over me at the thought of him feeding from someone else—of his fangs digging into another woman's flesh and I walked with new intent toward the tent flap I saw him enter.

I braced myself as I opened the flap and saw a handful of vampry soldiers, exhausted and still in their armor, feeding off of others, fangs clamping into mortal flesh, biting down as they fed. But I hardly processed the soldier beside me as he traced his fingers against a woman's exposed throat, before digging his fangs in. Instead, my eyes scanned the tent until I caught sight of him, speaking to a woman to the side, pointing to her wrist even while she tilted her neck at an angle for him.

"What the *fuck* do you think you're doing?" The words flew from my mouth before I could stop them, and every vampry in the tent paused their activity, bloodlust abided as their eyes laid on me.

Exhausted amber eyes, flaked with gold, latched onto mine, and a flicker of amusement passed through them at my outburst.

"Now, little venom, how many times do I need to tell you to watch that pretty little mouth of yours?" he purred as he dropped the woman's wrist to face me fully. Silence fell across the tent, all eyes looking between me and their king, before I whirled on my heel and stormed out of the tent.

My mind reeled, I couldn't believe that I'd just done that, that I'd just questioned their king in front of an audience like that. I made it all of five steps before I felt his hand on my wrist, the chilled breeze of my bonded wrapping over me, halting my retreat as he spun me into his hard body.

"Well," Kodrayn spoke, his eyes assessing me as he did, "you certainly gave my men something to talk about tonight."

"Sorry," I muttered half-heartedly, still unable to get the image of him about to feed from someone else out of my mind. I yanked my arm from his grasp, taking another step away from him, to which he simply fell into step with me, matching me step for step as I walked toward where Cass had told me I'd be staying.

"You do know I have to feed, right?"

"Obviously," I snapped toward him as I kept my quick pace, stalking through the camp.

"And you realize that if I don't feed, I won't regain the strength expended during battle today?"

"Again, yes, I'm aware of that."

His eyes flickered with another look of amusement before he spoke again.

"And unless you're offering yourself up as a viable option, I have to feed from another mortal." His words hit me and I spun to glare at him.

"Yes, Kodrayn," I snarked, unaware of why I was so angered by the thought of him feeding. "I'm aware that all vamprys have to feed from mortals. I'm aware of *why* they have to feed from mortals."

"So," he added.

"It doesn't mean I have to like this particular situation," I answered angrily.

"Are you jealous, little venom?" Kodrayn asked as he led me in through a tent flap. The onyx material flapped in the breeze as I walked through.

"No," I replied quickly, maybe too quickly. I looked around at my surroundings, noting the dark bedroll on the floor, the male armor to the side, and the number of weapons, freshly polished by the entrance. This was *his* tent.

"No?" Kodrayn asked, suddenly towering over me, as he reached out, tilting my head up to meet his gaze. "The thought of me biting another mortal, feeding from them instead of you, doesn't bother you at all? Doesn't fill you with a venomous, fiery rage?" his voice purred the question against my ear and my pulse increased at his words.

I flicked my eyes toward him, my breath caught in my throat as I stared at his face, taking in his tanned skin, the small scars that were barely visible, and the large scar across his eye. "Tell me you're not jealous, little venom. Tell me that it doesn't matter to you if I feed from someone else."

But it does, the tiny part of my soul longed to scream. I chewed on my lip, contemplating how to answer his question when his lips fell on mine, prying them apart as he sought entrance. My anger melted as he consumed me, his lips dancing across mine, demanding mine as he took control. The taste of citrus, of *him*, flooded my senses. His hand tangled through my hair, tilting my chin up as his tongue slipped into my mouth. I moaned against him, circling his tongue with my own as he claimed my lips, my tongue, taking what he wanted.

He broke the kiss, leaving me breathless and wanting him as his gold-flecked eyes peered into mine. I watched as the right side of his lip tugged upward, a cocky grin pulling across his face.

"Tell me, little venom," he said as he tugged his own shirt over his head, exposing an expanse of finely toned muscles that rippled with every movement. My eyes drank him in, taking in every line, every scar imprinted on his olive brown skin. "Were you jealous?"

Heat flooded to my cheeks as I held his gaze, my body shifting as I pressed closer to him. "And if I was?" The words dropped from my lips slowly.

His gaze pierced mine, his lips hovering tantalizingly close, and I felt his ice magic swirl around us. I could feel the heat radiating from his body, the pulsing length that pressed against my middle. "Why be jealous of what's already yours?" he purred as I lifted my fingers, slowly letting the pads trail across each mark of his body, over his back. Each scar held a story, just like mine.

"Do you trust me?" I glanced up at his question, my eyes holding his.

I didn't answer. Instead I dragged my tongue against the column of his neck, feeling him shudder against me as I reached his ear. "Against my better judgment, always. I will trust you until the end."

His responding growl sounded from deep within him as he reached the hem of my shirt, swiftly removing the material that separated his skin from mine. My nipples pebbled as I watched the warrior, the king before me, focus his entire gaze on me. Calloused hands traced circles over my exposed flesh, toying with me as skilled fingers kneaded my breasts.

"You know." Kodrayn's voice was husky, his eyes never leaving mine as his fingers pinched, drawing a gasp from my lips as fiery need coursed through me. "There are *other* places to feed . . ."

My stomach flipped as pressure built, the anticipation of his next move edging me on as his head lowered.

"Is that so?" I murmured as I ran my hands across his broad back, purposely digging my nails in deep as they raked over his skin, reveling in the feel of him. "Do you plan to show me?" I nearly whined as my body thrummed under his touch, as his tongue drew wet circles across my pebbled nipples, icy air dancing over them as he switched between the two.

He struck. His fangs pierced the tender skin of my breast as he drew blood and my mind hazed over, focused solely on him, *my bonded,* and his wicked tongue circling my nipple. The bloodlust flowed over me, the need pulsing through me while my bonded fed from me. I pressed into him, needing more. Needing to feel him on me, to remove the layers between us. I felt the hard muscle of his thighs as they nudged mine apart.

I felt his hands move near my stomach, and then I heard his pants being undone before they fell to the ground. A hard length pressed against the flat plane of my stomach, while his hand was in my hair and his fangs danced across my skin. All my mind could comprehend was the feel of him on me, his hands trailing across my skin.

We ended up on the ground, Kode's weight heavy over me as he pressed hungry kisses across my skin. His kisses drifted lower and lower, until my pants gave way and he ripped them off me. His eyes appraised me with pride, with hunger . . . with satisfaction. I stared at the king before me, breathless as he became the only thing that mattered.

"You." He kissed my stomach, his fangs lightly dancing across my skin. "Are absolutely." He kissed lower and my core turned molten, the need throbbing through me at his touch. "Breathtaking." His tongue licked up my left thigh and I moaned. I felt his hand touch my right thigh and my body tensed, immediately regretting this decision.

Panic raced through my mind as his hand was still on my right thigh and his eyes met mine. *I can't do this. Not like this. Not after that.* I recoiled in my own mind at the thought of the scar carved into my thigh.

You don't get to stop now, little venom. You're mine. Every inch of you. Every scar, every wound, every imperfect edge. I wouldn't want you any other way.

My heart stopped as I stared at the man in front of me. "I'm damaged. He made sure of that." Sorrow filled my eyes as I propped myself onto my elbows to see the purple-hued scar across my thigh. When my eyes flicked back up to Kodrayn's, all I saw was fury—anger and fury at my words.

"Damaged?" the word spit from his mouth, his eyes dark. "Listen to me carefully, *little venom.* Damaged is not a word I ever want to hear from your pretty little lips. You are many things, but damaged is *not* one of them."

"That mark, the scar will forever be there." Tears rimmed my eyes but never fell as I spoke, baring my darkest fear.

My mate shifted, his golden eyes holding mine hostage as he took my hand in his, bringing it to his body. He guided my fingers to trace along a jagged scar on his abdomen. "This was from the first battle I fought in. I was ten years old."

His hand shifted, bringing mine with it as my fingers glided across another scar over his chest. "This one, this was from my father. The first time I lost to him in the training pit."

"And these here." My fingers traced along the scars across his shoulder, before his hand dropped and I felt the ridges along his back. "Those were from the first time I lost a battle, and very nearly lost my life, had the Brotherhood not come to my rescue."

The raw, hollow tone in his voice surprised me. "We are all made up of scars, little venom. They tell the story of who we are, who we have been forced to become. But never once do they diminish any part of you. They only strengthen you, making you who you are, weaving a beautiful story across your skin."

My mouth felt dry as I stared at the man above me, wanting him, needing him to make me whole.

"Do you trust me?"

I smiled at the line. The question he'd asked me so many times before, and nodded my head as silver tears rimmed my eyes. "Yes," the word fell out in a shaky laugh.

I watched as his fangs lengthened, he struck again, lovingly, but harder than before, sinking his teeth in as he left yet another claiming mark across my skin, covering over the letter carved into my skin. My body writhed against his hold, his hands on my hips holding me in place as he left a permanent mark, a permanent reminder of himself on me.

He shifted, sitting up as he tugged me up toward him. I straddled him, need building in me as he kissed my forehead, then my lips, before pulling back. As Kodrayn's head came into view above mine, I stared at the man who rewrote the scars across my body. Who crossed enemy territory to free me. Who whispered down a bond to keep me company during my darkest hours. "I love you, Kode," the words fell from my lips as tears trickled down my cheeks.

"I've loved you since the moment you opened that poisonous

mouth, little venom," he replied in turn. "And every second after. You were always, and will always be mine."

Then his weight shifted, as he lifted me up slightly. Leaning forward, he pressed his lips against the mark on my neck, *his mark*. One. Two. Three kisses before he thrust forward as he brought me down on him, shattering my realm as he sheathed himself fully in me—barely giving me time to adjust to his size. I moaned atop him, feeling him pulse within me and then he was moving, lifting his hips to thrust in and out as I matched his movement, feeling him deeper in me with each thrust.

"Fuck, little venom," Kodrayn's growl sounded from beneath me, and I shifted my hips, taking him deeper. My thighs began to shake as I moved above him, needing him, wanting every inch of him. I moaned when his hands gripped my hips, holding me down on his length as he thrust, once, twice, and then he rolled, flipping our positions. He pinned me to the ground, his weight trapping me beneath him as his body caged me in.

I felt his breath across my neck as his rhythmic thrusts picked up speed, power radiating from him as he hit that spot over and over. "More," I murmured as my nails dug into his back, leaving my own mark on him. His fangs sank into my neck and I cried out as need overtook me, the build up edging me on.

"Kode," I gasped, breathless as he moved, pleasure building in me until I couldn't hold it back; until *we* couldn't hold it back and he moved within me, quicker and quicker, unleashing himself to the point of no return. Embers and ice collided as we shattered together, time and space irrelevant as the realm faded and my life became whole.

Our *bond* became whole.

EAST ENGLES

Chapter Thirty-Six

MY EYES CAUGHT on Kodrayn's half-dressed form as I woke up in his tent, and for a moment, all I wanted was to drag him back to bed and curl up with him for a while longer. Yet judging from his demeanor and the blades he was analyzing on the ground, I knew that option was still a long way off.

I watched him for a few moments longer, admiring the line work of the tattoos that inked his side, and the way his hair was tousled messily from sleeping beside me. His muscles rippled in tight cords as he laid out the pieces of armor he would be wearing today.

"Should I stand here a little bit longer for you to drool over, or do you plan to get up?" Kodrayn chuckled as he looked at me and heat rushed to my cheeks.

I pushed the blanket back as I answered, "Well if you're giving me a choice, I'd much rather the first option." I stood up, walking over to him and wrapped my arms around his torso, snuggling into his warmth, finding a small moment of peace before we faced the day.

A low growl sounded from his chest and I looked up, noting the feral look in his dark gold eyes and the elongated fangs on display. I smiled before saying, "And here you thought you were *so* much better than me." I pulled myself off of him, walking to the other side of the tent as I too began dressing for the coming day. The faint beat of drums echoing through the darkness of the camp told me that we were about to face another harrowing day.

"We won't have enough of the antidote to go around today," Everett announced as he walked into the war tent we were all crowded together in.

I listened to all four members of the Brotherhood discuss how they should best divide the narelle antidote amongst the troops as I scanned the map of Hallyus and the ancient city. I ran over the conversations I'd overheard from my time imprisoned at both Kyllios and Dyffin when an idea occurred to me.

"We don't need enough of the antidote to go around." At the sound of my voice, the men around me halted, all eyes focused on me as I spoke. "You just need enough to cover the fae here." I indicated to a spot on the far right of the city. "And here." I mimicked the spot on the left.

"That leaves the center open to attack," Dravyn said as he studied the map across from me.

I turned toward my bonded, knowing he wouldn't like what came out of my mouth next. "Not if you use us." I indicated toward Cass and myself.

"No." I couldn't tell who spoke first, my bonded or her mate. Both men stood up in anger at the suggestion. Darkened tendrils of black mist, mixed with iced winds whipped through the tent.

Please, I pleaded down the bond. *Just let me finish my thought before you shoot the idea down.*

I took Kodrayn's silence as enough of an answer while I continued. "We know that the antidote will ward off the effects of the Fantoms for long enough to take one down. But . . ." I paused as I looked around. "It doesn't seem like that's the only thing that is able to withstand their power."

Looking toward Kodrayn and Everett, I continued. "You were both there the night of the Moyros Festival. Which means, I know you both saw how the Fantom vanished once it—" I couldn't finish the sentence this time before both Kodrayn and Everett vehemently shouted their opposition at the use of the mark on my leg. It was Zaron though who cut in, telling them both to shut it, before I could continue.

Pointing to the map I went on. "If you put Cass and I here"—I indicated to a marker a little ways off from the center of the ancient city—"and we reopen the scar, like Carawn did . . ." I paused, breathing deeply as I pushed on, forcing myself not to think of everything that I'd done yesterday. "Cassandra and I should be able to merge our magic, working as one with the ability to fend off the Fantoms."

Sébastien stared at the map in consideration, before saying, "If we stationed men on all sides—here, here, and here." He pointed to the map. "Plus utilize the reinforcements from Ryker's aerial fleets, as Kateya mentioned, it could give us a fighting chance to at least make it off the island with troops still intact."

I watched while the men studied the map, talking over logistics.

"No." Kodrayn's voice cut through the air as the eyes of Sébastien, Ryker, and Dravyn met his. "You will not use my *bonded* as a lure for the Fantoms."

"Kode," I started, but was cut off.

We'll talk about this later. The snarled command came down the bond, an icy chill tightening in the center of my soul.

"What other option do we have, brother?" Sébastien's voice interrupted aloud. "We're running out of options, out of men. And until we get the next two artifacts, the prophecy won't unravel. We can't keep fighting endless battles."

Kodrayn's eyes darkened as he glared at his blood brothers.

"You have our word. We will all protect them," Dravyn added.

"Embers and Ash," Ryker's voice followed, his steely gaze firm on Kodrayn's.

It's the only thing that works, Kode, I added, in defense of my plan. *I know you don't like it. But the alternative leaves us dead, and I don't know about you but I'd much rather be alive.*

Are you going to be okay with reopening the scar on your leg? He asked, softer now, the concern for me blatant in his question.

No, I replied honestly. *But we've already established that our bond can shut it off when you bite me, and I would rather it be Cass, than the enemy controlling me.*

Amber eyes held mine until the conversation around us concluded. I slowly broke eye contact and looked around the room at the faces I'd grown to cherish. Unable to help the feeling that we wouldn't all make it back.

I stared at my sister as we found ourselves surrounded in the ancient city. "You ready to do this?"

"As ready as I'll ever be," she claimed, lifting the dagger slightly. "And just so you know, sis, for all the time I've claimed to be so angry at you I could hurt you, this is not what I meant," she said with a forced laugh that had me chuckling.

"Same, sis." I reach out toward her, passing purple sludge in a cup her way.

"Bottoms up." Cass grimaced as we both knocked back the narelle flower potion the magic assessors and healers had crafted.

"Void-damned," the curse fell from my lips once I swallowed. Cass coughed by my side, both of us disturbed by the taste. "Should I feel any different?"

"No," she replied. "I felt the exact same yesterday when I took it." Cass stared at me as the sounds of fighting began to draw closer and I knew our time was limited before we found ourselves mid fight. "Are you sure about this, Kat?" Cass confirmed once more as I took a steadying breath and nodded. "We don't even know if it will work."

"We have to try. Just get it over with."

"It's you and me until magic is restored to the realm," my sister whispered the same words to me that Aerilyn had in the present. And then I felt the blade hitting my skin and I gritted my teeth, familiar ancient magic circling around us. I couldn't help but wonder, as the blade cut through my flesh, what type of powers we were playing with. All magic demands a balance. What would this use of a corrupt magic left inside of me demand?

I trusted my sister to gain control of the magic as the sounds around me faded away. I saw her lips moving before I felt the first hesitant command, *Stand.* My body listened to her voice, relaxing at the softness of her tone as I trusted my sister.

And when the first wave of gryffins rained down on the ancient city, we were ready for them. Our magic ebbed into one force, flames dancing in and out of dark shadows as we struck the enemies that charged toward our people. We moved in tandem, brandishing weapons as a united force, just as our Father had taught us to growing up. We struck, ducked and parried around each other as we took on soldier after soldier, waiting for the first big strike.

As the first Fantom approached, I felt the purple haze surrounding me, leaping toward the magic. A familiar saying echoed in the back of my mind as the magic surrounding me drew toward that of the Fantom, a saying that like calls to like. We watched as the Fantom grew closer. I could make out the figure within its depths, a frown marring my face as the figure of my father hovered above the shadows of the Fantom.

"Fuck," Cass called out from my left as she saw the figure drawing closer. But I was already striking, shifting into fae form as I rose, dodging purple tendrils of mist while letting myself get closer to the Fantom. We waited, my wings flapping as I held myself in the air, and then the Fantom was in range, and the mist radiating from me shot out toward it, purple-hued mist circling around the shadowed creature as they spiraled up into the air. The Fantom vanishing in the air and becoming the first of many beasts to be destroyed.

Despite the success of our plan, the screams and cries that surrounded me as the battle raged on didn't relent. The number of Seefers didn't stop, and gryffins continued to swarm the skies as we fought them off. I whirled, ducking to avoid being clawed by a Seefer as I shifted into a wolvyn form, and my sister sent a black wave of shadows in front of me as I struck the beast in the darkness of her magic. Its sharp shrill died as my claws raked down its body.

I barely had time to catch my breath as two gryffins approached us, talons out as they dove from the sky. Cass and I shifted into vampry form, utilizing our speed to dodge their spiraling descent. Daggers raised, we ducked under them as they spread their talons preparing to land, the blades cutting the undersides of their bellies as we rolled out from under them.

Now.

The command rattled through my bones as Cass and I drew on our elemental magic, onyx shadows entwining with sapphire flames as we cast out our magic. My arms shook as we circled our magic around the gryffins; fiery flames engulfed in shadows as we seared our enemies in the darkness.

We took off running as a shrill snarl sounded from our left. Seefers were hot on our trail when an icy chill shot past us and I turned, glancing back to watch the beasts halt mid run, speared through with icy stakes.

Another Fantom burst through the forces, then another. Darkness shrouded the sky as they dove toward us, twisting in spirals as tendrils of magic flowed from them. The tug of a command rattled through my body and I was moving, pushing off the ground while Cassandra's magic swirled around me, my wings hidden from view as I blended into the darkness. I climbed higher and higher, my wings protesting in weary agony, and I pushed myself further until I knew I was in range. I stopped, and as I did,

Cassandra's shadows lifted, and the purple haze that surrounded me shot forward, circling the Fantoms.

I watched as like met like. Magic called to its own, and the mists swirled up, racing toward the sky as they battled, then collided into one, vanishing once again. I sighed a breath of relief, my wings sagging slightly, and lowered myself to the ground, rolling my shoulder to relieve the pressure of flying.

My limbs began to shake with every push of magic, and the ember of fire within me began to grow smaller. Still, we pushed on, battling gryffins and foot soldiers that broke past the ranks, then wielding our magic through the field, striking down approaching enemies. A Nordak soldier struck to my right, my duck barely avoiding the blow of his blade as I whirled, my arms wobbling while I went on defense. I matched him, blow for blow, my arms shaking. The soldier arched his blade, swinging wide then striking from both sides as a dagger appeared in his other hand. I cried in pain as the blade cut across my forearm between my armor, blood covering my skin.

Cass appeared to my right, her sword arched as she swung it through the air, her shadows tightening around the enemy as her sword cleaved through him.

You're hurt, the concerned snarl cut through my mind.

I'm fine, Kode. No life saving needed, I responded quickly as Cass began speaking by my side.

"It's letting up," Cass shouted beside me and I struggled to take a moment to breathe as I looked up and noticed that she was right, the number of soldiers advancing was reducing.

Sparing a glance behind me, I noted that the second part of our plan was already in motion. Ships departed from the shore filled with wolvyn and vamprys as we began the evacuation phase of this battle. Because we knew—we all did—that until the next two artifacts appeared, this war would never be over. My heart lurched when I took in the water lining the shores, the once clear liquid, now a bleeding tide of crimson that soaked into the sand. I wondered, not for the first time, what we were missing from the prophecy. What had truly happened when the Great Four cast the artifacts into the depths of time?

As I turned back toward my sister, I screamed, launching a dagger from my waist at the charging soldier, just as Cass turned around, bringing up her blade to deflect the blow. As she spun, striking back, the soldier put up a fight until black tendrils licked at his feet and he was swallowed whole by the shadows surrounding him.

We began to retreat, moving backward as a unit while we continued fighting the remaining gryffin across the ancient city. I heard the shouts and commands of the men, and watched as Ryker's aerial units continued monitoring the skies, pouncing on any gryffins that appeared over our evacuation zone. They wouldn't follow us across the Avyz, not when Dathrian believed the fourth artifact was located on the shores of the East Engles.

I turned, purple haze clouding my vision, but my gaze fell on amber eyes once more. The scent of blood orange and cedarwood surrounded me as he stalked toward me, tall and powerful as he approached. I stared at the warrior, at the king before me, as sparks of embers fluttered in the distance between us, colliding with his flurries of ice.

Suddenly, he was there, towering over me, his eyes sweeping over my features in concern, ensuring I was unharmed. He slowly sank his fangs deep into the claiming mark on my neck, and I moaned against him as the purple haze vanished from my view.

Testing my power, I realized that I'd spent nearly all of the flames residing within me. A hollow spark of ember barely flickering remained in my soul. "I—" I didn't know what to say as I stared at the man in front of me.

You did well, little venom. Let's get you home now.

A shout sounded from somewhere in the distance. Kodrayn and I both turned and scanned the battalions until we noticed the right wing of fae warriors charging toward the center of the battle field. That's when I saw it. The clouds above the battleground darkened, the sky ominous as the clouds began to swirl together, twisting violently.

I stared in shock and horror as something fell from the sky. Glimpses of auburn red fluttered around, surrounded by a black-and-gold mist as the form fell, before collapsing onto the ground in the middle of the battlefield.

Shouts rose from both sides as I watched the figure lay immobile on the battlefield, surrounded by the blood and gore of a day of fighting. I watched as Kodrayn and a few others began sprinting toward the frontline while Ryker's men continued their flight toward the fallen figure. Slowly, the person staggered to their feet, and I froze, recognizing the figure even from a far distance.

The sharp intake of breath from my side told me that my sister was seeing the same thing I was.

But it couldn't be, could it?

NOT AN ENEMY! I yelled down the bond. *Not an enemy.*

Do you know her? Kodrayn's winded voice answered my cry from down the bond as he continued moving forward.

Aerilyn, was all I could say as I stared at the face of my best friend, my roommate, and my sister's best friend, and processed the fact that she was here, because there could only be one reason she *was* here.

My heart began racing, pulse rushing as I pieced it all together in the brief instant that I had time to process what was happening. She'd found the artifact and had shattered it, traveling back through time to find us. I turned just in time to see Dathrian and Carawn charging toward my best friend from the other side of the battlefield, straight toward Aerilyn.

"No!" Cassandra and I screamed at the same time. My power sputtered, failing to come to life as I threw caution to the wind and began running toward the center of the battlefield—sprinting toward my best friend.

My lungs screamed in protest as I pushed myself toward her, trying to draw any remaining magic I had stored within me, when I felt strong arms shove into me from the side.

I flew through the air, watching as Everett collided with me, halting my advance as I hit the ground, my side screaming in pain. I rolled, trying to get up, but he pinned me to the ground. "No," he seethed, fury ablaze in his eyes in a way I'd never seen before. "It's a trap."

I watched, pinned under Everett, in horror as Dravyn, who was closest to my best friend, sprinted toward Aerilyn, with Dathrian and Carawn not far behind as they too began closing in on her. "RUN!" I screamed toward Aerilyn. Her face whipped around, her dazed eyes wide as she saw me being held down and processed the barrage of men racing toward her, all with weapons drawn and magic releasing.

I struggled against Everett, kicking as I tried to break free. As I tried to help my best friend in any way I could. "He's not going to make it to her. He's going to be too late! Do something!" I screamed but his hold on me didn't loosen, even though remorse filled his eyes.

"I can't, Silver, I promised Kodrayn I wouldn't let anything happen to you. I'm sorry."

Help her! I screamed down the bond to my mate. To the King of Avyon. *Do something! Help her please!* I screamed, my voice cracking as I watched helplessly.

I was useless as I watched. I saw the arrow Carawn fired as he sprinted toward my friend, propelled by water rushing on the ground a second too late. The arrow soared straight toward Dravyn, the singular target on the battleground, as he ran to the center of the battlefield, straight toward my best friend—toward the final key to ending the war raging around us.

I watched as the arrow, laced with purple-hued corrupt magic flew true, hitting its target. His body staggered against the strike, purple mist surrounding him as the arrow protruded from his body. He was falling, collapsing onto the ground in a crumpled form.

I screamed in terror as the Nordak King caught up to Aerilyn, yanking her against his body even as she struggled and tried to fight against him. Dathrian drew his blade and another scream fled from my lips as I watched him jam the hilt of his dagger against Aerilyn's skull, knocking her out cold. Before Ryker's men could get close enough, he shifted into his gryffin form and began pushing off the ground.

I watched on, helplessly, as Dathrian took to the skies, climbing higher and higher, until even the fae warriors wouldn't be able to reach them. His gold wings glistened as he flew off with Aerilyn—with the powers of the third artifact. With my best friend held precariously in the talons of our enemy, a purple mist encased them as they vanished from sight. And the realm shook.

Spice Rack

If you wish to be aware of any chapters that contain explicit, on-page intimate scenes, please review the following list.

- Chapter 15 - one brief scene
- Chapter 28 - one longer scene
- Chapter 31 - one short scene
- Chapter 35 - one longer scene

Acknowledgments

I would like to thank my family for encouraging me to keep pushing toward my dream. For always telling me to write whatever came to mind, and who believed in, and supported me as an author.

My dad, who has helped make it a possibility for me to continue publishing books.

My mom, who listens to every phone call I make (which is nearly daily) about being an author and what's coming up next on this journey.

My brother, who always encourages me to go for my dreams.

And my sister, who is convinced that Kateya will always be *her* character, who is always there for me and brings out the best of me.

My husband, for giving me a writing space and making sure I set aside time to write and edit.

My grandma, who gave me the best writing desk I could ask for . . . the desk where I wrote all of book two.

My alpha reader, Donna, who read the book chapter by chapter as I wrote it and helped me work out plot holes in the storyline.

My lovely beta readers, Leslie, Ashley, Shannon, and Chelsey. All of your feedback, thoughts, unhinged sidebar comments, and texting convos (looking at you Leslie) had me smiling through edits.

My editor, Caitlin, who answered every text I sent about the plot line—even if it was crazy late at night—has read through this book nearly as many times as I have, and helped me make WTE what it is today. Thank you!

My proofreader, Chelsey, for making sure this book was perfect and ready to go out into the world!

My real-life best friend, Ashley, who has gone with me to book signings, listened to me ramble about my books all day sometimes, helped look at every piece of artwork I commissioned to ensure the world would love it, and made sure that I didn't have the FMCs do anything too crazy.

All my author/booksta friends (you know how you are) who have hyped me up and cheered me on as I wrote book two, I'm so grateful for y'all.

And most importantly, God, for giving me an imaginative mind filled with words to put on paper, a wonderful life, and salvation through His son.

T.A. Reilly is an author of NA fantasy romance with equal levels of adventure, time travel, and romance mixed in. Reading came naturally to her at a young age, and the words began flowing shortly after that. She has traveled all over the world from a young age and is constantly counting down the days until her next trip! After graduating with a master's in Professional Communications, she decided to pursue her lifelong dream . . . bringing time travel to life on paper. Currently, she calls Florida home. In her free time, she loves rewatching *FRIENDS*, going to the beach, and staying up too late, lost in a good book.

Connect with her on Instagram and TikTok as @tareillybooks

Did you enjoy reading *Within the Embers*? Jump right in to Book 3, *Above the Shadows*!

Books by T.A. Reilly

Scattered Destinies Series

Beneath the Shatter

Within the Embers

Above the Shadows

Book 4 (TBA)

Aurelian Guild Series

Solis Falling